FACES OF THE GONE

To Laurie,

Thanks for sharing a
spot of tea!

FACES OF THE GONE

Brad Parks (signature)

Yorktown, VA
2/17/2016

B R A D   P A R K S

Minotaur Books ✺ New York
A Thomas Dunne Book

This is a work of fiction. All of the characters, organizations, and events portrayed in this novel are either products of the author's imagination or are used fictitiously.

A THOMAS DUNNE BOOK FOR MINOTAUR BOOKS.
An imprint of St. Martin's Publishing Group

www.thomasdunnebooks.com

www.minotaurbooks.com

Library of Congress Cataloging-in-Publication Data

Parks, Brad, 1974–
    Faces of the gone / Brad Parks.—1st ed.
        p. cm.
    ISBN 978-0-312-57477-2
    1. Reporters and reporting—Fiction.   2. Murder—Investigation—Fiction.   3. Newark (N. J.)—Fiction.   I. Title.
    PS3616.A7553F33 2009
    813'.6—dc22   2009028472

First Edition: December 2009

10   9   8   7   6   5   4   3   2   1

I had the great fortune to meet the love of my life when I was nineteen and she has since become more to me than I possibly have space to recite. So I will keep this brief: Thank you, Melissa, for being my everything.

With all the vacant lots in Newark, New Jersey—and there were thousands of them—the Director could afford to be picky.

He wanted one near public housing, a red herring for police, who always began their search for suspects in the projects. It had to be dark at night, lest any random passers-by had inquisitive eyes. But it also needed to be in plain sight once day broke. The sooner the bodies were discovered, the sooner the Director's message could be delivered.

After a brief but diligent search, the Director found the ideal vacant lot on Ludlow Street, in a forgotten South Ward neighborhood. There were projects in every direction, including some of the city's most notorious. The streetlights had been shot out, so there was no worrying about *late-night voyeurs. And—this was perfect—it was next to a church. The shock value would be priceless.*

With his second in command, Monty, the Director rounded up the four dealers. They came to their designated places as instructed, thinking they were simply collecting their weekly shipment. They loaded themselves in the back of the van and put on their blindfolds, all part of their training. Then they traveled in silence toward the vacant lot, because the Director ordered them not to speak.

At their destination, the Director guided the still-blindfolded dealers to the rear of the vacant lot and made them form a line. He told them it was new training, instructing them not to be alarmed if they heard gunfire.

Then he shot each one in the back of the head.

There had been no witnesses. No one could see them through all that unlit gloom. There were no shell casings left behind—the Director collected those before they hit the ground. He didn't even have blood on his gloves. The job was that clean.

As soon as the last body dropped, the Director gave Monty a digital camera and ordered him to take close-ups of each dead face. Monty balked at first. He worried about the flash attracting attention. But the Director reminded him it was an essential part of the plan.

Because punishing the four dealers—all of whom had strayed and broken a vital clause in their contract—wasn't enough. It had to be made clear to the others in the organization, especially those who might consider straying themselves, that this was the price for disobedience.

Thank goodness, the Director chuckled to himself, the news media would seize on this sensational story and help deliver his message. He couldn't have bought better advertising.

CHAPTER 1

If there had only been one dead body that day, I never would have heard about it. From a news standpoint, one dead body in Newark, New Jersey, is only slightly more interesting than planes landing safely at the airport. Assuming it's some anonymous gangbanger—and in Newark it's almost always an anonymous gangbanger—it's a four-paragraph story written by an intern whose primary concern is finishing quickly so he can return to inventing witty status updates on Facebook.

Two bodies is slightly more interesting. The intern has to come up with eight paragraphs, and maybe, if there's someone unfortunate enough to be hanging out in the photo department when an editor wanders by, a picture will run with the story.

Three bodies is worth a headline *and* a picture, even a follow-up or two, though the interest peters out quickly enough.

But four? Four means real news. Four gets a town buzzing, even a town as blood-jaded as Newark. And four bodies is what I was contemplating that Monday morning in early December as I arrived at the offices of the *Newark Eagle-Examiner* and opened up the paper.

We had managed to cram a quick story about it in our late edition. It was done by our night-shift rewrite guy, a man named Peterson who delighted in hyperbolizing gritty crime stories. He quoted a Newark police spokesman as saying four victims, each with a single bullet wound in the back of the head, had been found in a vacant lot next to a church on Ludlow Street.

The police spokesman didn't provide much color, so Peterson created his own, describing the "brazen execution-style slayings" as having "rocked an otherwise quiet Newark neighborhood." The bodies, he wrote, had been "stacked like cordwood in a weed-choked plot." The Newark police had not released the names of the victims, because next of kin had not been notified, so Peterson referred to them as "four John Does" every chance he got.

I was making it through the last of Peterson's compositional flourishes when I heard my editor, Sal Szanto.

"Crrttrr Rssss," Szanto growled. From experience, I knew he was at least attempting to say my name, Carter Ross.

"What's going on, boss?" I said, lurking in his doorway.

Now in his early fifties, Szanto often had trouble with vowels until his voice warmed up a bit. No one could say which of his vices—coffee, cigarettes, or antacid tablets—had taken the letters away.

"Ssttddnn."

4

Sit down. I think. As I entered the office and took the chair across from his desk, Szanto turned away and held up his left hand while coughing forcefully into his right, his jowls jiggling at the effort. He stopped for a moment, started to speak, then hacked a few more times until he finally dislodged the morning phlegm that had rendered him all but unintelligible.

"Ah, that's better," he said. "Anyway, Brodie is really pitching a tent over this Ludlow Street thing."

As far as anyone knew, Harold Brodie—the legendary *Eagle-Examiner* executive editor who was now pushing seventy—had not gotten an actual hard-on in years. He got stiffies for stories and, sadly for Mrs. Brodie, nothing else. And although they were erections only in the figurative sense, the impact they had on the rest of us was very real. When you heard the phrase "Brodie has a real hard-on for this one"—or any number of colorful derivations on that theme—you knew it was trouble. Once he was turned on to a story it could take days for the old man to tire of it. And, in the meantime, he was going to harass everyone in the newsroom on a half-hourly basis until he got the story he imagined existed.

"I've already sent Whitlow and Hays down there. They're going to do the daily stuff," Szanto said, then aimed a stubby finger at me. "You're going to get to the bottom of what the hell happened down there."

"And how am I going to do that?"

"I don't know. You're my investigative reporter. Figure it out yourself."

I enjoy the title "investigative reporter" because it impresses women in bars. And I was proud to have earned the job at an age, thirty-one, when some of my peers were still slaving away on backwater municipal beats in faraway bureaus. But it's just a line on a business card. It's not like there are files marked "for investigative reporters only." It certainly hasn't made me any smarter.

"So what do we know, besides 'four John Does stacked like cordwood in a weed-choked plot'?" I said, mimicking Peterson's style.

"That one of the John Does is actually a Jane."

"Whoops."

"Yeah," Szanto said, wincing as he sipped his still-too-hot coffee. "The police already called to bitch about that this morning."

"So what do you think Brodie wants from this?" I asked.

"You know exactly what he wants: a fascinating story with great art that gives us all piercing insight into the woes of New Jersey's largest city. And he wants it tomorrow."

"How about you give me a week and I'll try to turn in something that doesn't read like it was written by a lumberjack?"

"Hey, if it gets Brodie off my ass, you can rewrite *Tuesdays with Morrie* for all I care," Szanto said.

"Yeah, maybe I'll do that," I said as I departed his office.

"Tk Hrrrndzzz," Szanto hollered after me.

"Hear that?" I asked Tommy Hernandez, the aforementioned Facebook-obsessed intern.

"Yeah, it sounds like a lawnmower that won't start," he said, then looked at me with something far beyond disdain.

"How many times do I have to tell you that a wristwatch is an accessory and it should match your belt?" he demanded.

Tommy is only twenty-two, but he's blessed with a great reporter's instinct of noticing every small detail. He's handy to have on the streets, because he's second-generation Cuban-American and speaks flawless Spanish. He's also gay as the Mardi Gras parade.

"Come on, Tommy," I said. "Let's go embrace another beautiful day in Newark."

The abandoned lot on Ludlow Street was, true to Peterson's imagination, a sorrowful little patch of earth covered in dried weeds. The neighborhood around it wasn't bad, by Newark standards. Most of the houses appeared to be owner occupied and decently maintained, with either newish siding or fresh paint. The church, St. Mary's Catholic, was a century-old stone building with a tidy rectory next door. There was public housing across the street, but they were newly constructed town houses, the kind that wouldn't go to seed for at least another decade. Weequahic Golf Course, a charming little cow pasture county residents could play for fifteen bucks, was maybe two blocks down the street.

"This place is pretty decent," I said as Tommy and I pulled to a stop on Ludlow. He cast me a sideways glance.

"Yeah, let's start an upscale day spa here," he cracked.

"Okay, fair point," I corrected myself. "But look around. There's no one just hanging out. The cars are all gone. The people in this neighborhood work during the day."

"How far are we from Seth Boyden?"

The Seth Boyden projects were a festering den of urban despair. Even the toughest reporters got jittery about going there during the day. Going there after dark put you on the short list for a mugging.

"Three or four blocks," I said.

"Think it could have been someone from there? A lot of Blood sets hanging around."

"Could be. But would some Blood really go through the trouble of marching four people all the way down here? Those guys are hit-and-run types."

Tommy, who had written up nearly every shooting in Newark over the past six months, knew that as well as I did. We were really just stalling. The car was being buffeted by gusts of wind and neither of us was real keen to face them. A cold front had barreled down from Canada overnight and the winter season was giving New Jersey its first slap. Which figured. It's a meteorological fact that as soon as the weather gets extreme—in either direction—it coincides with me having to do man-on-the-street reporting. I've spent most of my career either sweating or shivering.

"I don't suppose the story will come to us in here, will it?" I asked.

"You know, for a superstar investigative reporter, you're a real pussy sometimes," Tommy said.

Grunting, I willed myself out of the car, across the street, and into the vacant lot. The Newark police's Crime Scene Unit had already retreated back to the warmth of their precinct. A few strips of windblown yellow tape were the only sign they had ever been there.

I gingerly picked my way toward the fence that lined the back of the lot, where a makeshift shrine was already forming. In the past few years, these shrines had become a ubiquitous part of the city landscape. As soon as some way-too-young kid gets gunned down, his boys come with candles and other mementos to memorialize the spot where he fell. If the victim is a Blood, you'll see red bandanas and "BIP"—Blood in Peace—spray-painted somewhere nearby. If he's a Crip, the bandanas will be blue and the graffiti will have some kind of number (Crip sets often have numbers). The Latin Kings decorate in black and gold, and so on.

I had interviewed kids who bragged about how big *their*

shrines would be when they got killed. They talked about it with a nonchalance that was chilling.

This shrine was small, so far. But it would undoubtedly grow over the next few days. Four bouquets of flowers, one for each victim, had already been attached to the fence. One of the bouquets had a card attached. I turned it over to read the inscription.

"Wanda," it read. "May you rest in peace forever. Love, Tynesha."

Tommy had walked up behind me. As I stared dumbly, Tommy was scribbling something in his pad.

"Let's find out who Tynesha is," he said as he copied the name of the florist.

"Good plan," I said, slightly chagrined the intern thought of it before I did.

"Someone's gotta do your work for you," he shot back.

Richard Whitlow approached us from the sidewalk, stepping carefully through the waist-high weeds. A beefy, dark-skinned black guy, he had been covering Newark for more than a decade and was, how to put it, a little bit inured to violent death. His greeted us with, "Hey, make sure you don't slip on the blood puddle."

"You journalists are so insensitive with your gallows humor," I joked back.

"I wish I was kidding. Check it out," he said, pointing to a bare patch of dirt that, sure enough, appeared to have been stained by something dark and red.

"Oh, nasty," Tommy said.

"Yeah, poor suckers bled out right there," Whitlow said, shaking his head.

"Police told you anything new?" I asked.

"Finally got the names out of them."

"They mean anything to you?"

"Nah. Not until I figure out their street names," Whitlow said. Aliases littered the hood like so much trash, especially among those who were employed in what you might call the city's informal economy. Your friendly neighborhood drug dealer could be known by up to a half-dozen different aliases, which bore scant resemblance to his real name. Depending on the name the police settled on, the victim's own mother might not recognize it. Or she might be the *only* one who recognized it.

"What names did they give you?"

Whitlow flipped open his notebook and shoved the page toward me so I could copy them down: Wanda Bass, Tyrone Scott, Shareef Thomas, Devin Whitehead. I had to press hard on my pen. The ink was already freezing.

"Cops say anything else?"

"Around ten, there were four shots, bang, bang, bang, bang," Whitlow said, turning to the next page in his notebook. "No one called the cops or even thought much of it because there's a bar down the street and people are always coming out drunk, shooting off their guns for the hell of it."

I always found strange comfort that the American propensity for mixing alcohol and firearms cut across racial, socioeconomic, and cultural divides, from rural redneck to ghetto gangbanger to skeet-shooting blue blood.

"Around eleven, some guy came out of the bar and happened to see four people lying in the back of the lot," Whitlow continued, flipping more pages as he went. "He told the cops he thought they were homeless and he was going to roust them and take them to a shelter, on account of the cold. Then he got close, saw the blood, and made the call."

"Wow, there are helpful citizens after all," I interjected.

"Yeah, anyway, that's about all I can tell you, other than that my ass is about to freeze off," Whitlow said, storing his notepad back in his jacket. "I got enough to write a daily. Hays is working some of his cop sources trying to get stuff out of them. Let me know if you find anything interesting around here."

Tommy and I decided to work the streets, which can be a wonderful source of information for the reporter who doesn't mind the trial-and-error method of walking up to random people until you bump into one who knows something.

Which is not to say it's easy. As a rule, Newark residents don't trust anyone. They especially don't trust anyone who looks official, be they cops, politicians, or newspaper reporters. And they *doubly* don't trust white folks, who are usually only there to arrest them or scam them.

Therefore, for someone of my pallor and profession, milking information from the streets involved bridging that rather huge chasm of natural distrust. Some white reporters running in the hood try to "act black"—talk the vernacular, quote rappers, dress like they're going on BET—but that was never going to work for me.

The fact of the matter is I'm Carter Ross, born to an upper-middle-class family in the privilege of Millburn, one of New Jersey's finer suburbs. I was raised by two doting parents alongside an older brother who's now a lawyer and a younger sister who's now a social worker. We vacationed down the shore every summer, skied in Vermont every winter, and were taught to view Newark as the kind of place you heard about but did not visit. I was sheltered by some of New Jersey's best prep schools until age eighteen, whereupon I went to Amherst College and spent four years around some of the nation's most elite students. I just don't have any street in me.

And anyone could see it. The things that allow me to blend into the tasteful décor at any of New Jersey's better suburban shopping malls—my side-parted brown hair, my preference for button-down-collared shirts and pressed slacks, my awkwardly upright carriage, my precise diction and bland anywhere-in-America accent—made me a circus freak in the hood. Most people I pass on the street are polite enough to merely stare. A few openly point. People are constantly asking me if I'm lost.

Yet through the years, I had come to realize a simple fact of reporting: if you approach people with respect, listen hard, and genuinely try to understand their point of view, they will talk to you, no matter how different your background is. So that's what I attempt to do.

Over the next three hours, I learned a lot about the neighborhood: how the vacant lot had once been home to a crack house, until the city got its act together and tore it down; how the public housing across the street, which had been slapped together by a developer known to be cozy with the mayor, was already falling apart; how the bar down the street, the Ludlow Tavern, just kept getting rougher, with the patrons leaving their knives at home and bringing their guns instead.

But I didn't learn anything about the four victims, which suggested they weren't from this part of town. Most Newark neighborhoods were tighter than outsiders realized, with familial connections that went back generations. If someone from the neighborhood got killed, you could always find a cousin or a friend—or a cousin of a friend whose aunt was distantly related to the victim's stepmother. Something. But I had struck out.

By the time I was done canvassing and had returned to the vacant lot, a truck from a New York TV station had pulled up outside the church. No doubt, they were ready to lend great insight and understanding with their ferociously dogged reporting,

12

which would consist of taking off just as soon as they had collected one usable five-second sound bite from the first "concerned citizen" they could find.

I don't want to launch into too much of a rant against local television reporters. But if I were a modern-day Noah, I'd take the bacteria that causes the clap on my ark before I took one of them.

This reporter (I loathe to even use that word) was a typical TV news chick whose good looks were an entirely artificial creation. It was possible, underneath the layers of eye makeup and expensively treated hair, she might have once been an attractive human being. But who could tell anymore?

"I'm standing outside St. Mary's Roman Catholic Church in Newark," she began breathlessly, "where four bodies were found stacked like cordwood in this . . . *dammit.*"

A gust of wind had sullied her hair, momentarily halting her unflappable dedication to delivering the news.

"Come on. My fingers are freezing," her cameraman complained.

"Shut *up*. You think I'm warm here?" she said testily, running a gloved hand through her hair.

Then she saw me, instantly dropped the bitchy act, and affected a huge smile, as if she were happy to see me—which, I knew, meant she was going to try to leach information out of me. TV chicks believe they can get stuff from male newspaper reporters simply by flipping their hair and batting their eyes a few times. They do this because they assume male newspaper reporters are hard up. Most of the time, they're absolutely correct. But I can proudly say I don't let Mr. Johnson do my thinking when I'm on the job. I save that for *after* work.

"Hiiiiiii," she said, managing to fire off two hair flips inside seven seconds. "Alexis Stewart, News 8 Action News Team."

13

"Hi," I said flatly.

"Do you know where any of the victims' families live, by any chance? I'd love to get a bite from a grieving mom."

"Yeah. They all live just a few blocks up that way," I lied. "They're in an apartment complex called Seth Boyden. You might want to hurry. I hear they're just about to hold a news conference."

The News 8 Action News Team rushed off like they were headed to a free hair spray handout, leaving me alone on Ludlow Street. A strong gust of wind sliced into me as I gazed at the vacant lot, trying to imagine what circumstances had led four people to this spot for the purpose of taking their last breaths.

Four bodies. It was a big number. There had only been one other quadruple homicide in Newark in the last quarter century, mostly because the drug-related killings that typified the city's murders tended to be one- or two-at-a-time type affairs. Contrary to what suburbanites believed, the drug trade in Newark was not highly organized. There were no kingpins, no major operators, no Evil Geniuses behind it all. The local gangs, who did most of the selling, were all neighborhood based, with little centralization beyond that. Even though all Bloods wore red and all Crips wore blue, each set operated independently. The violence they committed tended to be limited in scale.

So four bodies suggested something new, something much more pernicious. To herd together four people, lead them to a faraway vacant lot, and kill them? That took planning, organization, coordination. And those were higher-order skills we hadn't seen from the street before.

I soon realized I wasn't alone in staring at the lot. An older guy with long, salt-and-pepper dreadlocks was doing the same thing. He was wearing the uniform of a Newark Liberty

International Airport baggage handler and was carrying some flowers.

"Hi, there," I said.

"Hey, Bird Man," he said.

On the streets, the *Newark Eagle-Examiner* was known as "the Bird." Its reporters were called "Bird Man" or "Bird Woman." It was an unfortunate consequence of the long-ago marriage of the *Newark Eagle* and the *Newark Examiner* into the *Eagle-Examiner*. And while the merger made us New Jersey's largest and most respected daily newspaper, it also made us sound like we were the official publication of the Audubon Society. I suppose the reporters didn't have it as bad as some: the guys who tossed the papers onto people's front porches in the morning were called "Bird Flippers."

"Gee, what makes you think I'm a reporter?" I asked, trying not to sound too sarcastic.

"You got that nosy look."

"You can call me Carter," I said, sticking out my hand for him to shake. He looked a little surprised—people in the hood often are when a white person is friendly toward them—then grabbed it and pumped it twice. His hands felt like they had gripped a lot of Louis Vuitton knockoffs in their time.

"You know one of them?" I asked.

"Yeah. Tyrone Scott. Called himself 'Hundred Year.' He told people he was supposed to get himself a hundred years in jail for killing some guy."

"So I take it he got paroled."

"Ah, he was full of it," the man said. "You know how these young bucks are. Always trying to puff up their damn reputations, trying to make themselves all bad. He was just caught selling near a school."

That was one of the Catch-22s of urban drug sales in New

Jersey: there were stiffer penalties for dealing within a thousand feet of a school, the difference between jail time and no jail time. But the thousand-foot standard was set with the suburbs in mind. In the city, *everything* was within a thousand feet of a school. It was the main reason New Jersey led the nation in the disparity between its prison population (60 percent black) and its general population (12 percent black).

"So how'd you know him?"

"I go with his mama a little bit. She asked me to come down with this," he said, holding up the flowers.

"Any idea what he did to end up here?"

"What you think?"

"Dealer?"

"Nah," the man said. "He was just a hustler."

In Newark, the distinction between "dealer" and "hustler" was an important one. A "dealer" is a guy who does nothing but sell drugs, and is mostly despised. A "hustler" is a more sympathetic figure: he only sells drugs out of necessity, to keep the lights turned on.

Which is not to say a hustler couldn't get himself in the same kind of trouble a dealer did.

"What was his hustle?" I asked.

"Diesel," the man said. Heroin.

"Did he live around here?"

"Naw. His mama lives over off South Orange Avenue by the Garden State Parkway. He hustled in front of the chicken shack over there."

I was keeping mental notes at this point. Sometimes people clam up when you pull out a notebook and I didn't want to spook this guy.

"So how come he ended up down here?" I asked. "I mean, that neighborhood has to be three miles from here."

"His mama was asking the same question," he said, then started mimicking a woman's voice: "'What was that boy doin' down there? Why he leave his hood? Don't he know they ain't got no respect for nothing down there?'"

"She have any idea why this happened to him?"

"She didn't even know he hustled. She didn't want to know. He'd be out on that corner hustling all day and she'd say, 'Ain't it nice of Tyrone to keep an eye on the neighborhood? He's such a good boy.'"

"He in a gang?"

"Don't think so. He was too old for that."

"How old was he?"

"Tyrone? Hell. Twenty-eight, twenty-nine?"

In gang years, that was the equivalent of about ninety-seven. Gang members reached middle age by eighteen. By twenty-three or twenty-four, after a quick stint or two in jail, you were considered OG, an "Original Gangster." No one made it to thirty in a gang. By that age, you were either dead, in jail for an extended stretch, or you had finally found the good sense to change occupations.

"Well, I best be moving on," the man said. "My bones is getting cold."

"Mine too. Thanks for talking."

"Uh-huh. Just make sure the police catch whoever did this, okay?" the man said, as he began walking toward the shrine with his flowers. "I don't know if Tyrone's mama could take it if she don't get a little justice."

With early-stage hypothermia setting in, I was making the teeth-chattering walk back to the car when I saw Tommy emerge from a house at the far end of the street.

"Hurry up," I hollered. "Pretend there's a sale at John Varvatos."

"What's the matter?" he shot back as he caught up to me. "You're nervous because it's been four hours since you checked on your fantasy football team?"

"Hey, that's important stuff. I'm *thisclose* to pulling off a blockbuster deal for Peyton Manning."

"Let's just say my fantasies involving football teams are a little different from yours."

We hopped into my car to escape the cold just as a gust of wind rocked it. I got us rolling and clicked on the radio, where an all-news station was midway through another report about the troubled newspaper industry. For those of us who had been living with the devastation, this hardly qualified as news.

People think newspapers are struggling because the Internet stole our readers. But that's not the problem; when readers go online, they're still clicking on our sites for their news. Between print and online, most newspapers have more readers than they've ever had. We don't make much money off online readers at the moment, because most advertisers are still learning how best to utilize the Web. But we'll figure that out eventually.

The real problem is that the Internet stole our classified advertising. Every daily newspaper used to have a nice thick section stuffed with nothing but ads—used cars, apartments for rent, houses for sale, secondhand pianos, job postings, and so on. We were the community's marketplace and in most areas we were the only game in town. As an industry, our entire profit margin came from that one section.

That's gone now. Gone to Craigslist, to eBay, to Monster, to Autotrader. Combine that with some of our other issues—shrinking retail advertising budgets, soaring newsprint prices, increased distribution costs, and so on—and it made for a fiscal conflagration that was threatening to consume an entire American institution.

"Can we turn that off?" Tommy said. "It's like listening to someone narrate your own funeral."

"Happy to oblige," I said.

It was easy to get caught up in the sense of doom. The threat of layoff was constant and I didn't care to think about how many good people we had lost already. Yet for all the Internet had done to shake up newsrooms, the basics of what we did—gather information and disseminate it in a speedy and sensible manner—were unchanged. So I turned my attention back toward that job.

"You learn anything out there?" I said, holding my hand against the car's heater, which was finally spitting out lukewarm air.

"Not really. Nobody seems to know anything about these guys. I just keep hearing the same thing: there were four shots, no one called the police because gunfire in the neighborhood is so common, suddenly there are four dead bodies. Everyone is a little freaked out."

"Sounds like stuff you can feed to Whitlow and Hays for the daily."

"Yeah. What did you get?"

I related the conversation I had with Tyrone Scott's mama's boyfriend.

"Well, that's a little something," Tommy said. "Should we check out that chicken shack?"

"No, I'll do that. Let's split up. Why don't you visit that florist and see if they can tell you who 'Tynesha' is."

Tommy agreed and, as I drove back to the office, he subjected me to a harangue about how my shoes were just *wrong,* saying I should free myself from the bondage of laces and get slip-ons.

"Tommy, I'm born and bred WASP," I reminded him. "You ought to be proud of me for not wearing shoes with tassels."

Upon returning to the office, I made a quick Coke Zero pit stop at the break room vending machines. There, I found Tina Thompson, our city editor, reading *Fertility for Dummies*. Tina was excessively candid about her sex life, and the thunderous ticking of her thirty-eight-year-old biological clock could be heard as far away as the Pine Barrens. It never failed to amuse me how a woman whose life had until recently consisted of work, yoga, jogging—and a series of relationships that lasted between one night and two weeks—had suddenly entered a nesting phase. Her search for Mr. Right had taken on a highly procreative bent. She wasn't looking for a life partner, just a mating partner: a man who was, above all else, fecund.

"Hey, Tina," I said. "Gotten yourself knocked up yet?"

"Jesus Christ!" she said, without looking up. "Did you know that excessive time riding a bike can cause sterility in males? That's it. No more bike messengers for me."

She threw the book down.

"Might want to take it easy on the X-ray technicians, too," I suggested.

"Hey, if he's six foot one, a hundred eighty-five pounds, with dark hair and blue eyes, I might let him throw one in me anyway," she said with a flirty grin.

I'm six one. One hundred eighty-five. Dark hair. Blue eyes. I'm not a bad-looking guy. Occasionally, I'm even somewhat dashing. But I'm not under any illusion Tina is attracted to *me*. Just my sperm. So far, my little swimmers had held off on her overtures. Though I'm a little worried about what might happen if she got them drunk someday. They're weak-willed. And

Tina has that hot-older-woman thing going on, with yoga-toned arms, never-ending legs, and expressive brown eyes that seemed to be winking at me even when they were still.

"Too bad I'm a born-again virgin," I said. "I'm going to Virgins Anonymous and everything. Just celebrated my three-month anniversary of celibacy."

That last part was actually true, sadly, though not by choice. I was just in a little slump. That didn't mean I was going to hop into bed simply because Tina patted the pillow. I wasn't ready to become one of those Modern Fathers who parade around with Precious Bundle strapped to his chest in a Baby Bjorn all day. Nor was I particularly interested in spawning a child who would someday refer to me as "my biological father."

"Fine, have it your way," she said. "You'll cave someday."

Alas, she was probably right. Tina was wearing a button-down white blouse that was just slightly see-through and an above-the-knee charcoal-gray skirt with black tights. And in one motion—she recrossed her fabulous legs and tucked a lock of curly brown hair behind her ear—I could already feel my resolve crumbling.

"So you look like you've spent all day in a meat locker," she said. "You get anything out there?"

"Other than frostbite? No."

"Buster Hays has a cop source who says they're looking into a theory that this has something to do with a robbery at the Ludlow Tavern," Tina said.

"What's the theory?"

"That one of the victims helped stick up the place a couple months ago then had the balls to walk back into the place and order a drink. Supposedly, the owner had him whacked."

"Which one?"

"The one with the Muslim name . . . uh, Shareef Thomas."

21

"So who are the other three people?"

"Accomplices?" she said, sounding uncertain. "I'm not sure they know."

"The police got any good evidence to back up this theory?"

"Source won't say. But do the Newark police ever have *good* evidence?"

She had a point. I once covered a murder trial where—no lie—the whole case had been pinned on the eyewitness account of one drug addict who admitted to being high at the time of the shooting. "I was high," she said on the stand. "But I have a really good memory." The jury disagreed, deliberating for about thirty-five minutes before returning a not-guilty plea.

"What does Hays think?" I asked.

"That they may be on to something. His cop made it sound like this was a really hot lead."

"Huh," I said. "Brodie still got wood for this thing?"

"His flag has been at full staff all day long," Tina said.

Before that imagery developed any further, I ended our conversation and went back to my desk.

I started punching the victims' names into my computer, seeing what it might tell me. Between Lexis-Nexis, New Jersey voting records, the Department of Corrections Web site, and the other public records to which a reporter had instant access, you could usually piece together a solid bank of information on a person within a few minutes.

Unless their names are Wanda Bass, Tyrone Scott, and Shareef Thomas, all of which were too common for me to get anything definitive. The only name that returned much of anything was Devin Whitehead. I got his Department of Corrections profile, which included six convictions for possession and possession with intent to distribute. I also got his last known address, which was in the Clinton Hill section of Newark.

22

And that was a good break, because I happened to have a source there.

My guy in Clinton Hill is Reginald Jamison, but I think the only person who calls him "Reginald" is his wife. Everyone else calls him "the T-shirt Man," or just "Tee."

Tee has a small storefront on Clinton Avenue. He and I became acquainted a few years back when I did a story about RIP T-shirts, which happen to be Tee's specialty. RIPs had become a disturbingly prevalent urban fashion trend: anytime some too-young kid got killed, his boys rushed to have a T-shirt made in his memory. Every RIP T-shirt was different, but they followed a basic formula, featuring the deceased's photo, the dates of birth and death, and the words REST IN PEACE. The people who wore them essentially became walking tombstones.

More than half of Tee's business came from RIP T-shirts. And while he hated the idea that he was profiting from these kids' deaths, he was also a businessman who figured if he wasn't making these things, someone else would. He assuaged his guilt by putting extra care into the design, so each T-shirt would be special to the grieving family.

The story I wrote about Tee had given him some good publicity and I became a semiregular visitor to his store. We couldn't have been raised in more different circumstances— while I was taking SAT prep classes, Tee was dropping out of high school to support three younger siblings. But we were close to the same age, shared a fundamental curiosity for the world, and enjoyed each other's company because of it. Tee could explain the hood to me, while I translated white people for him. Plus, Tee had a natural eye for news. He could have made a great reporter.

Instead, he was just one of my best sources. And as soon as

I got buzzed into his store that afternoon, he greeted me with, "I wondered when I was going to hear from you."

"And why is that?"

"You're here about Dee-Dub, right?"

Dee-Dub. D.W. Devin Whitehead. Got it.

"Good guess."

"Everyone's talking about it. Figured you'd get here sooner or later. I'm making his T-shirt right now."

I walked over to Tee's computer, where he designed all his shirts. Sure enough, Devin Whitehead's face was on the screen, waiting to be immortalized on a Hanes Beefy-T. I did quick math on his dates. He was exactly two weeks shy of his twenty-first birthday.

"Can you believe that? Twenty years old." Tee shook his head and I could tell he had been near tears. Tee looks like a badass—five ten, at least two hundred fifty, most of it muscle, braids, and tattoos—but the dude could cry from watching a car commercial.

"You know him well?" I asked.

"A little bit. He was one of those knuckleheads who hang outside my store. But he was a good kid."

The definition of a "good kid" in Newark was perhaps a little different than it was in the suburbs. Out there, being a good kid meant you did your homework, made it home by curfew, and participated in resume-building extracurricular activities that would compare favorably on a college application. In Newark, it meant you hadn't shot anyone.

"Gang?"

"Allegedly."

"Allegedly" was one of Tee's favorite words. He used it with the appropriate sense of sarcasm.

"Which one?"

24

"You ain't gonna write nothing bad about him, are you?" Tee asked warily. "I know his mama. If his mama found out you got it from me, she'd smack me upside the head. And his mama is one big bitch."

"He's dead, Tee," I said. "I'm not gonna piss on the kid's grave. I'm just trying to figure out what he might have done to get himself killed."

"Okay, well, *allegedly* he was part of the Browns."

The Brick City Browns was one of Newark's more venerable street gangs—which meant it had been around since the late 1990s.

"Are the Browns at war with anyone right now?" I asked.

"No more or less than usual."

"Was he a dealer?"

"Allegedly."

"What did he sell?"

"Mostly smack, I think," Tee said. "I don't know. I ain't into that stuff. Hang on a sec."

Tee went outside his store and had a brief conversation with the aforementioned knuckleheads. Tee could get more information out of those kids in thirty seconds than I could get in half a lifetime.

"Yeah," Tee said as he came back in. "They said he used to sell cook-up"—street term for crack-cocaine—"but he kept getting popped for it"—street term for sent to jail—"and when he got out the last time he switched to smack. Allegedly."

That made two heroin sellers.

"So what are you hearing? What are people saying?" I asked.

"I don't know," Tee said. "This one is weird. You know how it is around here. Someone has a beef with you, they find you on a corner somewhere, they drive up and shoot your ass and then they drive off. That's a dime a dozen. You know what I'm saying? This don't make no sense."

"Tell me about it."

"I mean, what was he doing down there?"

"I'm trying to figure that out. Is it possible he knew anyone in that neighborhood?"

"Dee-Dub? The only times he left Clinton Hill was when he got arrested. He lived with his mama. He had a baby with a girl down the street. His boys are all here. He didn't have no reason to go down there."

We mulled that over for a moment. Tee busied himself by rearranging the used DVDs and CDs he sold as a side business.

"What are *you* hearing?" Tee asked.

"Not much, to be honest. The police think this was retribution for some kind of bar robbery the victims pulled. Is that possible?"

"I mean, possible? Yeah, it's possible. It's possible Busta Rhymes will decide to make his next video in the back of my store. But I don't think it's gonna happen, you know what I'm saying?"

"Uh, no."

"I'm saying, Dee-Dub wasn't no stick-up artist," Tee said. "He just didn't have that in him."

I pulled my pad out of my pocket and showed him the list of victims.

"Any of these other names mean anything to you?"

As he scanned my pad, I added, "Tyrone Scott goes by the name 'Hundred Year' sometimes."

"Nope. Don't know none of them besides Dee-Dub," Tee said.

"Huh. Well, keep your ears open, okay?"

"You got it," Tee said, then went back to the task of memorializing Devin Whitehead in the way he knew best.

My next stop was the South Orange Avenue chicken shack, hard by the Garden State Parkway. Like a number of Newark's finer providers of well-crisped fowl, this one was a shameless knockoff of Kentucky Fried Chicken. It was called Wyoming Fried Chicken. Its mascot was "Cowboy Kenny," who looked like the Colonel after a hot shower. It featured "the Cowboy's" secret blend of herbs and spices—as if salt, pepper, and MSG were a secret.

Any corporate lawyer would have filed a lawsuit quicker than he could eat a five-piece basket. But that was the blessing of Newark that protected every bootlegger, boondoggler, and copyright infringer within the city limits: anyone who might have the inclination to file such a suit wouldn't come within three zip codes of the place.

I pulled up in front of the WFC, which had roughly a dozen guys hanging out in front of it—or at least it did until one of them saw my pasty face, at which point there was a rapid scattering. The sight of a well-dressed white man in the ghetto often has that effect. Only one of the loiterers stayed behind. He was wearing a North Face jacket, which was all the rage among discerning urban pharmaceutical salesmen. Lots of pockets.

"What you want?" North Face asked, eyeing me suspiciously.

"I'm a reporter with the *Eagle-Examiner*. I'm just working on a story. You know a guy named Tyrone Scott? Goes by the name Hundred Year?"

"Never heard of him," North Face said, spitting his sentence out almost before I finished mine. I could have asked him if he

27

knew Mickey Mouse and the answer would have been the same.

"Really? That's funny, because someone told me he hustles around here."

"Well, good for him," North Face said, getting agitated. "But you can't stand here."

"Excuse me? This is a public sidewalk."

"It's *my* sidewalk. Get out of here. You're scaring away all the customers."

"Well, we can do this one of two ways," I said. "Either you tell me about Hundred Year, or I stand here all night until I find someone who knows him. What's it gonna be?"

He glanced around, clearly not liking either choice. And perhaps he was considering a third option—pulling a piece out from under his jacket and reducing me to a bloody speed bump on Cowboy Kenny's sidewalk—but I think he realized having dozens of cops responding to a homicide call was going to be an even greater business disruption.

"I talk and then you leave?"

"You have my word," I said. "What was his deal?"

"I don't know. He went to jail for a while. Then he got out."

"What was he in for?"

"Dealing, I guess. He told people he shot someone, but if he did, it wasn't no one around here. I ain't never heard no one saying, 'Yeah, Tyrone, that nigga shot me.' "

"Was he in a gang?"

"Naw. Tyrone's just a mama's boy."

"Did he hustle?"

"Yeah, sometimes. Not all the time, you know what I mean? But more lately."

"What did he sell? Diesel?"

"Diesel?" North Face said, screwing up his face like he had never heard the word.

"You really want me out here all night, don't you?"

"Okay, yeah, he was selling diesel."

"You think it got him killed?"

"I don't know. Look, it wasn't me or any of my boys, okay?"

"Convince me."

North Face looked left, then right, like he wanted to make sure no one was eavesdropping. Or maybe it was just a reflex to keep your head on a swivel in his line of work.

"Man, I'm saying, he just did his own thing, you know?" he said. "He had his own customers, the real hard-core junkies. He got a reputation for selling really good junk and then, bam, all the junkies started going to him."

"Didn't that piss you off?"

"Naw, man. I don't sell drugs."

"For a guy who doesn't sell drugs, you sure know a lot about it," I said, cracking an I'm-kidding-please-don't-shoot-me smile.

"Who me?" he said. "I just read that in *National Geographic*."

I made good on my word to leave him and his business dealings in peace, and it was probably about time to do so anyway. It was getting dark. The streets of Newark aren't quite as treacherous as outsiders think. But they're still no place to dawdle once the sun sets.

I returned to the newsroom to find it humming with its usual five o'clock buzz as deadline loomed. Our newsroom, like most newsrooms, had offices only along the outer walls and only for the most high-level editors. The majority of the editors—and all of the reporters—sat in a sea of desks that sprawled uninterrupted, without walls or partitions, over a vast open space.

So it wasn't hard to monitor the daily ebb and flow, and sometimes the newsman in me—the part of me that is incurably ink-stained—delighted in watching what we in the business call "the daily miracle." My mother always wondered why her handsome son didn't seek the greater fame and fortune to be had on TV (her dream for me was to be the next Charles Gibson). But there were too many things about the newspaper business I loved.

The early-evening newsroom scene was one of them: reporters straining to burnish their prose before deadline; editors roaming about, hungry for copy, pestering and pressuring the reporters to give it to them; designers forcing the jigsaw-puzzle pieces of stories, artwork, and advertisements to fit on a page. Once upon a time, in the hoary old days of our business, the primary motivation for finishing was getting to the bar. The local watering hole was essentially a second newsroom. Going to work the next day hungover and wearing yesterday's clothes was not frowned upon. It may have even been encouraged.

Today's newsroom bears little resemblance to the newsroom of yore. Sometime during the seventies, inspired by Watergate and the notion that a newspaper had the power to overthrow a president, journalism sobered out and grew up. Reporters became responsible members of society with degrees from respectable colleges and paychecks you could actually live on.

So the end-of-day hurry-up was about getting home to the family, where a respectable, SUV-driving, diet-soda-drinking life would continue to be led. The old-timers will tell you something was lost along the way, that journalism went so corporate it surrendered its soul. But I disagree. To me, journalism is still a calling, just as it was to our ruffled, alcoholic forefathers.

I believe the stories I write matter. I believe the world is a wonderful, chaotic, fascinating place and that I've done my job if I can help people understand it just a little better. I believe a free and vibrant press is an essential part of a free and great society.

And sure, it gets messy sometimes. What used to be known as journalism has morphed into this ugly, chimeralike beast collectively called "the media." And "the media" has its faults, what with all the princess-chasing paparazzi, the sleazy tabloid folks, and, of course, the cliché-drenched local TV newscasters. But I'll link arms with all those malcontents and proudly state the world is a much better place with us than it would be without us.

Take my current assignment. I'm sure someone who loves to bash "the media" would say I'm exploiting the death of four people by writing a story that sensationalizes violent crime. I disagree entirely. To me, I'm helping people make sense of a profoundly tragic act: the intentional taking of four human lives. And it would become even more tragic if we in the media—who have both the privilege and obligation of being society's vocal cords—allowed such a terrible act to pass without commenting on it.

I was lost in that thought when the voice of Buster Hays, our resident aging crank, jolted me out of my reverie.

"Hey, Ivy, come over here a second," he hollered. Hays grew up on 133rd Street in the Bronx and felt his common-man roots made him a superior journalist to an overeducated prep school boy like me. So he called me Ivy, no matter how many times I told him Amherst was not part of the Ivy League.

"What can I do for you," I said as I walked up to his desk.

"This may be a shock to your delicate system, but it seems we're putting out a newspaper that we plan to sell *tomorrow*," Hays said. "You got anything to add to that effort or are we going to have to wait until January to read what's in your notebook?"

31

Hays was of the general opinion that reporters like me—who spent weeks developing more complex stories—were about as useful as paper cuts.

"Well, I think this thing might be drug related," I said. "Tyrone Scott and Devin Whitehead both sold heroin."

"Well, stop the presses," Hays said, then announced to no one in particular, "Hey, Ivy boy here says two of the Ludlow Four were *drug dealers*! Can you imagine that? Drug dealers! In Newark!"

"Dammit, Hays, this guy—"

"Look, Ivy, let me explain a little something to you," Hays interrupted in a condescending manner, peering at me over the top of his reading glasses. "Just because someone who sold drugs is involved in a crime, it doesn't make the crime drug related, okay?"

"Well, I know that, Hays, I just think your cop sources may be throwing this bar-robbery theory against the wall to see if it sticks," I said, sounding whinier than I wanted to.

"Tell you what, Ivy, you get someone credible to say this thing is drug related, I'll put it in tomorrow's paper."

"And who, in your mind, is credible?"

"I dunno. Why don't you call the National Drug Bureau?" he suggested with a smirk.

The National Drug Bureau was a federal agency that targeted international drug smuggling. Every so often, we'd quote them crowing about another big bust at the airport, along with a picture of NDB agents preening in front of a pile of controlled dangerous substances. But they didn't really concern themselves with street-level drug trafficking. Hays telling me to call the NDB for a story about Newark homicides was like phoning the Democratic National Committee and asking for comment on the Barringer High School student council race.

Then again, if I could convince some bored federal flak to give me a line or two, it'd be fun to throw it back in Hays's sneering face.

"You know what, Hays? Fine. I'll call the National Drug Bureau," I said.

"Have fun wasting your time."

"Yeah, well," I said, groping for something to put Hays in his place. "It's my time to waste."

Retreating from the Dinosaur's Den, I stomped back to my desk, all the while stewing that I hadn't come up with a snappier rejoinder. *It's my time to waste*? Dammit. Couldn't I have at least managed some kind of comeback that involved him filing his stories on an IBM Correcting Selectric II?

I hauled up the National Drug Bureau's Web site, which featured whole photo galleries of agents posing in front of large piles of powdery junk, then clicked on their "For the Media" link. After about sixteen more clicks—government efficiency at work—I found a number for their Newark Field Office and the contact name L. Peter Sampson, Press Agent.

Agent Sampson's voice mail informed me he was in the office today but currently unavailable. I looked at the clock. Five thirty-two. No way a federal bureaucrat was still hanging around. Luckily for me, his recording concluded by saying that if I was a reporter on deadline, I could call his cell phone.

"Why, yes, I just so happen to be a reporter on deadline," I said out loud, to no one in particular, copying down the number. I hung up and immediately dialed it.

"Agent Sampson," an enthusiastic, Boy Scout–sounding voice answered.

"Hi, Agent Sampson, Carter Ross from the *Eagle-Examiner*."

There was a long pause on the other end. It has been explained to me that low- and mid-level PR people live in constant fear they'll be fired because of something a miscreant like me puts in the newspaper. It turns them into sad little creatures, analogous to any timid, furry animal of your choosing. With few exceptions, they're not all that smart, startle easily, and don't like leaving their holes for long. Above all else, they hate surprises. And a reporter calling unsolicited after hours qualified as a surprise.

"What, what can I do for you?" he said cautiously.

He sounded very much like a guy who didn't want the world to know his first name—L. Peter Sampson, indeed. I wondered what his friends called him. L. Pete? L. Peter? Or just plain L.?

"We're working on a follow-up story about this quadruple homicide in Newark, the one down on Ludlow Street," I said. "I'm looking into the theory that it's drug related."

"What makes you think it's drug related?" L. Pete said, his voice quickening, sounding even more panicked.

I went into a brief summary of my reporting, glossing over the parts I didn't really know and concluding, ". . . so, it'd just be nice to have a quote from you guys saying a crime of this nature could be drug related."

"I'm, I'm not authorized to give a quote."

A PR guy not authorized to give a quote? What's next, a plumber not authorized to flush toilets?

"I'm not trying to say you guys did anything wrong," I explained in an attempt to calm him. "I just want an authoritative voice on drugs to add to the story. How about a quick interview with your boss?"

My attempt to soothe his nerves—to lure the timid, furry animal out of his hole with a few kind words and some bits of bread—was backfiring. I was only scaring him more.

"My, my boss?"

"Yeah." I scanned the Web site and pulled the name off the roster. "Randall N. Meyers."

"What's he got to do with it? We don't have anything to do with this case."

"I know, but it's a big case and I thought, with all the times we put news about your guys' airport busts in the paper, Randall Meyers would be a name our readers would recognize and trust on this subject."

That's it. Soften him up. C'mere, little guy. C'mere . . .

"Randy won't . . . uh, Agent Meyers won't . . . is unavailable for comment."

"So you guys are a no comment," I said. I didn't know if I would stoop this low, but no comments could be useful as a sleazy, backdoor way to force unverified news into the paper, the classic being "Senator Gobble D. Gook had no comment on whether he was beating his wife."

"No, no," L. Pete corrected me. "I didn't say 'no comment.' I said 'unavailable for comment.' It's different."

So it was. It was also less useful. And frankly, I was beginning to lose interest in this exchange, which wasn't at all going the way I hoped.

"All right," I said. "If you guys don't want to be mentioned as respected experts on this subject, that's up to you, I guess."

It was my last attempt and I thought he just might take the bait. But no, he took it as his exit strategy, quickly thanked me for calling, then hung up.

I was still pouting a little when Tommy returned from the flower shop.

"What's the matter?" he said.

"Just a conversation that didn't go well," I huffed. "My life needs better scriptwriters."

"Yeah. You should get those people from *Will and Grace*. They're not doing anything these days. You could stand to get in touch with your queer side."

"I thought hanging out with you filled my daily gay quota."

"You can *never* get too much gay in your day," Tommy said.

"Now what would your father think if he heard you say that?" I asked. Tommy still lived with his parents. At home, he was so far in the closet he was rearranging his sweaters.

"He's so clueless, he'd probably think I was talking about vitamin supplements," Tommy replied.

"Very nice. How was the flower shop anyway?"

"Helpful," Tommy said, flipping open his notebook. "The owner was this sweet little Costa Rican lady. She kept talking about how she had a daughter my age and how I looked like such a nice boy and how I should come back when her daughter was around."

Tommy is a good-looking guy, to be sure—dark, handsome features; small, wiry body; neat, natty clothing. But his sexual orientation is as obvious as three snaps in a Z-formation.

"So we have a flower shop owner with no gaydar whatso-ever," I said.

"Yeah, but luckily she does have caller ID. Tynesha placed the order from this number," he said, showing me his pad.

"Great," I said, hauling up a reverse lookup service on my screen. I typed in the number. No luck.

"Well, so much for the easy way," I said. "Let's try it the old-fashioned way."

I dialed the number. Tommy leaned over by the earpiece so he could eavesdrop.

"Hello," said a female voice I assumed belonged to Tynesha. It was cold, impersonal.

"Hi, is Tynesha there?" I said.

"Heeyyy, baby," Tynesha said, having suddenly warmed up by a hundred degrees. "How you doin' today, cutie-pie?"

"Uh, I'm fine," I said, confused.

"Where you get my number from, honey? Lucious give you my number?"

"Lucious?"

"Yeah, what price he give you?"

"Uhh," I said, trying not to sound like an utter imbecile. "I'm not sure."

"Okay, let's just call it a hundred, okay? A hundred and you can do whatever you want for an hour. One-fifty for two."

My confusion instantly evaporated. Tynesha was a hooker.

Tommy doubled over in noiseless laughter.

"An hour . . . an hour would be great," I said, blushing. "Where can I find you?"

"You know where the Stop-In Go-Go is?" she said.

"The Stop-In Go-Go," I said. "You mean that place in Irvington?"

"Yeah, baby. I'll be dancing there tonight," she purred. "I'd looove to see you there. I can just tell from your voice you're a gorgeous white boy."

Tommy was now quietly hitting his fist on the table as he bit his lip to keep from laughing aloud. I swatted at him. This was hard enough without his histrionics.

"What time are you dancing?" I said.

"I'm on stage from six to seven and again from nine to ten. In between, I'm all yours, baby."

"Great," I said, unsure of what else to say. My career in journalism had helped me develop a great many skills. Soliciting prostitution had not been one of them.

"So," I continued, "how does this, you know, happen? I've never done this before."

"Of course not, baby," she said. "Neither have I."

I didn't want to think about how thoroughly untrue that was.

"No, I mean, how will you know who I am?"

"Oh, don't worry, baby, I'll know who you are," she said. "You'll be the one who tips me the most during my dance."

I had to admit, she was good.

"Right," I said. "Of course I will be. I guess I'll see you later on, then?"

"Bye, baby. I'm looking forward to it."

I hung up the phone and Tommy finally let his pent-up laughter explode outward.

"Nice job, stud!" he howled when he was done, then started another laughing fit.

Half the heads in the newsroom turned our way.

"Carter has a date with a hooker tonight!" Tommy exclaimed.

Suddenly, Tommy wasn't the only one laughing. They all were—and hooting, and whistling, and mocking. Some comedian from over on the copy desk started clapping, and soon I was getting a full standing ovation. I could feel my face, which had already been red, cycling through about six different shades of scarlet until it settled on something close to purple.

"You know me, anything for a story," I said, waving my hand in the air to acknowledge the cheers, which slowly died down. "Let's get out of here, Tommy."

I walked out of the newsroom to a variety of catcalls—"Go get 'er, Casanova," "Remember, she won't kiss on the mouth," and, lastly, "Don't forget to double-bag."

The Director enjoyed the irony of how he had gotten into business in the first place. He was always reminding Monty: they owed all their success to the U.S. government and the things it had done unwittingly to prop up the East Coast heroin trade.

The first was to declare war on Colombian cocaine during the mid and late eighties. For a while, the Colombian cartels stubbornly continued to harvest their coca crop. But even they couldn't fight glyphosate—an herbicide better known by its stateside brand name, Roundup. Using spy satellites to determine where coca crops were being planted, the U.S. government helped the Colombian government dump tons of the gook on the countryside from airplanes. The Aerial Eradication Program, as it was known, was hailed as a tremendous success in the War on Drugs.

But while the government was congratulating itself on the plummeting cocaine traffic on America's streets, the Colombians were busy rolling out a new product line. And it was one the feds and their spy satellites weren't looking for: heroin. It was an almost instant hit. The Colombians had been hooking America on cocaine for years and had the supply routes, distribution systems, and retail muscle to move massive quantities of the drug at never-before-seen purity levels.

The heroin of the seventies was perhaps 5 or 10 percent pure. The rest of it was baking soda or aspirin or whatever additive a dealer could find to cut it with. The heroin of the new millennium was 50, 70, even 90 percent pure and delivered its high—and addictive powers—with corresponding efficiency.

The second thing Uncle Sam did to help the Director's operation was to declare a War on Terror. After 9/11, America's picture of evil changed overnight. It was no longer the swarthy Colombian drug lord in a linen suit. It was now the straggly bearded Muslim extremist. For every new wall of protection the U.S. built against the Middle East menace, a piece of the wall that once kept the Colombians at bay came tumbling down.

New Jersey proved a particularly ideal entry point. It had the infrastructure, with a major international airport, a bustling seaport, and a vast highway network sprawling in every direction. It had the geography, being wedged in between New York and Philadelphia in the heart of the Northeast corridor. And it had the demography, with a densely packed population spread over urban areas (where most drugs are sold) and suburban areas (where most drugs are stashed and, yes, consumed).

The third thing the U.S. government did was kick the Taliban out of Afghanistan. The Taliban had ruthlessly suppressed poppy production. But with the Taliban out, Afghani farmers who had been growing poppies for generations got right back into business. All it took was a few growing seasons for Afghanistan to transform into the world's newest narco-state.

That meant the Colombians had competition. They responded by pushing even more product across the borders in an effort to keep up, to the point where they were getting sloppy with it.

And it was the Colombians' sloppiness that was allowing the Director to grow rich.

CHAPTER 2

My four-year-old Chevy Malibu—practical, dependable, and the last vehicle any self-respecting Newark carjacker would ever want—was parked in the garage across the street. When I bought it a year ago, I had taken endless ribbing from my newspaper friends. Apparently, a used Malibu isn't considered the car of choice among highly eligible bachelors such as myself. My friends from Amherst, most of whom made Michael Moore look like a Bush family toady, chided me for not buying a hybrid that ran on lawn clippings.

But while I wholeheartedly support the development of renewable energy sources, damn if I'm going to drive some oversized golf cart. I'll give up my gas-powered V6 just as soon as someone gives me an alternative that actually moves when I press down the accelerator.

As I got in the car, I turned on the radio, switching to a Top 40 station. The same liberal friends who disapproved of my choice of transportation also rolled their eyes at my music. But there's only so much NPR a man can take.

"Oooh, I love this song," Tommy said.

"Should I be worried I agree with you?"

"What do you mean? You're worried you might actually have good taste for once?" Tommy said, turning it up and singing along, loud and off-key. Nothing like driving through Newark blasting music that announces, "We're not from here."

We soon crossed into Irvington, a city that's like Newark but with fewer redeeming qualities. Irvington was once a blue-collar town that was only slightly down on its luck. Then Newark demolished its public housing high-rises, dispersing all the crime and dysfunction that had once been concentrated there. Irvington, like other towns nearby, had been caught completely unprepared and went into the toilet practically overnight.

The Stop-In Go-Go was no exception. Occupying a dingy, windowless corner storefront, it had as its only neighbors a bodega and a liquor store. Its backlit sign—which featured the silhouette of a curvaceous, long-legged dancer—had to be at least half a century old.

"If it gets out in the gay community I went to a place like this, I'll be forever ostracized," Tommy said as we parked and exited the car.

Intellectually, I knew strip clubs were offensive: they objectified the female gender, perpetuated wrongheaded ideas about sexuality, and opened young women to all kinds of potential exploitation. For those reasons, I avoided them.

Unless, of course, I was drunk. If you threw a couple beers

in me, I had to admit I didn't mind watching a woman take off her clothes. And judging by how much it lightened my wallet by the end of the evening, I could make a fair argument the exploitation went both ways.

The Stop-In Go-Go was not actually a strip club, mind you. It was a go-go bar, and in Jersey there was a difference: strip clubs could go all-nude but didn't have booze; go-go bars had alcohol, but the dancer's choicer bits needed to stay covered. Granted, a careless dancer might "unintentionally" flash a little nipple or a bit of muff. Accidents happen in every industry.

As we entered, we were barreled over by a smell that was one part male pheromone, two parts Coors Light, and three parts stale sweat. The Stop-In Go-Go may have been poisoning the environment in any number of ways, but the overuse of cleaning products wasn't one of them.

"I'm afraid to sit down," Tommy whispered. "I might stick to something."

"That's half the charm," I said. "What are you drinking? This is no place to be sober."

"How about a cran-apple Cosmo?" he asked.

"I don't think they've heard of those here," I said as I caught the attention of the bartender. "Two Buds, please."

"We're not going to start talking about sports now, are we?" Tommy asked.

"No, I think just being here is sufficient torture for you," I said, then flipped two twenties down on the bar and turned to the bartender. "Mind giving me change in singles?"

"Oh, my God, you're not really going to?" Tommy asked, horrified.

"Of course I am. I've got to play the part. I'm just wondering how exactly I'm going to put this down on my expense report."

I grabbed the two beers and my pile of singles, then turned my attention to the small stage in the middle of the room. There, two dancers gyrated in robotic fashion to some tiresome bit of club music, their expressions blank, their minds elsewhere. The only person who could have possibly been more bored was Tommy.

One of the women was a thick-legged, bleached blonde who occasionally graced one of the patrons with a come-on in Russian-accented English. The other woman had to be Tynesha, a not-insubstantial black woman wearing just enough clothing to keep the Stop-In Go-Go from getting fined.

I sat down at one of the barstools ringing the stage and gestured for Tommy to sit next to me. Tynesha started dancing our way, wasting no time pouncing on fresh meat. I pulled a single out of my pocket and held it in the air. Chum couldn't have made a shark come quicker.

"Thanks, baby," she said as I slipped her a dollar, being careful not to let my hand linger in a way that might later be deemed professional misconduct.

"You're welcome," I said.

"Oohhh. You're my white boy. I knew you'd be gorgeous."

I forced a smile. Her eyes were amber-colored, from contact lenses. And when she smiled back it gave her a freaky look—the golden-eyed harlot.

I went to introduce Tommy, but he had vanished. He was probably off in a back room, swapping skin-care regimens with one of the dancers.

The hour went quickly enough and Tynesha shrank my stack of singles with professional efficiency. As soon as she was relieved of her duties, she cruised up behind me and let her hand get familiar with my tush.

"Mmmm," she said. "You got yourself one firm behind. I'm going to have fun with you."

Tynesha was only about five seven. But I was betting if she did try to "have fun" with me, I'd end up in traction. I'm delicate that way.

"Where can we go talk?" I asked in a low voice.

"I've got a private room upstairs," she whispered, giving my butt a final squeeze.

"Sounds great," I said. She led me behind a curtain then up a narrow flight of stairs, opening the first door and turning into a small cubbyhole of a room. It contained a bed, a dresser, and more clutter than my eyes could begin to focus on.

"Okay, baby, so what it's going to be?" she said, expertly ditching her top and pushing her breasts on my forearm in one motion. "You want the full two hours?"

"Uh, actually, I'm not here for that," I said as I pulled out my notebook, and she froze.

"Dammit, I told Lucious not to send me no cops! Come on, baby, give me a break and I'll—"

"Relax, I'm not a cop," I said. "I'm a newspaper reporter. I work for the *Eagle-Examiner*. I'm writing a story about Wanda Bass. I saw the flowers you sent her. I wanted to talk to you about her."

She crossed her arms over her bare chest and shot me a look from behind those amber contacts that said an ass-kicking might be forthcoming.

"Why, so you can write that an exotic dancer got herself killed?" she spat. "You know, you newspaper guys really piss me off. All your stories are like, 'Oh, well, a dancer got smoked, but who cares, she was just a ho.' Why you always got to write that it's a dancer?"

This was uncomfortable. I had a personal policy about not getting into journalism ethics arguments with topless women in bordellos. Especially not when I needed them as sources.

46

"Well, we write it because it's true," I said. "If a car mechanic gets killed, we write it was a car mechanic. We can't control what the profession is."

"Oh, come on, you know it ain't the same. You write that some banker gets killed and everyone goes, 'Poor little white boy.' You write that an exotic dancer gets killed, and everyone is, like, 'Well, she was probably a hooker. She had it coming.' And Wanda sold drugs on the side. So people will think, 'a hooker *and* a drug dealer, she deserved to die twice.' But let me tell you, Wanda had a *family*. She had *kids*. She was a *person*. Why don't you write that for a change?"

"I'd like to, that's why I'm here," I said, trying to turn the conversation to something more productive. "I want you to tell me about who Wanda was as a person."

Tynesha eyed me.

"Look, if I wanted to write another hooker got killed, I could have done that from the office, without bothering to talk to her friend," I pressed. "Why would I have come out here and let you grope my ass if I didn't truly care about who Wanda was?"

Finally, a break. "You know you *liked it* when I groped your ass," Tynesha said, not smiling but at least not frowning anymore.

"Every second of it," I said, allowing just the slightest bit of a grin.

"What you say your name was?"

"I didn't. It's Carter Ross."

"Damn, that's a white boy name all right."

"Is your real name Tynesha?"

"Tynesha Dales. I dance under my real name. I know I ain't supposed to. But I'm too damn tired half the time to keep up with fake names."

"Okay." I paused. This was a little awkward: "I'd like to shake your hand, but maybe you should put your top on first."

"What, this embarrass you?" she said, shaking her breasts at me. Then, thankfully, she pulled a T-shirt out of the dresser.

"You're a prude," she said.

"No, just Protestant," I said, opening my notebook. "So how long did you and Wanda know each other?"

"Oh, I don't know. Since she came here. I was already here. Three years, maybe?"

"What kind of family did she have?"

"No dad, of course. Her mom is a decent woman but she's disabled and can't work. So she watches Wanda's kids and Wanda supported all of them."

"How many kids?"

"Four."

"Yikes."

"Yeah, it was kind of a, what do you call it? When bad stuff just keeps happening over and over and over?"

"A vicious cycle?"

"Yeah, that's it. A vicious circle. She was a real pretty girl. Long legs. Beautiful hair. Beautiful eyes. She was *too* pretty. She got pregnant the first time when she was fifteen, sixteen. Then the dad took off. As soon as he did, she was out trying to find herself a man to take care of her and the baby. That got her another baby, then that guy took off, so she started trying to find another guy. And it just kept going like that. A vicious circle."

"How old are the kids?"

"The oldest is maybe eight? Nine? The youngest was born about six months ago."

"Damn. That's a handful."

"Yeah. An expensive handful. She didn't want to do what I do—she couldn't when she was popping out all them kids—so she started selling drugs to my clients. We was kind of a one-stop shop: I'd give them love, she'd get them high, and the men would leave real happy."

"And a couple hundred bucks poorer," I said.

"Damn straight," she said. "Speaking of which, this is costing me money, sitting here talking to you and not doing my thang. I got, you know, customers to serve."

"When can we talk again?"

"I don't know if I got much more to say."

"Come on. Let me buy you lunch tomorrow."

An eyebrow arched. "You'd buy me lunch?" she asked.

"Sure," I said.

"What kind of lunch?"

"Any kind you wanted, I suppose."

"Yeah? Even a nice place? Like . . . Red Lobster?"

"We could even do better than that," I ventured.

"Yeah?" she said. "You mean, like, we could go to that, um, Australian place?"

Australian place? Then it clicked.

"You mean an Outback Steakhouse?"

"That's right!" she said. "An Outback Steakhouse! I always wanted a white boy to take me to an Outback Steakhouse."

"Well, then, be here tomorrow at noon," I said. "Your white boy will be awaiting you."

I had half a mind to bolt the Stop-In Go-Go and leave Tommy inside. But for as funny as that struck me—ditching a gay guy at a titty bar—it also met the constitutional threshold for cruel and unusual punishment. I found him at the bar, by himself, sulking.

"Can we get out of here?" he said. "It's too hetero."

I led him outside, where the night air smelled crisp, like snow—a nice change from the dankness of the Stop-In Go-Go.

"So, did you conquer the Sure Thing?" Tommy asked as we neared my car.

"Yeah, we had mad, wild sex."

"Oh, so that's why you were out so quickly," Tommy shot back. "Anyway, she tell you anything useful?"

"Told me Wanda Bass was selling drugs to her clients."

"Let me guess: she sold heroin, too."

"I don't know. She broke it off before I got any further. But we have a lunch date tomorrow. She insisted we go to a fancy foreign restaurant."

"The International House of Pancakes?"

"Close. The Outback Steakhouse."

"Well, just try not to get her pregnant when you end up going for a little afternoon delight."

"Uh, I wouldn't worry about that much," I said, as we climbed back into the Malibu. "I wouldn't call her my type. I try to avoid women who could break me in half during lovemaking."

"Well, I try to avoid women, period, so I guess I can't blame you."

I cut off our banter so I could concentrate on my driving. It was getting closer to that crazy time of night. Much of Newark's reputation as the Scary Capital of the Eastern Time Zone is undeserved. During daylight hours, I feel as safe in Newark as I do on the streets of Manhattan. It's nighttime that gives the place a bad rap. Around eight o'clock, the city's crazy quotient slowly begins to rise, with steady increases in addictions being serviced, darkly clothed people cutting across the street at odd angles, and questionable characters on nefarious errands. The crazy quotient usually crests around 1 A.M.—slightly later on weekend nights— then gently decreases until the sun rises. It's the familiar beat of the city's daily rhythm.

"So, what's the plan for tomorrow?" Tommy asked as we pulled into the parking lot.

"Well, we don't know anything about Shareef Thomas yet," I said. "I guess that would be a good place to start."

He nodded and slipped away to do . . . whatever it was Tommy did after work. I considered heading inside for a quick e-mail check. But when I thought of what was likely waiting for me—pointless press releases from PR firms and notices about ergonomics training from the Human Resources Department that were marked "High Importance"—I decided to call it a night.

My home is a tidy bungalow in Nutley, a nearby town known for its ballsy name and for being the childhood home of Martha Stewart. If that makes Nutley sound like a place where everyone spends their time scrapbooking and making decorative birds' nests out of matchsticks, it shouldn't. Nutley isn't really a Martha Stewart kind of town. It's more of a Roseanne Barr kind of town. No one in Nutley is quite sure how Martha sprang from our ranks. If you saw how tacky the Christmas decorations are, you'd understand.

Nutley is just a solid, middle-class Jersey suburb. Everyone works a decent job, drives a mid-sized car, gripes about their property taxes, obsesses over their minuscule lawn, orders pizza on Friday night, and watches football on Sunday afternoon. And while it may have a few too many twenty-something Italian guys who still live with their mothers, I like it all the same. The truth is, I enjoy lawn care. There's nothing like pulling a few dandelions to soothe job stress.

By the time I got home, my cat, Deadline, was pacing back and forth, waiting to be fed. But that was really nothing unusual. Deadline spends most of his waking hours—both of them—pacing, waiting to be fed. As soon as you come near him, he runs to his bowl and looks at you expectantly, even if it's already full. Sometimes, I reach my hand into the bowl and rustle the food around to make him think he has been fed again. You know how most cat owners will rave about how smart, sensitive, and intuitive their pet is? Not me. I can admit it: Deadline was pretty much last on line when they handed out the kitty brains.

And in some ways it was appropriate, because he was the last vestige of what had been a truly brainless relationship. I adopted Deadline—then a cute, black-and-white domestic shorthair kitten—at a time when I foolishly thought I was going to be able to provide a stable, happy, two-parent home for him. The girl I was with at the time had moved in. There was talk of more serious things to come. There was even a shared Netflix account.

Then Deadline's mommy decided life in Nutley, New Jersey, just wasn't for her. I should have seen it coming. She wanted a guy you might find in the pages of *Esquire*. I'm more a *Sports Illustrated* kind of guy. She ended up leaving me for a designer at her advertising agency, a dandy fellow who used lots of product in his hair, lived in a loft in SoHo, and didn't worry so much about staying faithful to the Scotts' four-cycle lawn care program.

That left me and Deadline to our shared bachelorhood. Which was fine. Deadline never liked her much. Maybe he wasn't so dumb after all.

The next morning, Hays's story led the front page:
"A return trip to the scene of a previous crime proved deadly for Shareef Thomas and three accomplices, who Newark police believe orchestrated a robbery at the Ludlow Tavern several months ago—and have now paid the ultimate price."

The story went on with the necessary background about

how police had now identified the "Ludlow Four," and how they hoped to have a quick resolution to the heinous crime. And, sadly, there was no quote from a National Drug Bureau spokesman, since one L. Peter Sampson was afraid of his own shadow and one Carter Ross couldn't make him believe it was cloudy.

I poured myself some Lucky Charms—they *are* magically delicious, after all—and finished reading the story, at the end of which I felt like chucking my bowl against the wall. Hays's cops were just so wrong. Newark bar owners get held up all the time. If they put contracts out on everyone who did it, there would be no one left at the bar to drink.

I made my commute in seventeen minutes and had just settled in to wade through my daily helping of pointless press releases when Sal Szanto suddenly became aware of my presence.

"Crtr!" he croaked. I entered his office just as he cleared his throat explosively.

"What's up, boss?"

"Brodie still has major wood for this Ludlow thing. What's the deal with the bar these people held up? Who owns it? Why hasn't the guy been arrested yet? And how did he plan this hit? I'm seeing some kind of profile of this bar. You know: 'It appears to be just another neighborhood bar, but the Ludlow Tavern had something more sinister going on inside.' Something like that. How does that sound?"

"Sounds like you can write it yourself," I said.

"Aw, don't start that. Come on, what do we know that we didn't know this time yesterday?"

"That Hays is an old-fashioned screwup."

"No," Szanto said, "I actually *did* know that yesterday."

"Yeah, but you probably didn't know he was going to strip a story across the top of A1 that's just wrong."

53

Szanto put his elbow on the arm of his chair, resting one of his chins in his palm. As the managing editor for local news, he ultimately had responsibility for this story. If Hays screwed up, it meant Szanto screwed up. So Szanto—and, for that matter, the *Eagle-Examiner* as a whole—was now invested in Hays's story being right.

"The Associated Press picked it up and gave us credit, you know," he said gravely. "Radio, TV, they're all giving us credit, too. And you want to tell me it's wrong? You got anything to back that up or are you just in the mood to make my ulcer bark at me?"

"Nothing concrete," I admitted. "But I got a pretty strong hunch. Hays is taking the word of his cop source. And I think the cop is just throwing something out there. You know how it is for those guys: if they don't at least pretend they've got *something* while a story like this is hot, everyone just assumes they're not doing their job, starting with the mayor. When the story cools down, they'll quietly arrest someone else or just drop it. But for now, they can't let everyone know they're clueless."

Szanto ground his teeth for a moment.

"Aw, Jesus Christ," he said at last. "So what's your theory?"

"Well, I don't necessarily have one yet," I said. I just had three drug dealers in three different parts of the city and a fourth victim who was still a big question mark.

Szanto grumbled something as he reached for some Tums.

"So since you don't have a theory, Hays's story still *could* be right," Szanto said.

"I guess," I admitted.

"I've got to be straight with you, I think everyone around here would be a lot happier if you just wrote about that bar," Szanto said. "If the cops are wrong, that's on them. Put the damn bar story in the newspaper and let's move on."

In other words: don't rock the boat.

"Uh-huh," I said, purposely agreeing in as tepid a way as possible.

"Great. Look, I'm not going to tell Brodie about this Hays thing. It's not smart to upset him when he's aroused."

"You're the boss," I said as I left his office.

"So you're doing the bar story," he shouted after me. I pretended not to hear him.

I went back to my desk and finished reading my e-mail, which allowed me to learn I could get a discount if I signed up for Weight Watchers at Work. I lingered over the rest of the newspaper, then stalled rather than face the inevitable moral crisis: follow my conscience or follow the boss?

Maybe I *could* just do the bar story. It would be easy enough. I could turn it around in two days. The police would like it. Brodie would be happy. Szanto would be thrilled.

The only problem was, I would have to remove all the mirrors from my house because I wouldn't be able to stand the sight of myself. I mentally shelved the idea of the bar story and returned to fleshing out my theory—whatever my theory was.

I clearly needed to learn more about Shareef Thomas before I even had a theory, so I started doing some public-record searching. I soon identified at least three Shareef Thomases running around Newark—at seven different addresses. It was time to start knocking on doors.

Better yet, make the intern do it.

"Hey, Tommy," I said as he slinked into the office. "You look like you could use an errand or seven."

While Tommy was out knocking on doors, I had a date— with a hooker and a Bloomin' Onion.

I threaded my way through the ghetto, which seemed especially empty on this frigid morning. The wind had been fierce overnight, strong enough to knock over garbage cans. Trash was blowing everywhere—Jersey tumbleweed.

I pulled up in front of the Stop-In Go-Go at 11:58—habitual punctuality is a WASP curse—and waited for fifteen minutes. I was beginning to wonder if I had been stood up when Tynesha came out the front door, dressed in off-duty clothes: a pair of unflattering jeans, a puffy black jacket, and low-heeled boots. I beeped lightly and waved for her to hop in, but she stormed up to the driver's side and gave me an icy amber glare. I lowered the window.

"I ain't going to lunch with you. I just came to give you a piece of my mind," she spat.

"About what?"

"About that crap in your newspaper today. I thought you said you wanted to write about what kind of person she was. Instead you write that she robbed a bar? Are you kidding me? Wanda didn't rob no bar! She didn't know no Shareef, or whoever he was. You know how much that upset her mother to read that? I thought—"

"Hang on, hang on," I said, holding my hands out like a traffic cop. "I know the story was wrong. And I'm sorry."

She inhaled like she was going to keep on yelling, then stopped.

"You know it's wrong?"

"Yes."

"So why did you write it?"

"I didn't. Another reporter at our paper wrote it. He took the story straight from the cops. I told him he was making a mistake. He wouldn't listen to me."

"So y'all just write a story that's not true?"

"It sort of works that way sometimes," I said. "We write what we think is correct at the time, relying on sources we believe to be credible. Sometimes those sources turn out to be wrong. It's not perfect. All I can tell you is I'll try to set the record straight later."

She was still having a tough time believing me. I took advantage of her indecision.

"Look, why don't you hop in and we can talk about it on the way. I'd still like to buy you lunch. You can stay pissed off at me, but at least get a good steak out of it."

She nodded—few things are as persuasive as free meat—and walked around to the other side of the car. I opened the door for her from the inside.

"The nearest Outback is over on Route 22. It'll probably take about twenty minutes to get there."

"That's fine," she said, still sounding a little surly but coming out of it. "My shift don't start until five."

"Great," I said as I got us under way, running over at least three plastic bags in the first two blocks.

"So, how many days a week do you dance?" I asked.

"Six."

"And how many days a week do you . . . uhh," I began, immediately regretting the question.

"Turn tricks?" she asked.

"Yeah, I guess."

"As many as I can. I can't do this forever, you know. I'm thirty-six. I figure I got six, maybe eight, years until I'm all saggy and nasty. I want to have enough saved up by then to open one of them fancy clothing stores."

"You mean like a boutique?"

"Yeah, a boutique."

"That's cool," I said.

"I know what you're thinking: 'What does a ho know about starting a business?' "

"No, actually, I'm thinking it's great to have a dream," I said. "Everyone ought to have one."

She looked at me thoughtfully. "Yeah, what's your dream?"

The question caught me off guard. What was *my* dream? Maybe it used to be working for *The New York Times,* but the Old Gray Lady had long ago stopped hiring, just like every other newspaper. Or maybe it was winning a Pulitzer Prize. That'd be nice. But, really, that wasn't something I thought about a lot.

"Maybe this sounds corny," I said after a pause. "But this is my dream already. I get to make my living telling people's stories. I think of that as a privilege. I can't really imagine doing anything else. And even if I could, I'm not sure I'd want to."

She thought about this for a moment.

"I like you, Mr. Carter Ross. You seem like you got a good heart. And I got this little voice in my head—maybe it's Wanda, I don't know—telling me I ought to trust you. Just don't make me regret it."

"Yes, ma'am," I said, merging onto the five lanes of road-raging good times that is the Garden State Parkway.

We drove in comfortable silence for a while and I felt pleased with my progress. In order to tell any story successfully, you have to cross the threshold where your source stops looking at you like a reporter and starts seeing a fellow human being. I thought—I hoped—I had just reached that point with Tynesha.

"So what made you and Wanda hit it off?" I asked.

"I don't know. I don't get along well with the other girls. But me and Wanda just clicked—sisters from a different mother or something. All her kids called me 'Aunt T.' "

"You have any kids yourself?"

"Can't. A guy messed me up real bad one time. Couldn't get his own equipment working so he knocked me around for a while then did me with a broom handle."

I flinched and reflexively moved my legs together.

"Yeah. Doctor said he busted my insides," she continued. "Probably just as well. I would have messed up raising my kids just like my mama messed up raising me."

I let the comment pass. She didn't need me playing amateur psychologist.

"So who's taking care of Wanda's kids?"

"The grandma for now, but I think the state is gonna take them eventually. Wanda's mama don't got no money and she has that diabetes. She ain't in good shape. They'll split those kids up in a thousand different directions. The baby will probably get adopted because everyone wants babies. I don't know about the older ones."

I did. Unless they got really lucky, they were going to live in a succession of foster homes and group homes until they were turned out onto the street at age eighteen. We all get dealt a hand to play in this life. Being orphaned in Newark, New Jersey, had to rank among the worst.

As we made our way through midday traffic toward the Outback, we downshifted to small talk. It's amazing how much hookers and reporters have in common: we have to walk the streets in all kinds of weather, we have to relate to people from a variety of backgrounds, and we're constantly getting dicked around by politicians.

We arrived at the restaurant to find it mostly empty and got seated in a corner booth. After we ordered our meal and received our salads, I got down to business.

"So how is it you and Wanda started working together?"

"You mean with me doing it and her dealing?"

"Yeah."

"I guess it was when she got pregnant with her fourth baby

and couldn't dance no more," Tynesha said. "We were pretty tight by then. I knew she had to do something to support those kids of hers, and there ain't exactly a lot of jobs out there for pregnant dancers. I mean, there were a few guys out there who wanted to get themselves with a pregnant girl . . ."

I made a face.

"Yeah, all kinds of weird suckers out there," she said. "But Tynesha didn't want to turn tricks. She was real firm about that. You should put that in your article. Anyway, once her baby started showing, the owner wouldn't let her dance no more, so she started selling. See, that's the side I want to come out. She sold to support her kids. She wasn't no bad person."

"I'll make sure that gets in," I said, using it as an excuse to remove my notepad and start taking notes.

"So where did she get her drugs from?" I asked.

"At first, she got it from Lucious, my pimp. Then one of her boyfriends hooked her up with some stuff. She got it from all over, I guess. I don't know. I didn't ask."

"What did she sell?"

"Oh, man, I don't even know. All kinds of stuff. Whatever she could get her hands on. She was just trying to survive, you know what I'm saying?"

"She sell heroin?"

"Yeah, some of that."

"She ever get caught?"

"Yeah, once," Tynesha said. "She was selling to some guy who turned out to be a cop. Ended up doing some time for that."

"When did she get out?"

Tynesha thought for a moment.

"Well, she got pregnant right after she got out. I mean, like, she was going to find herself a man to take care of her and she was going to do it *fast*. She got herself another loser, of course.

And he ran off. But that was . . . let's see . . . that baby is six months and she was pregnant for nine months . . . so she got out . . . a year and a half ago?"

"Didn't getting sent to jail make her want to stop dealing?"

"Naw. It made her more careful," Tynesha said. "It's like she learned how to be a better dealer in jail, like it was dealer Vo-Tech or something. Before she went to jail she was just selling to people in the bar, you know? But then after she got out, she was selling inside the bar, outside the bar. People would seek her out. It was like, man, she made it. I mean, maybe this sounds weird or something, but I was proud of her."

"So why did she keep dancing if she was doing such good business?"

"I guess it was like a front, you know? If she stopped dancing, it would be suspicious. We get cops who come in all the time. They know all the dancers. They'd notice if she quit. I guess she just didn't want them asking questions."

"Do you know what she was selling at that point?" I asked as our meat arrived.

Tynesha got this look like she was trying to remember something.

"I mean, there was this one guy. I was sucking him off and he was just jabbering on and on—some guys really like to talk, you know? And he said something like, 'Man, I love this place. You give me the best head ever and your girl gives me the best H ever.'"

H. As in heroin.

"Was that before or after she got out of jail?" I asked.

"Definitely after," Tynesha said with half a mouthful of filet mignon.

Another confirmed heroin seller. Another ex-con. It was definitely starting to become a pattern.

61

"So if she suddenly has this best-ever heroin after she gets out of jail, you think she hooked up with a source in prison?"

"I don't know. Maybe. I guess."

"She ever talk about where she was getting it from?" I asked.

Tynesha looked at me solemnly.

"In the hood, if you have a really good source for junk, you don't never talk about it. Never," she said. "Not with your neighbor. Not with your boyfriend. Not even with your best friend."

Our date finished uneventfully, and I dropped off Tynesha in Irvington with an exchange of cell phone numbers. When I got back to the office, it was nearing 3 P.M. and Tommy was deep into the Edun jeans Web site.

"My butt would look *so* killer in these," he said wistfully. "Too bad they're like $195."

"Who would want to drop two bills on a friggin' pair of jeans?"

"*Bono* wears Edun jeans," Tommy said with the utmost gravity.

"And Bono has a great ass? He's old enough to be your father."

"I hope my ass looks half that good when I'm his age."

"So Bono has set the standard for aging asses?"

"It's not just his ass," Tommy said, getting frustrated with me. "It's his whole *aura*. I wouldn't expect someone who wears pleated pants to understand."

"What's wrong with pleated pants?"

"Nothing, if it was still 1996," Tommy said. "Although I guess they match your 1998 shoes."

"Okay, meanwhile, back in the present, please tell me you managed to find out something about Shareef Thomas?"

"Well, of the seven addresses you gave me, I found two

vacant lots, an abandoned building, one Shareef Thomas who is alive and well—and *totally* mental—and two places where, to quote one woman, 'I ain't never heard of no Thomas Shareef.'"

"And the seventh address?"

"I got a door slammed in my face."

"That's promising," I said, and I wasn't kidding.

"You think?"

"Absolutely. Think of all the things a slammed door represents: a little bit of anger, some fear, definitely something to hide. I'd say you hit paydirt. Which address was it?"

Tommy shuffled some papers. "One-nine-eight South Twelfth Street," he said.

"That's . . . where?"

"Up off Central Avenue," Tommy said. "I kicked three plastic vodka bottles on my way from the car to the front door. There's a homeless shelter next door. It's pretty much wino heaven."

"Any of the neighbors know Shareef?"

Tommy paused, a little embarrassed.

"You didn't talk to any neighbors?"

"It was like the fifth or sixth address I looked at," he whined. "I was getting cold. All the other addresses had been dead ends. I just thought . . ."

"No, that's okay," I said. "Look on the bright side: now you have something to do this afternoon."

Tommy sighed and sank low into his seat.

"That street was *so* nasty," he said.

"C'mon. All you need to do is find someone who will be willing to admit to a perfect stranger that Shareef Thomas was a heroin dealer who recently got out of prison. How difficult can that be?"

"See you later," Tommy said, sighing more as he grudgingly lifted himself from his chair. "If I don't make it back alive, I'm bequeathing you my wardrobe. At least I'll die knowing it went to a truly needy recipient."

I returned to my desk but quickly found myself yawning, always a sign the needle on my caffeine-o-meter was dipping low. I went to get a Coke Zero from the break room, where the reproductive-minded Tina Thompson was eating a late lunch, probably laced with ground-up fertility drugs. She was wearing a tight, rust-colored V-neck sweater that rather nicely show-cased her upper half. I'm definitely a sucker for a woman with a nice set of shoulders, and Tina's were better than most.

"You should avoid that stuff," she said as I fed money into the soda machine. "Excessive caffeine has been shown to lower sperm count."

"Really?" I said. "In that case, does this thing sell Red Bull?"

"I thought all men wanted to spread their seed," Tina said. "Isn't it supposed to be some kind of biological imperative?"

"Actually, I come from a long line of sterile males. Goes back generations."

"Har har," Tina said. It was a pretend laugh but she still rewarded me with a real smile. I don't know what it was, but Tina had this one particular smile she used on occasion. It was at once coquettish and demure, but it also left little doubt she could make your toes curl in bed.

I distracted myself with the soda machine, which refused to dislodge my Coke Zero without a gentle bump. Sometimes you really had to rock the thing, which inevitably prompted someone to inform you that ten people a year die from vending machines falling on them.

"So what are we offering our readers tomorrow with regards to the Ludlow Four?" I asked.

"Oh, the usual shock and outrage. The mayor is promising to put more police officers on the streets. The antiviolence groups are clamoring to get their names in the paper. Some of the people on Ludlow Street are forming a neighborhood watch group. That sort of thing."

"Team Bird coverage continues."

"Yeah. Brodie has been humping my leg like a horny leprechaun all day," Tina said. "And I might be flattered by that. But after he's done with me, he goes over to Szanto and humps him. Besides, you ever notice Brodie has old-man hair issues? He's got it coming out his ears, his nose, and he's got those eyebrows that are sprouting like old potatoes. It's a little gross.

"How's your bar story going?" she asked.

"Uh, it's not."

"Oh?" she said, giving me the toe-curling smile again. "Swimming upstream, are we?"

"Off the record? Yeah."

"Good. I'm with you," Tina said. "I just can't believe how much everyone hopped into bed with Hays's story. Yeah, great, radio and TV picked it up. I just hate it that being first with a story has taken precedence over being right. What's your angle?"

I thought of telling her my suspicion that all four victims were jailbird heroin dealers. But hard experience had taught me you didn't share a story idea with an editor until you knew it was true.

"I'm still working on that," I said.

Tina crinkled her brow and I admired her collarbones for a second.

"Well, whatever it is, keep working it," she said. "I'll cover for your little upstream swim as best I can."

"Oh, Tina, how can I ever repay you," I said, grinning.

She winked. "I'm sure I'll figure out something."

returned to my desk, keeping a wary eye out for Sal Szanto.

I think, deep down, Szanto knew I would rather gargle razors than propagate the error that was Hays's story. And therefore he had to know I was ignoring my assignment. Eventually, that would work out okay, because he would come around to the conclusion that getting the story right was a triumph for journalism— even it meant wiping some egg off the paper's face.

But in the meantime, he would be much happier if I at least *pretended* I was working on the bar story. There were two ways to continue the charade: lying to him when he asked me for an update, which made me feel uncomfortable; or avoiding any meaningful interaction with him, which is the option I chose.

So when I saw Szanto lugging his pear-shaped body toward my desk, I immediately flipped out my cell phone.

"Carter Ross," I said into the mouthpiece then paused a beat so my imaginary friend could answer.

"Oh, hey, how are you?" I said, giving Szanto the "one minute" finger. "That's great. Thanks for calling me back. It's wonderful to hear from you."

I had almost succeeded in turning Szanto away when my phone rang for real. Szanto looked at me quizzically.

"Uh, hi," I said, scrambling to answer. "We must have gotten cut off. Can you hear me now?"

"What the hell you talking about?" answered Tee Jamison, my T-shirt man.

"So, anyway, where were we?" I said. Szanto was still staring at me.

"We wasn't anywhere," Tee said. "You forget to take your pills this morning or something?"

Finally, Szanto turned back to his office, apparently satisfied I was going to be a while.

"Sorry, I just had to . . . never mind," I said. "Anyway, what's up?"

"You been down to the vacant lot where they found them bodies yet today?"

"No, why?"

"I'm just hearing some weird stuff. Meet me down there in fifteen?"

"You got it," I said. Tee hung up, but I kept the phone at my ear until I was around the corner, out of Szanto's sight.

I made good time to Ludlow Street. That was one of the advantages of working in an economically devastated city: less traffic. In short order, Tee rolled up behind me in a new Chevy Tahoe that could have swallowed my Malibu whole and still had room for dessert.

"Why is the poor black man driving this big fancy SUV while the rich white kid is driving this little tin can?" I asked.

"How many times I got to tell you: there's money in the hood," Tee said. "We just make sure you white people don't know nothing about it."

"Ah, my tax dollars at work," I said.

Tee was dressed in a camouflage jacket with a black hooded sweatshirt underneath, having perfectly dressed the part of the urban tough. I wore a charcoal-gray peacoat and dressed the part of the insurance salesman.

"So why am I out here in the cold?" I asked.

"You gonna have to check this out," Tee said, walking toward the shrine that had, as predicted, grown substantially. "Damn, it's just like everyone's been saying."

"What is?"

"His shrine, man."

"Dee-Dub's shrine?"

"Yeah."

I looked at the small cluster of candles and flowers dedicated to the memory of Devin Whitehead. It looked no different from the other victims' memorials.

"Uhh . . . okay, what am I missing?" I asked.

"It's what *the shrine* is missing," Tee said. "It ain't got no brown in it."

"And that means . . . ?"

"Damn. Didn't they teach you nothing in college about the hood?" Tee said. "Dee-Dub was supposed to be one of the Browns, you know what I'm saying? When one of them dudes gets killed, there is *always* a big-assed shrine filled with everything brown you can find. Brown bandanas. Brown bags. Brown teddy bears. One of them niggas even stole a UPS truck once."

"A UPS truck?"

"Yeah, you know them commercials . . . What can brown do for you?"

"Oh, right," I said. "So the fact that there's no UPS truck here means . . ."

"It means Dee-Dub wasn't with the gang no more."

"Is it possible he got kicked out?"

"Oh, it's possible," Tee said. "It's possible Tyra Banks is going to ask me to father her baby. I just don't think it's going to happen, you know what I'm saying?"

"No, Tee, I have *no idea* what you're saying."

"I'm saying, dudes like Dee-Dub don't get kicked out of gangs like the Browns. It just don't happen. Not to an OG like him."

"So maybe he tried to leave the gang and they killed him?"

"Nah, because that don't account for the other three cats that got smoked with him," Tee said, crossing his arms as if preparing for a scholarly lecture in Hood Studies. "The Browns are pretty old-school. If they had a beef with Dee-Dub, they would put him down nice and quiet, not make some big thing out of it."

"Good point," I said, shifting my weight and fixing my eyes on a blob of melted wax that had once been a candle.

"However," Tee said, pointing one finger in a professorial manner, "they might know something about what happened, being that it involved a former member. You know what I'm saying?"

"For once, yes, I know what you're saying," I said. "You got any kind of in with the Browns?"

Tee looked thoughtful for a moment.

"Well, let me ask you something," he said.

"Shoot."

"That cat of yours. You got someone who will take care of it in the event of your untimely death? I don't want no orphaned cats in this world."

"Don't worry," I said, cracking a smile. "It's dealt with in my will."

Tee had me follow him back to his store. It shouldn't have been hard to trail Tee's mammoth truck, except he squeezed it through the tiniest holes in traffic. He and I had once had a debate about what made a "good" driver. To me, it was someone who didn't get in accidents. To him, it was someone who could make a fifteen-minute trip in ten by doing a grand slalom through three lanes of traffic, one of which was oncoming.

I could see he was talking on his cell phone, and by the time we pulled up in front of his store, he had already made some arrangements. I parked behind him and rolled down my window as he walked toward my car.

"Okay," he said, "I got you an interview with the Browns."

"Great."

"There's just one condition."

"Okay."

"At some point they're going to offer you some weed," Tee said. "I strongly suggest you smoke it."

"And if I don't?"

"They'll think you're a cop and they'll shoot you."

"Well, then, tell them to put on Marley and bring on Mary Jane!" I said.

"I thought you'd see it that way."

"You coming along?"

"Hellllll, no," Tee said. "Those dudes is messed up. I mean, I know them. If they come in my store, I'll talk with them. But that don't mean I hang out with them. Besides, if my wife found out I was smoking weed while I was supposed to be at the store? She'd beat me silly."

That was another way Tee's tough-guy look belied what was underneath: he readily admitted to being afraid of his wife.

"Well, I sure don't want to go pissing off Mrs. Jamison."

"Damn straight," Tee said. "I keep telling you, that bitch is scary."

Tee told me to drive to an intersection a few blocks down on Clinton Place, get out of my car, and wait for the Browns to find me—which, he assured me, wouldn't take long.

I drove to the designated spot and immediately began hoping the Browns got to me before someone else did. Dusk had come quickly, and the corner had an ominous feel to it. An intersection with three abandoned houses tends to be a bit foreboding that way. None of the houses had been boarded up—or if they had, the boards had been removed. You don't want to know about what kind of stuff goes on in an abandoned house in Newark.

Down the street, there was a row of particularly slummy-looking brick apartments, the kind where the front door hadn't existed in decades, allowing the drug dealers free access. Each apartment had a NO LOITERING sign near the entrance, promising that Newark police would arrest anyone who disobeyed. It was a sure indication a building was bad news.

But on this block it wasn't the only indication. There were enough shoes hanging from the telephone wires to start a Footlocker warehouse. Broken glass—some of it old booze bottles, some of it used crack vials—littered the sidewalk. And a row of brown bandanas flying from the traffic light stanchion told me I was clearly in Browns territory.

But where were the Browns?

I got my answer quickly enough when I felt something hard and metallic sticking in my back. "Don't turn around," said a voice that could put skid marks in even the bravest man's underwear.

I raised my hands.

"Put yo' hands down, fool. You want some cop driving by here thinking this is a stickup?"

"I thought it was," I said.

"You the Bird Man, right?" my friend said.

"Yeah."

"Well, then this ain't no stickup. We just going to take you for a little ride is all. And you gonna have to put this on."

I saw a hand reach around in front of me. It was clutching a brown bandana.

"Can't I just promise to keep my eyes closed?"

"This ain't no comedy club, Bird Man. Put it on. And put it on tight."

"You got it," I said, and tied a sturdy knot around the back of my head. He tugged on it, then came around in front of me. I felt a rush of air on my face, like a punch had been pulled just inches short of my nose. My friend was checking if I could see through

71

my blindfold. But I didn't flinch. In truth, I didn't really *want* to see what was going on.

I heard a car—no, a van?—pull up beside me. The next thing I knew, someone picked me up, bride-across-the-threshold-style, and carried me a few steps toward the sound of the engine. From the ease with which he handled my 185 pounds—think child carrying rag doll and you've got the idea—I knew I didn't want to pick a fight with him.

"Watch your fingers, Bird Man," my friend said, and I heard two doors slam.

"Thanks," I said, not sure if he could hear me.

Soon the van was rattling down the street and around several corners. After a while, I got the distinct feeling we were really just driving in a circle—we kept making right turns. But if that's what they had to do to feel comfortable with me, I was fine playing along.

Finally, I felt the van coming to a stop and heard the engine cut. Someone opened the back doors.

"Come on, Bird Man," my friend said. "We going to Brown Town."

The Director was not a religious man. Far from it. But if he was ever moved to prayer, it was for the continued existence and prosperity of Newark Liberty International Airport. Those ten thousand acres of paved swampland were the world's most fertile source of heroin.

One flight came directly each day from Colombia. The rest came through Miami, Atlanta, or other points south. Then there were the cargo planes. Altogether, it kept the heroin pouring in day and night, 365 days a year, helping to nurse addictions up and down the Eastern Seaboard one landing at a time.

The heroin entered in the lining of suitcases, hidden in freight, sewn in clothing, tucked in nooks and crannies. Powder is an easy thing to conceal and a 747 is a massive piece of real estate with plenty of hiding places. The liquid form of heroin—which could then be extracted using methylene chloride and baked into a solid—offered other possibilities for the creative smuggler.

One kilo of heroin—2.2 pounds of powdery white gold—cost roughly $8,000 on the streets of Bogotá. That same kilo was worth at least $60,000 on the streets of America, even before it was cut with cheaper products. With a cost ratio like that, there was a tremendous market-driven incentive to import as much product as possible. Caution didn't pay. Daring did.

No one knew how much heroin poured through Newark airport. The Director wondered if his competition—primarily ethnic mobs—was getting even more of it than he was.

But, as the Director often told Monty, he got his share. He made sure of it.

CHAPTER 3

I was escorted up a flight of steps, and from the creaking I could guess it was a typical specimen of Newark's mostly wooden, mostly dilapidated housing stock. Once inside, I was led to a room and made to sit on a sofa that felt and smelled like expensive leather.

"Mind if I take off this blindfold?" I asked, but didn't get an answer.

I heard the door open and could sense the lights dimming. I felt someone come up from behind me and untie the knot on my blindfold. Except when the bandana came off my face, I couldn't see a damn thing; someone was shining a huge flashlight in my eyes.

"You have *got* to be kidding me," I said. "You guys saw this in a movie once, right?"

"I thought I told you this wasn't no comedy club," said my friend, who was the one holding the flashlight.

"Look, guys, I just need a little information here. Can we drop the KGB act?"

My friend looked over to someone else, who must have consented, because the flashlight switched off. As soon as my eyes adjusted, I saw I was in a faintly lit room, surrounded by members of the 1987 Cleveland Browns. Or at least with guys wearing their retro uniforms. Number 34, Kevin Mack, was my friend, the one who approached me on the street. The big guy, the one who had picked me up, was wearing Number 63, an offensive lineman's number. Was that Cody Risien? Could be. He was the only offensive lineman from that team I could remember.

And the one who appeared to be the leader was wearing Number 19. Bernie Kosar.

"How you know Tee?" Bernie Kosar asked.

"I wrote a story about him once. We've been buddies ever since."

"Yeah? Tee says you all right."

"I try to be," I said.

I furtively glanced around to get a better sense of my surroundings. It was a good-sized room, expensively furnished with the spoils of the Browns' prosperity. The sofa was a never-ending sectional that felt sturdier than the house it sat in. There was a massive flat-screen TV directly in front of me, a similarly enormous fish tank to my right, and floor-to-ceiling boxes against the wall to my left.

"So what you want with the Browns?" Bernie asked, making some kind of quick hand gesture when he said the word

"Browns," almost as if he were a Catholic genuflecting after the Lord's Prayer.

"Well, I want to know a little about Devin Whitehead."

"Man, we ain't got nothing to do with that," Bernie said. "How come everyone thinks we did it?"

"Well, he used to run with you, didn't he?"

"Yeah."

"So . . ." My voice trailed off.

"Yeah, but he hadn't run with us in a long time," Bernie said. "He went to jail and when he got out he didn't want nothing to do with us no more."

"Yeah, why is that?"

Bernie looked at Kevin Mack and Cody Risien, sharing some silent communication. Then he turned back to me.

"So tell me something, Bird Man: you like to party?"

I laughed despite myself.

"Are you asking me if I want to smoke pot?" I said.

"What if I was?"

"I'd say I hope you have a lighter because I left mine at home."

Bernie produced a lighter and marijuana cigarette that was the length of my hand and the thickness of my thumb. It could have almost doubled as a nightstick.

"My God." I choked. "Are we going to watch *Pink Floyd—The Wall* after this?"

No one laughed. So I lit the end and took a drag, holding the smoke in my lungs for as long as I could bear, then handed off to Kevin Mack. I had smoked maybe half a dozen times in my life, and not at all since college. By the third pass, I already felt like my head was a helium balloon floating on a string, somewhere above my shoulders.

"Damn," I said. "This is smooth."

"We grow it ourselves," Bernie said proudly.

"Where?"

"In the basement. We got the high-intensity sodium-chloride grow lights, the heating mats for optimal germination, the liquid seaweed fertilizer. The fertilizer is key—it packs some high-quality nitrates, yo. Nothing but the best. That's pure, hydroponic pot you're smoking, Bird Man."

"You guys must make a fortune off this stuff," I said, taking another hit.

"Naw, man, this is just for us," Bernie said. "We don't sell it."

"Come on, cut the crap," I said, blowing out a large cloud of smoke. "How many hits do I have to take before you believe I'm not a cop?"

"Naw, man. I'm serious. That's why Dee-Dub left us. While he was in jail, we switched operations. We don't sell drugs no more."

"Really? So how can you afford all this?" I said, looking around the room.

"C'mere, I'll show you," Bernie said.

I tried to rise from the couch, but as soon as I got about halfway up, my buzz caught me and took me out at the knees. Suddenly the room got slanty. I could feel myself going over and made an attempt to stay upright, but my legs wouldn't bear any weight. I staggered one step, two steps, then lost it, slamming into the wall of boxes as I went down. Several of them came toppling over on my head, spilling their contents on the floor.

The Browns thought this was hysterical—the white man who couldn't handle his weed. As they were high-fiving and enjoying my distress, I sat there dumbly, staring at what had slipped out of the box. It was DVDs of a new Adam Sandler movie, one that wasn't even out at the box office yet.

"What the . . ." I started, and then it dawned on me. "Bootlegs? You guys sell bootleg movies?"

"Hell, yeah," Bernie said, still laughing a little. "There's more money in bootlegs than there is in drugs. Every brother in this city wants to sell you drugs. So now a dime bag of dope goes for six, seven bucks. A bootleg movie goes for five, and ain't no one blow your head off because you selling bootlegs on their corner. Plus, a whole lot more people in this city watch movies than do dope. Hell, most of them are afraid to go out at night because of the dope, so all they *do* is watch movies."

"I'll be damned," I said, feeling so high I was unsure if the whole thing was real.

"Yeah, and the Newark cops don't bother us none," Bernie said. "Bootlegging movies is a federal crime. It's FBI business. And the FBI, man, once they figure out you ain't a terrorist, they ain't interested. So we got the best of all worlds: less competition, more demand, no police."

A sound business model. I was impressed.

"So why wouldn't Dee-Dub want a piece of this?" I asked.

"I don't know. When he got out of the joint, he was all hot about this new source he had for smack. Kept talking about how it was the best in the world."

"How long ago did he get out?"

"Dee-Dub? Like a year ago?" Bernie paused and looked to Kevin Mack, who nodded.

"Yeah, a year ago," Bernie said. "He was all fired up. He said this stuff could make us all rich. And I'm like, 'Yo, dawg, we *already* getting rich selling bootlegs. And ain't nobody shooting at us.' But he wouldn't hear it."

"So you let him go?"

"Man, this ain't slavery. If he don't want the Browns, the Browns don't want him," Bernie said, and suddenly all three were genuflecting again. "He had been doing his own thing for a while. Make sure you put that in your article because I'm sick of people talking bad about us. The Browns didn't have nothing to do with this."

I knew I should ask more questions, pump them for as much information as I could. But my usual journalistic vigor and innate curiosity was being sapped by one simple thing:

I was as high as the Himalayas.

Within an hour, the pot made us instant friends. They taught me everything there was to know about the production of bootleg movies. I somehow ended up giving them a geology lecture, most of which I probably invented, because I don't think I know a thing about geology. They offered me honorary membership in the Brick City Browns, saying they could use a token white man for diversity purposes. I asked if honorary membership involved initiation in the form of participating in illegal activities. They informed me that, in my case, they could waive that requirement.

As Cody Risien drifted off into a contented slumber, Bernie Kosar informed me I was allowed to come and go as I wished, provided I swore to uphold the secrecy of Brown Town's location. I consented, allowing me to stumble out of the Browns' secret hideout without my blindfold.

It turned out the house was right in front of where I had parked. I was still stoned, but deemed myself sufficiently sober to drive, which was only the first of several bad decisions that night.

It was, by this point, completely dark. I wasn't sure how much more I was going to be able to get accomplished on the story given my condition. And I was getting a killer case of the munchies.

All of these were perfectly good reasons to call it quits and head back to my Nutley bungalow and dim-witted cat. But somehow, in my mentally diminished state, I convinced myself I should make an appearance at the office. All I had to do was keep a low profile and avoid Szanto.

Right. Low profile. I was invisible. Like Wonder Woman's airplane. The only way the viewers at home could see me was because of the pencil-thin outline drawn for their benefit.

I crept back to the office, going five miles under the speed limit the whole way. I parked (crookedly) in the far corner of the company garage. I moseyed my invisible self toward the front entrance, kept my head down . . .

. . . And damn near barreled over Harold Brodie.

Luckily, it was enough of a glancing blow that it only knocked the old man to the side. The *Eagle-Examiner*'s executive editor looked appropriately startled. I guess it wasn't every day one of his reporters hip-checked him. But as my mind started racing—*how did Wonder Woman get the invisible plane to work if she couldn't see the controls?*—Brodie, to my horror, had recovered and seemed to want to stop and chat.

"Good evening, Carter," he said. Brodie's voice was this pleasant, grandfatherly falsetto. "In a hurry?" he asked.

Words started pouring out of my mouth without stopping to check in at my brain.

"Yes, sir. Time is money, you know. And money makes the world go round. And the world wasn't built in a day. And you've got to take it one day at a time. Which brings us back to time being money. So I guess you could say I'm trying not to waste money, time, or the day."

Oh, God, I began to think, *I'm going to get myself fired.*

"I thought it was 'Rome wasn't built in a day,'" Brodie said, still pleasant, still grandpa.

81

"Well, that's true, too, but Rome *is* part of the world. And I don't want to single out Italians as being slow builders. I mean, frankly, who would even *want* to live in a city that had been built in a day? It's like those suburban tract houses that get tossed together in a week and a half—they're always crap."

Okay, not fired. Worse than fired. The high school sports agate desk.

"I suppose that's true," Brodie said, as if I had just offered some piercing philosophical insight. "So how's that bar story going?"

Oh, crap. Oh, crap. Oh, crap.

I was certain things couldn't get any worse for me, but then they did. Because instead of answering him, I started laughing.

Actually, not laughing. Laughing merely would have been awful. I was acting like a twelve-year-old girl reading the sex column in *Cosmo.* I was *giggling.*

"What's so funny?" Brodie said, looking confused. He had been the paper's executive editor for the last quarter century. I'm pretty sure no one had giggled in his presence before.

"Oh, nothing, sir," I said, and only giggled harder. "Well, gotta go!" I said, and tried to make for the front door.

"Wait a second," Brodie said, grabbing my arm and sniffing loudly. "Why do you smell like you've just been at a Grateful Dead concert?"

"Uh, I'm working on this Jerry Garcia retrospective . . ."

"Son, don't give me that poppycock. I was born at night, but not last night. Have you been smoking marijuana?"

"Carter Ross, 31, of Nutley, committed career suicide yesterday . . .

"Yes, but I can explain," I said.

Brodie stood there with fists stuck into his hips. Grandpa was pissed. "I'm listening," he said, his helium-sucker voice managing to take on an ominous tone.

"Oh, you want the explanation *now*?" I asked.

. . . He left behind no note. Police said there was no sign of foul play . . .

"That's the general idea," Brodie said.

"Well," I said, trying to wrest the story from my racing mind. "It started when Tee said there wasn't a UPS truck at Dee-Dub's shrine—you know, the whole 'What can brown do for you' thing? And then he told me to stand on the corner, where gangbangers blindfolded me and took me for a ride around the block and around the block and around the block. We were in this van."

. . . He is survived by the world's dumbest cat. A funeral service for his dead career will be held every day between now and his retirement from some sad-sack PR firm 25 years from now."

"And then," I plowed ahead, "and then they took me into this room where I had to toke up with the Cleveland Browns so they knew I wasn't a cop. And then they were cool with me and we talked. And then I knocked over the boxes of the Adam Sandler movie? And then I decided to come back to the office like I was in Wonder Woman's plane, except apparently I'm not in it anymore, because you can see me."

I stopped there, because somewhere in my head there was this tiny voice telling me I had said enough. Brodie fixed me with a hard stare from underneath his overgrown, Mr. Potato Head eyebrows.

"So, what I think you're saying is, you smoked marijuana with some sources to get them to trust you?" Brodie asked.

"Well, actually, so they wouldn't shoot me. But yes."

Brodie lifted his hand, and for a second, I thought he was going to smack me right across the face. I flinched, except he was . . . patting my shoulder?

"That's fantastic!" Brodie shouted with a high-pitched hoot, his eyebrows waving at me from above his delighted eyes. "Well done, Carter! Very well done, my boy! You did what you had to do to get the story. That's the kind of dedication I want to see in all my reporters. I'm proud of you. Keep up the good work, son!"

Brodie charged down the steps, still cackling.

"Smokin' pot to get the story!" he exclaimed as he walked away.

"Reports of the demise of Carter Ross's career were greatly exaggerated . . ."

Having gained the endorsement of the executive editor, I felt emboldened as I entered the newsroom and flopped noisily into my chair.

"I am *so high*," I said, and laughed when I realized I was talking to myself.

I tried to look at my e-mail, but the words kept floating off the screen and freaking me out. So I decided to relax and savor the feeling of being utterly baked at the office. I'm sure that was by no means a first in the *Eagle-Examiner*'s illustrious history. But it was a first for me.

Still, for as much as I was enjoying myself, there didn't seem to be any point in being stoned alone, with no one to play with. I gathered my things, and went to the elevator, where I was joined at the last moment by Tina Thompson.

"How come you're grinning like the cat who ate the canary?" she asked.

"To be honest, I'm a little stoned," I said. "Actually, I think I'm *a lot* stoned."

"Really?" she said. "You mean, for real?"

"I kind of had to pass the peace pipe with the boys from the Brick City Browns to convince them I wasn't a member of the law enforcement community," I said.

"No."

I nodded, feeling like a life-sized bobble-head doll, my skull wobbling on top of my shoulders. Tina clapped her hands together and laughed. It was a delightful laugh. We boarded the elevator together.

"Well, then you must be hungry by now," she said.

"I'm favished."

"What the hell is 'favished'?"

"I don't know. I think it's a combination of 'famished' and 'ravenous.'"

"Then you're definitely not driving. I'm taking you to dinner."

She quickly slid her arm through mine and pressed against me, allowing me to feel the firmness of her breast against my triceps. Before I knew it, I was being escorted through the parking lot, to her car, which would take us . . . on a date? How exactly had this happened again? The executive editor had congratulated me for getting stoned on company time and now I was going out on a date with the city editor.

We hopped in her new Volvo—the perfect car for a safety-conscious mother-to-be—and I was soon being treated to the spectacular natural beauty of one of New Jersey's most scenic roadways, the Pulaski Skyway. That was the way to Hoboken, which is where Tina lived. It was not especially near Nutley. I was starting to get that feeling this might turn into a sleepover.

Tina was quiet. Which meant I wasn't the only one contemplating the very adult act that might be taking place by the end of the evening.

"So how did this happen to you?" I asked as we made a left turn away from the Holland Tunnel traffic, toward Hoboken.

"How did what happen?" Tina said.

"This whole biological clock thing. You used to take your

birth control pills in the break room. Now you wear a watch on your wrist that tells you the exact hour when you're ovulating."

"Oh, you noticed that, huh?"

"Hey, I have to know when to keep my guard up," I said.

She laughed and playfully patted my thigh. My upper thigh.

"Well, first of all, the whole biological clock thing is a load of crap."

"Oh, come on," I said. "You turn thirty-eight and you start picking up brochures for birthing centers just like that?"

"Well, yeah, but I don't think it's an age thing. I think I just reached the point where I was tired of being the most important person in my life. I've been so selfish for so long. I'm sick of focusing on myself. I want to put someone else's needs first."

It was as good a reason as I've heard for wanting to have a child. It was also about as far from my own experience as I could imagine. I had enough problems just taking care of myself.

At the same time, I had this vague feeling that Tina's life was heading in a more meaningful direction than mine. And the truth was, this career-minded, hard-running, yoga-disciplined woman was going to make a great mother—the kind of mother I'd want my own kid to have. I could suddenly imagine a tiny little Tina: the curly brown hair, the twinkling eyes, the mischievous laugh. And in that moment I resigned myself to allow whatever was about to happen between us.

It's not that I had suddenly given myself over to believing in fate or destiny or any of that malarkey. Because that quickly leads you to a place where free will doesn't exist, and that's no fun whatsoever. I did, however, feel that previous decisions had put me in a circumstance where my next action had become a foregone conclusion. So I might as well stop fighting it.

Or maybe that was the pot talking.

Either way, when Tina got us a romantic table in the back corner, I didn't protest. And when she ordered a bottle of red wine, I nodded in approval. And when her leg brushed against mine under the table, I enjoyed the sensation. And when a second bottle of red wine appeared, I didn't let it go to waste. And when Tina announced at the end of the meal she was in no shape to drive me back to Nutley—so I had to come over to her place—I complied.

We walked arm in arm back to her condo, a one-bedroom with a view of Manhattan, leaning on each other the whole way. It was closing in on midnight and I had been buzzing constantly since about five in the afternoon, with the red wine taking over where the pot left off. I was ready for love.

As we rode up the elevator, she nestled against me. I enjoyed the smell of her hair and the faint note of her perfume. I had half a mind to pin that lithe body of hers against the wall as soon as we walked in her front door.

But no. This was her seduction scene. I was going to let it unfold her way. She unlocked the door and pointed me toward the couch.

"I'll be right back," she whispered.

"I'm looking forward to it," I said in a deep, lusty growl.

I did a quick survey of the landscape. Tina's pad was filled with sturdy, sensible furnishings—and no shortage of potential landings for two adventurous lovers. The chair. The sofa. The coffee table. They'd all hold just fine. I was beginning to toy with the possible combinations when Tina returned, still dressed in the same clothes, carrying a blanket.

She immediately interpreted my confused look.

"We're both far too drunk," she said, handing me the blanket and pushing me down on the couch. "It's not right."

She bent over and kissed me on the cheek.

"Besides," she whispered in my ear, "I don't reach peak fertility until Friday."

My only wish that next morning was that I be allowed to file a motion for clemency in the Court of Hangover Appeals. Hangovers are supposed to be punishment for wicked behavior. My argument, therefore, was that I didn't *deserve* this hangover—especially not a red wine hangover, known to be among the most vicious in nature.

After all, I had merely been acting in self-defense. In their infinite wisdom, the judges would surely see the logic: the reason I drank wine was because I had smoked pot; I had smoked pot because I didn't want to get shot by gang members; therefore, I drank wine because I didn't want to get shot by gang members. Self-defense.

Alas, there was no court in the land with the benevolence to hold such proceedings nor the power to commute my sentence. So I awoke with a skull full of broken glass, a stomach full of bile, and a mouth full of squirrel excrement.

"How was I last night?" I said as I wandered into Tina's kitchen, squinting at the brilliance of her track lighting.

"Since I didn't have to fake anything before I fell asleep? I'd say you were just fine."

Tina was wearing Lycra leggings, a windbreaker, and running shoes.

"Don't tell me you've already been jogging," I said.

"It's the best way to get over a hangover. Blows the whole thing right out of your system."

"I'll stick with water and aspirin, thanks."

"Suit yourself. Want some eggs?" she asked, pointing to a

fry pan full of them. I have a general rule about eggs: I will eat a chicken's leg, wing, or breast, but I draw the line at eating its embryonic fluid.

"Thanks, no," I said. "But a toothbrush might be nice."

"There's a new one in the medicine cabinet. I had been hoping the baby's father would use it the morning after we conceived. But I suppose you can have it."

I laughed. "So, let me get it straight: in exchange for some random guy's sperm, you're planning to give him a toothbrush?"

"Hey, I'm going to feed him breakfast, too," Tina said.

I wandered into Tina's bathroom, and instantly wished it hadn't been mirrored. I know most folks don't think thirty-one is old. But thirty-one never looks more decrepit than when it's been smoking weed, drinking wine, eating salty food, and sleeping in its clothes. It was like I went to bed as Carter Ross and woke up as Yoda.

I brushed, rinsed, brushed again, rinsed again, and still felt like I hadn't rid my mouth of the squirrel turds. Only time, and the proper amount of penitence in the Church of the Throbbing Headache, would do that.

I returned to find Tina removing a bagel from the toaster.

"Well, if you won't eat eggs, you will most certainly take a bagel. You can't start a day on an empty stomach."

She stopped herself and looked surprised. "Wow, I really sounded like a mother, didn't I?"

"Right down to the shrill inflection. Are you sure I didn't get you knocked up last night?"

"I'm hoping you'll be a little more memorable than that," she said.

The use of the future tense was a little worrisome. Alas, it was probably accurate. On the Easy Lay Scale—where 1 is a nympho-maniac crack whore and 10 is a fair maiden whose chastity belt key is guarded by a fierce army of eunuchs—my performance the night before rated about a 1.3.

I sat down with the bagel and was soon joined by Tina and her omelet.

"So, not to overtax your tender mind," she asked. "But what do you think your plan of attack is with Ludlow Street this morning?"

"I was thinking of eating this bagel, bumming a ride back to my car, then sleeping off this yucky feeling until mid-afternoon while Tommy does all my work for me."

"What's your backup plan? Your first plan sucks."

I bit off a large chunk of bagel, chewed and swallowed—not an easy task, being as my mouth was still a little low on saliva. But it gave me the necessary moment to regroup my thoughts.

"First order of business is to chat up Wanda Bass's family," I said. "I've gotten in good with her former best friend."

"Is that the, uh, prostitute you visited the other night?"

"One and the same."

"By the way, you didn't, uh . . ."

"Jesus, Tina, no!" I said, and tried my best to appear injured by her impudence.

"Sorry," she said quickly. "I just had to check. Can never be too careful."

This was getting uncomfortable, having my city editor taking a personal interest in whether I was dipping my pen in dirty inkwells. I made a mental note to never start another flirtatious, potentially sexual relationship with a city editor for as long as I lived. Then again, since most city editors were rumpled, bald-ing, middle-aged men, that probably wasn't going to be a real tough covenant to keep.

"As I was saying," I said, shooting her one last wounded glance, "I think I can manage to get a little closer with Wanda Bass's mother. Maybe she'll know something."

"Great. Anything I can do to help?"

"Well, for one, stop asking me if I'm banging hookers," I said, and she actually blushed. "Two, if you can keep Szanto off my ass, I'd sure appreciate it."

"No problem," Tina said. "I'll just mention at the morning story meeting that I spoke with you and that you're making excellent progress. I just won't say on what."

Tina showered then spent the next twenty minutes walking around her apartment in a towel as she got ready, seemingly going out of her way to let me see that, yes, her collarbones were every bit as wonderful as I thought. And her legs were even better. The evil temptress was back on the job, getting me primed for when her wristwatch told her the moment was right.

If there's one good thing about having a hangover in Hoboken, New Jersey, it's that you're not alone. Hoboken's typical resident is a recent college graduate who's living like he's still the pledge captain at Alpha Beta Chi. So as we walked to Tina's parking garage, I was at least comforted in knowing Brother Flounder was out there somewhere, grimacing his way through the morning with me. The only difference between us was I should have been old enough to know better.

Tina drove us to the office as gently as she could, though I felt like I was about to redecorate her Volvo with the contents of my stomach every time we hit a pothole. Good thing the ten-mile trip between Hoboken and Newark only has about three million of them.

As we approached the building, I became aware of another

91

potential danger. If anyone saw me hopping out of Tina's Volvo wearing yesterday's rumpled clothing, they wouldn't exactly have a tough time deducing where I spent the evening. They would fill in their own conclusions from there.

And once that rumor got started, there would be no stopping it. Journalists are essentially trained gossips, which makes newsrooms absolute cesspools for loose talk. Before long, even the delivery boys would believe Tina and I were knocking boots.

The key was for no one to witness me getting out of Tina's car. But that hope was killed—make that: hung, drawn, and quartered—when Tommy Hernandez pulled up next to us in the parking garage. Tommy was perhaps the worst gossip at the paper: not only a journalist, but a gay one.

"Well," I said as I unbuckled my seat belt. "This is going to be awkward."

"What is?" Tina asked.

"Did you see who just pulled in?"

"Who?"

"Tommy."

"So?"

"So by lunchtime half of Newark is going to think we're shagging."

"Oh, don't be ridiculous," she said as she got out. "He probably won't even notice."

But Tommy noticed. His eyes had already tripled in size and he had clapped his hand over his mouth in sheer delight.

"Oh . . . my . . . God!" he said, gleefully pointing at us. "You two are doing it!"

"Would you believe me if I denied it?" I asked.

Tommy thought for a moment, head tilted. "No," he said.

"Well, we're not."

Another moment's reflection, this time with the hand on the chin. "You're right," he said. "I don't believe you."

"No, honestly, I got drunk. She let me crash at her place. That's it."

"Oh, *come on*," Tommy said. "You have to do a little better than that. Couldn't you at least say you had car trouble and she was giving you a ride? Or that you were coming from the same breakfast meeting? Or that you're wearing the exact same ugly pleated pants from yesterday by accident?"

I could only shake my head.

"Even better," Tommy continued. "You could tell me you *were* doing it and throw in all kinds of salacious details and brag you're the world's greatest lovemaking superhero—which would lead me to believe you *weren't* doing it."

"Listen to me," I said. "There's nothing going on. Can you please just pretend you didn't see this?"

"The golden-boy investigative reporter and the hotshot city editor arrive for work in the *same car* and you expect me to say nothing? Nothing?? It's just not possible."

"Look," I said, growing desperate. "If you gossip about this—which would be slander, since it isn't true—Tina is going to assign you to the Hunterdon County livestock beat."

"Hey, leave me out of it," Tina said. "And since when is it slanderous to say you slept with me?"

"But I didn't!" I said, exasperated.

"Yeah, but so what if people think you did?" she demanded, crossing her arms. "Would that be so awful?"

"Wait a second, he didn't sleep with you?" Tommy said.

"No," Tina replied.

"Oh, that sucks," Tommy said, pouting.

"Wait, you believe her and not me?" I asked.

"Think about it," Tommy said. "Tina tells everyone everything about her sex life anyway. You're the only one who's a priss about it. So if Tina says you didn't do it, you must not have done it."

I didn't know whether to be exasperated or relieved. Tina was still pissed, albeit more in a theoretical way than a real way. Then again, when applying female logic, I doubted the distinction mattered much.

"No, seriously, what would be wrong with people thinking we slept together?" she demanded. "You find that embarrassing or something?"

"She's got a point," Tommy said. "She's a lot hotter than you are. If anything, *she* should be embarrassed to have slept with *you*."

"Thank you, Tommy," Tina said self-righteously.

Tommy moved to Tina's side and put his arm around her to emphasize that I was now facing a united front. This was clearly going nowhere good. I was outnumbered in a hypothetical debate about something I hadn't even done. And, on top of that, my head was pounding, my mouth was dry, and my stomach was still feeling all those potholes.

"If I were you, I'd be *proud* to have slept with such a fine-looking woman," Tommy said. "Well, I mean, I'd rather be sleeping with her younger brother. But I'd still be proud."

"Can I just please surrender?" I asked. "This is too much to handle before I've showered for the day."

Tina narrowed her eyes and shook an index finger in my direction.

"You're lucky I'm only after your sperm," she said.

"*Men,*" Tommy huffed.

They turned and walked into the office together without another word.

---

thought about following them, then remembered my clothes still smelled like happy grass. So I returned to my peaceful Nutley bungalow, where Deadline was pacing nervously in front of his empty food bowl. I poured in an extra helping, and he hungrily attacked. Eating was one of the few things Deadline did well. Sleeping and pooping were the others.

A day of sleeping, eating, and pooping was sounding like a fine idea at the moment. But I forced myself into the shower. I was the toughest man alive. It was the 1970 NBA Finals and I was Willis Reed. I would play hurt.

By the time I completed my heroic comeback, it was after eleven, which I deemed fashionably late enough to call Tynesha.

I deemed wrong.

"lllo?" her sleepy voice answered.

"Tynesha, I'm sorry. It's Carter Ross from the *Eagle-Examiner*. I thought you'd be up by now."

"Not unless the building's on fire," she said, coming to a little.

"Right, sorry. I'll call you later."

"Don't worry about it, baby. What's up?"

"I was wondering if I could talk to Wanda's mama. You said Wanda lived with her mama, right?"

"More like her mama lived with her," Tynesha said, not bothering to stifle a yawn. "Wanda paid the rent."

"Think her mama knew what was going on?"

"Her mama's a pretty sharp lady. Miss B knew a lot, probably more than Wanda realized. But I'm not sure she'll talk about it with you."

"I'll take my chances, if that's all right."

"I'm supposed to see Miss B this afternoon to help her pick out a casket at the funeral home. You want to come with us?"

Picking out caskets ranked pretty low on my list of favorite activities. Funeral homes ranked even lower on my list of favorite places. But it was either that or hang around the office and duck under my desk whenever Szanto came near.

"Do you think she'll mind some random white guy tagging along?" I asked.

"It's okay. You're with me. Besides, she ain't got no car and neither do I. Without you, we'd be taking the damn bus."

A half hour later, I met Tynesha in front of the Stop-In Go-Go. She tumbled into my car offering several choice complaints about the cold, which felt like it had come to New Jersey on a Get Out of the Arctic Free card. I cranked up the Malibu's heater a little more, and we made our way to Wanda's place, a rundown, four-story brick apartment building on South 18th Street.

Out front were three obvious markers of urban malaise: the obligatory NO LOITERING sign; another sign that read WE ACCEPT SECTION 8, the federal rent vouchers given to low-income families; and, finally, a pair of teenaged boys—lookouts—who might as well have had bullhorns and been screaming, "Drugs here. Get your drugs here."

We got out of the car and walked up the front steps, hearing the familiar tweeting of Nextel phones on walkie-talkie mode, the preferred method of communication among the well-connected gangsta set. The alert was being sent out: a white man was entering the building.

Once inside, we were serenaded by another familiar song on the urban soundtrack: the chirping of smoke detectors in need of batteries. A landlord once explained to me the tenants stole the batteries almost as fast as you could put them in, so most landlords stopped bothering.

Knocking on the door to Wanda's apartment, I was expecting the worst—trash-strewn floors, leak-stained ceilings, the stench of ages—and instead got June Cleaver's house. The smell of baking pie practically knocked me over as the door opened. Fresh flowers were tastefully arranged on a tiny table in the alcove. Framed artwork decorated the wall above it.

"Hi, Miss B," Tynesha said.

"My baby," Miss B said, smothering Tynesha with a motherly hug. Not many women would have been big enough to envelop Tynesha that way. But Miss B was living on the bottom right corner of the panty hose size chart.

"Hello," she said to me as soon as she released Tynesha. "I'm Brenda Bass."

She said it cordially enough, but it had a steely *I'm Brenda Bass, who the heck are you?* ring to it.

"Hi, Miss Bass, I'm Carter Ross, I'm a reporter with the *Eagle-Examiner*. I'm writing a story about Wanda."

"Oh, no thank you," Miss B said instantly. "Wanda doesn't need any stories written about her."

"It's okay, Miss B," Tynesha said. "He wants to write about the human side of things—like a personal story."

I bounced my head up and down in earnest agreement.

"And how's he going to do that?" she said, talking as if I weren't there.

"He just wants to chat with you a little bit, maybe look around for clues."

More head bouncing.

"I don't like the idea of some man"—she looked at me and downgraded my status—"some *reporter* going through her things."

"It's okay, Miss B. He's all right."

Miss B gave me a once-over, starting at my toes and working her way up, which I took as the cue to begin my sales pitch. Any reporter who doesn't know how to sell himself is going to end up being a reporter who doesn't get many good stories.

"The police are just ready to sweep this thing under the rug," I said. "And they're going to get away with it if we let them."

Miss B had made it up to my shoulders by this point.

"They're trying to push this story that your daughter held up some bar," I continued. "I don't think that's true, but I need to prove it and I need your help."

She was now at eye-contact level, which she held for a moment. Her next question took me off guard.

"Do you like apple pie, Mr. Ross?"

I grinned. "It's Carter. And, yes, I adore it."

"Well, good. When I grieve, I bake. Except with my diabetes, I can't eat it. And Lord knows those children get too much sugar as it is, especially now. You want some pie, Tynesha?"

"You ever know me to turn it down?"

"Good girl. Come on in, you two. But keep your voices down, the baby is asleep."

Miss B limped toward the kitchen, leaning on a cane and flinging the right side of her body forward. I swear, Newark might lead the nation in limpers. It seems like most adults of AARP-eligible age have developed one. Decades of dreadful nutrition and poor health care tend to do that.

Tynesha and I followed slowly behind. The Bass apartment was every bit as well kept inside as it was in the alcove. Everywhere I looked, there were nice little touches—and pictures of a young woman that stopped me cold.

It was Wanda. And she was gorgeous: dark, flawless skin; warm, brown eyes; high, perfect cheekbones; long, thick eyelashes.

In all the pictures, she had the same smile. It was nice, but there was something in it, this hint of vulnerability that caught me. She had been this girl who just wanted to love and be loved back, even though she only found men who thought of love as a strictly one-way, strictly physical thing. It made her ripe for exploitation and there were all too many people around her who did just that.

I could feel this lump rising in my throat. Up until that moment—for all my bluster about wanting to know Wanda as a person—she hadn't really been human to me. She had just been a story. Her death was this abstraction, a piece of a narrative I was forming in my head.

She was real now. And I could see her life all over these walls. Wanda as a baby. Wanda at her baptism. Wanda in dance classes. Wanda at an eighth-grade graduation ceremony. Wanda heading off to the prom. Wanda with her own babies.

"I told you she was too pretty," Tynesha said in a low voice.

"I see what you mean."

"Damn," she said.

"Yeah," I replied, still battling the lump. "How did she get into dancing, anyway?"

"She used to talk about how she had wanted to be a Rockette. She had the legs for it. Then she got knocked up when she was just a kid and it changed everything. The Rockettes don't want no pregnant high school dropout from Newark."

"I guess not."

"Anyway, the baby's father was just some no-good punk who talked about how he was going to support his child—and then he took off. So she started dancing go-go. I always told her she would have made a lot more money in Manhattan dancing for white guys. She was too skinny for guys here. They want a little junk in the trunk, you know?"

Tynesha clearly was not lacking in the trunk junk department.

"But she wanted to stay close to her baby," she continued. "And when she got knocked up again, there was no way she was

99

going anywhere else. Then she got knocked up again. Then she started dealing. Then she got caught. Then . . . I don't know, she just got caught."

Miss B dragged herself back into the living room with that lopsided gait, somehow managing to walk with her cane and carry two slices of pie at the same time.

"C'mon, eat something," she said, setting the pie down on the coffee table and gesturing toward the couch. "You're both too skinny. Sit yourself down."

I took a seat, took the pie, and suddenly realized I had entered the voracious phase of hangover recovery.

"That crust is made with real lard, Mr. Ross," Miss B said, parking herself in an easy chair. "Don't let any old fool Betty Crocker recipe mess with your head. The only way to make a crust is to make it with lard."

I took a bite, then three more. It was dynamite. I shoveled in most of the piece before I realized I should probably, y'know, chew once or twice.

"You make a great pie, Miss B," I said, having reduced a generous wedge to a smattering of crumbs. "And I must say, you keep a lovely home."

"I just wish the building weren't so awful," she said. "It used to be a real nice building, with nice families who cared about how things looked. You should have seen it back in the day."

"So maybe it's a dumb question, but why do you stay?" I asked.

"Oh, I don't know. It's home, I guess. My husband died right in that bedroom," she said, pointing behind her. "He was thirty-nine. Heart attack. Just like that. Wanda was maybe eight or nine. After that, I just felt like if I left, I'd be leaving him. So I stayed for a little while. And then a little while turned into a long while."

I looked at Miss B, trying to guess her age. Wanda had been twenty-five. That put Miss B in her mid-fifties, assuming she had been roughly the same age as her husband. She looked older. I suppose losing your husband and your daughter would do that.

"How did Wanda handle her father's death?"

"Oh, I don't know," Miss B said, sighing. "Wanda was such a daddy's girl. Sometimes I can't help but think maybe if her daddy had stayed around, things would have turned out different. Maybe all those boys she had babies with would have been more respectful."

Or maybe, the amateur shrink in me thought, Wanda wouldn't have been so desperate for male approval if her father were still in her life.

"Tynesha was telling me Wanda wanted to be a Rockette," I said. "Did she dance a lot as a little girl?"

Miss B sighed again, this time more forcefully. She shifted her weight, folding and unfolding her hands across her lap.

"Mr. Ross," she said finally. "I appreciate you showing an interest in Wanda. But I, I know what she was. I know what she did for men—"

"I told you, Miss B, she never turned no tricks!" Tynesha interrupted, but Miss B held up her hand.

"And I know she sold drugs. She didn't tell me, but I knew. A mother knows."

"That still doesn't mean whoever killed her should get away with it," I said.

"I know that. But, I don't know, Wanda wasn't real happy. She was a sweet girl, real sweet. Oh, honey, if you could have seen her with her babies"—Miss B paused to collect herself—"she just had a big heart.

"But she kept thinking that having these babies with these men was the answer. What ghetto girl thinks that way? That Prince Charming is waiting for her on the corner? And by the time she had two or three, you tell me, is Daddy Number Four really going to stick around and support another man's kids? And every time her baby daddy would run off and crush her dreams, it just made her that much more empty."

Miss B started dabbing her eyes with a tissue.

"Wanda was a Christian," she continued. "I know you think that sounds strange, doing what she did. And maybe I'm a fool but, I don't know, I just think she's in a better place now."

"You know she is, Miss B," Tynesha said. She reached out across the arm of the easy chair and grabbed one of Miss B's hands. Miss B had stopped dabbing and was just letting her tears flow. She exhaled loudly.

"I'm sorry, I have got to stop carrying on like this," she said in a broken voice.

"Oh, no, it's really okay. I understand," I said, feeling like a jackass, because, let's face it, I didn't have the slightest clue what it felt like to have a daughter die facedown in a vacant lot. Miss B straightened herself and fixed her red-rimmed eyes on me.

"Mr. Ross, let me just take you to what you came for," she said. She stood and wobbled into one of the bedrooms. I followed.

"This was Wanda's room," Miss B said. "The baby's crib was in my room. The three kids were in the other bedroom. Wanda had this room to herself."

The shades were drawn, making the room darker than the others. It was also messier. There were clothes and dance costumes strewn about the floor, panty hose draped on the lamp-shade, a small Macy's worth of makeup piled next to the vanity. The bed hadn't been made. The air smelled stale. No one had been in here since Wanda's death.

"I wanted her to have her own bedroom because, well, I knew what she was doing in here and I didn't want the children to see it," Miss B said, heading toward the closet. "She thought I didn't know about this."

"Did you ever ask her to stop?" I said, and it came off sounding more judgmental than I wanted.

"I don't think she would have," Miss B said. "Maybe it sounds odd to you, but I didn't think it was my place. A single mother trying to do for her children, that's a powerful thing, Mr. Ross. She always talked about how badly she wanted these kids to have opportunities like suburban kids and I think that's what she was trying to provide—in her own way. She would have died for those kids."

Miss B led me over to the closet, opening the door and pulling on a chain that caused a bare lightbulb to illuminate. She parted some of the clothes and pointed to a cardboard box.

"It's all in there," she said, still holding the clothes aside, not wanting to go any further.

"Thanks," I said, bending low to pick it up. It didn't have much weight to it.

"I don't think I can be in here. I'm going in the other room with Tynesha. Holler if you need anything," she said, closing the door behind her.

I gingerly sat on the chair in front of the vanity, shoved aside some of the cosmetics to make room for the box, and pulled open a flap to look inside. I didn't have a great deal of experience pawing into dealers' stash boxes, but I had to assume this was fairly typical: there was a jar of baking powder, a few straight-edged razors, a tiny scale, and a heaping pile of dime bags.

Even though they were called "bags," they actually resembled tiny envelopes. Each was filled with one tenth of a gram of heroin. Ten bags was known as a bundle. Five bundles was a brick. A brick went for about $300 wholesale—or about $6 a bag. The dealer selling a dime bag for $10 each was going to clear $200 for his $300 investment, but only dealers in the suburbs could get away with charging that much. In the inner city, where there was more competition, dime bags went for $7 or $8.

Wanda's stash consisted of two bricks, two bundles, and a large pile of loose bags, some of which appeared to have been opened. Most of the bags had the same brand-name stamp on them. Yeah, heroin really does come in different brands. People unfamiliar with drug culture always get a kick out of that.

Some of the brands seized in drug busts we had written about had names like Body Bag, Blood River, Head Bang, Power Puff, Instant Overdose—the idea being that the more dangerous your brand sounded, the more potent your dope must be. When a brand got hot, people would line up around the corner just to get it.

Wanda's brand was a name we hadn't written about before. It was called "The Stuff."

The Director came up with the brand name himself and was proud of it. It was an easy name to remember, straightforward and instantly identifiable. People always used the word "stuff" when they talked about drugs.

Now they could talk about The Stuff. It was simple, yet distinguished. The Director also designed the logo: an American bald eagle whose talons clutched a needle. The words "The Stuff" were written in fancy script underneath.

He had several stamps of the logo created and spread them around the production department. Each of his technicians was reminded to make sure every dime bag of The Stuff had the logo stamped on it. But the Director always spot-checked each shipment, just to make sure.

He even kept a The Stuff stamp on his desk. He loved that logo.

The Director's dealers loved it, too. Within the crowded heroin marketplace, it was a logo—and a name—that stood out. You didn't have stuff unless you had The Stuff.

The Director scoffed at all those cretins who tried to outdo each other with gory, violent names. Who really wanted to be snorting something called "Walk of Death" or "Corpse Powder"? It was so literal. It would be like naming a tissue brand "Sir Sneez-A-Lot."

The Director liked to think of The Stuff as being the Kleenex of the heroin world. He imagined a day when the brand went national, when people everywhere would ask for it by name, when only injecting a batch of The Stuff would do. Just like everyone asked for a Kleenex. It had a ring to it.

And, really, the principle behind branding heroin and branding tissues—or clothes, or cereal, or any other product—is identical. You need to be able to differentiate your product to the consumer. Then you build brand loyalty. That was true whether you were talking about denim jeans, corn cereal, or illegal narcotics.

The Director's only regret was that he couldn't push his brand out there even more. He sometimes fantasized about what he would do if he were allowed to advertise. He imagined billboards, radio spots, print advertisements, online campaigns, merchandising opportunities, a clothing line, all of it. And it was all terrific.

But the only person he could share his ideas with was Monty, who naturally told him how wonderful they were. And that didn't mean much. The Director could have defecated on Monty's shoes and Monty would have told him it was ice cream.

No, the Director told himself sadly, his marketing genius was never going to be appreciated. Sometimes, he would take the stamp on his desk and imprint it on a glossy piece of paper, just to see what it would look like on a magazine cover.

And then he would ball it up and throw it away, saddened that the world could never know the brilliant man behind The Stuff.

CHAPTER 4

I picked up one of the dime bags and examined the picture on it more closely. It was an eagle, sort of like the one on the back of a quarter, except instead of clutching arrows, this one had a syringe in its talons—a national symbol for junkies.

Then I started combing through the stash box, staring at its contents until suddenly it became obvious what Wanda had been doing: the empty bags, the razor, the baking soda, the scale. Wanda had been running her own cutting operation. It involved opening The Stuff bags, diluting it with the baking soda, then repackaging it in the unstamped bags. It was a quick way to augment supply.

The Stuff was obviously the top-of-the-line name-brand

product that she sold to her best customers. The blanks were like the generic brand that she sold to everyone else. On an impulse, I grabbed four of the bags—two of The Stuff and two of the generic—and dropped them in my pocket. I briefly debated the ethics of doing so, since I was sort of tampering with evidence. I also briefly debated the sanity . . .

Why, no, Officer, that heroin isn't mine. My interest is, uh, purely professional . . .

But, ultimately, I knew I'd regret it later if I didn't take some product samples while I had the chance. Heroin was clearly the link between those four bodies. Having some of it in my possession just seemed like a good idea. Maybe we could have it tested at a lab? Maybe it would make a nice photograph?

And maybe I was just out of my bleepin' mind. But before I chickened out, I repacked the box, replaced it in the back of the closet, then rejoined Tynesha and Miss B in the living room, where they were sniffling into their tissues.

"Should we head to the funeral home now?" I asked.

Miss B nodded and began preparing herself for a trip outside, allowing me a few more moments to dwell on all those pictures of Wanda.

We often ran head shots of people who died quick and violent deaths in our paper, and there was something about them I found endlessly fascinating. Especially when they captured some happy moment—a graduation, a wedding, a retirement, whatever. I just couldn't help but think: if the guy in that photo had known he had three years until he got splattered on some drunken trucker's grill plate, would he have lived differently? Would he have left his wife or spent every second with her? Would he have gone on a cruise around the world? Or just gone to the racetrack every day?

If Wanda had known the choices she was making would

have left her dead before her thirtieth birthday, would she have chosen differently? Maybe. Except, of course, Wanda probably never thought about her thirtieth birthday. It's a common problem among the impoverished, the lack of future focus. People are so worried about surviving today they don't have the luxury of thinking about tomorrow.

"Sometimes, I think I could just stare at her picture all day, too," Tynesha said, walking up alongside me. I suddenly became aware they were waiting for me.

"All right, let's go," I said.

Our departure brought about much less Nextel blurping than our arrival did. The white man hadn't been that interesting, after all—he had come and gone without arresting anyone or buying anything.

I fired up the Malibu, flipped the heater on high, and drove us downtown to one of the funeral homes that had been serving Newark's black community for more than a hundred years. I had never been to this one before, but knew the type. And I could practically guarantee the folks there were tired of burying people like Wanda Bass. In this city's death business, the customer demographics had skewed young far too long.

We didn't seem to have an appointment, but we were still ushered into the office of Mrs. Rosa Bricker, who had the role of funeral director down pat. She was friendly, but not too friendly. She cared, but not too much. She was warm, but in a detached kind of way. She dealt with death the same way an accountant deals with taxes: as a practical problem worthy of attention but not hysteria. She was, above all else, professional.

After we were properly introduced—having a reporter in the room didn't seem to faze her—she slid a packet labeled "Price List" across the desk at Miss B. The basic services included embalming, dressing, viewing ceremonies, transportation, and so on, and they went for around $3,500. That didn't include the casket, which ranged from your basic three-hundred-dollar pine box all the way up to the Z64 Classic Gold Solid Bronze Sealer With Velvet Interior. It went for a hair over 10 Large. Calculating in monetary terms I could understand, that was about 2.8 used Malibus.

Miss B was doing her best to keep her composure, but it wasn't hard to see how floored she was. She obviously didn't have enough savings to get Wanda near the cemetery, much less in the ground. There was a grim joke in the funeral home business that the shorter the driveway, the more expensive the funeral. Rich people just wanted to get on with probating the will. It was the poor folks—the ones who couldn't really afford it—who felt the need to have showy funerals.

Miss B didn't even have a driveway.

"Do you . . . do you offer payment plans?" she asked.

"Naturally," Mrs. Bricker said. "But if I might make a suggestion, you might want to make an application to the Violent Crimes Compensation Board. They pay up to $5,000 for funeral costs. We can assist you with that."

"I would appreciate that," Miss B said, then started breathing normally again.

Mrs. Bricker pulled some paperwork from her drawer. Much of it had been filled out in advance. This obviously wasn't her first time with a murder victim.

"We have a package we offer for families who are using Violent Crimes money," Mrs. Bricker said, pushing a piece of paper across her desk at Miss B. "It covers all essential services, including a burial in a sealed casket with a headstone. You would be responsible for any additional costs, although we've tried to make the package as inclusive as possible."

As Miss B began filling out the required form, I caught myself feeling relieved, which was odd. I didn't know Wanda. Up until an hour ago, I didn't know Miss B. And I grew up in a house with a long enough driveway that pricey funerals struck me as pointless. What did I care if Wanda Bass was buried in a pine box? More to the point: what did *she* care?

But I did care. I cared because of Miss B and Tynesha. I cared because the girl in those pictures had had a lousy life and an even lousier death. She deserved a little something unlousy coming her way, even if it was too late to do much good.

Miss B caught me off guard with her next question.

"Can I see Wanda now?"

My innards did a somersault–back handspring combination and for a moment I thought I was going to regret some of the previous night's overexertion. Mrs. Bricker's smooth surface didn't ripple for a moment. Instead, she folded her hands on her desk and looked straight at Miss B.

"We can certainly see her if you wish," Mrs. Bricker said. "But I will tell you we had to do quite a bit of restoration work. It may be difficult for you to view her right now. You may want to wait until we've had the chance to dress her, do her hair, and put on some makeup."

"I can handle it," Miss B said.

"It can be traumatic," Mrs. Bricker said, more firmly. "I'd advise against it. It will be a much more positive experience if you wait."

"I will see my daughter now," Miss B said with a certain edge that seemed to settle the matter.

"Very well," Mrs. Bricker replied, smoothly picking up the phone on her desk. She said a few soft words to the person on the other end and hung up.

"Come with me," she said, rising from her desk.

I was hoping someone would ask me to stay in the office, which I would have happily done. It's not that I have anything against dead bodies. I just prefer living ones.

Alas, no one said a word. So I brought up the rear as we were led downstairs and through a door marked STAFF ONLY. The room we entered was brightly lit, slightly chilly, and tiled from floor to ceiling. Jugs of pinkish liquid—embalming fluid, I assumed—were stacked against the far wall. In the middle were three stainless steel gurneys. Two were empty. The third was very much occupied and draped with a white sheet.

An underling, dressed in scrubs, nodded at Mrs. Bricker as he departed.

"We don't allow families in here if there is more than one body present—out of respect to the other families. But as you can see, Wanda is alone here today," Mrs. Bricker said, and it seemed to be for my benefit. I guess she didn't want *Eagle-Examiner* readers thinking her funeral home lacked discretion.

Miss B, who didn't seem to be hearing anything, stood about five feet from the gurney, her eyes locked on the figure underneath.

"I'm going to roll back the drape now," Mrs. Bricker said.

When Miss B nodded slightly, Mrs. Bricker neatly folded back the sheet.

It wasn't Wanda. Well, technically, it was. But it was some grotesque version of her. Her face barely resembled the beautiful woman I had seen in the pictures. The cheeks were swollen. The eyes were sunken. The forehead looked like it had been shattered and put together again—which it probably had been. All the features were just slightly off.

"Are you sure that's Wa—" Tynesha began, then stopped herself.

"We started the work as soon as we received the body from

the medical examiner yesterday," Mrs. Bricker said, answering the question Tynesha sort of asked.

Miss B uprooted herself and approached her daughter's corpse. She first touched the hair, then gently cupped the jaw, then brushed her fingers across the lips. The tears were rolling down both sides of Miss B's face, onto her chin, and into the folds of her neck. But no sounds were coming out.

"As I said, the restoration was extensive," Mrs. Bricker continued. "I worked on her myself for several hours."

"Can I just be alone with her for a moment or two?" Miss B asked.

"Of course," Mrs. Bricker said, nodding at me and Tynesha. I didn't need to be asked twice, and made quickly for the door.

"Oh, Tynesha baby, stay here," Miss B said.

Tynesha rushed to her side. As the door closed, I saw them embrace awkwardly. Miss B's eyes never left her daughter's broken face.

Back in the hallway, Mrs. Bricker leaned against the wall and crossed one foot over the other. The sudden relaxing of her posture surprised me. Up until that point, she had been nothing but formal. Now that she was out of eyeshot of the customer, she felt she could stand down just a little.

"Wow, that's tough," I said, slumping against the other wall.

"That's why I told her to wait," Mrs. Bricker said. "But I could tell she was going to be a stubborn one."

I nodded, as if I, too, knew Miss B was going to be a stubborn one.

"You get any of the other bodies from down on Ludlow Street?" I asked.

"No, just this one."

"You get used to stuff like that?"

"I'm around death all the time," she said. "Sometimes it agitates me our society has so many superstitions about it. It's really just a natural thing. It happens to everyone eventually."

"No, I mean do you get used to what happened to Wanda?" I said. "I mean, what *did* happen to her? You heard that in there. Her own best friend barely recognized her. I'm sure you did what you could, but . . ."

It was among the less articulate questions of my journalism career. Mrs. Bricker took it in stride. I suppose it was a nice change for her to talk with someone who wasn't near-hysterical with grief.

"I've seen worse, but that was a pretty difficult reconstruction," she said. "You have to understand, when that girl came here, she only had half a face."

"I thought she had been shot in the back of the head," I said.

"She was. And there was an entrance wound in the back of the head. It was pretty small. That was about a ten-minute patch job. It was the exit wound that was the problem. That bullet took a lot of the forehead with it."

I cringed a little but tried to hide my reaction. There was no room for sentimentality in a discussion like this.

"Any idea what kind of gun it was?" I asked.

"Forty caliber," she said without hesitation.

"That's odd," I said. "Are you sure it wasn't a .38?"

I'm no gun nut, but it was my understanding .40 caliber was used mostly by law enforcement—local, state, and, primarily, federal. The thug or thugs responsible for this must have somehow gotten their hands on some cop's gun.

"We serve the neighborhoods," Mrs. Bricker said. "Trust me when I tell you I've seen enough bullet wounds to tell the difference. It was a .40 caliber. A .38 wouldn't have done nearly as much damage."

"Well, then explain something to me," I said. "You said the bullet took out the forehead. I thought it would have come out lower."

"Why?"

"Well, the cops told us the killing was done execution style. To me, execution style means the victim is kneeling and the perp is standing, meaning the shot goes downward." I pantomimed a gun, putting a finger to the back of my head, tilting it at the appropriate angle. "Shouldn't it have blown off the nose or jaw or something?"

"Well, in this case, she was standing, not kneeling," Mrs. Bricker said definitively.

"Oh?"

"The entrance and exit wounds are parallel. That tells me she and the shooter were at the same level. You're probably looking for a gunman who is tall, six three to six five."

"I didn't realize you doubled as a forensics expert," I said, smiling despite the subject matter.

She smiled, too. It was her first one. "I'm not," she said. "But in this case the math is pretty simple. Wanda was tall, right? Let's say five nine or five ten?"

Tynesha had talked about what long legs Wanda had. "Sounds right," I said.

"Okay, so we know the perp was holding the gun straight, because the entrance and exit wounds are the same height," Mrs. Bricker said, now pantomiming her own gun. "Since he's able to hold the gun straight and still be pointing near the top of her head, the shooter must be roughly a head taller, call it six or seven inches. That's how you get six three to six five."

"You're good," I said.

She smiled again but stamped it out the moment Miss B and Tynesha emerged from the examining room, sniffling and

115

leaning on each other for support. Miss B's limp looked even worse than before.

"Thank you for trying to patch her up," Miss B said. "I think we'll keep the lid closed for the viewing."

"Of course," Mrs. Bricker said, having immediately resumed her former ramrod straightness. "We'll still want to get some clothes from you to put her in. If you don't have anything suitable, we work with a charity that provides burial outfits for needy families. And of course we'll bring someone in to do her hair. That's part of the package."

Miss B murmured something indistinct. Seeing her daughter laid out on a metal gurney in that cold room had taken all the starch out of her. It required some effort to get her back up the stairs and out into the street, where I feared even the smallest gust of wind was going to knock her over. Tynesha had her by one arm. I couldn't grab the other because of Miss B's cane, but I stayed close in case she toppled.

After a silent car ride back to Miss B's building, we got her back out of the car and I resumed spotting. The Nextel guys paid us little mind as we slowly hobbled up the steps. We were just a couple of people escorting a crippled old woman home.

Miss B went straight into her bedroom and Tynesha gave me a little wave as she followed. I took one last glance at Wanda's high school portrait, then departed.

I returned to the newsroom and to a desk that had been transformed into a veritable legalize-marijuana showcase. Someone had printed out twenty copies of a marijuana-leaf picture and taped them all around my computer. Another creative genius had twisted some used newsprint into a two-foot-long joint and left it next to the keyboard along with half a dozen smaller joints, a lighter, and a homemade bong that had been fashioned from a two-liter soda bottle.

Sitting on my chair was a brochure with a picture of a morose-looking guy and the headline "Seeking Help for Your Marijuana Problem?"

I had been hoping to surreptitiously slip the four pilfered heroin bags out of my pocket and into an envelope, which I would then hide in my desk for safekeeping. But that suddenly seemed like a very bad idea, what with half the newsroom wondering if I was developing a drug habit.

"Nice going, Ivy," Buster Hays hollered at me. "Let me guess: you didn't inhale, right?"

It was a tired joke, but some of Hays's cronies laughed. I began clearing away enough drug paraphernalia so I had some workspace.

"Ha ha," I said, with intentionally flat inflection. As usual, Hays had caught me completely without comeback.

Tommy sauntered over from his desk to snicker up close.

"So I guess I have you to thank for this lovely display?" I asked.

"Don't look at me," Tommy said. "Brodie made an announcement at the morning editor's meeting and then sent out an e-mail to everyone at the paper, saying you were an example for all of us to follow. What you see before you is a collaborative effort."

"I'm never going to live this down, am I?"

"By the time the night copy desk makes it in, you'll be the most famous stoner this side of Cheech and Chong," Tommy confirmed.

"Just what I always wanted."

"C'mon, you're a hero," Tommy said. "The hippies over in the features department are thrilled because now they think they're allowed to get high at work. I think they're out behind the building getting stoned as we speak."

"They do that all the time anyway."

"True, but now they feel justified. You might want to negotiate with the vending machine guy about getting a cut. Newsroom snack food sales are going to skyrocket."

I was just starting to enjoy our banter when the abominable Vowelless Monster became aware of my presence.

"Crrrrttrrrss!" Sal Szanto hollered, taking the trouble to lift his hairy girth from behind his desk so I could see him gesturing for me.

I immediately began formulating escape strategies. Would fake appendicitis be over-the-top?

"Hey, Sal," I said, strolling into his office and pulling up a chair as if nothing were awry.

"I know you're Brodie's new cuddle-buddy and all, but would you mind telling me what smoking dope with a bunch of gangbangers has to do with our bar story?"

"Why, yes, of course," I said.

"Well?"

"Glad you asked," I said, then started squirming as if something were gnawing on my leg.

"Hang on," I said, fishing my cell phone out of my pocket. "I gotta take this."

"It didn't even ring!" Szanto protested.

"It's on vibrate," I said as I flipped open the phone and gave my most officious "Carter Ross!"

"Like hell it is," Szanto said, raising his voice. "There's no one on the other end. I'm not falling for that again!"

"Huh," I said, taking the phone away from my ear and looking puzzled at it. "I lost him. This must be a dead reception area. Let me try it from the other side of the newsroom."

I lifted myself from the chair, but Szanto was having none of it.

"Sit your ass down. Give me a quick update on the bar story and you can go call from Botswana for all I care."

"I thought Tina gave you the update on the bar story," I said.

"If you're checking to see whether your accomplice covered for you, the answer is yes. She tells me you're making excellent progress. But when I asked her details she faked an intense menstrual cramp and ran out of my office."

Menstrual cramps. Why hadn't I thought of that?

"So stop dicking around," Szanto ordered. "Brodie is talking about this being a page one story on Sunday and he keeps asking me every eight minutes what it's going to say. I'd like to have an answer for him."

"Right," I said. "The bar story. It's this . . . bar . . . where everyone in the neighborhood went to, you know, drink. Except there was something, something"—what was the word Szanto had used the other day?—"something *sinister* going on inside."

"Fine. I like where we're heading on this," Szanto said. "Who have we talked to?"

"Oh, lots of people."

"Like who?"

"People in the, uh, neighborhood. You know . . . customers."

"Have we talked to the bar's owner yet? What does he say? When did these people rob him? Is he a suspect?"

"I'm sure he's a person of interest," I said, employing that wonderfully vague bit of cop talk.

"Goddammit, are you working on this story or not?" Szanto demanded.

He didn't wait for my answer. "You know what? I don't care. I'm going to make this real simple for you. You got this assignment on Monday. It's now Wednesday afternoon. I expect that bar story to be on my desk by Friday at noon or I'm sending you out to Sussex County to cover bear scat for the rest of your life."

I grinned despite myself. Sussex County was our farthest-flung bureau, about an hour away in the northeast corner of the state. Szanto threatened to reassign me there roughly every other month.

"Right," I said. "You'll have a story by Friday at noon."

And I meant it. I just didn't know what story it was going to be.

After my retreat from Szanto's office, I went straight to Tommy's desk, hoping he had made some progress in the past twenty-four hours.

"You might want to consider a smaller belt," he said as he saw me approach.

"And why is that?"

"You're going to need *something* to hold your pants up with the way Szanto just chewed your ass off," Tommy finished, pleased with himself.

"I really walked right into that one, didn't I?"

"Chin first, yeah."

"Then I need a soda to recover from my wounds. Come on, I'm buying."

Tommy trailed after me to the break room vending machine, which was in a cranky mood. After surrendering the first bottle with relative ease, there was no way it was giving up the second one without a fight. I gave the machine a slight shove, which did nothing. Neither did leaning into it a little harder. I was rocking the thing violently back and forth when Tommy spoke up.

"You know, ten people a year are—"

"Oh, stuff it already," I said, finally getting enough wobble going to dislodge a fresh Coke Zero.

Tommy sat down with his soda. I went over to another machine to do something about the rumbling in my stomach.

"So how was your return to Shareef Thomas's neighborhood?" I asked, selecting a sleeve of strawberry Pop-Tarts. Health food.

"Not bad if you like spending a lot of time with people who wear polyester blends," he said. "Though I did meet a drunk who claimed to be Shareef's uncle."

"Was he?"

"He had a Social Security card with the name Marlon Thomas on it."

"Okay, I guess that's legit," I said, tearing into my first Pop-Tart.

"He told me he'd tell me anything I wanted to know if I got him something to drink. So I bought him two bottles of Boone's Farm's finest sparkling wine from the corner liquor store."

"I hope you went with the 2007. Growing conditions were excellent that year."

"But of course," he said.

It's strictly unethical for us to pay a source for information. Tabloids do it all the time, but no serious newspaper would ever think about it. Information that has to be paid for is considered untrustworthy.

That said, what Tommy had done was more or less fine. I'm not saying I'd write in to *Columbia Journalism Review* to brag about it. But it wasn't really that much different than, say, picking up the tab when you lunched with the mayor. This was just a less conventional method of building rapport with a source—a liquid lunch, as it were.

"How do you think I expense that?" Tommy asked.

"Just put it under 'Miscellaneous Supplies.'"

"Sounds good," he said, pulling out his notebook and reading from it. "Anyway, here's what Uncle Booze-Breath had to say about his precious nephew. His daddy—Booze-Breath's brother—was apparently a pretty decent guy who got shot in some kind of mistaken-identity thing back in the eighties. After that, Shareef's mom started messing around with a drug dealer, and you know how that story ends."

"I'm guessing poorly," I said, moving on to my second Pop-Tart.

"You got it. Once Mama Shareef had enough possession charges, she got put away for ten years and Shareef got put in foster care."

"I'm guessing that went poorly, too."

"Very. There was no foster home that could hold him. He hightailed it out of every one they tried to put him in and always ended up back in the neighborhood, crashing with a different relative. The relative would usually put up with him for a few months. Then Shareef would do something to make the relative turn him back over to foster care, then he'd run away again. Somewhere along the line, he started stealing cars, landed in a juvenile lockup, and has pretty much spent the rest of his life in and out of jail. When even your wino uncle describes you as 'that boy ain't no good,' that ought to tell you something."

Pop-Tart No. 2 was now gone and I peered into the empty plastic wrapper, hoping that a third had somehow miraculously materialized. Alas, it was empty.

"That was your lunch, wasn't it?" he asked.

"No. I also had a slice of apple pie earlier."

"I'll remind you of this moment when you have to go to the Ugly Pants Store to buy a larger size."

I shrugged. My secret to weight loss: get busy enough at work and you end up skipping meals without realizing it.

"So did the uncle know anything about Shareef's most recent mode of employment?" I asked.

"The uncle didn't know much or didn't say much. But I talked to some other people. Shareef was a drug dealer, obviously. He was a solo operation. He didn't have any kind of crew or anything.

"Let's see, what else," Tommy said, continuing to scan his notes. "A couple of months ago he paid for a bunch of neighborhood kids to go to Great Adventure."

"Ah, a real Robin Hood, this one," I interjected.

"Yeah, it seems like business had been good lately. People said he bought himself a new Chrysler 300—you know, those Bentley knockoffs. Everyone in the neighborhood assumed he was getting too big for his britches so someone decided to permanently remove him from his turf. I guess he was starting to take customers away from other dealers."

"Sounds a lot like our other three victims."

"Uh-huh," Tommy said.

"He sold heroin, I assume?"

"Yep," Tommy said, still flipping pages. "Oh, this was kind of cute. Apparently the brand he sold was called 'The Stuff.'"

I felt a jolt, like the wind had been knocked out of me.

"The Stuff? Are you sure about that?"

Tommy turned some more pages. "Well, I wouldn't exactly stake my shoe collection on it," he said. "I got that from a junkie who kept asking if she could borrow twenty bucks. So I don't know if I could consider my sourcing beyond reproach. But, yeah, she said his brand was called 'The Stuff.' Pretty funny, huh?"

"In more ways than you know. That's the same brand Wanda

Bass was selling. I saw it myself in her bedroom when I visited her mother's house."

"Really? Huh. Think it's a coincidence?"

"I don't know. I mean, how many brands of heroin are sold in this city?"

"Beats me. A hundred?"

"At least. What are the chances two dealers from completely different parts of the city would end up selling the same brand?"

Lights were going on in Tommy's attic.

"About the same as the chances two dealers from different parts of the city would end up dead together in a vacant lot at the far end of the South Ward," he said.

I allowed myself to bask in the moment and savor the buzz I was feeling. There was nothing like the moment when a story started coming together.

"Tommy," I said. "I do believe we've just found the missing link between the Ludlow Four."

Of course, believing it and proving it were two different matters. And in the proof department, we still had some work to do. I knew I would only be able to talk Szanto out of that stupid bar story if I could definitively tell him that each of the Ludlow Four sold the same brand of heroin.

It would pain Szanto to hear it, of course. But in the twisted logic of newspapering, being wrong can be somewhat forgiven as long as you have something to right it with: another big scoop. And this story, if I could nail it down, would certainly qualify as one, especially with all the attention that was starting to surround the Ludlow Four.

The New York newspapers, which normally treated the other side of the Hudson River as if it were some distant curiosity, had been following the story each day. The grisly details of the crime and the brazen nature with which it was carried out made for good copy. One of the tabloids even put it on its cover, an unusual honor for out-of-state news.

With the newspapers beating the drums, the TV stations—who only decide how to play ongoing stories after they read the papers—had stayed on the bandwagon, too. Each local nightly news telecast was featuring sound bites from a steady stream of local antiviolence activists, who were eager to jump in front of the cameras and exclaim "this has to stop" or "enough is enough."

None of it was actually news, of course, just reaction to the news. Only the newspapers were going to push the story forward. And being able to establish the connection between the victims would definitely keep us out in front of the competition. Szanto would like that. Brodie would love it.

Now we just had to make sure it was true. Tommy volunteered to head back to Shareef's neighborhood and do some double-checking with his new friends there.

That left Devin Whitehead and Tyrone Scott. Devin would be easy enough. I picked up the phone and dialed my man Tee.

"Yeah," Tee said. He always answered his cell phone that way. I guess it was part of the tough-guy image.

"What's up, Tee?"

"You tell me, you're the one calling."

"Right. Are those knucklehead kids hanging around outside your store?"

"Of course."

"You mind asking them what brand of heroin Dee-Dub was selling."

"You mean what brand he was *allegedly* selling?" Tee corrected me.

"Right. Allegedly."

"Hang on," Tee said.

I heard the electronic *bee-baa* that went off whenever Tee's front door opened, then could make out the sounds of the street and some muffled voices. I drummed my fingers for a few moments, checking my e-mail as I waited. Great news: Human Resources had an upcoming series, "Cholesterolapalooza."

Tee brought his phone back to his mouth.

"You gotta do something for me," he said.

"What's that?"

"I'm going to put you on speakerphone. Just answer my questions honestly."

"No problem."

Suddenly the ambient noises were a lot louder.

"Carter, you there?" Tee asked, half yelling.

"Yeah," I said.

"Okay, first question, 'Are you Carter Ross, Bird Man extraordinaire?'"

"Correct."

"Are you, in fact, white?" Tee asked, and I heard some snickering.

"As white as they come."

"Just to be sure about this, I need to hear you say something really, really white."

I rolled my eyes.

"And can you explain to me what would qualify as really, really white?" I asked.

"Actually, that'll do it," Tee said, and the voices in the background erupted with laughter.

"Order in the court, order in the court!" Tee howled, though he was laughing, too. "Okay, okay, now that we have established you are a card-carrying member of the Caucasian persuasion"—more snickering—"can you please tell the court, 'Who you was hanging with last night?'"

"Uh . . . Well, this woman took me back to her place . . ."

"Oh, now you bragging," Tee said, and the voices cackled again. "Order! Order, I say! Okay, *before* you and your lady friend did whatever it is white people do, what did you do then?"

Where the hell was he going with this?

"I, uh, spent some quality time with the Brick City Browns," I said.

"Aha! And did that 'quality time' involve the use of any controlled dangerous substances? Let me remind you, Mr. Ross, you are under oath."

"Uh, Tee, you don't have any cops listening to this, do you?"

Tee clicked off his speakerphone, bringing the phone to his mouth.

"C'mon, man!" he said. "What self-respecting black man would be hanging out with the Jake?"

"The Jake?"

"Yeah, you remember that TV show, *Jake and the Fat Man*? Jake was the cop."

"Oh, right," I said, still thoroughly bewildered as to what he was driving at. "Anyway, what was the question?"

Tee put me back on speakerphone.

"The question, Mr. Ross, is, 'What was you and the Browns doing last night?'"

Suddenly, it started to make sense.

"Well, Judge Tee, I would have to say we were smoking some high-quality hydroponic ganja."

The background voices burst out in a chorus of disbelieving expletives.

"I told you! I told you!" I could hear Tee crowing. "Twenty bucks! Twenty bucks!"

I was taken off speakerphone again, though I could still

127

hear a lot of indistinct noises punctuated with occasional laughter. It took another minute for Tee to return to the phone.

"Mind telling me what that was about?" I asked.

"They didn't believe the story they've been hearing about the white guy who smoked up with the Browns then started falling all over the place."

"Oh, so now I'm a story?"

"You ain't a story. You like a legend. It's been all over the hood today. I must have heard about four different versions by now."

"I'm never going to live this down, am I," I said. When I had asked Tommy that earlier, it was a question. It was getting to be more of a statement now.

"Not a chance. By the way, did you really give them a lecture on how tsunamis are created?"

I searched my memory. I couldn't recall having done so. And I'm not sure, sober, I even knew myself. But the brain on drugs could cook up some interesting things.

"I suppose it's possible," I said.

"Huh. You'll have to explain that to me sometime. Because I always wondered."

"Right. Anyway, did you get the answer to my question?"

"What question?"

"About the brand Dee-Dub sold?

"Oh, yeah, that. *Allegedly* his brand was called 'The Stuff.' You know, like it was stuff but it was proper stuff so they called it 'The Stuff.' But remember, you didn't get that from me. His mama would whup my ass."

"Right," I said. I would worry about how exactly my story would deal with the sourcing later. A simple "according to people in his neighborhood" would probably suffice.

"Thanks for your help," I said.

"Anytime. Thanks for winning that bet for me," Tee said. "Talk to you later, you old pothead."

I hung up the phone and self-consciously fingered the dime bags of heroin that were burning a hole in my pocket. There were still too many wandering eyeballs around to make a safe transfer to my desk, so I turned to my notebook.

"Notebook," I said, using my internal voice because otherwise everyone would think I was still smoking something. "Notebook, please tell me something about Tyrone Scott."

I flipped the pages, ever hopeful. I know it seems desperate, asking a four-by-eight-inch pad of paper to be your savior. But there are times when this kind of pleading really does work, when you've buried some little treasure of a note that you uncover at just the right time. Maybe it's some scribbled observation that brings an entire picture into perfect relief. Or a name and a phone number you never followed up on. Or something you forgot having ever written that perfectly synthesizes your story.

Or you can just end up staring at a bunch of worthless scribbles for twenty minutes.

The only way I was going to discover more about Tyrone Scott was to head back out to that chicken shack and poke around.

By the time I arrived at the Wyoming Fried Chicken, home of Cowboy Kenny's secret blend, it was pitch-black. Still, the hooded figures who patrolled the sidewalk in front of the chicken shack became aware of my pale-faced presence the moment I stepped out of my car, and scurried off quickly.

Leaving behind only one guy. My friend North Face.

"What, you drew the short straw again?" I asked.

"Aw, come on, man. I already told you everything I know. Now you going to screw up my business again?"

"You can tell your customers your product is so good I just can't stop myself from coming back."

"Oh, great. We'll put it on a billboard: 'The guy who dresses like a narc only gets his stuff from one place.' Man, get out of here."

"Relax. I just got one question."

"And I'm supposed to give you the answer? Do I look like Alex Trebek to you?"

I laughed.

"I ain't trying to be funny, Bird Man," he said, reaching into his jacket and leaving his hand there, the all-purpose wintertime signal that a gun was being kept nice and cozy underneath.

The last time we met, North Face had just been giving me a hard time for the sake of giving me a hard time. It had been earlier in the day. I wasn't really costing him business. This was different. It was after five now—prime time for sales. A lot of Newark drug users are slightly more functional than they are stereotypically given credit for. They manage to hold down day jobs then go straight to their local dealer and buy enough to keep them high until the following morning. The early evening was rush hour for a guy like North Face.

"Okay, okay. Take it easy," I said. "Look, I just want to know what brand of heroin Tyrone sold and then I'll get out of your way."

"I ain't in that market."

"Can you point me toward someone who is?"

"I ain't the Yellow Pages, either. Now get the hell out of here."

"Do we really have to go through this again?" I asked. "You know I'm going to hang out here until I get the information I need. So why not just help me out?"

"You know what? I ain't helping you with nothin'. I ain't telling you nothin'. I'm gonna ask you to leave and if you don't I'm gonna stop asking nicely."

His hand dug a little farther into his jacket. A good 98 percent of me was certain it was an idle threat. The other 2 percent of me was sure my bowels were about to loosen.

"Look, pal, I'm just a reporter here doing a job, that's all," I said, trying hard to project an image of everymanness.

"Well, then, let me ask you, when my cousin got killed out here two months ago, where were you then, huh? Where was his story?"

North Face glared at me. The cold fact was, in our business, some deaths mattered more than others. But I don't think North Face needed to hear that. When I didn't immediately open my mouth to answer, he continued his tirade.

"Oh, so my cousin is just another dead nigga, but Tyrone Scott is some kind of cause for you people? Tyrone is better than my cousin, is that it? Because he got killed with three other people and my cousin got killed on his way to the store for some milk? That makes Tyrone better than my cousin?"

He glared some more, which I took as my invitation to speak.

"I'm sorry about your cousin," I said, keeping my voice as even as possible in an effort to deescalate the emotion of the moment.

I thought about adding more: that in a city where ninety or a hundred people are killed every year, no newspaper could write at length about every one; that we had to pick our spots or risk being tuned out altogether; that treating every single murder like it was a big deal, while it would honor the memory of the victim, could actually make the problem of urban violence worse by lending undue attention to it.

But those were all macro justifications for a micro problem. We *should* treat every murder as if it mattered, because what could be of graver concern to society than the intentional taking of human life?

So I just said: "You're right. I'm sorry."

It's tough to argue with someone who won't put up a fight. When he saw I had no more to say, North Face relaxed his shoulders and slowly slid his hand out of his jacket, then pointed up the street.

"You can go over to Booker T," he said. "All kinds of junkies there. Half of them used to buy from Tyrone."

"Thanks," I said. "I'll get out of your hair now. And I really am sorry about your cousin."

"No one reads the paper anyway," he grumbled.

I let him have that parting shot. And as I pulled away, I saw the hooded figures start to emerge from their hiding places and resume their posts.

The Booker T. Washington Public Housing Project, otherwise known as Booker T, was a few blocks away. Booker T's story was a sadly familiar one in Newark. Built not long after World War II—when it was hailed as a glistening, modern replacement for nineteenth-century tenement housing—it had once been a vibrant, thriving community where slightly down-on-their-luck families found their bootstraps and pulled themselves up.

But, in the long run, slack management, shoddy maintenance, and neglectful tenants made it just as bad as the tenements it replaced. And as the city died around it—with the middle class fleeing and the factory jobs disappearing—Booker T settled slowly into a mire from which there was no rescue. By the turn of the twenty-first century, it had gotten so bad the city decided there was only one way to fix Booker T: tear it down.

But even that wasn't easy. There were disagreements among city, state, and federal governments about who should pay for the demolition. There were residents who didn't want to leave. Then there were the illegal residents—the squatters, the drifters, the junkies, an entire underworld of people who hacked their way through the plywood that covered the windows and doors and used the buildings for their own shadowy purposes.

That was the Booker T I was venturing into, a place that was worse than a ghost town because the souls that haunted it were still alive. If you took a snapshot of Booker T at any one moment, you might not see anything living, besides perhaps one of the stray cats that came to hunt for rats.

But if you stayed for a while, you'd inevitably see some vagrant shuffling through. Or you might notice a tendril of smoke escaping from a window where someone had lit a fire inside a trash barrel.

Those were the people I was looking for, people who had slipped through society's safety net, past the dozens of nonprofits and churches that may have tried to catch them, and hit rock bottom. They were, to say the least, a difficult cohort to interview. Many of them suffered from delusions and paranoias that made their grasp on the real world anywhere from tenuous to nonexistent. Some would be so high they might as well be mentally ill.

Still, I had to try.

I parked my car along the street that ran outside Booker T, a collection of six block-long, four-story brick buildings. In the middle was a massive courtyard, around which Booker T's social life had rotated for fifty years.

The sense of desolation in the courtyard was overwhelming. This had once been a place where friends gathered, where stories were told, where summer days were passed, where lives were led. And now it had been surrendered to an eerie kind of urban emptiness: not the slightest bit of human activity greeted my arrival.

After maybe fifteen minutes, a lone woman wandered through, saw me, and turned in the other direction. It was no use trying to catch up to her.

Next came a man doing the junkie stumble, staggering in a chaotic pattern, unseeing and unknowing. He had a boisterous conversation going with himself, one that consisted of bits of words followed by loud, dry coughing. I considered talking to him but decided I'd be better off trying to interview one of the stray cats.

In the darkness, and with the cold numbing my senses, time became hard to judge. Had I been there thirty minutes or three hours? It didn't matter. I would stay as long as needed until . . .

There. A man. Walking at the far end of the courtyard. The buildings were numbered, one through six, and he was in between numbers one and two. The darkness and lack of moonlight made it difficult to see what he was doing, but, yes, he had momentarily halted. Had he seen me and frozen, hoping to elude detection? Was he going to flee?

No, he was turning. He was facing Building Two. And he was . . .

Pissing on it.

I waited for the man to dispense with his business, giving him the kind of time and distance I might appreciate were I urinating on a public building. Once he restored his gear, I moved in, approaching noisily so he knew I was coming. When I was still about forty feet away, I hollered out the biggest, friendliest "Hi, there!" I could summon.

"I'm sorry to bother you, sir," I continued, still trying to sound as harmless as I could.

I had gotten near enough to see the man was looking at me like I was his first extraterrestrial sighting. He was wearing sneakers that appeared several sizes too big and several decades too old. I guessed he was wearing all the clothes he owned, though even with all that padding he seemed gaunt and under-nourished. He had one of those patchy-bald heads, the kind older black men get when they don't have the good sense to just shave it all off. His age, as with most advanced addicts, was dif-ficult to guess—somewhere between forty-five and seventy-five. All you really knew for sure was that life had been hard on him.

"I'm a reporter with the *Eagle-Examiner*," I said, coming closer still.

"You sellin' newspapers?" he slurred, even more puzzled.

I laughed. I was now close enough to see *and* smell his breath, which could have flunked a Breathalyzer from ten paces away. That was actually a good sign. In my experience, the drunks were slightly more coherent than the druggies.

"No, sir. I'm a reporter. I don't sell the newspaper. I write it."

"Izzat so?" the man said, smiling curiously. Thank good-ness, an amiable drunk.

"Yes, sir. I'm working on a story about a drug dealer named Hundred Year."

He recoiled.

"He dead?" the man asked. "Thas what folks been saying."

I nodded. The man spat deliberately on the ground. "Good. I don't like to speak no ill of the dead, but he pick on ol' people for the hell of it. He one nasty bastard. You gonna tell people he wasn't no good in your newspaper, yeah?"

"If that's what's true. That's why I'm trying to talk to folks around here. You got any friends?"

"Oh, I got some friends. But let me ask you somethin'. You think if I help you write your newspaper, maybe you could help get me a little something to eat?"

Ah, Newark. The hustle never stops.

"That can be arranged," I said, smiling.

"Well, then, all right. You all right."

Having gained his approval, I decided I might as well get to the point. "I'm trying to figure out what brand of heroin he sold."

"Couldn't say. I don' touch that junk," the man said proudly. I love addicts and their logic: the guy who had been pickling his liver with alcohol for thirty years could express disdain at the thought of ever using a drug. Meanwhile the neighborhood crackhead was smugly thinking that at least she wasn't some slurring alchy.

"You know anyone who might have bought from him?"

"'Round here? Shoot. Jus' 'bout everyone."

He gestured as if we were at a crowded cocktail party. I looked around at the still-empty courtyard. "Know where I could find them?"

The man thought for a moment. "S'pose I do," he said.

"By the way, my name is Carter Ross," I said. Normally I would have stuck out my hand for him to shake. But having been subjected to such a graphic demonstration of where his hand had just been, I kept my fingers anchored in my pocket.

"Folks call me 'Red,' jus' like Red Sanford, 'cept my family name is Coles," he said. He was about 150 pounds shy of passing for Red Sanford. And he was so jaundiced, folks should have called him "Yellow Sanford."

"I'll follow you," I said. "You're my tour guide."

"Okay, now I know a woman, she like the mayor of this place. I'm goin' to see her now," he said, then elbowed me in a conspiratorial fashion. "I kind of mess aroun' with her a little bit."

God bless the male spirit: here was a man who had no home, no job, no money, a raging case of cirrhosis and Lord knows what other maladies. But he still wanted me to know he was getting some ass now and then.

I tailed Red toward Building Five and watched as he scampered up a Dumpster, onto a fire escape, up a flight of stairs, and through a vacant spot in a plywood window. I was impressed at how smoothly he moved, given his condition. Obviously, he had been doing this for a while. With all my youth and relative health, I was struggling to keep up. When I reached the window, Red was inside gesturing for me. There was no sign of light or life.

"C'mon," he said.

"How can you see a damn thing in there?"

"I cain't."

"So how do you walk?"

"Jus' trust your feet. They know how to do it."

I scooted through the small opening, then did my best to navigate the dark, trash-strewn room. Maybe *Red's* feet knew. Mine were tripping over everything.

I followed Red's voice into the hallway, where there was an array of candles casting a dim light. There were also two old mattresses and assorted flotsam and jetsam—a box of Ritz crackers, one woman's high-heeled pump, a brass lamp that looked like it once belonged to Aladdin, bloodstained rags, and trash. Lots of trash. There was so much trash it was hard for my eyes to focus on what exactly it was. I was suddenly glad it was cold. I didn't want to imagine what this place smelled like in summertime.

A human form was lying on one of the mattresses.

"Mary," Red said. "Hey, Mary, wake up."

Mary rolled over, slow and drowsy. Her eyes got huge the moment she saw me.

"What you bring a cop in here for!" she shouted.

"He ain't no cop," Red said. "Mary, this here a reporter. He doin' a story on that nasty sum'bitch that jus' got hisself killed. And then he said he gonna get us something to eat."

Red turned to me. "This here Mary Moss. Folks call her Queen Mary, 'cause she been 'round here so long she like the queen."

Queen Mary, Ruler of Refuse, Regent of Building Five.

"Hi, Mary, it's a real pleasure to meet you," I said. "I'm Carter Ross from the *Eagle-Examiner*."

"Oh," she said. She propped herself up on her elbow. There wasn't much to Queen Mary, maybe a hundred pounds of loose skin and brittle bones. Her hair was a tangled, matted mess— easily one of the worst bed heads in human history.

"Did you know a drug dealer named Tyrone Scott?" I asked. "He went by the name Hundred Year."

"Yeah, I knew him. Bastard."

"I hear he sold a particular brand of heroin. Do you know what his brand was?"

Queen Mary peered at me blankly. Her face was so skeletal it made her eyeballs bulge halfway out of her head.

"You know how there's a stamp on the bag?" I continued, making large gestures as if I were playing charades. "What did the stamp look like?"

"Oh!" she said. "Yeah, yeah! It was . . . You know . . . umm . . . Oh, damn! I just . . ."

Mary kept mumbling to herself until I remembered; I had a product sample in my pocket. I pulled it out, then picked up one of the candles so Queen Mary could see it.

"Did it look like this?" I asked.

Suddenly, from somewhere deep within the parts of her brain that still functioned, you could see about ten thousand neurons fire off at once.

"Yeah!" she said. "Yeah, that's it! Hang on."

She crawled off her pad and started sifting through the trash, then produced a torn dime bag, which she handed to me. Sure enough, I could see the familiar eagle with the syringe clutched in its talons. It was The Stuff.

"You mind if I keep this?" I asked.

"Depends. You really gonna buy us some food?" she asked hopefully.

"You bet." I smiled and pocketed the empty packet.

With that, Red Coles, Queen Mary, and I collected ourselves, climbed back out the window into the night, and made our way to the corner bodega, where I bought them all the fruit juice, crackers, and cookies they could carry.

It was the best $37.12 the *Eagle-Examiner* could have spent.

The Director knew how crucial it was to maintain his brand's quality. He understood it far better than any of those business-magazine cover boys.

The car company that once boasted "quality is job one" should have tried out the heroin trade for a few weeks. If automakers were as accountable to their customers as the Director was, they never would have needed a bailout. Fact was, an automobile manufacturer could skimp on the kind of head gasket it used, and it would take years for the buyers to notice—if they ever did. Likewise, soft drink companies freely switched between sugar and corn syrup based on whatever was cheaper at the moment. Consumers were never the wiser.

The Director's customers noticed everything, immediately. A hard-

core junkie may not know what day, week, or year it is, but he knows the instant someone is messing with his heroin. He knows from the way it makes him feel, from how high he gets, from how long the high lasts. He knows the instant it starts coursing through his veins. He knows because the drug has essentially turned his body into a finely tuned device for measuring heroin quality.

That was the entire principle behind The Stuff: that junkies knew. That's why the Director had to guarantee The Stuff was the best, purest heroin they could find. If—and only if—he could establish and maintain his brand in that lofty spot, he knew he could eventually control the entire Newark market.

It was an ambitious goal, one others had tried—but failed—to achieve. Their mistake was attempting to control the supply side, thinking that if they simply crushed every other source of heroin coming into the city, they could own it. But the Director understood that the job couldn't be accomplished with simple muscle.

The Director took a different tack, one that focused on the demand side of the equation. If the customers came to want The Stuff and only The Stuff, refusing to buy from any dealer who didn't carry it, they would give the Director a monopoly all by themselves.

And once he had Newark, there was no telling what the Director could accomplish. Newark was the conduit between New York and Philadelphia, the linchpin of the entire East Coast. He could make countless millions.

Yet it all hung on the quality of The Stuff. The moment anyone started diluting it, the junkies would stop associating it with high quality and it would get lost amid all the other brands.

The Director had put Monty in charge of quality control, but was constantly checking on him. Was he sending enough straw buyers into the street for samples? Was he having the samples tested and retested for purity? Were the samples coming back as close to 100 percent as they had gone out?

Monty seemed to be doing fine. He had, after all, managed to catch the four dealers who had been cutting. He had told the Director about it immediately and the Director had acted accordingly.

It was unfortunate to lose four productive dealers. But the Director would kill many more if he had to—as many as it took until the rest got the message:

The brand was sacrosanct. And it would be protected at all costs.

CHAPTER 5

In most aspects of my life, I have little use for the concept of karma, the universal cycle of cause and effect, or anything that might help me achieve total consciousness. Total *un*consciousness just suits me better.

Yet when it comes to reporting, I am a deep believer in karma. It is the only way to explain the following phenomenon:

There are days as a reporter when you can do no right, when no one will return your phone calls, when all the elbow grease you put into a story gives you little more than tendonitis. Then there are times when you're the King Midas of the newsroom, when you can get the Holy Trinity on a conference call for quotes, when everything with your story falls into place so perfectly, you start to convince yourself maybe you *really are* that good.

But, no, it's just the karma. Eventually you start to accept that for every time you subject your hindquarters to four hours of deep freeze in some nasty project—and end up with nothing to show for it—there will be a time when some strung-out homeless lady named Queen Mary tells you exactly what you need to hear.

So all I could do as I drove back toward the world headquarters of the *Eagle-Examiner* was thank the karma. It was a pleasant feeling: the success of a hard day's reporting, the warmth of my Malibu, the buzz in my left thigh . . .

No, wait, that was my cell phone. It was Tommy.

"You won't believe the luck I had." His voice came bounding out of the earpiece.

"You finally had a threesome with the Hardy Boys?"

"Who are the Hardy Boys? You have gay friends you didn't tell me about?"

"They're . . . never mind. What's going on?"

"Well," Tommy said. "I was hanging around Shareef's neighborhood, just hanging around, looking for people to talk to, and this white kid pulls up in his daddy's Pathfinder and asks if I know where I can find Eef."

Huh? I pressed my ear harder against the phone. "Eef?"

"No, you idiot. RRRRReef. As in 'Shareef.' Try to keep up."

"Sorry."

"So anyway," Tommy continued, "I play it all coy and I'm like, 'Who's asking.' And this guy is like, 'I hear he's got The Stuff.' And I'm like, 'By The Stuff do you mean stuff? Or THE Stuff?' And the guy is like, 'Yeah, THE Stuff.'"

Apparently I wasn't the only one with good reporting karma.

"Anyway, this idiot kid thought I worked for Shareef or something, so he practically starts telling me his whole life story. He came from some high school in the suburbs—Livingston, I think—because word is out that this dealer named Reef was selling the best heroin ever and it was called 'The Stuff.' How's that for confirmation?" Tommy asked.

"Pretty good," I replied. "Thank you."

"You're welcome. But I got more," Tommy said. "I asked around the neighborhood a little more and apparently Shareef pretty much made a living selling to suburban kids. He would just hang out all day in that pimp-daddy Chrysler of his and wait for the SUVs to drive up."

It made sense. Shareef's neighborhood was right near the intersection of the Garden State Parkway and Route 280. Both roads led rather rapidly to a nearly infinite supply of rich suburban kids.

"I was thinking," Tommy said. "This probably means we can rule out Shareef being killed in some kind of turf battle, don't you think?"

"How so?"

"Well, it seems like Shareef didn't even have a turf. His turf was his car. Wherever he went, those idiot kids were going to find him. I mean, the kid I talked to was driving around looking for him."

I pulled into the company parking garage, letting the new information rattle around in my head for a bit. Sometimes when you're working on a story, it can be difficult to parse data as it comes, to see both the trees and the forest simultaneously.

But this time the big picture was becoming pretty clear to me. None of the Ludlow Four were killed because of turf. The cause of death, proximate or otherwise, had to be the one thing they shared: selling The Stuff.

"Good work, Tommy," I said. "Now, if you'll excuse me, I have to go tell Sal Szanto his bar story is deader than disco."

I t was past seven by the time I strolled into the newsroom. The reporters were starting to thin out, but the copy desk was humming through the process of assembling Thursday's newspaper, doing what copy desks have always done: think up misleading headlines, add mistakes into stories, and devise new ways to muddle clean writing.

No, actually, I'm a big fan of our desk. There were some odd ducks—as is often the case among people who think 4 P.M. is early in the day—but by and large they were solid, dependable folks who could spot a typo at twenty paces and delight in having won the New Jersey State spelling bee six years running. Collectively, they edited the equivalent of a novel every night.

I paused briefly at my desk-turned-drug-shrine—someone had left me a copy of *High Times*, the stoner magazine—then continued on toward Szanto's office. I might as well let him scream at me when there were fewer people around to hear it.

"Got a second, boss?" I asked, tapping gently on the frame to his open office door.

Szanto glanced up from his computer screen, aggrieved by the combination of Tums and Maxwell House sloshing around in his stomach.

"Srrtt," he grunted.

I was uncertain whether he was trying to say "sure" or "sit"—I had left my Szanto-English dictionary behind—but I took it as an invitation to come in.

"Jsss gvvmmm scccdd."

Szanto's attention had turned back to his screen, where he was trying to lay hands on some abysmal piece of copy. We had some very good writers at our paper, people who made words dance on a page. We also had people who wrote as if full sentences hadn't been discovered yet.

"Jzzss Krrsst," Szanto mumbled through a sigh, then coughed, rattling loose the small amphibian that was trying to apply for residence in his throat. "What the hell are they teaching in journalism school these days? You should see this crap."

I waited patiently. Szanto grimaced and grumbled for a few more minutes, then finally sent the story over to the copy desk with an emphatic "Aw, screw it."

"It'll be lining hamster cages by tomorrow afternoon anyway," I said, trying to be helpful. Szanto grunted again.

"Okay," he said, "what can I do for my star investigative reporter? Making good progress with the bar thing?"

In an effort to keep our discourse on a civil tone, I tried to say my next sentence in as small a voice as possible.

"Sal, the bar isn't the story."

My efforts failed. Szanto launched a string of obscenities so long and so loud it was difficult to untangle one from the other. All I know is I heard a thorough exercising of the Seven Words You Can Never Say on Television, including one in particular he used as a noun, verb, adverb, and adjective—all in the same sentence. He drew a breath and was about to relaunch when I put a halt to it with the Four Words Every Editor Loves to Hear:

"Boss, I got something."

He let the air leak out of his lungs, then tilted his head to listen.

"I've got the link between the Ludlow Four," I continued, getting up from my seat and walking over to the map of Newark he had on his side wall.

"It isn't geography," I said, then began pointing to different spots on the map. "Wanda Bass sold out of a go-go bar in Irvington. Tyrone Scott worked in and around a chicken shack on South Orange Avenue. Devin Whitehead was a Clinton Hill kid. And Shareef Thomas lived up off Central Avenue near the cemetery.

"It's not clientele, either," I continued as I returned to my seat. "Wanda sold to a hooker friend's clients and whoever else wandered into her go-go bar. Tyrone sold to junkies and beat-up old homeless people at an abandoned housing project. Devin sold to guys in the neighborhood. Shareef sold to suburban white kids."

Szanto was listening silently.

"The link," I said, drawing it out a little bit, "is the brand of heroin they sold."

I fished into my pocket and brought out my samples of The Stuff. I flipped one of the bags across Szanto's desk.

"I found this in Wanda Bass's apartment," I said. "She had been selling it to clients at the go-go bar where she worked. Notice the stamp on it."

As Szanto grabbed it and began examining the signature eagle-clutching-syringe logo, I held up the torn dime bag.

"I got this from a junkie who said she bought it from Tyrone Scott. It's got the same stamp."

Szanto squinted across his desk and I handed him the torn bag.

"I'll be damned," he said.

"As for the other two, I've got a very good source in Devin Whitehead's neighborhood who talked to some local miscreants for me, and they all said Devin's brand was called 'The Stuff.' Tommy spent a lot of time around Shareef Thomas's haunt and found a kid wandering around looking for a guy named 'Reef' who sold a brand called 'The Stuff.'"

Szanto started nodding. "Not bad," he said.

"Boss," I said. "The Stuff is the story."

Szanto grabbed his industrial-sized jar of antacid tablets, poured out a few, and started munching on them with a far-away look.

"Do the police know this?" he said through a mouthful of chalk.

"I doubt it."

He chewed a bit more, swallowed, picked up his phone and punched four numbers on the keypad.

"Hi, chief," he said. "You got a second?"

Szanto only called one person "chief," and that was our esteemed executive editor, Harold Brodie.

"Come on," Szanto said after he replaced the phone in its cradle. "Let's take a walk."

The corner office of the *Eagle-Examiner* newsroom was a strange and foreign land, one I almost never visited. It's not that Brodie was unfriendly or unapproachable. Quite the contrary. And with his unkempt eyebrows and womanly voice, he looked and sounded like your aging uncle Mortie—the guy who wasn't really your uncle but was such a dear family friend everyone called him "uncle" anyway. Yet for whatever reason he still scared the crap out of me.

I suppose it was a bit of a stormtrooper–Darth Vader thing. Because, in my dealings outside the newsroom, I got to be the badass stormtrooper. I had my body armor, my helmet, my blaster. I could do serious damage—to someone's reputation, anyway—and was treated with corresponding deference. Except when I was around Brodie, I knew all he had to do was wave his hand and I would end up writhing on the floor, gasping for my last breath.

More than anything, I just didn't know the man all that well. In the seven years I had been working for the *Eagle-Examiner*— ever since being hired from a much smaller daily paper in Pennsylvania—I had spoken with him one-on-one perhaps four times. And one of those I was stoned.

In the management structure of our paper, there was never a need for me to speak to him. I talked exclusively to editors who reported to him, or sometimes editors who reported to other editors who reported to him. It's like I had been playing telephone with him my entire career.

Szanto, who obviously had no such issues, walked into Brodie's office without knocking. The old man had been playing classical music on a tiny radio, which he turned down as we entered.

"Hi, chief," Szanto said.

I just smiled. This was my other problem with Brodie. I got so nervous around him I ended up sounding like a moron every time I opened my mouth. So I decided to keep it shut this time. I mean, think about it, do you ever hear a stormtrooper say anything around Darth Vader?

"Carter, my boy, how are you? A little headachy this morning, I guess?"

I kept smiling and nodded. The ganja guy was a man of few words.

"That's a good lad," Brodie said, his Mr. Potato Head eyebrows dancing. "So tell me about this new development."

Szanto did the talking, laying out everything I had just told him in slightly more succinct fashion. Brodie absorbed it, looking more amused than angry that the story his paper had been putting forth the past two days had been flat wrong.

"Sounds like the police were just whistling Dixie with that whole bar angle, eh?" Brodie said when Szanto was done. "I'll have to give the police director a hard time about that the next time I see him at a benefit."

Brodie tented his fingers for a moment, resting his lips on them.

"So, Carter, do you feel like you have a story you can put in the paper?" Brodie asked.

The dreaded direct question. Must speak.

"Well, yes and no, sir," I said.

"Which part is yes, and which part is no?" Brodie asked, managing to sound pleasant despite the rather pointed nature of the question.

"Yes, I feel certain that The Stuff is the connection between the four dead people. Yes, I'm fairly certain they all hooked up with their source in jail. No, I don't know who that source is. No, I haven't the slightest idea why it got them killed."

"Do you have any good leads?"

I gulped.

"Not especially," I admitted.

More tenting of fingers followed as the executive editor settled into what was known around here as the Brodie Think. The old man was legendary for it. Reporters who found themselves in his office more frequently than I did talked about it all the time. He would just sit there. And think. And think. And think. He would do it until an answer came to him, however long that was. Sometimes—as was the case here—he even closed his eyes. It had all the appearance of advanced narcolepsy.

Brodie didn't seem the least bit uncomfortable with the silence. Szanto was accustomed to it, as well. For infrequent visitors such as myself, it was agonizing.

Still, it had its benefits. There was nothing worse to a reporter than a lack of direction from the top. Because more often than not, there were at least three different ways you could go

151

with a story, any of which was at least somewhat defensible. You could reach your own conclusion about which way was best and start traveling that path. But if the executive editor decided differently, it meant you had gone the wrong way. Once the great Brodie Think was over, at least I'd know where to head.

Finally, he opened his eyes.

"Let's take this one step at a time," he proclaimed. "Eventually, we're going to need to figure out where The Stuff is coming from. But I think in the meantime, we should write what we know and see what happens when we put it in the paper."

I nodded.

"Have you heard any footsteps on this story?" he asked.

That was newspaper speak for "are there any other media outlets working on the same angle that might blow our scoop?"

"I don't think anyone is even near this," I said.

"TV has been repackaging sound bites," Szanto added. "The other papers are just going with the usual shock and outrage."

"Good. Then there's no need to rush this into tomorrow's editions. Think you can have it ready for Friday's paper?"

I nodded again.

"Good boy," Brodie said. "Now why don't you go home and get some rest?"

I excused myself from the great man's office, thankful to have escaped without sounding like an imbecile for once. And then I took the great man's advice. I owed myself some sack time.

I aimed my trusty Malibu toward Nutley, suddenly realizing how eager I was to get home. I needed to unwind in my tidy bungalow, away from the world. I know that personality test—the Myers-Whateveritscalled—says we're either extroverts or introverts. I think we're all a little bit of both. The last million years of evolution have turned us into social animals, but somewhere before that in our family tree, there was a branch that just wanted to be left alone. That's what my bungalow is: a place where I can be an introvert.

Deadline did not stir upon my entrance—Deadline could sleep through nuclear testing—and I settled into the couch and pondered Brodie's plan to write what we knew, even though we only had half the story. The more I thought, the more I liked it. There are times when it makes sense to hold back and drop a big bomb on people all at once, when you have the full picture. This didn't feel like one of them.

Truth was, publishing a story is one of the most underappreciated reporting techniques out there. Sometimes it lets the right person know you're on the right track and it makes them want to push you a little further along. You just never know what it flushes out.

After a night of uninterrupted, undrunk slumber, it would stand to reason I would feel unhungover, uncrappy, and in all other ways more human than I had the day before. Yet as the sun crept around the shades of my bungalow's master bedroom, I still felt lousy. Someday, science will have to explain why a bad night's sleep hits you harder the second day.

Deadline had commandeered a disproportionately large part of the middle of the bed, leaving me wedged to one side. He grunted when I stirred, opened his eyes partway to shoot me a dirty look, then yawned dramatically. With his morning exercises thus dispatched, he settled back in for a well-earned nap.

By the time I got out of the shower it was after ten and Deadline was engaged in his other primary activity—pacing in front of his food bowl. So I gave him some breakfast, gave myself some breakfast, then grabbed my laptop and flopped on the couch.

I considered doing a little more reporting, maybe calling up the National Drug Bureau, feeding them what I knew and getting them to repeat it back to me—just to give the story a little more of an official grounding. Then I thought about having to deal with their press agent, L. Peter Sampson, Mr. I'm Not Authorized to Blow My Own Nose. And I decided to spare everyone the hassle.

No, it was time for me to write. People don't always think of newspaper reporters as "writers," inasmuch as our compositions are seldom confused with art. You know the statistical theorem that says a bunch of monkeys sitting at typewriters would eventually reproduce the complete works of Shakespeare—if you gave 'em a couple trillion years to do it? It would take the monkeys about forty-five minutes to come up with some of the slop that passes for raw copy around our shop.

Still, when you take into account that a newspaper reporter's sole creation is the written word, we have to be considered writers. And, as writers go, we're tough, resilient, dependable. We quietly scoff at the softer breeds. I mean, really, some magazine writers consider themselves "on deadline" when they're three weeks away from having to deliver copy. Where I come from, that's not a deadline. That's two weeks off and a few leisurely days at the office.

Then there are those namby-pamby novelists who write what the critics deem to be "literature." They're the bichons frisés of the writing world—they're poofy, pretty, and everyone fawns over them. But the moment things get tough, they're hiding under the kitchen table, making a mess on the floor.

Newspaper reporters? We're the Australian cattle dogs of

the writing world. Maybe we don't look that great. We certainly don't smell that great. But you can kick us in the head, trample us, stick us out in the rain or heat. Whatever. We're still going to get the herd home, no excuses.

And so it was time for me to start herding. Or writing. Or whatever. I decided to start with something snappy. Something quick. Something smart.

"The Stuff wasn't the right stuff for four Newark drug dealers," I wrote, then immediately highlighted and erased it. Not only did it have a glaring cliché, it was about as smart as people who mistakenly drive in the EZ-Pass-only lane and then try to back up.

Okay. Maybe something a little straighter.

"The four people found murdered on Ludlow Street earlier this week sold the same brand of heroin, sources indicate," I wrote, then erased that, too. If it was any straighter, it'd be a candidate for the papacy.

Okay. Let's go back to snappy/quick/smart.

"It's the heroin, stupid," I typed, then immediately regretted the day I entered journalism.

I got up. It had been fifteen minutes, right? I peed, even though I didn't need to. I scratched Deadline's head. I noticed some cobwebs in the upper corner of my living room, grabbed some paper towels and cleaned them out.

Random bits of ideas started forming. Maybe I could start with something about the police being offtrack? No. It was possible they were just trying to throw us off with this bar-holdup angle, all the while knowing about The Stuff.

Perhaps I could start with something about Wanda, the beautiful girl whose dreams of being a dancer were cruelly snuffed out? No. It would take too long to get to the point.

155

The best thing I could do was follow the oldest and greatest newspaper advice ever given: write what you see. What had I really seen in this case?

Of course. Those dime bags. I sat back down and began typing a detailed description of them, and before I knew it, I was on my way. After a couple hours of typing—not to mention four Coke Zeros, two snacks, and thirteen mostly unnecessary trips to the bathroom—I was nearing something resembling a story when my cell phone rang. The caller ID was showing Szanto's number.

"This is Carter Ross," I said. "I'm sorry I can't answer the phone right now—"

"Shhvvttt," Szanto growled. "You got anything I can read yet?"

I glanced at the clock on my computer screen. "I'm close. But it's only two-thirty, what's the hurry?"

"The hurry is Brodie wants this to lead tomorrow's paper and I don't want to walk into the three-o'clock meeting without having seen it. So why don't you just stop pretending like you're the second coming of Bernard Malamud and send it in?"

That was one of Szanto's favorite sayings.

"Okay, I'll e-mail it to you in a second," I said.

"How long is it?"

We measured length of stories in column inches—how long it would be if laid out in standard type and column width.

"About thirty-five," I said, which is about twice the normal length.

"Maybe you haven't heard this yet," Szanto said. "But times are a wee bit tight in the newspaper industry. We've had a few little cutbacks in space that makes it difficult to run longer stories. Any of this ring a bell?"

"I know, Sal, I know," I said. And I did. On some days, the

number of column inches we devoted to news coverage was half what it used to be. I added: "Don't worry, it's worth it."

"Jzzss Krrsst," he grumbled, then hung up.

I gave the story one more quick read—it was decent, though Bernard Malamud had nothing to worry about—then sent it in.

"Well, Deadline," I said to my cat. "What now?"

Deadline, who had slipped into one of his twenty-eight daily comas, had no answer.

Against my better judgment, I decided to go into the office. It was time to see if I could find someone who might tell me a little more about my heroin samples, preferably someone with a white lab coat. I knew that with the right assortment of gadgets, the right chemist could tell me how pure my heroin was and where in the world it originated.

Sadly, such people do not advertise their services. My knowledgeable-though-often-misguided research assistant, Mr. Google, pointed me toward friendly people who wanted to help me beat my company's drug-testing program. I found one laboratory that claimed it specialized in identifying unknown substances and testing the composition of known ones. But when I called them and told a nice scientist the substance she'd be testing was heroin, she suddenly was in a hurry to get off the phone.

I called another lab where a chemist suggested I *not* tell him it was heroin, that way he could accept it without knowingly breaking any laws. He also said I could expect a three-to-six-week turnaround. For an additional fee, he told me they'd "put a rush on it" and get it to me in two weeks. I must not have mentioned I worked for a daily newspaper.

After a few more unsuccessful phone calls, I resigned myself to asking for help. Worse, I realized where that help was going to have to come from: Buster Hays.

157

Hays is a cantankerous son of a bitch, but he's also a cantankerous son of a bitch who has sources and connections all over law enforcement. Somehow, don't ask me how, he had managed to build up enough goodwill that everyone seemed to owe him favors. And ultimately he was enough of a team player—in his own grouchy, condescending way—that he'd didn't mind cashing in a favor to help you.

But only after you groveled for a bit. And from the self-satisfied grin on his face as I approached his desk, I think he knew he was about to be the recipient of some concentrated groveling.

"Hi, Buster, got a sec?"

"What's up, Ivy?" he said, practically taunting me.

I told him about The Stuff, about the story that was going in the next day's paper, and about what I needed done to the heroin samples I had found. As I talked, a change came over Hays's face. He didn't belittle me, nor did he try to stick up for his story. He seemed genuinely miffed he had gotten it wrong.

"So the thing about the bar robbery, you think the cops are just making it up?" he asked.

"I bet your cop source probably believes he's right. I mean, who knows? Maybe Shareef Thomas really did rob that bar at some point? Or maybe he just happened to look like the guy who did? In the absence of any other information, it's probably the best theory they had to go on. And once they committed themselves to that premise, maybe they overlooked evidence that pointed in another direction. You know how it goes."

Hays nodded. "I feel like printing a retraction," he said ruefully.

If I'd wanted to bust Hays's balls a little bit, I would have said something like, "Oh, we'll be printing one. It's thirty-five inches, it's leading tomorrow's paper, and it's got my name on it."

But I didn't need to be scoring rhetorical points at the moment. I needed his help.

"So I'm trying to find someone who can run some tests on those heroin samples I got," I said. "You know anyone like that?"

"You know, it's funny, but yesterday I got a call from a guy who does that sort of thing," Hays said.

I looked at him for a long second to see if he was busting *my* balls, but he appeared quite earnest. "You did?" I asked.

"Yeah, a guy named Irving Wallace. I hadn't heard from him in a month of Sundays, but he saw my byline on the Ludlow Street story and gave me a holler. He was all interested in it for some reason."

"You think he'd help me?"

"Maybe. He sure seemed curious about the story," Hays said. "You're not going to have to quote him, are you?"

"I guess not. He's just doing a test for us."

"Good, because he works for a part of the federal government where they don't like to see their names in the paper."

Hays started flipping through one of his Rolodexes. He had four of them—one from each century he had been working here. Naturally, he was one of the holdouts who refused to modernize and put his sources in a computer. He was into Rolodex number three by the time he found what he was looking for.

"Here he is. Irving Wallace," Hays said as he copied the number onto a piece of paper. "This guy is the best forensic chemist on the East Coast. Drop my name and promise you won't quote him. He'll have that test done for you by suppertime."

On my way back from Hays's desk, I saw Szanto, who was returning from the three o'clock meeting along with a pack of other editors.

"Everything okay with the story?" I asked.

"It's fine," he said.

In Szanto talk, "fine" was a high compliment. If you were waiting for something that actually sounded like praise, chances are you would be waiting a while. He handed out a "good" about three times a year. "Very good" was a biennial event. I'm not sure anything beyond that—great, spectacular, superior— was even in his vocabulary. I was pleased with my "fine."

Tina Thompson trailed Szanto out of the meeting. She gave me a thumbs-up. "Great work," she said.

"Yeah, you like it?"

"Well, it's a bit overwritten, but I would expect nothing less from you," she teased. "On the whole, it's a great piece of re-porting."

"How'd it go over in the meeting?"

"Well, Brodie made it clear he liked it, so . . ."

So I knew how that went. When Brodie hadn't made up his mind about a story, he'd be real quiet, which inevitably gave rise to spirited debate. But when he indicated he liked it, all the other editors would pile on to insist they also liked it—with the possible exception of Szanto, who was a notorious contrarian.

"Great," I said. "Thanks."

Tina was turning to walk away when something—the way her curls framed her face? the way her sweater hugged her body?—caused me to blurt out, "We should grab a drink tonight to celebrate."

"Okay," she said, like it was nothing.

"I'll check in with you later," I said.

"Okay," she said, and gave me a little wave.

It happened so quickly, almost like my subconscious had been doing the talking for me. What the hell was my problem? The woman was less than twenty-four hours from ovulation. Hell, for all I knew that little watch of hers was off and she was ovulating *right now*. Once we got to the bar and had a drink or two, nature would take over. I might as well have volunteered to be her sperm donor.

Deep down, did I want to get Tina pregnant? Or was I just an incurably horny male who—because of hormones or pheromones or whatever—recognized Tina as an easy mark?

Then again, maybe it could just stay innocent. A drink or two between colleagues. A hearty farewell handshake. A return to the peace and solitude of my Nutley bungalow.

Uh-huh.

I did my best to shelve all those thoughts as I sat back down and punched in the phone number Hays had given me.

"Yes," a terse voice said on the other end.

"Irving Wallace, please."

"Yes."

"Oh, this is Irving Wallace?"

"Yes."

"Hi, I'm Carter Ross with the *Eagle-Examiner*—"

"No comment."

He wasn't trying to be funny, but I laughed despite myself.

"I didn't even ask you a question yet," I said.

"No comment."

"Look, sir, I'm sorry to trouble you. But I'm working on a story about this quadruple homicide in Newark and I've got some heroin samples I need tested. Buster Hays tells me you can help."

A pause.

"Heroin samples, huh?" he said, sounding intrigued.

"Yes."

"And it relates to the Newark murders?"

"Yes."

"And you know Buster Hays?"

"Yeah, I work with him."

Another pause.

"I'll call you back," he said, and abruptly hung up.

"Sounds great," I said to the empty phone line.

Feds. They were always so paranoid. I placed the phone back in its cradle and checked my e-mail, where there was more of the usual spam from Human Resources. I was just beginning to learn about an important discussion group on peanut allergies when my phone rang.

"Carter Ross."

"Hi, Carter. Irving Wallace," he said, sounding like he had undergone a robotectomy and was now human. "Sorry for the runaround. I just wanted to check you out."

"Do people often call you up and impersonate newspaper reporters?"

"Can't be too careful these days," he said. "Buster says you're okay. Actually, Buster says you're a smart-ass Ivy League type. But he also said you're a fine young reporter and I should help you. So what can I do for you?"

"I'm hoping you can tell me the purity and origin of some heroin samples I got off the street."

"You want just standard GC/MS?"

"Uh . . ."

"Because I can do that, LC, FTIR/ATR, IRMS, ICP/MS, Raman, whatever you need. We're a full-service shop."

"You're talking to a newspaper reporter, remember?"

"Oh, right, sorry. GC/MS stands for gas chromatography/mass spectrometry. LC is liquid chromatography. FTIR/ATR is Fourier transform infrared . . . I've lost you, haven't I?"

"Thoroughly."

"Okay, let's start with remedial instruction," Wallace said

patiently. "Heroin is derived from poppy seeds. Poppy seeds come from poppy plants. Poppy plants grown in different parts of the world have unique chemical signatures. My equipment reads the signature."

"Gotcha. How soon you can turn it around?"

"You're in luck. My gear is calibrated for heroin right now. I can have it in a few hours."

"Terrific," I said. "I'll drop off the samples right now. Where can I find you?"

"It's better I have someone find you. Be outside your building in fifteen minutes."

"Great," I said. "What part of the government do you work for, anyway?"

"What, didn't Buster tell you?"

"No."

"That's because he doesn't know."

The next sound I heard was the line clicking dead.

Fifteen minutes later—possibly to the second—a young man with close-cropped blond hair and an inexpensive suit hopped out of a late model Crown Victoria in front of the *Eagle-Examiner* offices.

Obviously, my fed had arrived.

I had taken my two heroin samples—The Stuff and the blank one, both from Wanda's bedroom—and tucked them in an envelope, which I handed to the man.

"How did you know I'm the guy Irving Wallace sent?" he asked.

"As a newspaper reporter, I'm a trained observer of the human condition," I said with a grin, although he seemed to come from The Land Sarcasm Forgot. Probably Iowa.

"Yes, sir," he replied, got back into his car, and drove off.

It left me, for the moment, with nothing to do. I had figured I would need to spend the afternoon protecting my story from the ravages of editing. But it had apparently garnered enough fans so that wouldn't be necessary. So I drove back down to Ludlow Street, just to poke around. The shrine was more or less the same size as it had been two days earlier, although it was starting to look a little the worse for wear. Some of the candles had been knocked over and all of them had burned out. The cold nights had done a number on the flowers, which now looked like limp spinach.

I pulled on the door to the church, but it was locked. So I wandered around the neighborhood for an hour or two, half-heartedly interviewing a few more people to see if there was any interesting talk on the street. There wasn't. And with the sun disappearing and the wind picking up, I was losing my will to canvass any further.

I had just turned over the Malibu's engine when my cell phone rang. The number came up as "unavailable."

"Carter Ross."

"You're not recording this, are you?"

It was, naturally, Irving Wallace.

"Do they teach you to be this paranoid or does it come naturally?"

"Hey, I got to ask," he said.

"Fair enough. No, I'm not recording this."

"Good," he said. "And my name doesn't go in your story, right?"

"Right."

"Good. Question for you. Where did you get the sample that was labeled 'The Stuff'?"

"From a dealer's stash box," I said.

"From an active dealer? Or from one of the victims in the Newark murders?"

"One of the victims—a woman who had been dealing out of a go-go bar in Irvington. The box was hidden in a closet in her apartment."

"I see," he said, like he was trying to make sense of something. "So you're sure this is what she was selling on the street?"

"Yeah. Why do you sound so surprised?"

"Because it's more than ninety-nine percent pure."

"I take it that's a lot?"

"The only time I've seen it that pure is when it's been seized at the airport," he said. "Once it gets to the street, it's always cut at least a little bit. Now and then you get low nineties, but even the best heroin is usually seventy or eighty. I tested this one three times and each time it came back above ninety-nine percent. You can safely call it the purest heroin ever sold on the streets in America in your article and no one would call the paper to correct you."

"What about the other sample?"

"The blank one? That was more like fifty. Run-of-the-mill."

"Anything else you can tell me?" I asked.

"Without making your eyes glaze over with the details, I can tell you the chemical signature is consistent with South American heroin. I didn't run the full workup, but I'd be willing to bet this came from the central highlands of Colombia, not far from Bogotá."

"Both of them came from the same place?"

"Yes."

"And the purity is that extraordinary, huh?"

"Put it this way," Wallace said. "The government takes thousands of kilos of heroin off the street every year, and most of it comes through my lab in one way or another. Yet in ten years of testing those thousands of kilos, I've never seen anything this pure. Junkies must have gone nuts for this stuff."

Maybe a little too nuts, I thought.

"Well, I really appreciate the help with this," I said, revving my engine a few times just to get the heater going a little more.

"Not at all. Those Newark killings are a heck of a thing, huh?"

"Everyone seems pretty rattled by them," I confirmed.

"Yeah. Well, they should be. That's a terrible thing, four people killed like that," he said. "Is what you gave me the only samples you have?"

"I have one more of each—The Stuff and the generic."

"And you're keeping them in a safe place?"

"I'm going to tuck them away in my piggy bank at home."

"Good," he said. "Wouldn't want them getting out."

I assured him I didn't, either, and with one more reminder to leave his name out of the story, he hung up.

It was nearing six o'clock—time for him to get home and for me to return to the office and make sure no one had spent the afternoon rearranging letters in my story. The editing process often reminds me of my favorite joke: a writer and an editor are stranded together in the desert. They've been slogging over the dunes for days and are about to die of thirst when, miraculously, they come across an oasis. The writer dives in and begins happily drinking the water. Yet when he looks up, he finds the editor pissing in the oasis.

Aghast, the writer screams, "What the hell are you doing?"

The editor replies, "I'm making it better."

Still, once I returned to the office, I was relieved to find no one with a spastic bladder had been near my story. Szanto had made a few judicious nips and tucks, put a few train-wreck sen-

166

tences back on track. I added one paragraph about the lab test results and shipped it over to the copy editors, thankful no one had made it "better."

With my day's toil complete, I went to round up Tina, only to discover her still chained to her desk, editing copy. She glanced up when she saw me approach, stuck five fingers in the air and mouthed "five minutes." Then she winked.

I nodded and looked around to make sure no one had caught the wink. Like it mattered. Tina's love life was an open book, one without the word "discretion" in it. The trade-off for getting to enjoy that slender body of hers would be that everyone was going to know about it.

I returned to my desk, prepared to unclutter my e-mail inbox for at least the next half hour. No journalist's "five minutes" is ever really "five minutes."

Except Tina's was pretty close. After maybe ten she appeared, purse in hand, ready to depart.

"There's this new wine bar that's just opened up down the street from my building," she said. "I've been dying to try it."

"Great. Do they serve beer there?"

"I'm sure they keep something on tap for you and the other Neanderthals," she said.

"It gives me strength for when I pull you out of the place by your hair."

"Charming. I need to run home first real quick," she said. "Why don't you go and get us a table, order me a nice pinot, and I'll meet you there?"

"Look for me in the knuckle-dragger section," I said.

I made my way to Hoboken and easily found parking—a minor miracle—then proceeded to the bar, a cozy little yuppie breeding ground about a half block from Tina's place. It being a

Thursday night, the place wasn't too full. I selected a booth with a semicircular table along the far wall. It was designed for a couple, and the lighting was just right, the kind of setup that announced to the entire establishment you intended to bonk like bonobos later in the evening.

I picked up the wine menu, but it was mostly just to kill time. I'm a total wine ignoramus. Making sense of the Torah in the original Hebrew would be easier for me. Eventually, I ordered Tina her pinot noir, selecting the name Fetzer because it amused me. Then I ordered myself a beer, earning a witheringly snooty look from the waitress.

When Tina arrived, she had ditched her work clothes in favor of a knee-length black cocktail dress with bare shoulders and a keyhole neckline. She looked stunning. It was all I could do to keep my jaw on its hinge.

"I just couldn't stay in pants for another five minutes," she explained.

I went to make a lame joke about how I wished all my dates felt that way, but my mouth was dry. It didn't take much imagination to know that dress would go from body to floor in 2.1 seconds. As she sat down, the dress shimmied halfway up her thigh, making it impossible to decide which part of her to ogle first.

"You look great," I managed to say.

She gave me an "oh, what, this old thing?" shrug. I couldn't help but be impressed—not just at how stunning she looked, but at how effortlessly she was working me.

Most guys cling to this archaic notion we are the seducers and women are the seduced. And perhaps, where the less clever of the gender is concerned, that's true. But in the presence of the truly skilled female, such as Tina, the myth of male domination is just another one of those wrongheaded ideas women allow to be perpetuated so guys never turn around to see the marionette strings coming out our backs.

It's like lion prides. For years, researchers—sorry, *male* researchers—believed the boy lions duked it out for the right to breed with the girl lions, who were passive spectators in the whole thing. The record only got set straight when some female researchers came along and took a more careful look at the social dynamics in the pride that preceded the fight. It turns out much of the time the lionesses are really calling the shots, selecting the most fit breeding partner. The fights the boy lions have are merely a noisy confirmation of what the girl lions have already decided among themselves.

So there I was, as our drinks arrived, wondering if I had been selected to beat the other lions to the prize. I wanted to skip the flirting and head straight to the making out, because nothing is more fun than engaging in truly obnoxious displays of public affection—if only because it makes the loveless married couples so damn uncomfortable.

But Tina had subtly shifted her weight, crossing her legs in a way that made it impossible for me to move in without getting a knee in the thigh. Obviously, she wanted her puppet to talk for a while first. So she asked me about my story, and I answered.

Another round of drinks arrived, and I was still talking—but without her having to ask questions. By the third round, it really started pouring out of me, all the emotion of the previous few days that I had been suppressing for one reason or another.

I would say I was rambling, but it was worse than that. I was blubbering.

Somewhere along the line, a transformation occurred in Tina. She was no longer wooing me with her black dress and knockout legs. She was reassuring me with this look of tender concern. She had pulled a cardigan over her shoulders—where the hell had *that* come from?—and I could tell she was keeping a tissue at the ready, in case I started bawling.

What a nightmare. I had managed to wreck the surest thing this side of sunrise because I needed to share my *feelings*? What the hell was my problem?

By the time Tina had comforted me and I paid the bill—my one manly act of the evening—I was just sober enough to realize an eighty-dollar bar tab meant I wasn't going to be driving anywhere. As we departed, there was intimacy between us in that we had just shared an emotional experience. But there was no romance and certainly no lust. Nor should there have been. Don Juan never blubbered on his lover's shoulder.

Before long I was back in a familiar place: on Tina's couch, covered in a blanket, very much alone.

The Director awoke early, a habit he picked up in the military and had been unable to shake, even fifteen years after his last salute. It pleased him to know he started his day while most of the world slept. He noticed it was a trait common among the high-powered CEOs profiled on the cover of those business magazines. They were all early risers.

The Director considered himself their peer, even if he never got his due for it. So he set his alarm clock for 4 A.M.

He tiptoed down to the gym he had built in the basement of his suburban New Jersey home. His wife and three children complained about the noise of iron slapping iron interrupting their sleep, so he had soundproofed it like a recording studio. Only the softest ping escaped, not nearly enough noise to wake them.

The Director had been working out six days a week since he left the military. He once swore he would never allow himself to get soft—he would keep the same iron-hard stomach as when he had been the fittest colonel in the army.

Alas, civilian food agreed with him too much. And as his metabolism slowed with age, he made a new vow: he would never allow himself to get weak. He took pride in still being able to bench-press over three hundred pounds. At an age, fifty-five, when some men were thinking about whether or not they would be able to pick up their grandchildren, the Director was still putting up personal bests in his basement weight room.

He completed his workout and shower and was midway through a breakfast of bran cereal and yogurt when he heard the thudding of the newspaper against the door. The Director glanced at his watch, annoyed. It was 5:33. He liked to have his paper earlier.

All those high-powered executives the Director read about started their days by reading two or three newspapers. The Director felt one was sufficient, and his paper of choice was the Eagle-Examiner. He retrieved it from the front porch and took it to the breakfast table, but lost his appetite when he read the first headline: "Heroin links victims in quadruple murder."

The Director felt sweat pop on his brow. He wanted to break something. But no. His wife would ask what had him so upset. He had to control his rage.

How was this even possible? Had the police figured it out? It couldn't be. He had informants inside police headquarters. They'd mentioned nothing about this.

The Director started reading and realized this was just some reporter who had stumbled across some things and had managed to make a few lucky guesses. The Director relaxed. The situation could still be controlled *if he acted quickly. He picked up the phone and called Monty, waking him from a sound sleep.*

"What is it, Director?" Monty said groggily.

"Wake up, Monty," the Director told him. "We have some damage control to do."

CHAPTER 6

The next morning, I at least had one small consolation prize. The paper Tina thoughtfully left on the coffee table for me had my story stripped across the top of A1 with the headline "Heroin links victims in quadruple murder."

I don't mind admitting that, even after a couple thousand bylines, I still enjoyed seeing my name in the newspaper. I was just settling in to read the latest one when my phone rang. It was from the 973 area code, but it was a number I hadn't seen before.

"Carter Ross."

"Sir, this is the Nutley Police Department calling."

"Hi," I said, bewildered.

"Sir, I have some bad news about your house," he said. "There's been an explosion."

Before hanging up the phone, the cop told me "the incident" occurred at 7:29 A.M., when several 911 calls were received. The Nutley Fire Department arrived at "the residence" by 7:34. EMS arrived at 7:35 but there were no known injuries. I tried to stick the details in my mostly numb brain and agreed to meet the police at my house. I hung up before I had the presence of mind to ask any meaningful questions, such as, "Explosion? What the hell do you mean by explosion?"

I staggered into Tina's kitchen, where I found a sticky note: "7:45. Went jogging. Bagels in the cabinet next to the fridge. Back by 8:30. Tina."

I considered waiting for her to return, because it might be nice to have some company, then decided against it. She had already seen enough of me blubbering for one lifetime.

Grabbing a pen, I scribbled, "8:10. Had to leave in a hurry. Call you later. Carter."

I swiped a bagel then went down to my Malibu, wondering if it was now the only thing I owned besides the wrinkled clothes on my back. This thought alone should have freaked me out, but I still felt detached, like this wasn't really happening. House fires were something I wrote about, not something I experienced firsthand.

As I drove toward Nutley, I forced myself to think rationally. Had I left the stove on? Couldn't be. My last meal at home was cold cereal. Lightning? No. It was December. Faulty wiring? Gas leak? Had to be something like that. The house is old. Was old.

I tried to become aware of my breathing and remind myself there were worse things. Sure, all my belongings were probably destroyed. But most of it could be replaced. And, sure, there was

175

some irreplaceable stuff—the pictures, the keepsakes, the school yearbooks, every newspaper article I had ever written . . .

But, hell, it could have been *me* in there. Most any other morning, it *would* have been me in there. This was clearly a rare triumph for the power of thinking with the little brain: if I hadn't been trying to get into Tina's pants, the Nutley fire chief would be explaining to my parents that his crew was busy picking up my remains with tweezers.

Really, as long as Deadline had managed to find a way out, the insurance would cover everything else, right? I would get a new house, a whole bunch of new stuff. I'd probably even get new golf clubs out of the deal. And how bad would that be?

As I approached my street, I began hearing this awful chorus of car alarms—there had to be fifty of them going off at once. I made the turn on my street but could only get partway down, what with the logjam of emergency vehicles.

Then I saw it, amid the usual neat row of houses along my street: this big, gaping hole, like someone had punched out a tooth. As I got closer, I saw a scrap heap where my bungalow once stood. There were pieces of siding and other various splinters on the lawn and street—even a few pieces stuck in my neighbors' trees—but nothing that resembled a house remained.

A small clump of my neighbors, most of whom only knew me as the childless bachelor who wasn't home very much, had formed at a safe distance on the sidewalk. As I got out of my car, my next-door neighbor, Mrs. Scalabrine, rushed up to me. Mrs. Scalabrine was a youngish widow, maybe sixty-five, and I don't think we had talked about anything more than the weather the entire time I lived there.

But she was suddenly my best friend.

"Oh, Carter, thank goodness," she said, giving me an awkwardly intense hug. "We thought you were inside."

176

I hugged her back, even though I didn't want to. The rest of my neighbors were just staring at me, ashen-faced, as though they were expecting something dramatic: ranting, raving, collapsing on the sidewalk, flipping out. I got the feeling they were mostly there for the theater of it and now they were expecting a show.

Speaking of which, where were the TV trucks? It was odd they weren't here. Generally those guys religiously monitored the incident pager, a network of nuts who listen in on fire and police frequency and send out real-time messages about what's going on. My house blowing up certainly would have been mentioned. A good house explosion usually got the TV trucks swarming from all angles.

Instead, it was just me, the broken remains of my home, a variety of people in uniforms, and my gawking neighbors.

"So what happened?" I said. They all looked at me like, *What do you think happened, you halfwit? Your house blew up.* Then they all started looking at Mrs. Scalabrine, who clearly had something to say.

"I saw a man in a white van," she said nervously. "I mean, I saw him getting out of a white van. I didn't see his face—the police asked me if I did, but I really didn't. All I saw is he was white and he was big, like six five, and real husky, like three hundred pounds at least."

The other neighbors, who had heard this story already, were nodding in corroboration. I thought about what Rosa Bricker had said about the size of the shooter, and how it was probably someone between six three and six five.

"I saw him run up on your lawn, right over there," she said, gesturing in the direction of the pile of lumber where my house once stood. "And it looked like he threw something inside. And then he ran back to the van and was gone."

Another neighbor, whose name was probably Cavanaugh—he was an actuary, I think—took the story from there.

"I heard the wheels squealing as I got out of the shower," he said. "It was like the guy wanted to get away fast. And all of a sudden there was this huge *BaaBOOOM*. It was just like that: first it went *baa* and then it went *boom*."

The other neighbors nodded, confirming that the "baa" and the "boom" had been recorded as separate incidents.

"It was like a bomb went off," said one of my neighbors, who was either Nancy, Pat, or Angela—I could never quite remember.

"All of my windows on this side of the house blew out," Mrs. Scalabrine said, pointing toward her place.

"Some of my unicorn figurines fell off my mantel," Nancy-PatAngela said.

I nodded, as if I shared concern for NancyPatAngela's unicorns, unable to quite grasp the absurdity that they were talking about their windows and knickknacks when I had lost my entire house and everything inside it.

"Anyone seen my cat?" I asked.

No one answered.

The neighbors eventually filtered out, wandering off to work or the gym or whatever it was they had planned for their mornings. I had a brief conversation with the Nutley police, who said they were starting an investigation based on Mrs. Scalabrine's eyewitness account—though, as I already knew, she wasn't giving them much to go on.

Before long, I was left alone with the realization that someone in this world wanted me dead. It was a surprisingly difficult concept to grasp, especially for a typically healthy thirty-something guy who lumped in dying with hearing aids, estate planning, and regularity in the category of Things I'll Worry About in Forty Years.

People at cocktail parties who find out what I do for a living somehow think I must receive death threats all the time, because I so frequently find myself writing bad things about scary people. But I had only gotten one death threat in my career—and even that was from a guy who was just blowing off steam. He was a local slumlord I had exposed for keeping his tenants without heat. The day the story ran, he yelled into my cell phone that I had ruined his life and he was going to kill me. He called back later in the day to apologize. I told him he could make it up to me by filling his building's oil tank.

Fact is, even the scary people recognize the newspaper reporter is merely the messenger. They might not like me writing about them very much. They might hope I stop doing it. They might wish I fall through an empty manhole cover and be devoured by a sewer-dwelling alligator. But ultimately the scary people are smart enough to know killing a newspaper reporter will only add to their problems. It's an extension of the old Mark Twain saw about not picking a fight with people who buy ink by the barrel.

Think about it: how often do you hear about a newspaper reporter in this country being killed for something they wrote? It just doesn't happen.

Except it came close to happening to me. And when I thought about how close, I started to shake. I've heard it said—mostly by blowhard World War II veterans—that a man doesn't really know what he's made of until he faces death head-on. Based on this experience, I think I was made of something resembling lime Jell-O.

I was scared out of my quivering, gelatinous mind. Whoever I was dealing with had killed four people already—perhaps more—and obviously didn't mind adding to the body count. In this case, he had read one article, decided his world would be better off without me in it, and clearly had the means to make that happen.

And he did it in frighteningly short order. I tried to do the math: our distributors were guaranteed to get their daily supply of papers by 4 A.M. From the distributor it went to the carriers around five. So the story was pretty much everywhere in New Jersey by six, at the latest. That meant it had taken this guy a mere hour and a half to make it look like the Big Bad Wolf had visited my little straw house, huffed, puffed, and blown it down.

He knew where I lived—or used to live, anyway. He knew where I worked. It was possible he knew what I looked like, too: my head shot had been in the paper on occasion. Did he also know what car I drove? Did he have people watching me? Should I worry about rounding some corner and having a gun pointing in my face?

I didn't know. I guess that was the most terrifying thing of all; someone was trying to kill me and I didn't know who, what, when, or how.

All I really knew was why. That damn article. The more I thought about it, the more I realized how much different it was than so many of the others I had written. This *wasn't* just a case of shooting the messenger. It's not like I was merely quoting some prosecutor or digging through documents. This was news I'd uncovered myself. And whoever was trying to kill me wanted to make damn sure I didn't find anything else.

Having nowhere else to go, I started driving toward Newark. I was midway through my journey when my cell phone rang. It was Tina.

"Hi," I said.

"Well, someone disappeared pretty quickly this morning,"

she said, her voice full of flirtatious energy. "Were you afraid I was going to make you eat eggs or something?"

"No," I said.

There was a pause on the end.

"Don't play that game with me," she said.

"Huh?" I mustered.

"The 'I'm embarrassed I got emotional and now I'm going to shut you out' game," she said. "Look, I know last night took a different turn from where we thought it was going and you ended up crying on my shoulder a little bit. It doesn't make you less of a man. I thought you were more evolved than that. It's no big—"

"Tina, *shut up*," I said. "My house blew up, okay?"

Her response was confusion, then alarm, then concern. Over the next several minutes, I took her through what I had seen and heard. "So, basically," I concluded, "someone doesn't like me very much."

"Do you think it's the same someone who killed those people on Ludlow Street?"

"I can't think of anyone else who'd want me dead that badly."

"Wait a second," Tina said. "Oh, Jesus. Oh, no."

"What?"

"The incident pager has been going nuts all morning and I didn't figure it out until just now. Oh, my God."

"Figure what out?"

She started reading like she was ticking off a list: "House explosion in Nutley. Fire on Eighteenth Street in Newark. Fire at Go-Go Bar in Irvington. Carter, those are all places you wrote about in your story!"

I was speechless. The man in the white van wasn't merely going after me. He was covering his tracks. He was destroying the places where I had found evidence or might have kept evidence, making sure no one else—like, say, the police—could retrace my steps.

"Tina, I gotta go," I said.

"Wait, why?"

"I'm heading to that fire on Eighteenth Street."

"Carter, you're in no shape to be chasing fire trucks. You're out of your mind."

"Probably, but I'm hanging up now."

"Please don't," she said. "Come into the newsroom. I don't want you out there. You'll be safer here."

"No," I said. "Until I figure out who's doing this, I won't be safe anywhere."

I shut off my cell phone so Tina couldn't bug me and turned in the direction of Miss B's apartment on 18th Street. I was still two blocks away when I came to a police barricade, but I could already see her building. It was mostly untouched, except for the upper right quarter of it, where Miss B lived. That part was streaked by black scorch marks and still steaming slightly. It looked soggy. The street outside was filled with puddles and fire trucks.

I left the safety of the Malibu, and as I got closer, I had this sense that whatever had been used on Miss B's apartment was different from what razed my bungalow. First off, the building was structurally sound. There were no pieces of it scattered hither and yon, as there had been with my place. For that matter, none of the surrounding buildings appeared to have been touched— there were no blown-out windows. I also didn't hear any car alarms.

It looked more like any of the number of slum-building fires I had written about: the cause of the fire always turned out to be a shorted-out space heater, an oven someone had left open for warmth, a cigarette igniting a couch, or something similarly banal.

I was now directly across the street from the building. Two TV stations were already there, which may have explained why my house blowing up hadn't attracted any coverage. The TV guys had decided an apartment fire in Newark was more interesting.

One of the cameras was busy filming a man-on-the-street reporter who was pretending to be compassionate as he interviewed the shocked and bewildered neighbors. The other camera was shooting B-roll of the smoldering building while a pissy-looking blond reporter bitched into her cell phone about how she should be somewhere else.

Still, I was a little surprised more camera crews weren't there. Fires combined the three elements necessary for local TV news: human tragedy, an easy-to-tell story, and great visuals. Where was the rest of the horde?

Not that I was complaining. And since neither crew seemed to be concerned with what had actually happened, I was able to sidle up to the Newark Fire Department captain who was overseeing the operation. He was a former high school basketball star—good enough to get himself a D1 scholarship, not good enough to take it any further—and still thought of himself as a local hero. I did nothing to disavow him of that and put his name in the newspaper whenever I got the chance. We were pals.

"Hey, Captain," I said.

"This can't possibly be the most interesting thing going on in Newark today," he said. "Shouldn't you be off trying to figure out who the city council is stealing from?"

"I was just driving into the office, saw the smoke, and wanted to see Newark's bravest in action," I said, trying to keep my tone nonchalant. "So what's this one? Crack addicts get sloppy with their lighters again?"

"Nope, someone wanted themselves a bonfire," he said. "You'll have to get it officially from the chief's office, but off the record, this sucker was set intentionally."

"Oh?" I said.

"Whoever did it was quick and sloppy about it. You could still smell the gasoline when we arrived."

"No kidding. When did you guys get here?"

"Call came in at seven thirty-six, I think. Chief will have that, too. We were here in four minutes—I don't want to hear any more of that crap about slow response times. We were able to contain it pretty quickly. Only the upper two floors on that one end got it. But they got it good. There was definitely an accelerant involved."

I looked down at my feet, sorting things out. The call in Nutley had come in at 7:29, right after the man in the white van tossed his little present through my living room window. At that time of the morning, it was at least fifteen minutes from my place in Nutley to 18th Street, even if you drove like it was Indy qualifying. There was just no way Van Man could have gotten here, doused the place with gasoline, and gotten a good fire roaring so quickly. Obviously, Van Man had friends. This was a coordinated attack.

"Everyone get out okay?" I asked.

"Yeah, looks that way. Except for this one woman on the fourth floor. She wasn't breathing too well when she got carted out of here."

"Her name Brenda Bass, by any chance?"

"You know her?"

"I interviewed her once," I said, skipping the details.

"Yeah, that's her," the captain said. "Brave lady. We're pretty sure the fire got started in the apartment below hers—the super said it was empty. She must have smelled it pretty quickly,

184

because she threw her four kids in the bathroom, stuffed some wet towels under the door, and got the shower going. Then she started looking for the fire to put it out. We found her in the living room with an empty fire extinguisher. The smoke got her."

"Why didn't she just take her kids and run out of the building like all the others?"

The captain looked over his shoulder at the TV crews then back at the building, then at me.

"I shouldn't be telling you this," he said. "And you didn't get it from me. But someone barricaded her in that apartment."

"Barricaded?"

"You didn't get this from me, right?" he said.

"Right. Of course. We didn't talk."

"Good," he said, speaking quickly in a low voice. "Some of my guys told me there was a board over her door."

"Oh, dear God."

"Yeah. You know how a landlord who is kicking out tenants will put plywood over the doors of the empty apartments to stop vagrants from breaking in?"

"Uh-huh."

"That's what someone did to this place, except the apartment wasn't empty. That lady and her kids were trapped in there. Someone wanted to burn them alive."

The captain's radio squawked something unintelligible, but it was enough to get him moving.

"Interview over," he said, as he walked away. "Call the chief's office."

A s I watched water drip down from Miss B's building, I wondered if this was how bugs who lived near the highway felt. They knew there was danger all around but they told

185

themselves if they just kept flying, everything would be fine. And then all of a sudden, splat, there comes the one fast-moving windshield they couldn't avoid.

I was nearly lost in that thought when I suddenly became aware of someone approaching behind me. With a surge of adrenaline, I whirled around in a crouched position, ready to be staring at a six-foot-five, white-van-driving brute.

Instead, it was just Tommy.

"Relax, I come in peace," he said, holding his hands up.

"You scared the crap out of me," I said, putting my hand over my fast-beating heart.

"Tina told me what happened to your place. She's right. You *are* a mess."

"I'm just a little edgy is all."

"A little? I've never seen a white man jump so high."

I could still feel the pounding in my chest.

"You shouldn't have turned off your cell phone," he said. "Tina is really freaked out."

"Excuse me if I'm not awash in pity for her."

"Well, she sent me out here to fetch you. She wants you to come into the office immediately. She said to tell you Szanto and Brodie said the same thing."

"Then I'm going to ask you to pretend you didn't see me."

"Carter, I don't know. This is pretty serious. I mean, this guy is a wacko. And Szanto and Brodie . . ." Tommy said, looking stricken. He was a twenty-two-year-old kid. He had yet to learn the finer art of ignoring the higher-ups.

"There is no way I can figure out who is doing this while cowering in the office," I said. "At least if I'm cowering out here, I can keep my mind off it a little."

Tommy said nothing, turning his attention toward the sodden, blackened building.

"What a mess," he said. "Everyone get out okay?"

I related what my fire captain had told me about the plywood on Brenda Bass's door.

"Oh, my God, that's terrible," Tommy said. "This is real, isn't it? This guy is really going after you, her, everyone."

"Yeah, and don't forget your name was at the bottom of that story as a contributor," I said. "You better watch yourself, too."

He nodded silently, looking down at a broken spot in the sidewalk, nervously shifting his weight from side to side.

"I'm sorry, I shouldn't have said that," I said. "There's no need for you to panic. There are a lot of guys named Tommy Hernandez in the world. There's no way these psychos are going to be able to find you."

"I guess they would have done it already," Tommy said. "I don't know whether to find that comforting or terrifying."

We hadn't really been looking at each other, but suddenly he was staring me straight in the eye.

"Carter, please come into the office," he pleaded. "Tina is right. You shouldn't be running around the city right now."

"I'll be fine," I said, trying to convince myself more than him. "If it makes you feel better, I'll call Tina myself. That way, you'll be off the hook."

"It's not about being on or off the hook. It's about you being dead or not."

"Tommy, I just feel like my best chance to stay alive is to keep moving and get to the bottom of all this. And I need to have you on my side. Please help me."

Tommy held my glance for another ten or fifteen seconds, which feels like an awful long time when you're looking straight at another human being.

"Okay," he said, finally.

"Thank you. I promise I'll be careful."

"You better be," he said. He looked down at his shoes, then added: "I'm not supposed to tell you this part, but there's been another explosion this morning."

"Let me guess: Booker T."

Tommy nodded.

"Initial reports are that Building Five is a big pile of rubble," he said.

"When did it happen?"

"It's tough to say because we think it wasn't called in right away—there's no one up there with a phone. Maybe an hour after your house blew its top."

I shook my head, thinking about Queen Mary and Red, hoping they weren't inside. And who knows how many other vagrants might be sleeping there? How high would the body count get?

"I'm scared," I said.

"Me, too," he replied.

We stared at the building for a while, a couple of guys feeling the weight of the bull's-eyes on their backs. I put my arm around Tommy. It felt nice to have a little human contact.

Actually, I was starting to feel a lot better in general, like I was coming out of the shock that had gripped me since my phone call from the Nutley police. If anything, the shock was being replaced by euphoria. I was alive. And it felt damn good.

I turned and gave Tommy a hug, patting him on the back.

"Thanks," I said.

"No problem."

"Well," I said, breaking the embrace. "If we wait here much longer, Tina is going to come out here with handcuffs for both of us. I'm heading to the Stop-In Go-Go. You mind checking out the scene at Booker T?"

"Okay," Tommy said.

"Do me a favor and ask around for Red Coles and Queen Mary," I said. "And, for God's sake, watch out for tall men in white vans."

My trip to the Stop-In Go-Go slowed to a trudge shortly after I turned onto Springfield Avenue, which was doing its best impersonation of a mall parking lot at Christmastime. I remained calm at first, using the time to call Tina. She didn't pick up her phone—which was perfect—so I left a message telling her that although my cell phone had been turned off, I had not been.

Once I hung up, I reminded myself I shouldn't let something as trifling and pedestrian as a traffic jam bother me. I'd just had a near-death experience. My thoughts should be more transcendental. I should be glad for *the gift* that was sitting in traffic.

Instead, all I could think was, why, in the name of all that is most holy, was any road gridlocked at ten-thirty in the morning? It's a lot harder to be grateful for one's continued existence when those precious extra moments are being spent stuck behind a Nissan Pulsar with a noisy muffler and an I STOP FOR SALSA bumper sticker.

I finally just parked and hoofed it, and thirteen blocks later figured out the problem: the Stop-In Go-Go had become the command center for the entire metropolitan New York mass media market.

Now it was clear why such scant attention had been paid to the other two catastrophes. Everyone who was anyone in the local infotainment world had set up shop outside the charred remains of this dubiously venerable Irvington institution. The TV trucks outnumbered the fire trucks, ten to two, which was troubling: just think of the flammable potential of all the petroleum-based

189

cosmetics concentrated in such a small area. I could only hope there weren't any burning embers still floating on the breeze.

As I drew closer, I noticed none of the cameras were pointed at the building. Every last one of them had focused on the five women holding an impromptu press conference on the sidewalk outside—five exotic dancers in varying states of dress and undress.

Channels 6 and 12 were tag-teaming the husky, fake-blond Russian I recognized from my earlier visit to the Stop-In Go-Go. She was dressed in a leopard-print unitard that was being pushed to the theoretical limits of spandex's tensile strength. Her interview seemed to have ended, but her attempts to spell her name—Svetlana Kachintsova—for the two Hairspray Heads in front of her was something straight out of an English as a Second Language class. And it wasn't the Russian who was struggling.

Channel 7 was interviewing a woman who had saved not only herself from the fire, but also managed to wrest from the peril her knee-high spike-heeled boots. She would have been five eleven barefooted, but the boots boosted her to six three. She was being interviewed by a Smurf-sized guy who was struggling to maintain eye contact, what with his face being at the same level as her massive, silicone-aided bosom.

Channels 11 and 32, the Spanish-speaking station, were sharing two apparently close friends who had escaped the conflagration in matching kimonos. They insisted on doing their interviews with their arms wrapped around each other—as if the male viewers needed their imaginations prodded any further—and you got the sense they were waiting for *Girls Gone Wild* to show up so they could start chewing on each other's tongues.

But the biggest star was Tynesha, who was captivating

Channels 2, 4, 9, 22, and 47 with her rendition of the morning's harrowing events. Wearing her amber contact lenses, furry slippers, and a brief robe, she was telling her story in animated fashion, waving her arms about in a manner the robe wasn't built to contain. She kept tugging it closed, but every once in a while, when she got too excited, it resulted in a shot that would not have been appreciated by the FCC.

In short, everyone was making great hay out of the scene at the Stop-In Go-Go, which combined the necessary local-TV elements of human tragedy, an easy-to-tell story, and great visuals—with the added bonus of involving strippers.

From a brief bit of eavesdropping on the interviews, I was amused to find the dancers' stories contradicted each other in nearly every detail—who first became aware of the fire, who had alerted whom to the danger, who had been the most selfless heroine putting herself in harm's way to save others, and so on.

But they seemed to agree on one basic fact: that sometime after eight that morning, when the five inhabitants of the upstairs apartments were still snoozing in their beds and dreaming of aging sugar daddies, all hell broke loose.

I sidestepped the cameras and looked for someone who resembled a spokesman for the Irvington Fire Department to get the official word, but the only firemen remaining were just as mesmerized by the dancers as everyone else.

With their attention thus occupied, I was able to slink close to the seared building and examine the damage for myself, letting my nostrils tell me the story of what happened. Gasoline. It wasn't as fresh as if someone had just soaked the rags. It was more like a little-used Exxon station, with the faint remains of an eighty-seven-octane fill-up still lingering in the air.

Or maybe ninety-three. Whatever it was, it had done the job. The tar-paper roof was more or less gone, reduced to a few scant islands of singed material remaining atop the blackened joists. The yellow aluminum siding had gone brown in spots, warped and buckled from the heat. The signature Stop-In Go-Go sign, with its curvaceously outlined dancer, was hanging askew, half melted so the dancer appeared to be some freakish doppelgänger of her former lovely self.

It was sad. That sign, that bar, had been a fixture for at least half a century in Irvington. It had seen the city through every economic and social shift, offered dancers good money and patrons a chance to blow off steam (and perhaps a little more) in a relatively safe, structured environment. I suppose you could say it had been a place of comfort for workingmen and a place of work for comfort women.

And now it was no more. I doubted it would be rebuilt. The owner, who had probably been looking for a way out, would take the insurance money and run, selling the land to someone who would open an auto parts franchise or a chain drugstore.

I know it's a little strange to get sentimental about go-go bars. I certainly wouldn't recommend running for city council on a progo-go platform.

But to me, go-go bars get a bad rap from outsiders who don't understand the culture, people who want to see them as dens of vice and smut and nothing else. They *are* dens of vice and smut, but they're also communities of people who, in their own bizarre way, really care about each other. They're wholesome places, albeit in an unwholesome way, and each time one of them gets bumped out for an auto parts store, some important bit of a town's character is lost.

The circus behind me was still playing in all four rings as I started mentally assembling a timeline of the morning's events.

My house had been blown up at the same time Miss B's place had been doused and lit ablaze. That seemed to be the first wave of attack, and it hit around seven-thirty. The second wave, which came during the eight o'clock hour, was the go-go bar being torched and Booker T detonating.

So, obviously, my two pyromaniacs preferred different methodologies: one knew what to do with a stick of dynamite; the other was a gas man—slosh it around, throw the match, run like hell. Each had effectively destroyed whatever evidence might have been left in their respective locations. I thought about distance between the sites and the time it might take to make the necessary arrangements. The timing fit nicely.

I had just worked it out when I heard the scuffling of Tynesha's furry slippers behind me.

"You!" she thundered. "This is all your fault!"

Her voice had been loud enough to attract the attention of all ten cameras—not to mention the firemen, the sidewalk loiterers, and the traffic stopped on Springfield Avenue—and I suddenly found all those eyes and lenses focused on me.

"That's right," she hollered, even louder. "Put his picture on TV. It's all his fault. Put his picture on TV under a thingie that says 'bastard.'"

Tynesha was staring at me with her arms crossed. The cameramen quickly arranged themselves to form a wall on one side of her, standing at enough distance to be able to catch a wide-angle shot of the dancer and the recipient of her ire. They clearly didn't have a clue what Tynesha was talking about, but they recognized potentially great footage when they saw it.

"Uh-huh!" she kept railing, her head bobbing from side to side as she spoke. "*Bastard*. Oh, he act like he's a nice white boy who takes a girl to the Outback Steakhouse and plays all friendly. And then the next thing you know you wake up and all your stuff's on fire."

Tynesha glared some more, challenging me to answer. But I wasn't saying a word, not with all those cameras rolling. I know how that stuff gets cut. If I said, "It's not like I'm guilty as sin," what would go on TV is me saying, "I'm guilty as sin." Plus, making the six o'clock news for arguing with an exotic dancer in front of a go-go bar was not a career-enhancing move.

The Smurf from Channel 7, undaunted by his ignorance, pointed his microphone at me.

"This woman seems to be saying you set this fire," he said. "Do you have a response?"

I sighed and shook my head but kept my lips clamped.

"Aw, hell, he might as well have set it," Tynesha proclaimed, walking over to the Smurf and snatching his microphone, then using it like it was hooked up to a loudspeaker system. She wanted to be heard. All the cameras instantly readjusted so their shot wasn't screwed up.

"He didn't strike the match but he put it in the hands of the guy who did," Tynesha declared, emphasizing every couple of words like a Sunday-morning preacher who has gotten on a roll.

The Smurf just stood there. His journalistic wits were apparently at their end—plus, he was impotent without his microphone—but the guy from Channel 12, the one who couldn't spell, was determined to apply his hard-nosed-reporter's instincts to get to the bottom of this important story.

"Are you an accomplice?" he asked me, with all due drama. "Are you a coconspirator in some way?"

I slapped my hand to my forehead and finally just couldn't keep quiet any longer. "No," I said. "No, no, no—"

"That's right!" Tynesha crowed. "That's exactly what he is. He's a Coke conspirator and a Pepsi conspirator and everything else!"

The hairdos stayed straight-faced, but I could see the cameramen smirking. Nothing like a little malapropism to make everyone's day.

"Look, guys, I'm a reporter for the *Eagle-Examiner*," I said. "I didn't set any fires. I wrote a story, that's all I did. You can turn your cameras off. There's no news here."

I thought it sounded like a reasonable request but, of course, I wasn't thinking like a TV person. Of course there wasn't any news. But there *was* controversy—which is far better than actual news.

"You keep those cameras rolling!" Tynesha commanded, still gripping the Smurf's microphone. "He put my friend Wanda's business out there. And now all my stuff's burnt."

"Tynesha, can we please have this conversation somewhere else?" I asked.

"No way. We're having it right here. All my stuff's burnt and you don't want to talk about it with all the cameras? Why, because it don't make you look good?"

"It has nothing to do with looking good," I countered. "There are some things I need to tell you. In private."

The hairdos had not yet put A (that Tynesha was talking about the story I had written in that day's *Eagle-Examiner*) together with B (that the places I had written about were under attack), so I could only assume they thought they were watching some kind of bizarre lover's quarrel. The cameras had started swiveling back and forth between me and Tynesha, as if they were covering a tennis match.

"No, I'm through with your crap," Tynesha bellowed. "Why

didn't y'all just put a map in the damn newspaper, maybe some directions, too. I'm going to get me a lawyer and sue the damn hell out of you and your newspaper."

I finally lost my patience.

"Tynesha, look, I've lost everything, too, okay?" I said. "Whoever did this threw a bundle of dynamite through my living room window this morning. He blew up my house. He blew up everything I own. He even blew up my cat."

I hated to play the cat card, but I needed to invoke a little bit of sympathy—if not for me then at least for Deadline.

It didn't work.

"Serves you right!" she snapped. "You just wait until I tell Miss B what happened. She ain't gonna give you no pie. She ain't gonna talk to you no more. She ain't going to answer the door when you knock."

"Tynesha," I said as quietly as I could, turning my back to the cameras in the hopes they couldn't hear me. "Miss B's place got burned, too. She's not . . . she's not looking too good."

Tynesha came at me with fresh rage, fists flying.

"You bastard!" she screamed, veins bulging. "You bastard! You killed her, you killed her!"

She was flailing at me more than she was punching me. I was able to hold her off easily enough—long arms are nice sometimes—though midway through the attack, the belt on her robe slipped loose. With her breasts flopping everywhere, I had to be a little more delicate about the manner in which I restrained her.

Tynesha either didn't know or didn't care that her goods were being aired for public consumption—perhaps mass public consumption. She just kept screaming obscenities at me until the big blond Russian grabbed her. Eventually, Tynesha allowed herself to be corralled away. She had been choking back sobs so she would still have breath to berate me, but she couldn't hold them forever.

"You bastard!" she shrieked one more time, then collapsed into the Russian, who offered her a protective, motherly embrace and shot me a Siberia-cold glower.

The cameras had, naturally, caught the whole ugly thing and they stayed trained on Tynesha and her grief. That left me alone with my thoughts. If I had felt like rationalizing, I could have told myself I was only doing my job, that I hadn't set anything on fire or blown anything up, that I was just as much of a victim as anyone else.

But knowing the ruin my article was causing—even if the ruin wasn't my fault—I couldn't help but think Tynesha right. I *was* a bastard.

With Tynesha having captured every bit of available attention, I slipped away unnoticed and began walking toward my car. About five blocks later, it occurred to me I should go back and offer the TV morons some kind of explanation for the bizarre thing they had just witnessed. After all, that's the first rule of public relations: if you've got a side of the story to tell, get it out quickly and in an attractive manner.

But the more I thought about it, the more I realized a psychopathic, pyromaniac drug kingpin was on the loose, and it was at least partly my fault. For as awful as the TV news was going to make me look, I should leave bad enough alone. After all, there's also the second rule of public relations: if you're in the wrong, shut the hell up, take your beating like a man, and hope everyone forgets about it by the next news cycle.

So I completed my walk down Springfield Avenue to my trusty Malibu, which soon delivered me to the relative safety (I hoped) of the *Eagle-Examiner* offices. By the time I arrived,

197

the morning editor's meeting was already under way, so I was able to settle into my desk without worrying about immediate ambush from Tina or Szanto.

Reassuringly, my e-mail in-box had the usual mix of worthless press releases and urgent reminders from Human Resources, one of which was about making sure the batteries in my home's carbon monoxide detector were working properly. Oh, irony.

There were also some messages from colleagues who'd heard about the kindling box my house had become. And over the next half hour, as I called my insurance company and began filing my claim, a number of them stopped by and offered condolences and iftheresanythingicandos. Even Buster Hays dropped his usual persona and offered some kind words.

You wouldn't necessarily think of newsrooms as dens of altruism, but in times of personal crises, the *Eagle-Examiner* staff was known for going above and beyond to help its own. I had a half-dozen offers for free lodging by the time Szanto and Tina appeared from the morning meeting.

Tina didn't bother with words. She came straight for me and hugged me before I could even get out of my chair. It was a bit awkward, having my face mashed into her chest. And I'm sure it was noted by the newsroom gossips, who undoubtedly knew why I hadn't been at home to be blown up along with the rest of my belongings. But it felt so nice I didn't care.

"When you're done molesting him, send him into my office," Szanto said as he walked by.

Unembarrassed, Tina kept clinging to me. "I'm just glad you're okay," she said, kissing the top of my head fiercely. "Now stop scaring the crap out of me."

I offered my best winsome smile. "Don't worry," I said. "If what Billy Joel says is true and only the good die young, I got a long way to go before I check out."

"You're staying with me until this is over," she said. "No arguments. We're locking the doors and putting on the security system."

"Okay, but no eggs for breakfast."

"Deal," she said, releasing me and exhaling sharply. "Okay. I'm done."

"Thanks," I said, and went into Szanto's office before anyone could get a full look at just how much I was blushing.

"I hope you don't expect me to hug you like that," he said. It was as close as Szanto came to a joke.

"Probably for the best," I said. "I have a pet peeve about hairy backs anyway."

He almost grinned, but I knew what was coming: the Sal Szanto I'm-a-gruff-bastard-but-I-care-about-my-people speech.

"Hell of a thing this morning," he said, leaning back in his chair. "How are you holding up?"

"I'm still here, aren't I?"

"No, really. How are you doing?"

"I'm fine, boss," I said. "Honest. I had my happy-to-be-alive epiphany. I've talked with my insurance company. The only thing I can't replace is my own wonderfully unique DNA sequence, and that managed to come out unscathed."

Szanto bent forward for a moment to grab his coffee, then returned to a recline, sipping thoughtfully.

"Sometimes these things take a little bit of time to sink in, you know," he said. "I want you to take some time off. Get away somewhere until this cools down. I talked to Brodie about it and he agreed the paper will handle the tab, so pick yourself a nice island and get lost for a couple of weeks. Drink some fruity drinks. Meet some local girls. Whatever works for you. Hays and Hernandez can pick up the story from here."

"Like hell they will," I said.

"Carter, I'm offering you a free vacation."

"And I'm telling you thanks but no thanks. This is my story and I couldn't live with myself if I quit on it. At least one woman—and who knows how many Booker T vagrants—may die because of something I put in the damn newspaper. You think a few banana daiquiris will make me feel better about that?"

Szanto moved forward in his chair and placed his coffee back on the desk.

"Yeah, I thought you were going to say that," he said. "If you wake up tomorrow and change your mind, no one here will think less of you."

"*I'll* think less of me."

That seemed to settle matters. Szanto asked about my morning and I gave him the full narrative. Then he caught me up on the latest from inside the nest of Mother Eagle. Apparently, the county prosecutor had called up and asked us to be a little more careful about what we put in the paper. Brodie, God bless him, had politely told the prosecutor to shove it up his ass.

Such bravado aside, we all knew that as long as we had a homicidal maniac receiving home delivery, the rules about what we did and did not print needed to change. We had to hold our cards closer to the chest.

". . . and the Newark police want a statement from you," Szanto finished.

"Can't you just tell them to buy the newspaper like everyone else?"

"Don't know if that's going to work this time," Szanto said. "We've had some success stalling them in the past when these sorts of things came up. But, ultimately, you're going to have to cooperate. You might as well get it out of the way."

That was how, in short order, I ended up taking a walk down the hill, across Broad Street, and onto Green Street for a visit with my good friends at the Newark Police Department. Tina had insisted on accompanying me, which gave me some small comfort: at least if the man in the white van suddenly appeared and decided my brain would look better decorating the sidewalk, there would be a witness.

Otherwise, I doubted Tina's yoga classes, for as shapely as they made her arms, were going to do much to help in the event of an attack. Fact was, if the guy still wanted me dead, I was going to be dead one way or another.

"Whatchya thinking about, Mr. Stare Off in the Distance Man?" Tina asked.

I looked at her and thought about telling the truth: death, Tina. I'm thinking about death. I'm wondering whether I'll be reunited with my harp-strumming grandparents atop cotton-candy clouds or whether I'll have all the afterlife of a junked television. I'm wondering if this lunatic is done for the moment or if he's merely having a Rooty Tooty Fresh N' Fruity at a local IHOP and will be back to finish me after he's done with the funnel cake he ordered for dessert. I'm wondering how my blood would look as it poured out of me and spread in a nice circle on the pavement, which is probably the last thing I'd ever see.

Which means I'm also wondering whether I should really just save my own ass and hop on a plane for St. Thomas, taking Tina with me so we can spend the next two weeks finding creative and entertaining ways to start a family.

Tina was still waiting for my answer.

"Oh, nothing," I said instead. "I was just realizing that I've spent my entire career interviewing cops and never once had the tables turned on me. Funny, isn't it?"

"You're lying," she said. "That wasn't what you were thinking about at all."

"I wasn't?"

"I *know* when you're lying. I hope you don't play poker. Your tells are as obvious as turnpike billboards."

The implication—that I couldn't tell a lie to a woman I might end up sleeping with—was too immense for my head to process at a time like this. So we walked in silence the rest of the way to police headquarters. I went up to the desk sergeant on duty, announced myself, then was asked to take a seat in a lounge area that reminded me of a hospital waiting room except that it had Wanted posters for wall hangings.

A battered television was bolted into the ceiling in the corner, and we arrived just in time for the *News at Noon* update. The TV was muted—as all TV news should be—and I was going to keep it that way until I saw they were leading their broadcast with the Stop-In Go-Go fire. I walked over and pumped up the volume in time to catch the words "Let's go live to Irvington."

The scene cut directly to the Channel 7 Smurf, who no longer looked so small now that he was appearing alone on camera with nothing to set his diminutiveness in perspective. The word "LIVE" appeared in the upper left-hand corner of the screen, and the blackened remains of the Stop-In Go-Go were framed perfectly in the background.

"Thanks, Tom," the Smurf said. "A bizarre story here, where police say an unknown arsonist has torched this and several other buildings, apparently in revenge for something written in a *newspaper* article."

The next scene was a quick scan of the top of that day's *Eagle-Examiner,* then footage of Miss B's place, then of the heap of rubble that remained of Booker T. The Smurf was talking over it the entire time and I was mostly ignoring him until he said, ". . . and we have this footage of a dramatic confrontation between one of the dancers and the man who wrote the article, *Eagle-Examiner* reporter Carter Ross."

I cringed. Other than Van Man, this was the last thing in the world I wanted to see: Tynesha raving at me, and me pleading in return.

Even having participated in the original event, it was hard to follow the clip they had chosen. They used a special effect to strategically blur her wardrobe malfunctions. They used a bleeping sound every time she swore. The net effect was that most of the clip was either blurred or bleeped.

"That was entertaining," Tina said when it was over. "Did you really just try to engender sympathy with a source by telling her about your dead cat?"

"Yes, I'm afraid I played the cat card."

"Interesting," she said. "At least we don't have to worry about losing you to network news."

"Be honest," I said. "How bad was it?"

"Remember that movie with Winona Ryder and Richard Gere?"

"Ouch."

Just then, Hakeem Rogers, the Newark Police Department's spokesman, appeared. Actually, calling Hakeem Rogers a spokesman was a bit of a stretch, since most of the time he was paid to say nothing. We had a relationship based on sarcasm and mutual irritation.

"Hi, Carter," he said, pretending he was happy to see me.

"Hello, Officer Rogers," I said.

"Gee, it really breaks my heart you wasted your time coming down here. We don't need you."

"What do you mean?"

"It's not our case anymore."

203

"So whose case is it?"

"We turned it over to the feds," Rogers said, like I should have somehow known this already.

"Which feds?"

"The Newark Field Office of the National Drug Bureau," he said. "They told us they had reason to believe the crime involved international drug smuggling and they claimed jurisdiction over it."

"Huh," was all I could say.

"Yeah, so you can go bother them now," Rogers said. "I'm glad we're rid of it. We got enough murders we can't solve. If you ask me, they're not going to do any better with it than we did."

The Director wasted little time pondering his morning's work. There was another job to do, and he knew it was going to take several hours: he had a lot of pictures to print out, and ink-jet printers were simply not built for speed. The Director didn't like using his own printer—in addition to the printer being slow, it meant fussing with those annoying ink cartridges—but he had no choice in the matter. These were not the kind of pictures he could take to the local Fotomat.

They were the snapshots the Director had ordered Monty to take of Wanda Bass, Tyrone Scott, Shareef Thomas, and Devin Whitehead in the moments after their deaths. They were postmortem portraits. Faces of the gone.

And now that the news of the four dealers' deaths was in every newspaper and on every television—and had no doubt captured his employees' attention—the time was right to deliver the high-impact message the Director wanted to impart.

He made forty-two packets, one for each of his remaining dealers, to be delivered along with their weekly shipment. Each packet included a set of the photos and a memo:

TO: All Employees

FROM: The Director

RE: Reminder about cutting

It has recently come to my attention that four of our employees were cutting The Stuff as a way of stretching out supply. The pictures enclosed can be considered the consequences of that decision. A similar penalty will await any other employees who make a similar mistake. We have put strict quality control measures in place and we will continue to perform spot checks in the field to ensure compliance on the part of all employees. Only with 100 percent purity can we achieve our goals.

It is my hope this is the last such directive I will have to issue on this subject.

The Director read the memo over three times to make sure it struck the right tone. Then, because he liked how it looked, he found "The Stuff" stamp on his desk and imprinted its logo at the top of each memo—one last sign of authenticity.

In a rare display of initiative, Monty tried to convince the Director it was madness to send out the packets. Mathematically, weren't there good odds one of them could slip into the wrong hands? Couldn't this be used as evidence against them?

But the Director only laughed at Monty's anxiousness. Even if one of his dealers took the package directly to the chief of police and spilled everything, it would have no impact on the Director's operation. The Director had the local police under control. Besides, each level of his organization was essentially blind to the level above it.

The Stuff could never be traced back to him.

CHAPTER 7

Now that Van Man had Uncle Sam on his ass, my chances of celebrating my thirty-second birthday had improved slightly. A smart bad guy could screw around with the Newark cops, who had never been accused of being the world's sharpest crime-solving unit. The feds were a different matter. The feds had resources, know-how, and a certain no-nonsense attitude about things. And if they decided a case was a priority, they had a much longer attention span, as well.

Hopefully it was enough to convince Van Man to go underground and not risk emerging to, say, grease a local newspaper reporter.

Yet while these were all good developments for my personal

208

life, it was not as promising for me professionally. Prying information out of local law enforcement was like playing with an old fire hydrant: if you kept taking whacks at it, you could eventually get it to leak. Feds were made of different material, stuff that was sealed a lot tighter.

Especially since I already had some inkling of who I was dealing with. My first experience with L. Peter Sampson, the NDB's press guy, had set a world record for Fastest Flak Blow-off (Federal Division). The guy couldn't wait to get me off the phone.

I quickly concluded there was only one way to solve that problem: pay him a visit. Maybe that personal touch would convince poor, frightened L. Pete that I wasn't one of those scary reporters who was going to get him fired.

I walked Tina back to the newsroom and promised her I would spend the afternoon safely at my desk, doing my expense report. Then I went to my computer for three minutes—just long enough to get an address for the National Drug Bureau's Newark Field Office—and scooted across town.

The NDB was housed in an appropriately stern federal building, a solidly built rectangular edifice without much in the way of architectural imagination. Upon entering, I was met by a metal detector and three square-jawed U.S. marshals.

"Can I help you, sir?" one asked.

"I'm a reporter with the *Eagle-Examiner*," I said. "I'm here to see L. Peter Sampson at the National Drug Bureau."

"Do you have an appointment?"

"No."

He nodded, went to a nearby phone, and immediately started talking in a voice that was inaudible from twenty feet away. One of his partners, meanwhile, eyed me like I was something that had crawled out of the sewer.

As a general rule, making unannounced visits to federal

agencies was not a very efficient use of a reporter's time. Bureaucracies abhorred such displays of spontaneity from the Fourth Estate. And they discouraged them by assuring that such attempts would be met with minimum cooperation and maximum fuss.

"Can I see some identification?" the marshal asked me after he got off the phone, and I obliged him with a business card and my New Jersey State Police Press ID.

"Driver's license, please," he said.

"I came here on foot," I said pleasantly. I hadn't, of course. But I didn't like the idea of giving Big Brother more information about myself than absolutely necessary. Plus, the guy was being a dick. The marshal frowned and returned to low-talking at the telephone. The partner was now staring at me even more contemptuously. I gave him an exaggerated smile—merely because I felt sticking out my tongue would be too juvenile.

Meanwhile, I considered how I might approach L. Pete differently this time. I had exactly zero leverage on the guy. One of the reasons the feds were so much harder to crack than the locals was that, in short, feds didn't really need good publicity. The local police chief knows his boss, the mayor, is eventually going to have to win an election and that friendly relations with the newspaper will help him do that.

A place like the NDB doesn't have nearly that level of local accountability. Its money comes from faraway Washington committee meetings and its employees enjoy the kind of job security only the world's most powerful government can offer. Sure, it doesn't mind good pub. But, more than anything, it looks to avoid *bad* pub.

And that, I realized, was my only recourse with L. Pete. If the carrot didn't work, I'd have to make him think I had a big stick. Somewhere.

The marshal eventually hung up the phone and instructed me to go through the metal detector. Then the second marshal passed a wand over me. The third one patted me down.

Having been sufficiently probed, I was led across a polished floor to a small padded bench near an elevator, where I was instructed to wait. The elevator soon produced a cheerless man in a suit, who relieved the marshal and took over his job: making sure I didn't cause trouble.

"Nice day today, huh?" I said.

"Yes, sir," he said, his expression unchanging.

"Any big plans for the weekend?" I asked.

"No, sir," he said, and I decided to stop antagonizing the poor guy.

Fifteen minutes passed, during which time suit guy remained grim-faced and I grew bored. I'm sure, somewhere in the building, L. Pete was simply hoping I'd leave. But I wasn't going to give him that pleasure. After a half hour passed, I took a quarter out of my pocket and began flipping it, gangster style. I thought I noticed a slight change in the suit's face, like he was a little jealous I was getting to have all the fun.

Finally—prompted by nothing I could discern—the suit said, "Come with me."

He slid a card into the control panel, punched the up button, then took me to the fifteenth floor. The top floor. I was escorted to an office next to a corner office, whose name plate announced it belonged to L. Peter Sampson.

"Wait here," the suit told me. "Agent Sampson will see you shortly."

Agent Sampson was apparently a very big fan of the New York Jets.

He had one of those Jets firemen helmets sitting on one of

his bookcases, a miniature Jets helmet next to it, and a framed ticket hanging on the wall from Super Bowl III, one of the rare proud moments in the franchise's otherwise abysmal history.

Behind his desk was one of those panoramic photos of Giants Stadium from a Jets-Bills game. On the desk, next to the usual wife-and-kid pictures, there was an autographed picture of Richard Todd and a football that had been signed by Joe Klecko, Marty Lyons, and Mark Gastineau.

A short, thin, energetic man with thinning hair and a dark suit walked in the room.

"Hi, Pete Sampson," he said affably. "Nice to meet you in person."

"Carter Ross, *Eagle-Examiner*," I said as we exchanged an extra-firm, manly-man handshake.

"Sorry about the wait," he said, smiling thinly. "I was in a meeting."

"The wait wasn't that bad. It gave me time to put my anus back in place after the body cavity search I got at the front door."

"Yeah, that," L. Pete said. "But, you know—Oklahoma City, 9/11—the rules have all changed. When the threat level is high, this place gets locked down tighter than a duck's ass."

Lovely image. Don't get me wrong, a little small talk was a good way to start an interview. But since I didn't want that talk to center around a duck's anatomy, I switched topics.

"So, I'm guessing from your decorations you're a fan of the Sack Exchange," I said.

"Best defensive line in football. Too bad Miami was able to slow 'em down in the mud at the Orange Bowl that one year."

"A. J. Duhe," I said.

He shuddered. Having lived in New Jersey most of my life, I was accustomed to the inner torment suffered by Jets fans.

212

"Well," he said. "I'm guessing you didn't come here to interview me about how the AFC East is stacking up."

"Not really," I said. "But to keep this in football terms, my friends at the Newark police tell me they've handed off the Ludlow Street quadruple homicide to you guys."

L. Pete paused for a beat, just long enough for me to hear the gears switching in his mind.

"Well, as you know, the National Drug Bureau is a federal agency ultimately responsible for fighting this nation's war against illegal narcotics smuggling both at home and abroad," he said, like he was quoting from a brochure. "And from time to time, we here at the Newark Field Office use that authority to claim jurisdiction over crimes we believe are extensions of that war."

"Uh-huh," I said. "So . . . you've got this Ludlow Street thing all figured out, then?"

"I can't comment on an ongoing investigation," he said, smiling at me.

I matched his insincere smile with one of my own. Time to use the stick.

"Well, don't take this the wrong way, Pete," I said. "But this son of a bitch blew up my house this morning and killed my cat. So I didn't really come here to get a polite no comment.

"Now, we can do this one of two ways," I continued. "I can team up with a forensic accountant and crawl through every line of your budget. No matter what we find, we'll run a headline that says, 'The drug war's answer to the $1,000 hammer,' along with grainy head shots of you and your bosses that make you look like criminals. And your wife can explain to her friends at playdates that the article wasn't really *that* bad.

"Or you can spare me the runaround and we can play nice and share some information. It's up to you."

It was empty saber rattling, of course. My bosses frowned on using the newspaper to carry out reporters' vendettas. And, in any event, I didn't really have the time—or the interest—to do the kind of intensive reporting I had just described.

But L. Pete, who looked like he had just taken a very large bite of lemon, didn't necessarily know that. I think my sudden lack of house and cat gave me just enough credibility as a crazy that he was taking me seriously.

"I, uh . . ." he began. "Will you excuse me for a moment?"

He left without another word and, I'm sure, headed next door to ask his boss what to do with the lunatic reporter in his office. I hoped they would come to the conclusion I needed to be placated.

He returned five minutes later.

"Can we be off the record?" he asked.

"Sure."

"Good," he said. "I've been authorized to tell you certain things but not other things. You understand we have people in the field working on this and the wrong information in the wrong hands could be disastrous. We're not putting our people at risk, no matter how many exposés you write about us."

"Fair enough," I said.

He paused then said, "The first thing I'm authorized to tell you is that we have good reason to believe this is the work of José de Jesús Encarcerón."

"I'm supposed to know who he is?"

"Colombian drug lord, and a real badass one," L. Pete said. "Some of the things he's done make other drug lords look like street-corner hustlers. Our agency has a file on this guy that could fill your garage."

"I don't have a garage anymore."

"Right. Sorry. Point is, we've been after this guy for more

than five years now. And I don't mean to sound insensitive, but those bodies down on Ludlow Street are just four more debits on a very large tab."

"So this guy sits in his palace in Bogotá, orders the hit, and the local muscle takes care of it?"

"Something like that, yes," L. Pete said.

"So why don't you start by going after the local muscle?"

"I'm afraid that falls under the category of things I can't tell you."

"And Encarcerón's people are responsible for distributing 'The Stuff' brand?"

"Can't tell you that, either," L. Pete said, shifting his weight uneasily.

"Why, because he's slipping it past you guys at the airport and you're embarrassed by it?" I said.

He just shrugged. "Despite what you might assume about how we're spending taxpayer money here, we're actually quite close to putting a case together against this guy. But we have to proceed carefully or we could screw up the whole thing."

Now it was my turn to shrug.

"Look," I said. "I don't care if or when you get around to putting away this José de Whatever guy. I care about the guy who tried to put a stick of dynamite up my ass this morning. Specifically, I'm a little worried he'll return to finish off the job."

"Well, that gets around to the other thing I'm authorized to tell you."

"Which is?"

"I wouldn't press too hard if I were you," L. Pete said.

"Oh?"

"We have good reason to believe Encarcerón's people consider this matter settled. All the loose ends are tied up. All the evidence is destroyed. They want to go back to business as usual.

But if a certain newspaper reporter kept nosing around, kept making himself a pest, they might feel the need to exterminate the pest."

"That sounds a bit ominous," I said.

"Call it what you want," L. Pete replied. "I call it prudent advice. These are some bad *hombres* we're dealing with. I am urging you in the strongest possible terms to leave the Ludlow Street investigation to our agents and trust we'll get the job done. We can't guarantee your safety if you keep sniffing around."

"I see," I said. "Are you authorized to tell me anything else?"

"Nope," he said cheerfully. "But when we're ready to announce our charges against Encarcerón, I promise we'll give you an exclusive interview. Seems like you're owed the pleasure."

"Terrific," I said, though I really meant the opposite of terrific. I had no intention of waiting for L. Pete and his fellow flatfoots to get around to making a case against some international drug lord.

But, at least for the time being, I had to keep up appearances.

L Pete and I swapped phone numbers and bid each other a fake-fond adieu, then I departed the National Drug Bureau's fortress with a friendly wave to the square-jaw boys. Despite my new information, I still felt wary of large men in white vans. Not to say I didn't trust our government but . . . well . . . I didn't trust our government. And since them being wrong could result in me being dead, I felt caution was still advisable.

At the very least, I wanted to educate myself more about this José de Jesús character. So I spurred my Malibu back to the office, where an hour of trolling through clips on Lexis-Nexis laid out a fairly complete life story. He was young for an intercontinental villain, just thirty-four. A poor street thug from

Bogotá, he got his start in the business in the mid-1990s, which turned out to be a fortuitous time for an ambitious would-be drug lord: Pablo Escobar had just been killed, and the instability created by his passing made it easy enough for Encarcerón to rise up the ranks.

He was pretty much your garden-variety ruthless sociopath. He terrorized and/or eliminated anyone who dared oppose him, kidnapped and/or imprisoned anyone he didn't feel like killing, bribed and/or murdered any government official who tried to slow him down, and generally didn't play well with others.

His nickname, La Cabra—the Goat—derived from an infamous episode early in his career. He'd killed a rival's entire family, decapitating them and placing goats' heads on top of the stumps. Charming.

As L. Pete said, U.S. law enforcement and U.S.-backed Colombian authorities had been after the guy for a while. Within the past few years, La Cabra had climbed the ranks of the NDB's Most Wanted and the price on his head had reached $2 million.

But Bogotá was a big city and Colombia was an even bigger country. He never stayed in the same place long. And he was generous enough with the spoils of his enterprise—hosting huge cookouts, sponsoring sports teams, paying hospital bills for indigents—that people in the *barrio* never gave him up. Of course, fear played a part, too. Legend had it, he had once been tipped off that someone in the neighborhood was going to inform on him. The would-be snitch's body was dragged through the streets by two horses. One towed the head and torso, the other the butt and legs.

So, yeah, he was on Santa's naughty list. But I couldn't drive away the thought that something didn't feel right. Why would a drug lord in Colombia concern himself with a few Newark street dealers? And, even if he did, why kill all four at once? And why leave their bodies where they could be so easily discovered? I can't pretend I knew a lot about the preferred modus operandi of the Colombian cartels, but this didn't feel like it.

Besides, the identity of the person giving the orders in South America was, in some ways, just academic. There was still someone on this side of the equator pulling the trigger. And it bothered me that my government, in its zeal to put La Cabra's head on its mantel, was treating this trigger-puller like he was such a trivial piece in a larger game.

Because I knew how this stuff worked. The foot soldiers would be given lighter sentences in exchange for their testimony against the Big Boss. *Yes, Your Honor, I murdered four people and torched all those buildings, but La Cabra made me do it.* Van Man would do twenty or thirty years but would end up enjoying his old age as a free man. Meanwhile, his victims got no reprieve on being dead.

But there was one way to possibly change that equation: if I could get to the foot soldier first and put his name in the paper, there would be pressure for the NDB to do something about it. The families of the victims would be clamoring for justice, and this crime had become high profile enough that they might be able to get someone with pull—a congressman, maybe—to listen.

So I just had to find a way to infiltrate a Colombian drug lord's local organization, implicate it in a major international drug-smuggling ring, and find compelling evidence it had committed a series of heinous crimes. I could have that wrapped up by, what, dinnertime?

Or not.

Knowing L. Pete wasn't going to be any assistance mapping out La Cabra's network, I had to leverage the information he had given me to try to get more from somewhere else. And, really, I could only think of one guy I knew who might even *have* more information. I picked up the phone and dialed Irving Wallace, hoping his part of the government—whatever part that was—had an agenda different enough from the NDB that he wouldn't mind being helpful.

"Yes," he said.

"Hi, Irving, Carter Ross from the *Eagle-Examiner.*"

Pause. "Are you in your office?"

"Yeah."

Click.

Ten seconds later, my phone rang.

"Carter Ross."

"Hi, it's Irving."

"You want to explain to me why that was necessary?" I asked.

"Because someone could have been impersonating you."

"Besides Buster Hays, no one knows we've ever spoken," I said. "And I'm sure Buster isn't sharing."

"Good thing, too," he said. "I understand your sources get their houses blown up."

Obviously, someone had been watching the news.

"Cheap shot," I said. "Now that you've hurt my feelings, you have to help me. What can you tell me about José de Jesús Encarcerón?"

"I don't know. That he's not very nice, I guess," Wallace said. "I'm just a lab guy, remember? I know what his drugs look like after they've been passed through a spectrometer."

"Aw, come on. I'm sure you hear little tidbits from . . . whoever it is you work for."

"Say the magic words."

Magic words? What magic words? Oh.

"Off the record," I said.

"Very good," he said. "What do you want to know?"

"Well, I want to know what kind of muscle he has on the street here."

"Where, in Newark?"

"Yeah."

"He doesn't," Wallace said.

"What do you mean? Of course he does."

"In the Northeast, guys like Encarcerón just supply the product. They've never been able to get down to the street level. I'm not sure they even want to. They've always left it to the local thugs."

"Someone told me—off the record, of course—that Encarcerón's people here are responsible for Ludlow Street," I said.

"Really?" Wallace said, sounding surprised. "Is it someone who knows what they're talking about?"

"They ought to."

"Huh," he said. "Sounds to me like someone is trying to snow you."

I made Irving Wallace promise to call me if he heard anything—a lot of good that would probably do—and was just about to settle in for some serious head scratching when the three o'clock editor's meeting let out and Hurricane Tina washed ashore on my desk.

"Goddammit, Carter. Where the hell have you been?" she said with quiet intensity.

"I had an errand to run," I said. "We were out of nondairy creamer in the break room."

"You prick," she bristled. "If I have to surgically attach an electronic monitoring bracelet to your balls, I will."

"Watch out," I said. "That might lower my sperm count."

"Yeah? You should see what dying does to your sperm count."

220

"Ah," I said. "So *that's* why you haven't gotten into necrophilia."

She had clearly been outzinged. So rather than hit me with another comeback, she put her hands on her hips and pursed her lips. A lock of hair fell across her face and I felt the urge to tuck it behind her ear for her. But Tina was determined to stay indignant, so she blew it out of the way and continued scowling at me.

"So do you want to fill me in on what's been going on around here?" I asked.

"No. I want to wring your neck. But I'll tell you anyway: Whitlow, Hays, and Hernandez have been putting together a story on today's series of fires and explosions that we will link to the *Eagle-Examiner*'s front-page report about the Ludlow Street murders."

I nodded.

"Their story will not carry a byline," she said. "That's our new policy. Until this Unabomber-wannabe is caught, all Ludlow Street stories are unbylined."

"What, no one else wanted the joy that is filing a total home destruction insurance claim?"

"In other news," she continued. "We've received and declined about twenty interview requests for star investigative reporter Carter Ross."

"Aw, damn," I said. "How am I supposed to get my fifteen minutes of fame?"

"Well, given how you did with your first five on the *News at Noon*, I'd say we're doing you a favor."

Now I was outzinged. I thought about sharing what I had learned from my new buddies at the NDB but decided it could wait.

"I'm still pissed at you," Tina said. "But if you behave yourself for the rest of the day, I'll make you my world-famous veal sca-loppine when we get home tonight."

"Consider me on my best behavior," I said, raising three fin-gers. "Scout's honor."

"Yeah, I almost believe that. I'm telling the security guards in the parking lot that if they see you unaccompanied, they should shoot to maim."

"Good thing they're old and blind," I said.

"You better hope so," she said.

She stormed off, taking her Category 5 wrath with her. I was just starting to scan my e-mail box—spaces in Human Re-sources' Ramadan Awareness seminar were going fast—but be-fore I could learn what I needed to be aware of (besides hungry Muslims) Tommy approached my desk.

"Is it safe?" he asked.

"You mean if you continue standing here will someone try to firebomb you and your Gucci shoes? I make no guarantees."

"No, I was talking about Tina," Tommy said. "I think I'd rather take my chances with the bomb."

"She'll get over it. How was Booker T?"

"I would say your friend in the van saved the City of Newark a lot of money in demolition."

"You ask about Red and Queen Mary?"

"Yeah. No one had seen them this morning. But as of a half hour ago the fire department hadn't recovered any bodies, so maybe there are none to recover."

The cynical side of me wondered how hard they were actu-ally looking. Anyone trapped in that building would be a person who long ago ceased to be of much consequence to society.

"What about Brenda Bass?" I asked.

"I made the usual round of calls to the hospitals and got the usual crap about confidentiality laws. But on a hunch I called the burn unit at University Hospital and one of the nurses slipped."

"Slipped?"

"Yeah, she was like, 'How did you know she was here?' And I was like, 'I didn't, honey, you just told me.'"

"Wow. The intern with the veteran move. Nice job," I said. "Anyway, how's your story coming?"

"Eh, you know what a joy it is working with Buster. If he calls me 'little girl' one more time he's going to have to remove my queer Cuban foot from his ass."

"I love it when you get all butch."

"I really sounded tough just now, huh?" he said, then giggled.

"I was definitely scared for a second. Look at me, I'm trembling," I said, holding out my hand, which was rock steady.

"Yeah, anyway, screw you," Tommy said. "I only came over here to tell you about this guy who called for you. The clerk transferred the calls to me, because the guy said it was about Ludlow Street. But he only wanted to talk to you."

Tommy handed me a number on a torn piece of Chinese menu.

"The guy have a name?" I asked.

"He wouldn't say. He sounded like some gangbanger. That's why I didn't want to give him your cell number. He sounded pretty scary."

"I'm not afraid of him. I've got a queer Cuban ass-kicker who will protect me."

"Don't you forget it," Tommy said as he walked away.

I looked at the menu/message slip for a moment. I generally have a pretty good memory for phone numbers, but this one wasn't jostling any brain cells (though it was making me hungry for mu shu pork).

I briefly debated whether to call the number. I was, at least according to some, a known enemy of La Cabra. There was no telling who might be trying to lure me into certain doom. Why wouldn't the guy give his name? Why insist on only talking to me? It had the classic markings of a trap.

But I gave in pretty quickly. Ultimately, the journalistic flesh is weak: an anonymous source calling with information is just far too great a temptation to resist. I mean, maybe this was my Deep Throat, the guy who would meet me in the parking garage and tell me everything. Besides, what would one little phone call hurt?

So I dialed.

"Yo," said a voice I couldn't place.

"Hi, this is Carter Ross, from the *Eagle-Examiner*," I said.

"Yo, Bird Man! Thanks for putting in your article that we didn't have nothing to do with Dee-Dub."

It wasn't Deep Throat. It was Bernie Kosar from the Brick City Browns.

"I promised you I would," I said. "I mean, you made me an honorary member. It seems to be the least I could do for you guys."

Especially with sources who, on occasion, shoot people.

"Yeah, it was cool. My mom even clipped it out and saved it. It's the first time we been mentioned in the paper for something positive, you know?"

"Well, I'm not sure I'm going to be able to feature you in the 'Good Neighbors' section just yet, but I'm glad it's something," I said. "Anyway, what's up?"

"I got someone here you want to talk to. Can you come out to Brown Town right away?"

"Brown Town?"

"Yeah, you know, the place where we, you know . . ."

"Smoked that fine marijuana?"

"Yeah," Bernie said, laughing. He cupped the phone, but I could hear him say to his buddies: "Bird Man wants to know if this is where we 'smoked that fine marijuana,'" he said, imitating my voice with exaggerated diction, then got back on the phone.

"You got a funny way of talking, Bird Man. It's like listening to the announcer in one of them antidrug videos. Where do white people learn to talk like that, anyway?"

"We take special classes," I replied. "I'll be right over."

"Okay, hurry up. This guy ain't going to hang around all day."

When I arrived at Brown Town, I realized Bernie Kosar was being quite literal when he talked about the source hanging around: in the darkened living room, next to the fish tank, there was a chubby young black man dangling from his heels.

He had been tied to an exposed pipe in the ceiling and was suspended upside down, bat-style. He had a sock in his mouth that had been secured by duct tape wrapped around his head. He was wearing boxers—and only boxers. He did not seem pleased about any of this.

In addition to Bernie, the guy in the Kevin Mack jersey was also standing sentry.

"We caught this nigga trying to steal a Drew Barrymore movie," Bernie said, giving the guy an evil look as we walked past.

He and Kevin Mack guided me down the hallway into the kitchen, out of earshot of the prisoner.

"We don't really give a damn about the Drew Barrymore thing," Bernie told me. "That bitch's movies are all the same anyway.

"But he was carrying this backpack," Bernie continued, holding up a nylon bag with a key chain full of soda can tabs attached. "And we found this in it."

Bernie flipped me an envelope. I looked inside to find four glossy eight-by-ten photographs that made me flinch. Each picture was an extreme close-up of a lifeless, shattered, bloody face. It was, to my utter astonishment, the Ludlow Four. Overcoming my revulsion, I pulled the pictures toward me for closer inspection.

I held up one of the pictures and blurted, "That's Wanda Bass. I saw her in the funeral home after they patched her up. That's definitely her."

"Yeah, and that's Dee-Dub," Bernie said, pointing to another photo. Then he held up a single sheet of paper that bore The Stuff's stamp at the top. "This came with it," he said.

It was written like a corporate memo: "TO: All Employees, FROM: The Director, RE: Reminder about cutting." I read it quickly, then went back over it more slowly. It answered some of the questions that had confounded me. Why kill the dealers? They had diluted the brand. Why kill all four at once and leave them together in a way that would garner so much attention? Because being noticed was the point. Who did the killing? The Director.

Whoever that was.

"Where the hell did he get this?" I asked.

"He won't talk to us," Bernie said. "But we figured he'd have to talk to you, you being a reporter and all."

If only that were true.

"Well, it's not like I have subpoena power," I said. "Why didn't you just call the cops?"

"We ain't exactly the cop-calling type, Bird Man," Bernie said matter-of-factly.

"No, I guess you're not," I said, frowning until an idea came to me. "Okay, but we can still act like cops. You guys be the bad cops. You know, the tough guys, threatening him and stuff. I'll be the good cop, protecting him from you. We'll work him that way. Okay?"

I didn't think playing bad cop would be too much of a stretch for either of them.

"Cool," Bernie said, clearly enjoying the idea. Of course he did. It was just like a scene from one of his bootleg movies.

"Just follow my lead," I said.

We went back into the living room, where Bat Boy eyed us. He couldn't have been older than twenty-two or twenty-three. And the baby fat made him look even younger.

"I'm telling you, I don't think that's a good idea," I said, as if we were in the middle of a conversation. "I don't think we should hurt him."

I turned my back on Bat Boy and winked, then faced him again. Bernie was a little slow to react, but Kevin Mack caught on perfectly.

"Forget it. I'm cutting his dick off," he said angrily, pulling out a thick-bladed hunting knife. From under the sock, a muffled scream escaped Bat Boy's throat. I turned away again so Bat Boy couldn't see how hard I was working to suppress a laugh.

"Look, let's at least give him a *chance* to talk," I pleaded. "*Then* you can cut his dick off."

"A'right," Kevin said, walking over to Bat Boy. "I'm going to take this thing off his face now. But if he screams, I'm cutting his dick off. You hear that, sucker?"

Bat Boy nodded, and Kevin Mack roughly ripped off the duct tape. The guy didn't have a lot of hair, but it still couldn't have felt good.

"Owww," he whined.

227

"Keep it down," Kevin Mack said, putting the point of the knife on the fly opening of the guy's boxers. Yes, bad cop was definitely well within Kevin Mack's theatrical repertoire.

"Okay, okay, okay," Bat Boy said in a high, panicked voice.

"Take it easy," I told Kevin Mack. Bat Boy was legitimately scared witless and I had this brief moment of ethical pause. Should I be interviewing a source who was being forced to talk against his will? For that matter, was it a good idea to willingly participate in what was essentially a forceful kidnapping? What would *Editor & Publisher* have to say about such journalistic tactics?

And then I thought, oh right, screw *Editor & Publisher.* No one was trying to kill them.

"Remember what happened the last time you did that?" I said. "Remember all the blood? I am *not* helping you clean that up again."

I turned to Bat Boy. "Nothing bleeds quite like a penis wound," I said, in a scholarly manner. "I'm not sure how familiar you are with anatomy, but the dorsal gonadal artery and the medial erectile vein converge at the base of the penis. If you sever both, you get a real gusher on your hands. You should have seen the last guy. He was hanging upside down just like you and he ended up with a face full of penis blood."

Bat Boy looked like he was buying it. I turned to Kevin Mack.

"Hey, what did you end up doing with that last guy's Johnson anyway?"

"Fed it to the fish, remember?" Kevin Mack said with perfect timing.

"I swear," I said to Bat Boy. "I think this bloodthirsty bastard enjoys this."

"Well, the fish sure did," Kevin Mack said. "They kept pecking at it, knocking it around, having fun with it. The big fish would gnaw on it for a while, then the little fish would dart out and take a chunk. That little blue one over there in the corner, he was a penis-eatin' fool. I swear, he's been begging for another one ever since."

Even though it was hard to tell through his chocolate-brown skin, I thought I detected Bat Boy blanching.

"Look, I'm sure this guy is going to be more reasonable than the last one," I said. "Maybe if you could give me a little time alone with him, we can get this resolved, okay?"

"A'right," Kevin said, heading back into the kitchen with Bernie, leaving me alone with Bat Boy.

I bent down on one knee, so Bat Boy and I could be face-to-face.

"Listen," I said in a soothing voice. "I'm a nice guy. Really, I am. These other two guys? They're not so nice. But I did them a favor recently so maybe now they'll do me a favor and let you off easy. But you're going to have to cooperate, or I can't guarantee you'll ever be able to pee standing up again. Got it?"

He nodded.

"Good, now what's your name?"

"Rashan Reeves."

"Very good, Rashan. That package with the pictures in it, where did you get it?"

"It was in my last shipment," Rashan said. "I was getting four bricks and they just put it in there."

"Who is 'they'?"

Rashan whimpered, his eyes shifting wildly about. He bucked a little bit, but wasn't going anywhere. The Brick City Browns were handy with knots.

"Don't make me call in my friends," I warned.

"I don't know, man," he said quickly. "They make me wear

this blindfold. Honest. *I do not know.* The boss is called 'the Di-rector' and that's the only name I ever heard anyone call him. They say it like he all-powerful, like 'nobody mess with the Di-rector.' His people come in this white van, and as soon as I seen the van, I put on the blindfold. And that's it."

I believed him. This Director guy seemed nothing if not or-ganized—he was sending out memos, for goodness sake. No-body with that level of competence would allow a street-level hustler to know much about the operation.

"So how do you know when it's time to pick up another shipment?"

"I do it the same time every week."

"Same place?"

"Naw, they call me and tell me where to meet them. Then I put on a blindfold and get in a van so I can't see nothing."

"A white van?"

"Yeah."

Of course it was a white van. I wondered if the Director had a fleet of them, or just one. Bat Boy, still upside down, patiently awaited my next query.

"They always call you from the same number?" I asked.

"Different numbers. I think they use them throw-away cell phones."

"They always give you the same amount of product?"

"Yeah."

"But what if you haven't sold all your product from the week before?"

"Don't matter. I signed a contract."

"A contract?" I said. Generally speaking, distributors of Class 1 narcotics were not known to be real caught up in the use of legal instruments.

"Yeah, I sign a new one every couple of months. It's basically, like, I agree to sell so much product and they agree to provide it to me, and it's all done out ahead of time. My contract right now is for four bricks."

I did the math. Four bricks was two hundred bags. Even assuming he sold each bag at a $2 profit, that was still only $400 a week. So, basically, he was risking jail, getting smoked by a fellow dealer, stabbed by a wacked-out customer, or killed by his own employer—all for twenty grand a year. True, the hours were flexible. And it was tax free. But I was guessing the health plan sucked.

"And how did you hook up with these guys? Who recruited you?"

"This dude in prison."

"Which dude?"

"The drug counselor dude," Rashan said. "One of my boys told me all I had to do was *pretend* I had a drug problem, get treatment for it, and then *pretend* I was cured, and they would let me out early. So that's what I did. Knocked six months off my stretch."

Ah, the redemptive power of recovery.

"So you met a guy in counseling who hooked you up?" I asked.

"No, no. The dude who hooked me up *was* the counselor."

"The substance abuse counselor?" I asked. Just when I thought I'd heard everything.

"Yeah. He took me aside one day and asked me if I wanted to make easy money selling the best stuff on the market. I heard all kinds of stories about how hard it was to get a job when you get out because no one hires ex-cons, so I was like, 'Yeah.' And when I got out, one of his boys found me."

"What's the counselor's name?"

"Umm . . ."

"Don't make me call my friend in the next room."

"No, no, come on, man," he pleaded. "I'm just trying to think . . . It was Mr. Hector . . . Mr. Hector . . . Alvarez. Yeah, that's it. Hector Alvarez."

Hector Alvarez. I guess that sounded like a plausible name for someone who worked for José de Jesús Encarcerón. But it also sounded like a name my pal Rashan Reeves could have made up on the spot. There was one way to check. I pulled out my cell phone and dialed Tommy.

"You have a lot riding on this phone call, Rashan," I said as I waited for Tommy to pick up.

He answered on the second ring.

"Hey, Tommy, it's Carter."

"Where have you been? Tina just asked me if I had seen you."

"What did you tell her?"

"That you were in the bathroom."

"Good man," I said. "Now can you do me a favor real quick? Look up and see if a guy named Hector Alvarez works for the Department of Corrections."

We had a database of all state and local employees that, from an information standpoint, was nothing short of gold. It came to us courtesy of an Open Public Records Act request our newspaper made each year. It made snooping on public employees as simple as a few mouse clicks.

"Yeah, got him," Tommy said. "Hector I. Alvarez. Born 10/25/1963. Hired 11/01/2003. He made $38,835 last year."

"Excellent. Can you get an address for him?"

"Hang on," Tommy said, and I heard his keyboard chattering away. I cupped my cell phone and turned upside down so I could look at Rashan.

"When you get out of here, you might want to send a thank-you note to Tommy Hernandez, care of the *Eagle-Examiner*," I said. "He just saved something precious to you."

It didn't take much convincing to get Rashan to join my field trip to Hector Alvarez's house. Anything that didn't involve his penis in close proximity to Kevin Mack's hunting knife sounded like a pretty good idea to Rashan.

By the time he was untied, redressed, and debriefed—a short, scary lecture from Bernie Kosar about the consequences of ever again tussling with the Browns—it was after five. A cold, blustery night was settling in outside. Rashan had his backpack returned to him, soda can tabs still attached, then was blindfolded and released into my recognizance. As an honorary member of the Brick City Browns, I was bound to protect the secrecy of Brown Town's location. So I escorted him to my car, then drove around for a few blocks before allowing him to remove his blindfold.

It wouldn't have surprised me at any point if Rashan had simply bolted. After all, it was clear I wasn't the muscle. It was possible Rashan was afraid the Browns would hunt him down if he ran. Or he might have felt beholden to me for having helped save him from horrible disfigurement. Either way, he had become quite docile, even cooperative.

And as we drove across town toward Hector Alvarez's home—the address Tommy gave me was on Sanford Avenue, in Newark's West Ward—he seemed amenable to chatting.

"So tell me again how Alvarez picked you out," I asked.

"I don't know, man. I was just going through the program like everyone else. I was getting toward the end. I think he knew I was about to be released. And he asked me what I was planning to do when I got out. I told him I didn't know. Then he started telling me about The Stuff."

"What did he tell you?"

"That it was the best. That I'd make a lot of money. That junkies went wild for it."

"Did they?"

"Oh, hell yeah. I got out like four months ago. My first contract was for two bricks—I was a little worried about biting off more than I could chew. But I didn't have no problems selling it. So I went up to four. I sold out every week. I didn't even have to find customers. They was finding me. I was thinking about going up to six or eight bricks, but now I don't know. I might quit."

"Why?" You know, besides the fact that it was illegal, immoral, and dangerous.

We idled at a stoplight. Rashan was staring out the passenger side window as he spoke. "That Ludlow Street thing, man," he said. "That's some cold business. I don't want to end up like that because some dude thinks I didn't follow my contract."

"Was that really in the contract you signed? The part about not cutting?"

"Yeah, man. I mean, I guess it was. I didn't realize they were that serious about it, though."

"You keep a copy of the contract?" I asked hopefully.

"Nah."

"Too bad," I said. There's something about documents supporting a story—any kind of documents—that editors absolutely love. I would estimate documents were the source of a third of all Brodie's newsroom erections.

"So did you know any of the Ludlow Four?" I asked.

"Nah."

"None of them?"

"Nah. I don't know any of the other dealers," he said. "It's like we all got our separate little things going on. The guy who gives me The Stuff, he tells me I'll never have to worry about competition. He said we all got our own turf and we'll never bump into each other."

"So that's why you don't quit?"

"Yeah, man," he said. "It's like guaranteed profit. Where else is a guy like me going to make that kind of money?"

Twenty lousy grand a year? How about down at the ports. In a trade union. Driving a truck. In fact, there were dozens of jobs where a young man like Rashan Reeves could make much better money and do it legally—but only if he was willing to be a little patient, get some training, and establish a decent work history.

"I think this is it," I said as we pulled up across the street from the Sanford Avenue address Tommy had given me. It was a two-story duplex with separate entrances adjacent to each other. Both sides were dark and there were no cars in the short driveway.

"Hang here for a second," I said.

I got out just in time to get sideswiped by a cold gust of wind. I walked quickly up the five stairs on the front porch. Hector Alvarez's address had an *A* after it, so I rang the doorbell on the left.

I hadn't necessarily formulated a plan for what I would do if Alvarez actually answered but it didn't matter. There was no one home.

Still, there were signs of continued occupancy: only one day's worth of mail in the box, a girl's bike chained to the railing, jackets hanging in the foyer. There was definitely a lived-in aura. It seemed worthwhile to stay for a while to see who might show up.

"Mind hanging here for a little bit?" I asked when I returned to the warmth of the Malibu.

"You mean, like a stakeout?" Rashan asked.

235

"Yeah, I guess."

"Cool," he said, sounding genuinely enthused. "You got your-self a pretty cool job, huh?"

"There are lots of cool jobs out there, Rashan," I said. "We'll have to find you one someday."

Ten minutes later, I was in the midst of explaining to Rashan the process of how a story got into the newspaper when a brand-new red Audi A4 rolled slowly past us and turned into the driveway. A short, round, middle-aged Hispanic man got out and Rashan practically jumped over the dashboard.

"That's him," he said. "That's Mr. Hector."

"Come on, Rashan," I said. "If you want to see how a reporter gets a story, this is a good place to start."

Or at least it was a good start if he wanted to get a feeling for ambush-style journalism, which is what this situation demanded. I closed in fast, with Rashan right behind me. Alvarez was barely out of his car when we were already on top of him.

"Hi, Hector, Carter Ross from the *Eagle-Examiner,*" I said. "And I'm sure you remember Rashan here."

Alvarez rocked back on his heels. He pretty clearly did remember Rashan and was too stunned to open his mouth.

"Rashan tells me you recruited him on behalf of a local drug syndicate," I continued. "You want to tell me who you're working for?"

Rashan and I had Hector more or less pinned against the open door of his Audi, which still had a faint new-car smell to it. Alvarez had a broad, fleshy face that was registering complete surprise.

"I, I don't know what you're talking about," he said, trying to recover from his shock but not doing very well.

"Well, then, let me remind you: Rashan was one of your patients in a drug and alcohol rehab program at East Jersey State Prison. When you realized he was nearing the end of his sentence and going back home to Newark, you offered to hook him up with a source for heroin."

"I don't know who he is. He's got me confused with someone else," Alvarez said halfheartedly. Rashan just scoffed.

"Sure, sure he does," I said. "Let me lay this out for you right now, Hector. You've been doing something very bad, something I'm sure the commissioner of the corrections department would be eager to hear about. Now, if you can help me out and tell me who you work for, maybe I can forget your name, you can forget your little sideline business, and everyone can move happily on with their lives. Or if you don't tell me who you're working for, I'll plaster your name in a nice big headline, and you'll not only lose your job, you'll end up serving time with some of the very same people you're counseling now."

I was pretty sure I had the man soundly beaten and just moments away from full confession. But apparently Hector Alvarez was a little more stubborn than I gave him credit for. That, and the shock was wearing off.

"He's lying to you," Hector said. "I'm a certified drug and alcohol counselor. I got a degree. Who are you going to believe, me or some punk?"

I glanced at Rashan, then back at Hector.

"The punk," I said.

"Then you go ahead and print your story and I'll sue your ass off," Alvarez said. "My cousin is a journalist. I know how this stuff works. You can't just print something because someone says it's true. This punk is lying."

Rashan shouted a few excited obscenities and faked a charge at Alvarez, who cringed. I grabbed Rashan by his backpack, and he allowed himself to be restrained—basically because he wasn't planning on jumping Alvarez anyway.

"Calm down, Rashan," I said. "We're just having a conversation here. Because now Hector is going to explain how he can afford this very nice new automobile on a drug counselor's salary."

Alvarez gazed longingly at the Audi for a second then turned back to me like I was talking about stealing his firstborn.

"That's none of your business," he said.

"You make thirty-eight grand a year, Hector," I said. "I looked it up. I can also look up how much money you owe on your house. I'm guessing between your house payment and car payment, something won't add up. Unless, of course, there's some, you know, outside stream of income. But I'm sure you can explain that all to the IRS after I run my story."

"Screw you," Hector said.

I lost control of my inner wiseass and pulled out my notepad.

"Is that your official comment, Mr. Alvarez? 'Screw you'?"

"Suck my dick," he said.

"Interesting," I said, pretending I was writing that down, too. "Not only is he the Crooked Drug Counselor of the Year, Mr. Alvarez is also a homosexual."

Alvarez slammed the door to the Audi and stormed past us toward his house. "If you got anything more to say to me, you can talk to my lawyer," he said.

"I'm not going away, Hector," I called out as Alvarez fumbled with his keys. "But you can end this little problem in one sentence. Just give me a name and you get to keep your job."

He stuck the key in the lock, turned it, then looked at me.

"You just don't get it, do you?" he said, shortly before disappearing through his front door. "You think I'm worried about my *job*?"

The door slammed. I stuffed my notebook in my pocket and turned to walk back to the car. Rashan didn't follow.

"What!?" he said. "That's it? You're not going to go break the door down?"

"I'm a newspaper reporter, not a bounty hunter," I said.

"But he's lying!"

"I know. No law against lying to a newspaper reporter. It happens all the time."

"So you just let him go?"

"I may call him later—but only when he's cooled down," I said. "I took a chance that ambushing him like this would catch him off guard and he'd just start blabbing. It didn't work."

"But you're going to go write the story now, right?"

"Before I write it, I have to prove it," I said. "Rashan, I know you're telling the truth. And I could tell that guy was full of crap. But unfortunately, Hector is right: no one is going to believe a drug-dealing ex-con over someone who works for the Department of Corrections. I need to verify your story two or three different ways before my editors will even think about printing it."

Rashan stuck out his lower lip in a convincing pout, making it clear his first brush with journalism had left him rather unsatisfied.

"This isn't a Western, Rashan," I continued. "The guys in the white hats don't always win. At least not right away. Sometimes you got to keep at it for a long time before you get the payoff."

With that particular bit of advice, I was talking about more than just journalism. But it was hard to tell if Rashan was listening anymore. I had disappointed him and now he was tuning me out.

"Get in the car," I said. "I'll give you a ride home."

"Nah," he said. "I ain't going back there."

I didn't know if he meant now or ever.

"Okay. Well, here's my card," I said, handing it to him. "Give me a call sometime, okay?"

"Uh-huh," Rashan said, then, without looking at me, turned and walked off into the night, his soda can tabs jingling as he went. I watched him go until all I could see was the night reflector strip on his backpack bobbing up and down. Then I went back to the Malibu, feeling the weight of the day settle on me.

It was getting to be six, which felt a lot like quitting time. And on a normal Friday, after a rough week at the office, I might just head home, curl up with Deadline, and watch *Braveheart* for approximately the fiftieth time. Except now my copy of *Braveheart* was just one more piece of ruin in what used to be my house. And, sadly, so was Deadline.

Then there was the other standby Friday-night activity for the suddenly overstressed: going out to some local bar, getting mind-blowingly drunk, and hitting on anything under the age of forty that wasn't utterly repulsed by me. Except there was the small problem of what I would do if I actually succeeded in luring some lovely young lady into my clutches. *Hey, honey, what do you say we go back to my place. I've got this great little debris pile not far from here . . .*

No, I was pretty much cruising for another night on Tina's couch—or maybe, if I could stop being such a loser, Tina's bed.

I just had one last errand to accomplish before I started traveling that way. Call it a mission of guilt: I wanted to see if I could find anyone who had seen Red or Queen Mary since their building got blown up. It wasn't going to do them a lot of good if they were, in fact, underneath the rubble of Building Five. But I felt like I at least owed it to them to check.

So I made the turn off South Orange Avenue, not far from the Wyoming Fried Chicken where my buddy North Face was likely on patrol, and soon found myself back in the odd netherworld that was the remains of the Booker T. Washington Public Housing Project.

It was its usual empty, forlorn self—though instead of six large, empty brick buildings, there were now five. The search-and-rescue mission had been called off. So it was just me and the ghosts again.

I started looking around for signs of life, peering in the corners and behind the shadows just like I had been doing a few days earlier. The wind was managing to find a way to blow up my pants, which felt even less pleasant than it sounds. I pulled my jacket closer to my body and kept hoping for that whiff of smoke or glimpse of light that would indicate I was not alone.

But I was. Obviously I was. And yet I kept standing there as, what, self-punishment? As if I could somehow atone for Red and Queen Mary dying a horrible death by standing out in the cold and looking for them? What the hell was I doing here?

I was losing it. I must be, right? Why else would I be shivering in the courtyard of an abandoned Newark housing project waiting for two dead people to show up? I felt this hysteria creeping all over me, like my rational mind was separating from me, slipping off into the ether where it would never again be found. I cupped my hands to my mouth and started yelling as loud as I could.

"Rrrreeeedddd," I hollered. "Rrrreeeedddd!"

I kept bellowing, each time pausing to listen for a response but only hearing the sound of my own voice echoing off cold, hard brick walls.

The Director picked up the call on the second ring, looking at his cell phone like it offended him. It was unusual for one of his people to call at this hour—or any hour for that matter. They were instructed to contact Monty on routine matters. And the Director had set up his organization so most matters had become routine.

"Speak," the Director said.

"It's Hector. Hector Alvarez."

The Director could practically hear Alvarez gulping through the phone. The Director did not like Alvarez, a former drug addict turned counselor. The Director had little respect for addicts. He viewed them as weak, lacking self-control.

But dealer recruitment was not something the Director wanted to do himself. He came up with the idea for recruiting in prisons early on. It just made sense. Most of the inmates were there for dealing drugs in the first place, so they already knew the business. Plus, recruiting in jail meant you weren't taking the unnecessarily dangerous step of swiping active dealers from other syndicates or gangs.

It hadn't taken long working through the Director's various Department of Corrections contacts to find Alvarez. He and the Director had a few beat-around-the-bush conversations, but the Director knew the first time they spoke he had found the right man. Alvarez had the taste for the finer things in life but not the paycheck. He had that sense of grandiosity, common among addicts, that convinced him he was due more than what life was giving him.

The arrangement with Alvarez, as it was with the recruiters in the other prisons, was simple: he received a cash bounty for every dealer he channeled to the Director. Yet while the Director valued Alvarez's service, he had little patience for the man himself—especially when he was being hysterical like this.

"Get a hold of yourself," the Director commanded.

"I'm sorry. I just got a visit from a reporter, a guy from the Eagle-Examiner," Alvarez said through shallow breaths. "I think he's on to us."

"Explain."

"Well, he had one of the dealers with him. Rashan Reeves. I got him for you a couple months ago. Remember him?"

"I do," the Director said. The Director knew who all his dealers were, even if they didn't know him.

"Yeah, so the reporter is like, 'Rashan here tells me you're recruiting drug dealers from jail. I'm going to write a story about you if you don't tell me who you work for.'"

"And you told him . . . what?"

"Nothing," Alvarez said, his voice cracking slightly. "I told him to screw off, and that was it."

"So by 'on to us,' you really mean 'on to you,' " the Director said coolly.

Alvarez did not reply.

"Well, you're calling me," the Director said. "Is there something you want me to do about this?"

"I just . . . I thought you should know."

"Fine. What's this reporter's name?" the Director asked, even though he already knew the answer.

"I don't know. He said his name so fast."

"Carter Ross."

"Yeah, that's it!" Alvarez said. "I swear, I didn't tell him anything."

"And where is Mr. Ross now?"

"I don't know. He just left."

The Director frowned. The Director thought he had rid the world of Carter Ross with one push of a wireless detonator. It had surprised the Director to see Ross alive and breathing on the News at Noon. Clearly, he needed to be dealt with. Immediately.

As for Alvarez . . .

"So, tell me, Hector, how old is that little girl of yours?" the Director asked.

"She just turned nine," Alvarez replied, his voice faltering.

"How nice," the Director said. "Tell her happy birthday."

CHAPTER 8

I must have yelled Red's name twenty or thirty times, with each repetition a little louder, a little more desperate than the last. I yelled until my throat went raw and I lost the breath to yell anymore.

But he wasn't there. Or perhaps he was, but only as a corpse buried under several tons of debris. I started walking toward Building Five to, I don't know, say a prayer or something. Then somewhere off in the distance, I heard a faint voice.

"Who there?" it said.

"Red?" I shouted one final time.

"What you want?" the voice said, and this time I could trace it a little better. It was coming from Building Three. And it sounded like Red.

I ran toward Building Three, pushing my numb legs to move as fast as they could. As I got closer, I saw Red's patchy-bald head sticking out of a second-story window. I never thought I would be so happy to see an old homeless man in Newark.

"Hey, Red!" I said, feeling some warmth returning to my body. "Remember me? Carter Ross from the *Eagle-Examiner.*"

"Yessir. I got Queen Mary right here," he said, then lowered his voice for a moment. "I'm trying to get me a little some, you know what I mean?"

I was so happy to see him alive, it didn't bother me that the image of two aging addicts in the throes of passion was now drifting through my mind.

"Why aren't you dead right now?" I asked.

"Oh, you mean with the building and all that? Shoooot," he said. Red was directly above me, one story up. I was still on ground level, which made me feel like the world's weirdest Romeo looking up at the world's ugliest Juliet.

"Yeah, you weren't in Building Five this morning?"

"Oh, I was there," Red said.

"Then how did you not get blown up?"

"Aw, hell, youngster, I got more lives than a kitty cat," Red boasted. "Can't nothing blow me up."

"You mean you were inside?"

"Well, I was jus' layin' in there with Queen Mary"—more bad visuals—"when I heard this racket coming from the fire escape," he began, and I imagined this was not his first time telling the story today. "An' I was thinking, 'Who's comin' visitin' at this time of the mornin'?' Our friends ain't exactly early risers, you know?"

I nodded. Red sounded a little less drunk than the first time

246

I spoke with him, which was to say he might have only been two sheets to the wind instead of the usual three.

"So I stole a peek around the corner, an' I saw this guy with a bunch of dy-no-mite. An' I thought he was from the city, come to blow the buildin' up. They's always talking about how they gonna blow it up. An' I jus' thought maybe today was the day, an' they jus' hadn't told none of us street people, you know?"

"Right," I said.

"So I watch him go 'bout his bidness, pickin' out a wall and tapin' his dy-no-mite and fussin' with all his doodads. And then he musta gone and taped it to some other walls or something, I don't know. But as soon as he was gone, I went an' got Mary. An' I said, 'Mary, we best be gettin' usselves outta here. It about to blow.' An' you know what she said?"

"What?"

"She said, 'Awww, there you go again,'" Red said, and then started howling with hee-haws, punctuating it with some woo-hoos, then finishing with some hoo-wees. I laughed to be polite, having no idea what he found so funny. Then again, I'm not sure it was fair to expect total clarity from a guy whose last sober day had probably been while I was in the first grade.

"So I said, 'No, no, Mary, we got to go. I mean, we got to go *now*,'" Red said. "An' she didn't say nothin'. An' I said, 'Mary, we got to *go*.' An' I done picked her up and carried her out, jus' like I was Superman."

I was having a tough time believing Red could carry a well-mannered lapdog—much less an inert old woman—down a fire escape. And apparently so did Queen Mary.

"There you go again!" she hollered from somewhere inside the building. And Red, finding this every bit as inexplicably hysterical as last time, started with a fresh round of har-hars, tee-hees, and ho-hos. I let him finish and he continued.

"Now, we wasn't out of the buildin' mo' than three minutes and, *WHAMBO*, the whole damn place done gone sky-high, and then it fell down, jus' like it was a deck of cards fallin' in on is-self. It was a terrible noise like you ain' never heard. And you know what?"

"What?"

"It wasn't no man from the city after all. Folks here is sayin' it was jus' a man up to no good, jus' wantin' to blow up our buildin' because he don' wan' it here no more. Can you believe that?"

"Actually, I can," I said. "He blew up my house, too."

Red couldn't have looked more surprised if a bottle of Majorska vodka up and started talking to him.

"You don' say!" he said. "Mary, you hear that? Remember that white boy who got us the food? That big feller with the dy-no-mite, he done blowed up the white boy's house, too!"

"I heard him the first time," Mary said tersely from inside the building.

"Well, don' get all sore. I was jus' sayin'," Red said, then turned and gave me the universal male shrug that loosely translated to, *Women, what can you do?*

"Red, tell me something. The guy with the bunch of dynamite, how big was he?"

"Little bit taller than you an' about twice as wide. He had hisself a neck like a bull."

Red held his hands a fair distance apart to signify a substantial width. That sounded like Van Man to me.

"Did you get a good look at him?" I asked.

"Sho' as I'm lookin' at you right now, youngster."

This was getting too good to be true. Not only was Red alive, he was possibly the only living witness who could ID a serial murdering arsonist. And, yes, there was the small problem of what, exactly, Red had managed to see through his Mad Dog 20/20 goggles. But it was still a hell of a lot better than nothing.

"What did he look like?"

"Well, like I said, he was a big feller an . . ."

"Do you think you could describe him to a sketch artist?" I said, cutting to the chase.

With that, Red leaned back from the window for a moment, straightening himself.

"Well, now," he said. "That all depend, don't it?"

I caught his drift immediately.

"Another trip to the store on me," I said.

Red flashed a smile that displayed his teeth—both of them— and said, "Make it three."

With the issue of compensation settled, Red and I hopped into the Malibu, which I turned in the direction of police headquarters. I drove quickly, mostly because Red was stinking up my car so badly I was afraid the upholstery might need to be detoxed if he stayed in there too long. With my non-driving hand, I called Tina.

She answered the phone with all the warmth I expected.

"You're a total ass," she said.

"I know, I know."

"No, you don't know. I'm sitting here wondering if you're dead or alive like I'm some kind of damn war bride. *I am not a damn war bride!*"

Tina was clearly a little crazed (is there such a thing as mind-altering ovulation hormones?). And while in my younger days I'd tried reasoning with crazy women, I had reached the conclusion, sometime in the wisdom of my late twenties, that it was simply not possible. As long as she was immersed in crazy, it was better to just agree with whatever she said until she emerged from said state. I guess you could say I had become a conscientious nonob-jecter.

"You're right," I said. "You're not a war bride."

"If you think you're getting any tonight, you are so mis-taken."

"I never thought that for a moment," I said.

"For a while, I was thinking about teasing you and leaving you with a crippling case of blue-balls. But the fact is, I am so *repulsed* by you right now, I'm not sure I even want to be in the same room with you."

"Definitely separate rooms," I concurred.

"Make that separate zip codes."

"So should I find another place to spend the night?"

"Of course not," she spat. "Don't be an ass."

"Sorry."

"You have no idea how sorry you are!" she said, and then all I heard was the slamming of a phone.

I looked over at Red, who had this knowing smile on his face.

"I'm not sure I understand what just happened," I said.

"Sounds like you got woman problems," he observed.

"I suppose I do."

"Ain' nothing you can do 'bout it," Red said with what was, for him, a philosophical air. "Sometimes those women, they jus' love you so much they gotta yell at you to show it."

"Is that so?"

"Trus' me. I've had mo' women love me like that than I can count."

I nodded. Red started scratching himself. And we left it at that. I found a metered space not far from the Green Street en-trance to police headquarters and herded Red inside.

After sliding my business card through a slot in the bullet-proof glass, I explained to the desk sergeant that the musty-looking gentleman with me had gotten a good look at the guy who blew up the Booker T building this morning.

The desk sergeant, an older guy with a white flattop who was probably just trying to hang on for another year or two until retirement, gave me this you-gotta-be-kiddin'-me look and picked up the phone. He talked for a few moments, then clicked on the microphone that allowed his voice to be heard in the lobby.

"One minute," he said.

Red had already settled into the ancient couch in the lobby. He probably knew as well as anyone, when you were waiting for the Newark police, you might as well get comfortable.

"So, have you always lived around here?" I asked.

"Naw, I been all over," he said. "North Carolina. Maryland. Georgia. Served in Germany when I was in the army."

"You were in the army?"

"What? You think I been a bum all my life?"

"I didn't mean it like that," I began.

"Tha's okay," he said, laughing. "I'm jus' messin' witchya. I like bein' a bum. Can't nobody tell you what to do when you don't got no boss to please and no landlord to pay."

Tough to argue with that worldview . . . y'know, as long as you don't mind sleeping in abandoned buildings in Newark.

"So how long have you, uh . . ."—been a bum—"lived in Newark?"

"I dunno. What year is it now?"

"Two thousand and—" I started.

But he was laughing again. "Come on, now, still messin' witchya. I guess I been here, off an' on, for 'bout twenty year. Used to go down South for the winter, jus' thumb my way down then thumb my way back. But I'm getting' too ol' for that. Thumbin' ain' what it used to be. An', besides, Mary'd miss me."

251

"How long you and Mary been, uh . . ."—knocking boots—"with each other?"

"Oh, I'd say fo' or five year now. Off an' on. Can't tie me down to jus' one woman, you know. But sometimes I wonder what woulda happen if we met when we was younger. Maybe things woulda been different. Maybe we woulda had a family . . ." Red said, his voice trailing off.

How about that. Red Coles was not only homeless by choice, he was also a bit of a romantic. I was about to comment on it when Hakeem Rogers emerged from behind a door and motioned toward Red.

"Three shoppin' trips, right?" Red said.

"Three trips," I said with a nod, and Red bounced off the couch and through the door. I gave chase but was stopped by the lieutenant's outstretched hand.

"You his daddy?" Rogers asked.

"Huh? No."

"His mommy?

"No."

"Then you can't come with him," Rogers said, pleased with himself.

"No fair outwiseassing a wiseass," I said.

"They give me bonus pay for pissing you off," Rogers replied. "Can't wait to spend that check."

"Yeah, now you'll finally be able to get your mother that syphilis treatment she's been needing," I said. Then I called out to Red, "I'll see you when you're done."

Figuring I had a little time to kill, I went to a nearby pizzeria for two much-needed slices and a much-more-needed Coke Zero. On the way back, I swung by my car and retrieved the envelope the Browns had taken off Rashan. I had only glanced at its contents earlier and wanted to give them more serious scrutiny.

I slid the photos out and shuffled through them one by one, trying to study each in a variety of different ways. It's amazing the things you can glean from a photo simply by breaking it down a little—looking at it piece by piece, instead of as a whole; cutting it up into an imaginary grid and only staring at one quadrant at a time; or holding it at certain angles or distances.

So that's what I did, poring over each picture detail by detail. It was gut-roiling work. The exit wounds had mangled the victims' features to the point where you weren't sure if you were looking at human beings or roadkill.

Still, you could (sort of) tell how beautiful Wanda Bass had once been. Tyrone Scott (kind of) looked like a guy who always grabbed a second helping at Sunday dinner. Shareef Thomas (maybe) had been a lady's man, with a scraggly little beard and a soul patch. Devin Whitehead? His shoulder-length dreadlocks covered part of his face, so it was hard to get much of a read on him.

Ordinarily, if you dissect a photograph long enough, it will gradually yield its secrets. It can tell you things not only about the scene being captured but the person who did the capturing. Over time, I think you can even begin to understand the intent of the photographer, how he felt about his subject and what he really wanted to show you.

But for as much as I examined these pictures, they never became more than what they appeared to be at first glance: four horrific portraits of people whose petty crime had been deemed worthy of death by a pitiless judge. Four faces of people now gone.

The memo wasn't much more useful. In its own way, it was every bit as cold and spare as the pictures, leaving almost no room for interpretation.

I leaned back in my seat and looked up, slightly bleary-eyed from having stared at the photos so long. I was getting tired of playing detective. And it was only when I slipped off my detective hat and started thinking like a journalist again that I remembered the materials in my lap would make for a fantastic story.

A deranged drug lord who sent corporate memos to his dealers like they were middle managers in cubicles? Yep, Brodie would get such a boner over that he wouldn't be able to walk.

I looked at the clock on my cell phone. 7:37 P.M. No point trying to squeeze it into tomorrow's paper. We had plenty of news already, what with buildings blowing up across the circulation area. Besides, the Sunday editor would be cruising for something that would keep us in the lead on the Ludlow Street story. This would fit that need.

It occurred to me I also might want to make some copies of the Director's gruesomely illustrated package and hand them over to the National Drug Bureau. But then I remembered my last interaction with L. Pete, which had left me hoping he contracted an incapacitating toe fungus. If he wasn't going to be better at sharing, I would just keep my toys to myself. He could read about the photos in Sunday's paper like everyone else; then *maybe* I would hand them over. If he promised to behave. Or if he subpoenaed me.

I looked at my phone again: 7:40. Red had been with the sketch artist for about an hour, and I couldn't decipher whether that was a good sign (because Red gave them a lot of detail for an accurate portrait) or a bad one (because Red was so incoherent he was making the perp look like the Elephant Man).

He reemerged a few minutes later, triumphantly waving a sheet of paper above his head.

254

"This is him," he said. "This is the guy."

This was Van Man. I looked at the sketch, hoping it might spark some recognition. Red had described a doughy-cheeked, thick-necked, middle-aged white man with a receding hairline. The guy looked more like a candidate for erectile dysfunction medicine than a serial murderer. I don't want to say the sketch was completely useless, inasmuch as I suppose it could rule out some people. But if you went by this picture alone, half the country club members in New Jersey had just become suspects.

"I tol' the computer what he look like and the computer done made this picture," Red said. "Tha's one smart computer."

"We just got the system," Rogers told me. "It lets us tweak things until we get it just right. Cuts the time to get a sketch done in half."

I looked down at the picture again, trying to imprint the face in my brain in case it should suddenly round a corner in my immediate future.

"So what will you guys do with this?" I asked.

"We'll send it to our many friends in the media, of course," Rogers said. "Then we'll show it to the officers in the patrol division."

"And then you give it to the National Drug Bureau?" I said.

"Yeah, I guess."

"What do you mean, you guess? You said they've taken over the case."

"Oh, they've taken it, all right. The lead guy in the Newark office called our chief and made a big stink. Then when our detectives paid them the courtesy of going over there with a box full of evidence, they gave 'em the usual 'we're feds, we're better than you' act. Bunch of jerk-offs, if you ask me. But you can't quote me on that."

Red wasn't any more eager to hang at police headquarters than I was. So we cleared out and I took us in the direction of the Pathmark on Bergen Street, the only major chain supermarket in Newark. A deal was, after all, a deal. I encouraged Red to buy whatever he wanted—after all, it was sort of my fault his last haul of groceries had blown up. But Red's tab only came to $41.05.

"Can't carry but so much anyway," he told me.

I took him back to Booker T with misgivings about dropping him back into such a cold night. The wind had picked up again, and the forecast was calling for a low of seventeen degrees. Red didn't seem concerned by it. He was shaking a bit, but I didn't think it was from the cold.

"Are you sure you don't want me to take you to a shelter?" I asked.

"Naw, I gotta get me a little something to drink. An' if you go to the shelter, they take it from you," he said as another tremor racked his body. He was nearly sober and his nervous system was starting to go haywire without booze.

"Suit yourself," I said as the car pulled to a stop outside Booker T.

"Say, you mind loanin' me a few bucks?" he asked nervously.

I reached into my wallet and pulled out a ten. Perhaps it wasn't the most responsible thing to do, enabling his disease. But it felt like the humane thing to do under the circumstances. "This do?" I asked.

"Oh, that'll do fine," he said, pocketing it quickly. "I sho' do 'preciate it."

"No problem. Is this where I can find you over the next couple days or will you be on the move?"

"Well, Mary 'n me got usselves set up in Building Three

256

pretty good," he said. "I s'pose we be staying there for a little while."

"All right," I said. "Stay warm."

Then I added, "Thanks for your help, Red," and stuck out my right hand.

He grasped it—which was like shaking hands with forty-grit sandpaper—and flashed me a two-tooth smile.

"You best watch out for yo'self, youngster," he said. "This ain' no place for a white boy after dark." He thought for a moment and, still holding the handshake, said, "This ain' no place for no one after dark."

"I'll be careful, promise," I said. He let go of my hand, grabbed his groceries, and stumbled off into the night.

I watched him until he disappeared around the corner, then got moving. I had pushed my luck long enough.

Having nowhere else to go, I drove back to the office to make peace with my new roommate, Tina. On the way in, I passed Buster Hays, who was in the lobby, pulling on a trench coat.

"Have a nice one, Ivy," Buster said.

"You, too, Hays," I said, and was about to get in the elevator when something stopped me, something that had been tickling my brain for the last few hours and had now developed into a full-blown itch.

"Hey, you got a quick second?" I said.

Hays finished wrestling with his coat and glanced at his watch. "I'm officially thirty-seven minutes overdue for my first Scotch of the weekend. Make it fast."

"It's about Irving Wallace."

"Ah, Irving. He help you out?"

"He did. Twice, actually. I'm just curious: how do you know him?"

"Aw, shoot, Irving?" Buster said. "When I met him, you weren't even a stain on your mom's sheets."

"So, it's been a while . . ."

"Oh, it's been a while," Hays said, enjoying himself. This was Hays in his glory: seizing the chance to remind a young whippersnapper how much more he knew about the world, how many more sources he had, or how much longer he had been around the neighborhood. And I, being a young whippersnapper in need of the information, had no choice but to listen.

"Let's see," Hays continued. "I met Irving Wallace in roughly 1970? Or 1972? The first couple years I worked for this paper, I covered high school sports. You might not believe it, but back in the day, Irving Wallace, the mild-mannered chemist, was a beast of a center for the Summit High School boys' basketball team."

"Really?" I said, genuinely surprised.

"Oh, yeah. You see more kids like it now, just because kids are bigger these days. But they didn't make 'em like Irving back then. He was big and mean. He couldn't shoot a lick from the outside, but he was a ferocious rebounder—on offense and defense. He made all-conference on put-backs alone."

I became aware that my heart was pounding.

"How tall was he exactly?"

"Jesus, Ivy, it's not like I'm still carrying the roster," he said, sighing.

"You think he was maybe six four, six five?"

"Sure."

"How much you think he weighs now?"

"I don't know. I haven't seen him in years. We talk on the phone."

"Any chance he might have ballooned up a little bit?"

"We all do," Hays said, patting his stomach. "You doing an exposé on old fat men now?"

"No, I just . . . Who *does* he work for, anyway?"

"I really don't know. He's real secretive about that and I never bothered to ask because he's always been good about helping me when I need his expertise. He must have been in the military for a while, because he went to West Point. Irving tells me I wrote a story about it when he got accepted and I take his word for it. Forty years' worth of stories can tend to blend together," Buster said, then got a faraway look for a moment.

He continued: "Anyway, I don't know how long he was in the army—we weren't pen pals or anything—and I think he was in the private sector for a while. Then he switched to the government and we got reconnected when he ended up helping some sources of mine on a case. He remembered me from the old days, I remembered him. I still don't know what part of the government he's with—he's big on that 'I'd tell you but I'd have to kill you' crap. But I do know his title is 'lab director.'"

"Lab *director*?" I said. "So the people who work for him, they would call him 'Director.'"

The pounding in my chest had now spread. I could feel it in my head now, a tiny little jackhammer going at the base of my skull.

"I don't know," Hays said. "I guess so, yeah. Why is your face getting red?"

"It's just getting hot in here," I said, taking off my jacket.

"Well, I hear that Scotch calling my name. I better be going," he said, pushing through the door into the cold.

So Irving Wallace was six four or six five, possibly three hundred pounds. He had been a ferocious rebounder back in the day, the kind of guy who might grow into someone who was ferocious at other things. He had no shortage of access to heroin. What had he told me? That his lab saw thousands of kilos of heroin a year? That would certainly be enough to fuel a major distribution ring.

Then there was the coincidence that Wallace had just so happened to call Buster Hays out of the blue a few days earlier. Hays had said something about not having talked to the guy in forever and then, bam, Wallace called to chat him up the moment Hays's byline appeared on the Ludlow Street story.

Finally, there was that itchy spot in my brain: in the article, I had mentioned the Stop-In Go-Go, Miss B's apartment, and Building Five at Booker T as places where I had found evidence of The Stuff, and they had all been torched.

I had never mentioned my house in the article. I had only mentioned it to one person.

Irving Wallace.

The elevator arrived, and as I rode up, I began to wonder if there was any other information I had gathered that might make Irving Wallace fit with the crime.

Of course. The gun. Rosa Bricker—the funeral director with the unexpectedly keen eye for forensics—had offered the professional opinion that the shooter had used a .40-caliber pistol. It had struck me as odd at the time, because .40 caliber is generally used by law enforcement. But I had dismissed it by assuming the perp had gotten his mitts on some pensioner's gun—never thinking the perp *was* a pensioner.

What else? I began replaying each of my interactions with Irving Wallace. The first time he wasn't even going to talk to me until I said the words "Ludlow Street," and suddenly he was interested. He had seemed pretty paranoid, which I had chalked up to him being a fed. Really, it's because he was a criminal.

Our next talk was after he did the testing for me. He freely told me the samples were more than 99 percent pure. Why tell me that? Wouldn't that just lead me closer to the truth?

Then it dawned on me: free advertising. He told me I could write it was the purest heroin ever sold on the streets in America. He knew I would write it—newspaper reporters are suckers for superlatives like that. And once New Jersey's largest newspaper reported The Stuff was 99-plus percent pure, junkies from Newark all the way out to the Delaware Water Gap would be trying to get their hands on it. If I had the dexterity to kick my own ass, I would have.

Then I thought about how he ended that conversation:

Is what you gave me the only samples you have?

I have one more bag of each—The Stuff and the generic.

And you're keeping them in a safe place?

I'm going to tuck them away in my piggy bank at home.

Good. Wouldn't want them getting out.

In my piggy bank at home. Lord. That one little throwaway line, which wasn't even true, had nearly gotten me killed.

Then I thought about our latest conversation, when he tried to put me off the theory that La Cabra was responsible for Ludlow Street. What had he said? That someone like La Cabra wouldn't reach down to the street level in Newark? That someone was "snowing" me?

I chortled. It might have been the only factual thing he told me—it just conveniently left out that he was the person doing the snowing. Of course he would steer me away from La Cabra: he wanted to protect his boss.

I wondered how Irving Wallace, high school basketball hero and proud graduate of the U.S. Military Academy, could have fallen so far as to get in with a scumbag like José de Jesús

Encarcerón. What a sad, fascinating tale—one I would no doubt flesh out in the coming days.

My legs had switched into autopilot and taken me to my desk, where I sat down and immediately went to our handy voter registration database. I typed in "Irving Wallace" and found three of them living in New Jersey.

One was in South Jersey, beyond commuting distance. One was in East Orange, which would have made him one of about three white people in the whole city. But one was in Summit, on New England Avenue. The onetime pride of Summit High School had stuck around his hometown.

I typed the address from voter registration into our property-ownership database and found out that, indeed, Irving and Sharon Wallace owned a home on New England Avenue. And it was valued at $1.4 million. Not a bad little shack for a humble government scientist.

I turned next to Lexis-Nexis, which told me, among other things, that Irving Wallace did not have a mortgage on his shack. He owned it free and clear, no liens, no nothing.

"Must be very frugal," I said to myself.

"What's that?" a familiar voice said.

I looked up and Tina Thompson was sitting across from me.

"Oh, hi," I said, a little startled.

"I've been here for ten minutes," she said. "You've had your head buried in that screen the whole time. Another five minutes and I was going to start peeling off clothing and see if you would notice."

"Well, in that case . . ." I said, sticking my face three inches away from the screen and banging on the keys.

Tina giggled, then added an adorable smile/hair flip/eye bat combination. A little more than an hour ago, she had been breathing fire at me through the phone. And now she was . . . flirting with me?

"I know it's not unusual for me to be slow on something like this," I said. "But I'm trying to keep up: weren't you pissed at me?"

"Oh, very."

"And now you're . . ."

"Sorry."

"Sorry?"

The female of the species is, indeed, a most confounding creature.

"Yeah," she said. "Look, I'm sorry I've been so hard on you. That's why I came over here. You've had an awful day, the kind of day I wouldn't wish on anyone. And as I was thinking about it, I realized I was probably only making matters worse being such a bitch. And I feel just terrible about that. So I want to apologize."

"Oh, well, okay," I said. As far as I could track, Tina had gone from nurturing consoler (last night), to worried friend (this morning), to overprotective bodyguard (this afternoon), to ranting quasi-girlfriend (earlier this evening), to remorseful suppliant (right now), to . . . whatever she would be in five minutes.

"This is usually the point in the conversation when you should say something like, 'apology accepted,'" Tina prompted.

"Oh, yeah, yeah. Definitely. Apology accepted. It's been a long day."

"So we're okay now?"

"We're great."

She moved over to sit in an empty seat at the desk across from mine. My reward—the superspecial toe-curl smile—was followed by a more serious countenance.

"Are we good enough that I can give you a lecture?" she asked.

"I suppose I have one coming."

"It's real simple. Just be careful, okay? I care about you."

"I thought you only cared about my reproductive capacity," I said, fixing her with what I hoped was an endearing grin.

"Well, that, too. But I don't want to have to tell my future child that his father got killed three days after conception."

"Conception? Who says I'm going to sleep with you? Since when am I that easy?"

"Since puberty, I'm guessing."

Couldn't exactly counter that point, so I decided to lecture back for a moment.

"Okay, I know you're just looking out for me. And it's sweet, it really is. It shows your maternal side."

She blushed a bit.

"But," I continued, "this thing is, I don't know, it's like my responsibility now. I mean, there are four people in the morgue whose chances for justice are slipping away by the hour and it doesn't look like anyone in an official capacity cares much whether they get it. Then there's the matter of the woman in the hospital struggling for her life because of something I wrote."

Tina reached out across the desk and grabbed my hand.

"That's not true. You didn't send that woman to the hospital. Some monster with a gasoline can and a lighter did that."

"And the monster never would have known about Brenda Bass if it weren't for me. It's not like we have a Hippocratic oath in this business. But if we did, I think it's pretty clear I violated it."

"You're being way too hard on yourself," she said firmly.

"Look, I don't kid myself into thinking I can fix this mess— it's already too broken for that. But maybe I can make it a little better.

"Besides," I said, with the requisite dramatic pause, "I think I may know who the bastard is."

"Yeah?" she said, releasing my hand and sitting back, like she wanted to get a wide-angle look at me.

"Yeah. I was just about to visit him. Want to go for a ride?"

She drew back even farther.

"I'm not talking about a guns-blazing visit," I continued. "Just an arm's-length visit."

She looked around at the copy desk, where the most pressing business seemed to be parceling out a group dinner order that had just come in.

"I don't know if I can leave," she said. "After I decided I wasn't sleeping with you tonight I agreed to fill in as night assignment editor. Technically the paper is under my command right now."

"Well, then I guess I just won't tell you—"

"Oh, dammit, you're impossible. Fine. First edition is pretty much done, anyway. It's just a drive-by, right?"

Within five minutes, having bundled up against the cold, we were in my car, speeding toward the suburbs. I told Tina about the latest, ending with my brilliant deduction that Irving Wallace was "the Director" from the memo. Tina mostly just listened.

"So, basically, it's that he's tall, his title has 'director' in it, and he heard you make an offhand comment about your piggy bank," she said when I finished.

"Yeah," I said. "*And* the murder weapon was a forty-caliber gun like a fed would use. *And* he seems to have an overdeveloped curiosity for our coverage of the Ludlow Street murders. *And* he just seems like the kind of uptight guy who would write memos about things."

"Uh-huh," Tina said, but I could hear her uncertainty.

"*And* he's got a fully paid-off house in Summit worth $1.4 million," I added. "How does a government lab director swing that?"

"He could have inherited it," she pointed out. "You said he grew up in town. Maybe that was the family manse?"

"He's not old enough to have lost both his parents."

"Mmm-hmm. And how did Irving Wallace find Hector Alvarez?"

"I haven't figured that out yet," I said. "But it stands to reason someone who does drug testing would have connections in the drug treatment community. The world isn't that big."

I turned off the interstate at the Summit exit, and not fifteen minutes after we departed Newark's gritty streets we were driving along the tree-lined avenues of one of New Jersey's nicest suburbs. This state could give you socioeconomic whiplash that way.

"But you think Irving Wallace works for this La Cabra fellow?" Tina said.

"Well, I'm not a hundred percent sure about that one," I admitted. "Call that a maybe. I mean, he did seem to go out of his way to try to throw me off that trail, like he was protecting someone. Why would he do that?"

"But, turn it around for a second, why would La Cabra want to work with Irving Wallace?" Tina asked as we climbed a hill, past rows of houses that got nicer as the elevation rose.

"What do you mean?"

"I'm saying, just imagine you're a Colombian drug lord. You can probably convince just about any bad guy in America to work with you. Why would you want to collaborate with someone who works for the government?"

"Well, because . . . because that way the government wouldn't come after you," I said. "Irving Wallace would be able to mislead them from the inside, push them in other directions."

"No good," Tina said. "I love conspiracy theories as much as the next girl. But there is just no way some bureaucrat with a chemistry set is going to convince the entire U.S. Department of Justice to call off the dogs on one of the world's most notorious drug kingpins."

"Good point," I said. I should have thought of that myself. The La Cabra thing may have just been the National Drug Bureau's ill-conceived way to explain four dead bodies, with no more credibility than the Newark police's ill-considered bar-stickup theory. "I suppose it's possible Irving Wallace is acting alone," I conceded.

"Okay, so without the Colombian drug lord, how did Irving Wallace get the product he needed for his operation?" Tina asked.

"His lab tests thousands of kilos a year," I said as we passed a sign for a hospital, then neared a train station. "He told me that himself."

"And you think he got his drugs by skimming off a portion of whatever his lab got sent for testing."

"Yeah, that's it."

"What about chain of custody?"

"What do you mean?"

"Well," she said, "any drug seized by a law enforcement agency is eventually going to be used as evidence in a trial, right?"

"If all goes well, yeah."

"So part of being used in evidence is having a clean chain of custody. Every person who handles it along the way has to sign something attesting that they didn't tamper with it."

"Uh-huh. And?" I asked, as we rolled past a YMCA, a library, a quaint little park, all the trappings of a well-tended, well-to-do town.

"I'm just saying that it's not like John Q. Detective is going to fork over ten kilos of heroin to the lab and then not notice when only five kilos come back," Tina said. "How did he get around that?"

"I don't know. He's a bright guy. He could have figured out something, I'm sure."

"Oh, of course," Tina said. "But then there's the issue of purity."

"What issue?" I asked, feeling increasingly worn down by Tina's cross-examination. It was like being a rookie reporter again, and the editor was asking me all the questions I had been too feebleminded to think of myself.

"Well, Wallace told you—what was it you put in the paper? That it was the purest heroin ever sold?"

"Right." I said, making a turn at a convenience store and passing several majestic Gothic churches.

"Okay, even assuming he was lying, everyone else has told you The Stuff was the best, that junkies adored it," she said. "So we can assume it was pretty high purity."

"Yeah, so?"

"So all Wallace has access to is heroin that has been seized off the street and comes into his lab. How is he possibly going to take that—a lot of which is garbage—and turn it into this product that drove all the junkies wild?"

"Christ, Tina," I finally exploded. "He's a chemist. Don't you think he knows how to do something like that?"

"Okay, okay. Don't get defensive. I'm just saying we have a few blanks to fill in, that's all."

"Editors," I huffed. And she let me leave it at that.

Our destination, New England Avenue, was just on the other side of the downtown area, opposite the Grand Summit Hotel. We passed some apartments, then some town houses, then some smaller houses, then some larger ones. Then we came to the Irving Wallace residence. The place was completely dark, but I didn't so much as tap the brakes as we rolled by.

"Hey, you passed it," Tina said.

"I know," I said, and drove two blocks farther down before turning around. On the way back, I turned off the headlights and we coasted to a stop. I didn't know if the subterfuge was necessary, but it couldn't hurt. Besides, with the lights off, it was less likely for a neighbor to notice a strange car and decide to call the cops. In Newark, my four-year-old Chevy Malibu was well camouflaged. In Summit, amid all the fancy imports and high-end domestics, it might as well have come with a neon sign that said JUST VISITING.

We took some time to stare at the house, looking for, I don't know, signs of evil aura or something. But it was just your basic Tudor, slightly on the large side but not a mansion by any stretch. I was guessing five bedrooms, three baths, no more. Don't get me wrong, it looked like it could keep the rain off your head. But it didn't entirely fit what I was envisioning.

"I guess $1.4 million doesn't buy that much anymore," I said.

"Not in Summit, New Jersey, it doesn't. Not even after a real estate slump."

"Where do you think he buries his money?"

"Isn't it always beneath the trapdoor that Scooby and Shaggy accidentally fall into?" Tina asked.

"Yeah, and he would have gotten away with it if not for us meddling kids," I said.

I turned my attention back toward the house. There was a basketball hoop in the driveway. The hedges were neatly trimmed. There were two large trees in the front lawn, each of which looked to be a minimum of a hundred years old. There were no cars in the driveway, no sign of white vans anywhere—

269

though I'm sure he would have been smart enough to stash his dirty-work vehicle elsewhere.

"I think I'll go ring the doorbell," I said.

Tina whirled to face me and voice her objections.

"Kidding," I said, before she could get them out.

I shifted the Malibu out of park, turning the headlights back on when we had gotten under way. There was nothing to be gained by confronting Irving Wallace at this point. Fact was, as Tina had so effectively pointed out, I hadn't even begun to figure out how his operation worked. And until I had a better idea, it was best that he not know I was closing in on him.

The newsroom was peaceful when we returned. By ten o'clock on a typical Friday night, there are usually more people working on the Sunday paper than are still fretting over Saturday's edition, so no one is in too big a hurry. It's not that we didn't take Saturday seriously, but . . . oh, hell, who am I kidding? We didn't take Saturday seriously. It was our smallest paper of the week and the one day a week that didn't count toward the numbers we gave to the Audit Bureau of Circulation. It was the closest a daily paper could come to taking a day off.

Tina had another two hours before she could abandon ship and focus her energies on entertaining me. I thought about borrowing her house key, crashing on her couch for a while, maybe rifling through her underwear drawer for fun. But—and maybe I just watch too many horror movies—I didn't want to be the male equivalent of the dumb blonde at home alone when the axe murderer was on the loose.

Besides, if I went back to Tina's place by myself, there would be nothing to do but mull things over, and there was no sense in letting my brain do too much catching up. I was afraid it would put me on the next flight to the Bahamas if it did.

So I ambled over to chat up Peterson, night rewrite man nonextraordinaire, to see what mayhem he was chronicling. Peterson started at the *Eagle-Examiner* as a clerk, when he was seventeen. As best I could tell, that had been 150 years ago—give or take. He moved into night work early in his career and had been doing it ever since.

Peterson's job essentially consisted of waiting for people to die. If they died of natural causes, he wrote an obit. If the cause was unnatural, he wrote a news story. It would be impossible to put an exact number on how many thousands of New Jerseyans had their demises chronicled by Peterson. But when you figure he averaged two hundred bylines a year, the numbers added up.

Yet it never seemed to grow old to him. He attacked each death with relish, eagerly ferreting out the details that would allow him to write that the deceased was beloved by all (if it was an obit) or that a death had shocked an otherwise quiet community (if it was a murder) or that the deceased met his end amid the squeal of skidding tires and the shriek of breaking glass (if it was a car crash). His penchant for cliché was legendary.

But on this night, he looked bored.

"Hey, how's it going?" I asked.

"Pretty quiet tonight," he said glumly. "Only one shooting."

"Is it anything you can turn into a story?"

"I don't think so. Just another Newark kid."

He yawned out of boredom. I yawned because yawning is contagious and because I had been going nonstop for fourteen hours—and was starting to feel it.

"Police give you an ID?" I asked, just to keep the conversation going.

"Nope. He's John Doe. They're still looking for next of kin. We'll be lucky if we get an ID in Monday's paper."

"Where'd it happen?"

"They won't say."

I cocked my head.

"What do you mean they won't say?" I asked. If nothing else, we could always get a location.

Peterson yawned again. "They were being coy with me. Gave me the old 'it's an ongoing investigation' and told me to call back later."

"What time did you have that conversation?"

"I don't know, an hour ago?"

"Well, it's later now, isn't it? What do you say you give our good friend Hakeem Rogers a call?"

"Good point," he said, grabbing the phone and jabbing at the numbers. Peterson was from the manual-typewriter generation and therefore believed all buttons needed to be depressed with brute force, lest they fail to register.

"Rogers, it's Peterson," he said into the handset. "What's going on with the kid who ate the bullet?" He waited. "I know you don't have an ID. But you gotta have a location for me." More pause. "Well, what gives, Rogers? How am I supposed to write a story that says someone got killed but we don't know who and we don't know where and we don't know how? This is a newspaper, not a game of Clue." Another pause. "Well, I don't give a rat's ass what your captain says. Tell your captain the law says the public has a right to know and I got a deadline." Briefer pause. "Fine. Put him on."

Peterson cupped the phone and looked at me. "I don't know why they're always playing these games with me. Every night, it's like Professor Plum with the wrench in the study."

Peterson returned the phone to his mouth. "Hi, Captain, it's Peterson. Am I going to have to sic our lawyers on you guys or can we get a little cooperation here?"

The captain started speaking and Peterson's hands suddenly

came to life. He flipped his notebook to a blank page and began scribbling madly. Peterson was excitable by nature, so it was hard to tell if this was routine or if he was onto something big. I did my best to divine what was happening from Peterson's half of the conversation:

"No kidding . . . Unbelievable . . . The exact same place? . . . Against the back fence? . . . How many? . . . Where? . . . Damn. And the call came in when? . . . Any witnesses? . . . You think it's connected to the thing from before? . . . Yeah, I'll hang on."

Peterson cupped the phone again. "You're not going to believe this," he said. "But they found another body in that vacant lot down on Ludlow Street."

didn't wait for Peterson to finish with the captain.

"I'm heading down there," I told him. "Call me."

Peterson nodded, returning his attention to his notepad. It occurred to me I should tell Tina where I was heading, partly as a courtesy and partly because she was in charge of the newspaper at the moment. But she was off in a far corner hovering over some page proofs with the copy desk chief, immersed in conversation. So I pit-stopped at her desk, grabbed a sticky note and scribbled, "Going to Ludlow St. Ask Peterson.—C." Then I attached it to her computer screen and hurried toward the exact last place I wanted to be: back in the hood.

But there was no choice, really. I was the only one who could go. I don't say that out of some overdeveloped hero complex. I mean I was *literally* the only one who could go. Between the hiring freezes, the layoffs, and the voluntary buyouts—all symptoms of the newspaper's unceasing economic decline—our staff was half the size it once was. The days of keeping around spare bodies to throw at breaking news were long over. During off hours, we were down to one reporter, who stayed tied to the desk.

So I went back into the frosty night, barely tapping the Malibu's brakes at red lights on the way down to Ludlow Street. I was most of the way there when my cell phone buzzed with Peterson's number flashing on the screen.

"What do we know?" I said.

"At eight thirty-seven, a caller who identifies herself as a Ludlow Street resident hears five shots and immediately calls the cops.

"The police say they were down there in less than ten minutes to comb the neighborhood," Peterson continued. "They were smart enough to start in the vacant lot next to the church, and they found a young black male against the fence in the back, exactly where they found the bodies earlier this week. And I mean exactly. There were fresh bloodstains on top of the old ones."

"Hooo-lee smokes," I interjected.

"The kid was apparently a real mess. Those five shots the caller heard? The cops think all five bullets went, *bam*, right in the coconut. The captain wouldn't give much detail, but can you imagine five shots to the head? If you're talking about a gun with any amount of punch at all, that kid probably doesn't have much of a head left. They'll be picking pieces of brain off that fence for hours."

Peterson's usual talent for embellishment wasn't failing him in this critical moment. I just hoped that particular bit of creative writing didn't make it into the next day's paper.

"Anyway," he went on, "they're not going to bother taking the kid to the hospital. He was pronounced dead at the scene. It will be straight to the morgue for him."

"Any ID?"

"No. Not that they'd tell us if there was. But the captain said half the reason he was giving us so much information so quickly was that they may need the public's help in figuring out who the kid is. He wasn't carrying a wallet and his face is so messed up they're going to have to hope his prints are in the system. If not, it's wait until his mama comes looking for him."

I felt a momentary sadness for this kid's mama, whoever she was.

"The captain say whether he thought it was the same killer from before or is it just some copycat?" I asked.

"Well, that's the million-dollar question, isn't it?" Peterson said. "The captain wouldn't even discuss it with me. I'll read you the quote: 'At this point, we're just sticking with what we know. We are not speculating as to motive or connection to other crimes.'"

"What do you think?"

"I don't know. I mean, the first thing got enough publicity that it *could* be a copycat. The first time it was one shot in the back of the head. This time it was five shots . . ."

"Unless that signifies it's the fifth victim," I interrupted.

"Yeah, I thought about that," Peterson said. "Look, I don't know. But I got a story to write. Thompson says we can get this thing in second edition if I hurry."

"No byline, remember?"

"Believe me, I remember. I don't want anyone blowing up *my* house."

The call ended just as I made the turn onto Ludlow Street. A few blocks down, I was stopped not by the police but by the size of the crowd that had gathered. A homicide provides this weird kind of live theater for people who grow accustomed to living around it. Once word gets out someone has gotten shot, it's not unusual to get a decent-sized collection of gawkers, gossips, and busybodies trying to sneak a glance at the victim to see if it's someone they know.

Plus, once all the flashing lights start whirring and the cops blanket the scene, there's no safer place in the city.

You have to be careful what questions you pose to bystanders at a crime scene, because the power of suggestion can be strong.

For example, I would never ask, "Did anyone see a white van driving off?" Because maybe the first person you talked to wouldn't have seen the van, nor the second. But eventually word gets around the Bird Man is asking about a white van and, lo and behold, someone who wants to get a little attention will say they've seen it.

So as I waded through the throng, I tried to stick to non-leading questions—simple stuff like if anyone knew who the victim was or had any ideas about what had gone down.

Over the next five or ten minutes, as I worked my way closer to the crime scene, I heard the usual assortment of theories. Half the people were absolutely certain it had something to do with the earlier Ludlow Street murders. An equal number were just as convinced it was unrelated. The shooter was believed to be a local drug dealer named Antoine, a rogue Newark cop who went by the street name "Radar," or a jealous boyfriend who found another guy making time with his girl.

The shooting was everything from five shots (the supposedly correct version), to one shot (always popular), to a massive gun battle that nearly clipped an innocent bystander (according to the man who claimed to be the innocent victim and wanted my opinion as to whether he could sue someone and recoup damages on account of the trauma he suffered).

But no one had much of an idea who the victim was. That was a constant.

Finally—after receiving enough double takes from people

who couldn't believe a white guy was in their neighborhood at such a late hour—I made it to where the yellow police tape separated the civilians from the professionals.

The cops had put up some portable lights, allowing me to see into the back of the vacant lot. Sure enough, the body appeared to be exactly where I had seen the bloodstains earlier in the week. The corpse was covered with a white sheet, with only the sneaker-clad feet sticking out. I was beginning to think we were just going to have to wait on the police for an ID.

And then I saw it, lying no more than three feet from the body: a backpack adorned with soda can tabs. Rashan Reeves's backpack.

I dropped to one knee. It was either take a knee or topple over. A few hours earlier, Rashan Reeves had been riding in my car, asking me about what it was like to be a newspaper reporter, alive and inquisitive, possibly beginning to consider a world with alternatives beyond pushing drugs. And now he was just one more dead drug dealer, his life—and whatever potential he had—oozing out of him onto the dried weeds in some frozen vacant lot.

I felt like crying. And screaming. And ripping out every damn last one of those weeds so that maybe, come springtime, I could plant flowers there instead.

But none of that was going to do any good. So I just did my job. I pulled out my cell phone and called Peterson, informing him the victim was Rashan Reeves of Newark.

"How do you know?" Peterson barked.

"Because I interviewed him earlier this evening. He copped to being a drug dealer in the network that sold 'The Stuff.' He even told me how he got recruited."

"Uh-huh," Peterson said, and I knew he was writing as fast as he could.

"Here, let me just dictate. You ready?"

"Shoot."

The words came racing out of me.

"Another dealer connected to the brand of heroin known as 'The Stuff' was killed in Newark late last night," I began.

"Rashan Reeves, twenty-two, appears to be the fifth victim in a lengthening chain of violence that continues to unsettle New Jersey's largest city. His body was discovered in the same Ludlow Street vacant lot where four of his fellow dealers were found dead earlier this week.

"Newark police have not yet confirmed that this most recent victim is Reeves, identifying him only as a young black man who was shot five times in the head. Police also would not speculate whether the two Ludlow Street crimes were connected.

"But shortly before his death, Reeves told an *Eagle-Examiner* reporter he had been dealing 'The Stuff' for four months, ever since his release from East Jersey State Prison.

"Reeves was carrying four gruesome postmortem photographs of the Ludlow Street victims and a memo penned by a person who claimed to have killed them. In the memo, the killer—identified only as 'the Director'—writes that he eliminated the four dealers as punishment for selling a weakened version of 'The Stuff' to their customers.

"Reeves was killed less than three hours after the interview ended, possibly in retribution for having spoken to a reporter."

"Slow down, slow down," Peterson said. "This is great. Are you sure it's all true?"

"Never been more sure," I said, then helped Peterson with the details and background he needed to finish off the story.

"Tell Tina to stick this on A1 next to the story about the fires," I said.

"Oh, and Peterson?" I added. "Screw the new policy. Put my byline on it. I want this guy to know I'm coming for him."

The Director had little trouble deciding what approach to take with Rashan Reeves. It was partly based on the psychological profile in Reeves's Department of Corrections dossier, which Alvarez had been nice enough to provide. But it was also based on the Director's instincts on where Reeves could be most easily exploited.

Greed. It was Reeves's weakness. It was many people's weakness.

The Director made the phone call himself, telling the young dealer he was aware of the visit he had just made to Hector Alvarez's house with the Eagle-Examiner *reporter. The Director did not hide his disappointment and told Reeves he had considered terminating their contract. But, the Director explained, that would scarcely solve the publicity problem if the reporter were to publish Reeves's story.*

So the Director made Reeves an offer he was sure the reporter could not match: in exchange for retracting his story and ending all contact with the reporter, Reeves would be given a leased Lexus. He would be allowed to use the car as long as he continued his loyal service. Did that sound fair? the Director asked.

Reeves had practically jumped out of his skin to accept. Sure he wanted a new Lexus. Didn't everyone?

Having thrown out the bait and set the hook, the Director needed only reel in his catch. It was easy enough. The Director told Reeves that, since he was to be the primary driver of the new Lexus, he would need to be a cosigner on the lease. Could he meet with the Director at eight o'clock with his blindfold on, like it was their normal weekly product delivery?

Of course he could. The young man was remarkably guileless. Reeves had asked only one question: "What kind of Lexus will it be?"

They settled on an LS 430 and the conversation ended.

The Director had the "lease" ready by the time he picked up Reeves. It was really just a sample lease Monty had downloaded off a car dealer's Web site and then hastily altered. The Director insisted Reeves read the entire thing before signing it. The young man anxiously pored over the document, skimming maybe a quarter of the paragraphs and understanding even less. Then he signed it, scarcely able to believe how his dung pile of a life had suddenly turned into a hill of diamonds.

The Director told Reeves they were going to pick up the car at the dealership, with a quick stop at Ludlow Street on the way. The Director spun a tale about wanting to clean up the four dealers' shrine just a bit, and asked if the young man might help. The Director could only chuckle later: Rashan Reeves didn't have the slightest inkling what was happening, not until nanoseconds before the first bullet entered his skull.

It had all been so easy. Then again, the Director reminded Monty as they drove off, the situation was only partly contained. There was still *the matter of the reporter. Carter Ross was clearly a more sophisticated enemy.*

But killing him would be just as easy. Because the Director had a plan, one that involved exploiting Ross's greatest weakness.

His curiosity.

CHAPTER 9

She came to me in the middle of the night, waking me without a sound. At first, I couldn't even be sure what was happening. I was on Tina's couch, but it was almost as if the couch were somewhere else. The living room of my boyhood home in Millburn? The mess hall at the summer camp I went to as a kid? I was still groggy, confused.

But it was definitely Tina's couch. It had to be, because it was Tina on top of me. She had changed into the black cocktail dress, the one with the keyhole neckline she wore the other night. I could feel her entire body pressing against mine with an urgency that didn't seem real.

I tried to get my bearings but there was no time. Tina was

demanding every last ounce of my attention. Her eyes were huge and sparkling. It was like nothing else existed but her face, her hips, her hair, her breasts. It was all perfect, all mine to explore, admire, and enjoy.

How had it happened? There had been no seduction that I remembered, no soft music, low lighting, or sloppy drinking. But I guess I knew it was never going to happen the conventional way with Tina. It was going to be her show, done in her way, fitting her schedule.

So, yes, it was happening in the small hours of morning, with her more or less attacking me while I slept. I had no memory of waking up nor of any conversation. Tina never gave me the chance to deny her. Not that I would have. I was just the innocent bystander in her not-so-innocent scheme, allowing her to dictate the action. I almost felt detached from it, watching it all happen from somewhere high above.

But then suddenly I was back in my body and it was time to take control. My mouth began exploring the soft spot where her neck and shoulders met. My hand caressed the curve from her hip to her breast. The keyhole dress slipped away and we were soon one.

It was incredible, the kind of incredible you almost never got the first time with a new partner. There was no awkwardness, no fumbling, no slowing down to make sure everyone was okay. It was just two bodies fitting perfectly into each other and nothing to interfere with the pleasure.

And then I went to finish and . . . couldn't. I kept at it, thinking I would feel the release any second. But it didn't happen. I increased my pace, then slowed it, then increased it again. Still nothing. And then I started smelling . . . bacon? And pancakes?

And then I woke up.

It was Saturday morning. Tina was nowhere near me and apparently never had been.

I tried to sit up but then immediately lay back down. I needed time to get my bearings and give the throbbing in my pants time to subside. I tried to recap how my Friday night ended: after deciding there was nothing more to be learned at Ludlow Street, I returned to the office and picked up a key from Tina, then went back to her place and fell asleep so quickly I'm not sure I was even aware of closing my eyes. The next thing I knew, it was morning.

So why did I feel so crappy? Let's see: I'd slept in the clothes I had been wearing for two days; I could carry everything I currently owned in my back pocket; my last three meals had consisted of a bagel, Pop-Tarts, and two slices of pizza; and my sources kept getting bombed, burned, and killed.

Yeah, that would do it. I looked at the clock on Tina's cable box. It was 9:18. I might have gone right back to sleep except for what had woken me up in the first place—a smell that had wafted in from the kitchen and worked its way up my nose, making my olfactory system convince the rest of me life was worthwhile after all.

Pancakes.

And bacon.

I suddenly found the strength to stand and wobble into the kitchen, where Tina was building a stack of pancakes that could have sated three hungry truckers.

"I think I'm in love with you," I said.

"Since you're the first man to say that to me this morning, I'll let you eat some of this with me."

Tina had her hair up in a ponytail. She was wearing jeans, a long-sleeved T-shirt, and not a hint of makeup. And she looked absolutely slammin'. ("Slammin' " is a word I heard from one of the kids answering the phones at work—apparently it's a good thing.) Most women could summon the right mix of hair spray, makeup, and clingy clothing to look good in a club on a Friday night. It was the true beauty who looked just as good over pancakes the next morning. Tina was one of those.

"Thanks for putting that extra blanket on me last night," I said.

"No problem. You were drooling a little bit. It was pretty cute."

She had that morning's paper sitting on the island in the middle of the kitchen. We had splashed the ongoing Ludlow Street story all over A1, and the layout people had done a nice job tiling together three photos: the Stop-In Go-Go dancers (all appropriately clad, of course) outside their scorched home; the remains of Booker T Building Five, shot from the top of one of the other buildings so you had a cool bird's-eye feel; and the sheet-draped body of Rashan Reeves with his sneakers sticking out.

Underneath were two articles: the nonbylined story of all the blitzed buildings that Tommy and Hays had done; and the late-breaking account of Rashan's murder, with my byline on it.

I was proud of the whole thing. Sometimes we pussed out and pulled our punches on stories like this. It was part of the endless battle that rages in newsrooms across the country, pitting those who worried we would offend readers if our words and images were too graphic against those who felt we were obligated to show the world as it really existed. I was naturally part of the latter camp: a newspaper existed to tell the news, not sugarcoat it.

Our camp was often outvoted. But not this time.

"This looks *great*," I said.

"Thanks."

"Your doing?"

"Once the murder happened, I took the night editor's prerogative to rip up the front page and start from scratch," Tina said. "I'm sure I'll take some flack for it on Monday, but I think it looks great, too."

"Thanks for using my byline."

"Peterson told me what you said. I wasn't going to do it, but Peterson fought for you. He pointed out it wasn't going to do more harm—this creep knows who you are already. And it might even do some good, if people in the community realize you're the guy on this story and they call you with more information."

I nodded and waited for more, but she was done. I debated telling Tina about the dream I just had, mostly because it was so vivid I couldn't get it out of my mind. But, really, how do you start that conversation? *So, Tina, I had this dream where you raped me last night . . .*

Nope. Not happening. Instead we dove into her stack of pancakes together, dividing the paper then switching sections when we were done with them.

After a leisurely half hour, she got up from her side of the table and came around behind me, placing a pair of warm hands on my shoulders. She began massaging, and I allowed myself to go limp.

"This is amazing," I murmured as she spent a few minutes working on several days' worth of adhesions.

Then she leaned over and, with her lips inches from my earlobe, said, "So what do you say we stay in and lay on the couch together watching movies until we get hungry enough to go out for an absurdly large steak? My treat."

"Ordinarily, that would sound heavenly," I began.

286

"But . . ." she interjected, sighing and standing up, releasing my shoulders from her grasp.

"But I've got a story to follow."

Tina excused herself by saying she had an errand to run, giving me a quick kiss on the cheek on her way out. I dawdled over the paper for a little while longer, did the dishes—I'm a supporter of federal You Cook I Clean legislation—then hit the shower.

I stayed in there a long time, letting the hot water erode some of my exhaustion. My thoughts started coming in disconnected bits, like ticker tape floating down from a skyscraper.

I should have someone keeping an eye on Irving Wallace, someone dependable like Tommy. It was possible his movements would give him away as being more than just a government scientist.

I should head into Rashan Reeves's old hood to see if I could find some of his buddies. Perhaps they would know something useful.

I should work on Hector Alvarez a little more, find some way to get more leverage on him.

I should visit Brenda Bass in the hospital. I didn't know if she would receive me—or if she was even in a condition to receive me—but it seemed like a decent thing to do.

I should pitch some kind of write-through on the whole week-long Ludlow Street saga to the Sunday editor, who would undoubtedly be looking for one.

I should work with Hays to get as complete a background on Irving Wallace as I could.

I should do something to expand my wardrobe, which at the moment consisted of one pair of soiled tan slacks and one extremely wrinkled blue button-down shirt.

287

I should eat more vegetables.

I should start exercising more.

Finally, I turned the water off. That was enough thoughts, especially when I didn't know if I'd get the time to do any of them. For all I knew, Irving Wallace had found my Malibu and I was one turn of the key away from being the subject of one of Peterson's obits.

I stepped out of the shower and had just gotten a towel wrapped around my middle when Tina nudged her way through the door.

"Knock, knock," she said after it was already open.

"Nothing to see here," I said.

"Too bad," she said. Then she lifted up a Banana Republic bag. "I hope I got the sizes right," she said.

She pulled out a new shirt, slacks, socks, and boxers.

"I take back what I said before," I said. "I don't *think* I'm in love with you. I *am* in love with you."

"Oh, you have no idea how true that is," Tina said, waving a plastic bag. She pulled out a brush, a razor, deodorant, shaving cream—all the things a boy like me needed to feel fresh scrubbed again.

"You're the best, Tina. Really. I don't know what else to say."

She just stood there, smiling sweetly at me, looking so damn hot. The dream was still fresh in my mind—as was the backrub and the sweet whispering—and I just couldn't help myself. I gently removed the bags from her hands and pulled her close for the kind of deep, wet kiss that was by now about three days overdue.

But somehow she dodged it, turning my big move into a hug. And it wasn't a full-body, this-is-about-to-turn-into-something-good hug. It was strictly shoulders and arms, the kind you'd expect to receive from your girlfriend's best friend.

"A simple 'thanks' will do," she said, giving my towel-covered butt a playful smack as she pulled away.

"Well, thanks," I said sheepishly.

"Get dressed. You've got work to do."

She left me to shave and inspect my new clothes, an open-collared shirt with enough Lycra in it to give it a little bit of a stretchy feel and pinstriped pants that were, naturally, flat-front.

"How come everyone is always pushing me toward flat-front pants?" I hollered. "What's wrong with pleats?"

"You're right," Tina called back from the living room. "There's nothing wrong with pleats—if you're seventy-two years old and need a little give so your pants won't rip during a particularly strenuous game of shuffleboard."

I harrumphed and finished dressing. When I emerged from the bathroom, Tina was seated at the kitchen table, her head in a crossword puzzle. She looked up and gave me a wolf whistle.

"Looking good there, Mr. Ross."

I gave her a model's half turn. "Yeah, *GQ* just won't stop calling."

"So what's your plan now that you're all spiffy?"

I went back to my various shower-stall brainstorms and tried to prioritize. Eating vegetables and exercising came in last. Putting Tommy on Irving Wallace watch and visiting Brenda Bass came first.

"Does Tommy Hernandez work on Saturdays?" I asked.

"Tommy is an intern. He works when I tell him to."

"Perfect. I was thinking it would be really nice to have a set of eyes on Irving Wallace. Think Tommy is up for a little game of Spy versus Spy?"

"Would you like to make the call or should I?"

"I'll do it," I said, pulling out my cell phone and selecting

Tommy's number. It rang five times before a very sleepy-sounding young man picked up.

"Hello?" he said. It wasn't Tommy. The voice was too deep.

"Hi. Can you put Tommy on?"

The young man was instantly on guard. "And who's this?" he said, the jealousy oozing through the phone.

"Relax. It's his boss."

"Oh," he said, then I heard him say, "Honey, it's your boss." Tommy picked up. "You're *not* my boss."

"Yeah, but I'm with your boss right now, so it's really the same thing."

"Does that mean you spent the night?"

"Yes."

"Does that mean you finally did it?"

"None of your business."

"That's a 'no,'" Tommy said, clearly disappointed. "How am I ever supposed to become Uncle Tommy to Tina's baby if you don't make the honorable move and shag her dirty?"

"No comment," I said. "And now I'm changing the subject. I need you to do something for me today."

"Oh, come on," he whined. "I have plans."

"Not anymore."

"But it's Saaaaturday," he persisted.

"Yes, and tomorrow is Sunday and the next day is Monday."

"Is he giving you a tough time?" Tina asked me.

"Of course," I said.

"Give me the phone," she said. "Let me show you how an enlightened manager deals with her people."

I tossed Tina the phone.

"Tommy, stop being a bitch," she said, waiting briefly for Tommy's response.

"I don't care, stop being a bitch," she said. "And whatever

290

you're about to say next, I don't care about that, either. So stop being a bitch. We're done. Get to work."

Tina held the phone out for me. "Problem solved," she said.

"Oh, yeah, that was really inspired leadership there," I said, walking over and taking it from her. "You learn that from reading a book or did you get it from the sensitivity seminars they make you attend?"

"Hey, it worked," she said. "You've got your spy, don't you?"

I filled Tommy in on the latest details and how I had come to believe Irving Wallace was the Director. Tommy listened well. As I wound down the conversation, I reminded him to stop in the office and pick up a copy of the police sketch Red had provided, then gave him one last warning.

"Remember to stay hidden," I said. "I don't want this guy to make you, because then Tina and I will have to explain to your father why there are all these homosexuals at his son's funeral."

I left Tina's apartment with a sisterly kiss on the cheek to speed me on my way. It was like being in middle school all over again, except I no longer felt it was appropriate to drape my arm around her shoulder in a lame attempt to cop a feel.

Still, between breakfast, the shower, and my new clothes, I felt like I had been reinvented. On the way to my car, I stopped at a flower shop and picked out an arrangement in a simple glass vase. The card I selected had a blank space for my own individual message. I wrote in neat script, "My sincerest apologies. Carter Ross."

Upon arriving at University Hospital, a sprawling, ever-expanding complex of buildings in the middle of Newark, I wandered around for twenty minutes before finding the burn unit. I asked at the nurse's station for Brenda Bass, and was pointed to a room just down the hall. I'm sure if they'd known I was with the newspaper, they would have thrown a fit. But I wasn't really there as a reporter. I was just another guy clutching flowers, looking for a sick person I cared about.

I walked softly into the room. Miss B was lying still with her eyes closed. The lower half of her face was covered in a mask connected to an oxygen tank. She was breathing on her own, though I thought I heard some raggedness with each inhalation. A bag of fluids hung to her left, slowly dripping into her through an IV in her arm. Other than that, she appeared quite peaceful. I didn't see any burns, any gauze, any sign of trauma.

Tynesha, who had been asleep in a chair pulled next to the bed, stirred as I entered. I wasn't sure what to expect from her, given the way she had received me outside the Stop-In Go-Go.

But it seemed her bedside vigil had taken some of the spite out of her. Or at least she didn't immediately move to claw out my eyeballs.

"Hi," I said cautiously.

"Hi," she said. There was no anger in her voice, just fatigue.

"I came to drop these off," I said, and placed the vase down on the ledge next to the window. The card dangled down and Tynesha grasped it, turning it over.

"You're apologizing?" she said.

"I owe her at least that much," I said. "I owe it to you, too. I . . . Look, I had no idea this was going to happen. To say I feel awful about it wouldn't even be a start. I wish I could go back to Monday and have myself hit by a bus. I just . . ."

I let my voice trail off. She turned toward the window and gazed out, maybe so she wouldn't have to look at me. She was wearing what appeared to be borrowed clothes—sweatpants with a nonmatching sweatshirt. Her hair was matted and I guessed she had spent the night in that chair. Her eyes, which

292

were brown without the aid of the amber contact lenses, had dark smudges underneath them.

"I shouldn't have been so rough on you yesterday," she said.

"I had it coming. Believe me, I did."

"Yeah, you did," she said, smiling slightly for the first time, and we left it at that. Miss B made a ragged, gasping noise, then quieted.

"How's she doing?" I asked.

"Not good. The doctors say her lungs are, like, melting or something. Maybe it starts getting better or maybe it don't. They say there ain't much they can do."

"Is she going to make it?"

"They don't know. They say she's holding on for now but they don't know how bad it'll get. They said sometimes it looks like someone ain't going to make it and they do, but sometimes someone who looks like they're going to make it don't."

Tynesha shook her head and continued. "I don't think these doctors know what the hell they're talking about. Half the time they talk to me like I'm stupid. The other half the time I feel stupid 'cause I don't know what they're saying."

"Are they giving her any drugs or anything?" I asked.

"Just painkillers."

"Has she been awake?"

"Not since I been here."

"It's probably better that way," I said.

We watched Miss B breathe for a minute or so. I had written about enough fires to know what was going on inside her. All the delicate mechanisms that normally kept the lungs clear of junk were failing and the congestion was building up. If it stabilized in time, she'd pull through. If not, she would drown in her own fluids.

"Wanda's funeral was supposed to be today," Tynesha said, breaking our silence. "We told 'em to hold off for a few days. The family decided Miss B wouldn't want to miss her daughter's funeral."

Or maybe, I thought grimly, the family was thinking the funeral might have to become a double feature.

"So you've been here all night?" I said. Tynesha nodded.

"I hope you don't take it the wrong way when I say you look like you could use some breakfast and a change of clothes," I said.

"Ain't got no clothes to change into. They all burnt up."

"Yeah, mine, too," I said. "But I had a guardian angel buy me a new outfit this morning. How about I do the same for you?"

Tynesha looked at Miss B, frowning.

"I don't think I should leave her," she said.

"Tynesha," I said, "I really don't think she's going anywhere."

That bit of logic was enough to convince Tynesha to join me for breakfast—or perhaps it was the combination of logic and hunger.

We went to an IHOP across the street, continuing the global theme to our dates, and were soon seated in a corner booth with formidable stacks of pancakes in front of us. This was, technically, my second breakfast of the day. But I found room.

"The cops get any further with Wanda?" Tynesha asked as she forked a bite of omelet into her mouth.

"Well, technically, it's not the cops' case anymore," I said. "They handed it over to a federal agency called the National Drug Bureau, which claimed jurisdiction over it."

"So have the National Drug Bureau cops figured it out?"

I thought about L. Pete and the toe fungus I hoped he was developing.

"Probably not," I said. "They think it has something to do with this guy, José de Jesús Encarcerón. Ever heard of him?"

Tynesha shook her head.

"Well, neither had I," I said. "But I'm pretty sure the NDB is just grasping at straws. They don't know the real answer so they pretend they know."

"Just like those doctors in there," Tynesha said, and I chuckled.

"Sometimes doctors are too smart for their own good," I said. "They get so used to being smart, they have a hard time admitting that they don't have the answers."

It was a cautionary tale for any profession, especially mine. The reporter who assumes he has all the answers is usually a reporter who finds his stories being mentioned in the correction column with considerable frequency. It's an easy trap to fall into when your job is to find the truth. The trick is never assuming your information is absolute or infallible. You have to stay flexible enough to still be able to recognize when your premise is all wrong. You also have to remember to keep going back to your sources with new knowledge and seeing what else they know.

With that in mind, I stopped chewing for a second and asked, "Did Wanda ever mention the name Irving Wallace?"

"Naw. That's a pretty unusual name. I think I would have remembered it. Who's he?"

"He's a chemist for the federal government."

Tynesha thought for a moment.

"Well, I don't know if this guy was a chemist or nothing," Tynesha said. "But I remember this one time a couple months ago Wanda brought me this guy who I thought was another client of hers. But then she said, no, he wasn't a client, he was like her boss or something."

"Her boss?" I said, sitting up in my seat a little and feeling a hankering for a notepad, like I should be writing this down. "How come you never mentioned this before?"

"I don't know. I just didn't think about it until you mentioned a government guy. Don't get all uptight."

"Sorry, sorry. Anyway, go on. You thought he was Wanda's boss . . ."

"Yeah. I guess he was some kind of grand poobah or something. They wasn't even supposed to be looking at each other, but he broke the rules with Wanda. I guess he got sweet on Wanda—a lot of guys got sweet on Wanda, you know? But she wouldn't turn no tricks. So she sent him to me so he could get his rocks off. But she said because he was like her boss, she asked if I could, you know, do him for free. As, like, a favor."

"So you, uh . . ."

"Yeah, I sucked him off."

"What did he look like?"

"I don't know," Tynesha said. "It's not like I spent a lot of time looking at his face, you know?"

"Was he a big guy?"

"Naw, he was a little guy." She paused, then snickered. "And I mean little in *every* way."

I realized my shoulders had gotten tensed up and I relaxed them. Certainly, if Tynesha had given Irving Wallace a hummer, it would have been stop-the-presses time. I'm not sure how I would have attributed it in an article—"according to a hooker who gave Wallace a blow job" just wasn't going to fly in our family newspaper—but it would have been a pleasant enough problem to worry about as I was plotting how to plaster Irving Wallace's name and picture all over the Sunday paper.

Alas, Tynesha describing her John as a "little guy" meant he couldn't have been the six-foot-five, three-hundred-pound van-driving menace I now surmised was Irving Wallace. But maybe he was an associate of Wallace's.

"So what made you think this guy worked for the government?"

"Well, he wore a suit. And he had one of them badges on his belt," Tynesha said. "He just looked like one of them guys that plays the government agent in the TV shows, like he was CIA or FBI. Well, not CIA, because they always have glasses and look all cool. So maybe he was FBI or something."

"You get his name by any chance?"

"Oh, yeah. I get all my customers' names. I get their names, their home addresses, their wives' and kids' names, and then we exchange Christmas cards."

"Okay, dumb question," I said.

"The only thing I remember about him is that when he was done he gave me all the usual, 'Oh, baby, that was great . . . Oh, baby, you're the best.' And then he didn't give me a tip or nothing. You know what he did?"

I spread my hands in an I-got-no-clue gesture.

"He told me maybe if I sucked him off again sometime he would take me to a game at Giants Stadium," Tynesha continued. "I didn't say nothing, because he was Wanda's boss. But I was thinking, 'A *game*? Are you for real?!?' Sometimes, guys are just too stupid for words."

Tynesha refused my offer of a quick trip to the Jersey Gardens Mall for a clothing run, saying she felt like she didn't want to spend that much time away from Miss B. We parted with promises to keep in touch and I went back to the office to regroup.

The Saturday newsroom is a relatively relaxed place, consisting mostly of interns who are still groggy from the night before.

Feeling a little woozy myself, I settled into my desk. Out of habit, I glanced at my office phone's voice mail light. It was off, but the caller ID was showing eleven missed calls. They were all from the same number, a 908 area code. Someone, who was apparently desperate to talk to me, didn't believe in leaving messages.

I was about to begin figuring out who my persistent caller was when my phone rang: the 908 number flashed on my caller ID for a twelfth time.

"Carter Ross," I said.

"Irving Wallace," came the reply.

I could feel my pulse surge and I instinctively drew in my breath. I didn't want to talk to Irving Wallace. Not right now. It's not that I avoid confrontation—hell, I'm a reporter, I *thrive* on confrontation—it's that I wasn't ready for this one yet. I liked to have my gun fully loaded before I went into a showdown with someone like Irving Wallace, and I felt like I had barely gotten the first bullet in the chamber.

"Why, hello, Irving. How are you this fine day?" I said through gritted teeth. I had a loathing for this man like I had never felt for another human being, but I had to try not to let my voice betray it.

"Fine, thanks," he said. "Just running around doing errands with the family, you know, the usual Saturday routine."

The breeziness in his tone was chilling. But wasn't that the essence of antisocial personality disorder? He could commit multiple murders and go on with his life as if nothing were happening. Because that's what killing people felt like to him: nothing.

"Right," I said. "Errands."

"We're off the record, yes?"

"Oh, off the record, sure," I said, shaking my head at the nerve this guy had.

"Okay, off the record, I've been figuring out some things

298

with regard to that heroin you gave me that I think you'd find interesting—*very* interesting," he said. "Ordinarily I might handle it through my own channels, but I really don't know who I can trust at this point. So I think if it just spills out in the newspaper, that'll be best."

"If *what* spills out?" I said.

The line went silent for a few moments. I tried to keep my breathing steady.

"It's not something we can discuss over the phone," he said, finally. "There are some things you'll have to see with your own eyes. We really need to talk about it in person."

Sure we did. It'd just be a cozy chat between Irving, me, and his .40-caliber handgun.

"When can we meet?" I asked, because I wanted to appear to be playing along.

"I'd like to do it right now, but I just can't—a ten-and-under girls' basketball team needs its coach," he said. "But let's do it tomorrow morning. Do you work on Sundays?"

Amazing, the calendar Irving Wallace kept. Let's see: shopping with the wife and kids on Saturday morning, check; coaching the girls' basketball team on Saturday afternoon, check; killing the pesky newspaper reporter on Sunday morning, check.

Still, the Summit Squirt Girls' Basketball League schedule was a break for me. It gave me time—time to do more reporting without looking over my shoulder, time to figure out a plan.

"We're a daily newspaper," I said. "I work whenever I have to."

"Great," he said. "I can't have you coming by my office—even on a weekend, someone might see you. So why don't you come to my house for brunch tomorrow? It's a Wallace family tradition. We do waffles, eggs, toast, the whole thing. Then after brunch we can go to my study and I'll lay everything out for you."

He'd lay me out, is more like it. I would go to the Wallace

household to find the wife and kids were gone. He'd offer some flimsy excuse then need to show me something—in the basement, probably, where he could kill me and clean up the mess easily. Then he'd eat his waffles and toast. Then he'd load my body in the white van parked in his garage, find some way to dispose of my corpse and my car, and no one would ever be the wiser. He even thought he had the ideal cover: everyone in our circulation area knew someone was trying to kill me. So when I turned up missing, he could just say I was still alive when I left his house and I must have been grabbed on the way back to the office. The smug bastard figured no one would suspect the gentle government scientist.

It was the perfect trap, except for one thing—it's not a trap when you know what's coming.

"Brunch it is," I said. "Can I bring anything?"

"What do you mean?" he asked.

"For brunch," I reminded him. "Can I make something? Bring some juice? Just trying to be a good guest."

How about that: I was keeping up his pretense better than he was.

"Oh, right," he said. "No, just a pen and a notepad. I'll take care of everything else."

The shopping. The cooking. The killing.

He gave me his address and directions, not that I needed either. He was so easy about the whole thing, almost charming. But isn't that what people always said about Ted Bundy?

"We go to the early church service, so we'll be home by ten-thirty," Wallace said. "Why don't you plan on being there around eleven?"

"Sounds fine. See you then," I said, hanging up.

The clock on my computer read 2:14. I had less than twenty-one hours to go.

looked around the newsroom with eyes that could barely focus. There were a dozen emotions and a hundred thoughts bouncing around inside me, each clamoring for my attention. There was rage and relief and nervousness. There were schemes and gambits and ploys. I couldn't untangle one thing from the other.

It was time to compartmentalize. If I didn't start dealing with things one at a time, I wasn't going to be able to accomplish anything. First order of business: I had a story to write. Irving Wallace had to wake up and find something in his Sunday paper, or he'd get suspicious. Plus, I'd promised the Sunday editor.

A story. No problem. I had written thousands of stories, I told myself. Just treat this one like all the rest. Quotes. I needed quotes. I started with the Newark police, calling their Public Noninformation Officer, Hakeem Rogers.

"What the hell do *you* want?" Rogers answered.

"Good afternoon, Lieutenant Rogers," I said, trying to ooze as much falseness as my voice could muster. "Carter Ross from the *Eagle-Examiner* here."

"Why are you calling me? You seem to know everything already."

"Why, whatever are you talking about, Officer?" I asked sweetly.

"Stop being a dick. You printed a victim ID before we located the family."

I dropped the courteous act: "Hey, it's not our fault you guys suck at finding next of kin."

I heard Rogers huffing through the phone. "Is there any reason you're calling or can I hang up on you?" he asked.

"Anything new on the Rashan Reeves investigation?"

"That investigation has been turned over to the National

301

Drug Bureau. Since it's no longer our investigation, I have no comment."

"Okay. Anything new on the explosions or fires?"

"National Drug Bureau. No comment," he said again.

"Fair enough. You ever give them that sketch my friend was nice enough to provide you last night?"

"Yeah, we gave it to them," Rogers said. "I think they're lining their trash cans with it as we speak."

"What do you mean?"

"I mean, when we told them the ID was offered by a drunk, homeless guy, they said it was useless."

"It's got to be worth *something*," I said.

"Yeah, well, that's their business now. Anyway, since we no longer have any investigations that are of interest to you, can I get on with enjoying a Saturday afternoon surrounded by people who love me?"

"Assuming you can find any? Sure," I said, happy to get one final shot in.

I leaned back in my chair, feeling a twinge of desperation. Sure, I could give the Sunday editor a nicely written rehash of what we had already reported—we had tossed enough out there that needed tying together. But journalistically, that was unsatisfying. Unless you had at least *some* new information to offer readers, you may as well have been a third-grader writing a book report.

It was just frustrating: the National Drug Bureau seemed to have been given jurisdiction over everything that mattered in Newark, and the NDB had been little more than a big stone wall of disinformation and nonanswers from the start. I was beginning to hope the toe fungus I had wished on L. Pete earlier was now spreading to his jock.

Just then, I got a call on my cell phone from a blocked number.

"Carter Ross."

"Carter, Pete Sampson from the National Drug Bureau."

"Hey, Pete. I was just thinking about you."

"That's great, just great," he said. "Your story today was really well done."

"Thanks. I understand you guys have taken over that investigation."

"Yes. Yes, we have," L. Pete said cautiously, then paused like he didn't dare to say anything else, lest it get him fired.

"To what do I owe the pleasure?" I prompted.

"Remember that exclusive interview I promised you?"

"Of course."

"Could you be at our offices in ten minutes? My boss wants to do it *right now*. With everything happening, he says time is of the essence."

An interview with L. Pete's boss. Maybe the big stone wall was about to come tumbling down.

"Sure," I said. "I'll see you in ten."

Before we hung up, L. Pete gave me instructions to park in a secure lot under the building—there would be plenty of room on a Saturday, and it would save me having to find a spot on the street.

"Thanks for agreeing to come so quickly," L. Pete said. "When this is all over, we'll have to go to a Jets game. I've got season tickets. We'll have a few beers, swap war stories."

"Sure," I said. "See you in a bit."

I hastily collected my notepad and threw on my jacket. Then, as an afterthought, I stuffed my digital recorder in my pocket, just in case L. Pete had a boss whose mouth moved faster than my pen.

As I drove toward the NDB's Newark Field Office, I was actually feeling optimistic for the first time since my house blew up. Maybe it was how L. Pete prefaced that one sentence—*when this is all over . . .* —but I was allowing myself to daydream about getting Irving Wallace locked up then putting my life back in order. I would use the insurance money to build a new bungalow—a better bungalow, one with a home theater instead of a living room. I would buy new electronics equipment, new clothes, new kitchen appliances. I would buy furniture with salsa-resistant fabric.

I was somewhere in the midst of thinking about the golf clubs I would buy—Callaway irons and TaylorMade woods? Or just go all Titleist?—when Tommy called me.

"Hey," he said in a hushed voice. "The guy finally came home . . . *in a van.*"

"What kind of van?" I asked in a whisper, even though I suppose I could have talked at normal volume.

"I don't know. I guess you would call it a minivan," Tommy said. "I couldn't give you make and model. But it's one of the big, boxy ones."

I realized I never got much description from Mrs. Scalabrine about exactly what kind of van Irving Wallace had been driving. That was a detail I'd have to sort out later.

"What color is it? White?"

"More of a tan, actually," Tommy said.

Which was close enough to white. Mrs. Scalabrine saw the van in the early morning. The rising sun can play tricks with colors, what with all that refracted light.

"What's he doing?" I asked.

"Well, he parked," Tommy narrated. "A blond woman—looks like bottle blond—popped out of the passenger side. Then three kids got out of the back. They're unloading groceries."

Well, at least Irving Wallace hadn't lied about one thing: he really was shopping with the family. I wondered if his wife knew she slept next to a murderer every night.

"How tall is he?" I asked.

"Oh, he's tall. I mean, it's hard to tell for sure, but I'd put him in the six-four, six-five range for sure."

"Does he look like the sketch?" I demanded.

Tommy hemmed for five seconds, then hawed for five more.

"Don't force it," I cautioned. "The sketch could be a bit off. I'm sure Red would be able to pick the guy out of a lineup."

"It's . . . it's just hard to tell," Tommy said. "He's got a hat on, so I can't see him that well. It's not easy going from a sketch to a real face, you know?"

"Okay, okay. That's okay," I said quickly, to reassure myself as much as anything. "No problem. Where are you watching him from?"

"Two houses down on the opposite side of the street."

"Good," I said. "By the way, Irving Wallace just called me in the office not long ago. He invited me to brunch tomorrow at his house—said he had an important story to give me."

"That's scary," Tommy said. "Are you going to go?"

"Oh, hell, no. Not when the quote he wants to give me goes, 'Bam, bam, you're dead,'" I said. "What I'm trying to figure out now is—"

"Oh, shoot," Tommy interrupted. "He's looking right at me. I gotta go."

Tommy hung up and I felt a little panic setting in. But, no, he would be fine. If he saw Wallace coming, he'd be able to get away in plenty of time.

There was the small problem that if Wallace spotted Tommy, he'd know someone was on to him—even if he didn't know it was us. It would make him more cautious.

Then again, this would all be a moot point in about fifteen minutes, when my new friends at the National Drug Bureau told me they were poised to arrest Wallace and execute a search warrant on his residence and office. I was about to get caught up in that daydream again when I reached the NDB's Newark Field Office. Following L. Pete's instruction, I pulled under the building. A guard stopped me for a moment, then waved me through after I identified myself.

The parking area was empty save for a smattering of dark, government-issue sedans. Apparently, anyone working on a Saturday was important enough to be furnished wheels courtesy of my tax dollars.

I took the elevator up to the lobby, where a couple of marshals—the same square-jawed types as before—were waiting for me. With a series of nods and polite gestures, they gave me the metal-detecting/wanding/patting routine. They took an extra moment or two over my recording device and let it slide only after I demonstrated it for them. But they paused over, of all things, my cell phone.

"Sir, I'm going to have to ask you for your phone," one of the square-jaws said.

"Why, you need to make a call?"

"No, sir. Elevated threat level today. Cell phones can be used as detonators."

"Okay," I said, waving it around, "but no dialing any of those nine-hundred numbers you fellas like so much. I know they say there are young boys waiting to turn you on, but those are really middle-aged women doing those voices."

"Sir?" he said, holding out his hand, unamused.

"Fine," I said, handing it to him. "Can't say I didn't warn you."

"Just a moment, sir," he said, then picked up the phone on the wall.

My wait was much briefer than it had been the last time—the key difference being that they were marginally happy to see me. L. Pete himself came down to the lobby to retrieve me.

"Hi," he said, extending his hand and smiling with far too much enthusiasm. "Thanks for being prompt."

We shook hands and he gripped as hard as he could. Why do some short guys always try to prove they possess superior forearm strength? Did they want us to know that, despite their lack of stature, they could still open stubborn mayonnaise jars?

"Nothing makes a journalist move faster than the promise of an easy scoop," I said.

"Right, right," he said, waving me onto the elevator. He slid his card through the slot on the control panel, then pushed the button for the fifteenth floor. "Don't worry," he said. "You'll be glad you came."

As the elevator launched us skyward, I took the opportunity to turn on the recorder in my pocket. I suppose it wasn't the most polite thing to be recording a conversation without the other party's knowledge. But in New Jersey it wasn't illegal. And what L. Pete's boss didn't know wouldn't hurt him.

When we disembarked, I was ushered past a succession of closed office doors until we reached the one in the corner, whose name plate announced it belonged to Field Director Randall N. Meyers. L. Pete knocked softly.

"Yes?" a powerful voice inquired from behind the door.

"It's me, sir," L. Pete said.

The powerful voice replied, "Come in, Monty."

"Who's Monty?" I asked as L. Pete opened the door.

"Oh, that's me," L. Pete said. "I've gone by 'Pete' since grade school. But when Randy found out my first name was Lamont, he started calling me 'Monty.'"

The Director surveyed the young man who followed Monty into his office and was almost disappointed. This was his nemesis? This was the greatest threat his operation had ever known? This was Carter Ross?

The Director buried his attention back into a pile of meaningless papers on his desk, not wanting the reporter to know he was being studied. In that quick glance, the Director had already seen enough to know Carter Ross would not pose any further difficulty.

He wasn't armed—the cut in his trendy clothing left no room for a concealed weapon. And, physically, the Director could crush him. Carter Ross was nothing more than a pretty boy. There was no real meat hanging on his shoulders, no thickness in the chest or arms that might suggest he was dangerous. He looked like any one of those yuppies who spend *time in the gym strictly for vanity, doing arm curls to get a small bulge in their biceps, with their only goal to look good in a tight T-shirt. They were not like the Director, who worked out for the express purpose of being able to overpower other men—for moments exactly like this.*

The only real challenge of killing Carter Ross was what to do with him afterward. You couldn't just dump his body down on Ludlow Street, like the Director had with the others. That would work for lowlife drug dealers, who would not be missed by anyone important. It wouldn't work for newspaper reporters.

So the Director had spent his morning planning Carter Ross's disappearance. Unbeknownst to him, "Carter Ross" had already booked an eight o'clock flight out of Newark airport to the Dominican Republic.

Making it appear Carter Ross was actually on the flight had taken a few hours of work. First, the Director asked one of the National Drug Bureau's computer technicians to hack into the Eagle-Examiner's network, telling the tech it was part of an investigation and he had a judge's order to do so. Once inside the mainframe, the Director accessed Carter Ross's account and poked around long enough to get a sense of Ross's e-mail style.

Then the Director wrote two e-mails— one to Harold Brodie, one to an e-mail account Ross had labeled "Mom & Dad" in his contact list. The e-mail to Brodie was more formal in its punctuation and sentence structure. The e-mail to Mom & Dad was more colloquial. Each said the same thing: their dear Carter had been so traumatized by the events of the past week, he felt he needed two weeks in the Dominican Republic to recover. The Director scheduled the e-mails to be sent at precisely 5:59 P.M. and 6:01 P.M., to make it appear "Carter Ross" had dashed off the e-mails then gone straight to the airport.

The next step was ensuring "Carter Ross" didn't miss his flight, but that was easy enough. The National Drug Bureau had authorization to create passports for agents traveling under assumed names, so the Director created one with Carter Ross's name and birthday—but Monty's picture.

Then, at six o'clock, Monty would drive Carter Ross's car to the airport, use the passport to check in for the flight and get through security, then use it again to get through customs on the other side. The next day, Lamont P. Sampson, using his own passport, would fly back—leaving "Carter Ross" on his Dominican vacation.

The Director knew someone would eventually notice when Ross didn't return, but he was less concerned about that. The authorities up here would locate Ross's car in long-term parking, check the airline manifold then conclude he had gotten on a plane for the Dominican Republic safe and sound.

To the authorities down there, Carter Ross would be just one more American who went on vacation and decided, for whatever reason, not to come back. The Director didn't know whether Ross's family had means to investigate his disappearance. But it didn't really matter. The Director knew how to weight down a body. Unless his family had a submarine, they were never going to find him.

It was all so perfect the Director was tempted to get it over with quickly: to stick a bullet in Ross's ear, dispose of the body somewhere wet and cold, and be home for supper with his family.

But no, a small amount of patience was required. First, the Director needed to find out if Carter Ross knew more than he had let on—and if he had shared those thoughts with anyone else. Maybe Ross would be unwitting enough to spill, maybe he wouldn't. Maybe the Director would have to coerce it out of him. The end result would be the same: Carter Ross's final hour on this earth was already well under way.

CHAPTER 10

The office of Randall N. Meyers had a large expanse of carpet that was a step up in quality from the thin, standard-issue floor covering his peons walked each day. In the middle of the room, a highly polished conference table was surrounded by eight cushy chairs. Along the side was a small living-roomlike setup, with a leather couch and matching recliners surrounding a low coffee table. On the two unwindowed walls, there were various plaques, diplomas, and newspaper articles, chronicling a long, successful climb to the higher reaches of law enforcement. Then there were the pictures: a portrait of Meyers as a young infantry officer, a pair of posed photos with two U.S. presidents, then a collection of more candid shots with three or four people who looked vaguely familiar as senators or congressmen.

It was all meant to convey the high standing of the man inhabiting the office. Because, obviously, anyone with enough juice to command from the federal bureaucracy such tremendous resources of square footage, carpeting, and furniture had to be someone around which solar systems rotated.

That someone, Randall N. Meyers, was sitting at the far end of the room behind a large, mahogany desk. He was a bear of a man who did not bother standing when I entered. He was casually dressed in a blue button-down shirt, which was wrinkled by the presence of a shoulder holster that was weighted down by his service weapon. Even seated, his considerable girth was obvious. I immediately pegged him as suffering from high cholesterol, hypertension, and occasional battles with gout. Some people just have that look.

Then again, he also looked like he could pick up a Honda if he put his mind and muscle to it. Somewhere in Randall N. Meyers's past there had been heavy manual labor or a lot of weightlifting.

"Uh," L. Pete said, clearing his throat. "Here you are, sir."

Meyers looked up briefly and told L. Pete, "Thank you, Monty. You can leave now."

But L. Pete was already slinking in that direction. His entire demeanor had changed the moment he entered that office. Gone was the little man with the firm handshake and the self-important—albeit Napoleonic—air about him. Around his boss, he was halting, uncertain, and deferential, like a puppy accustomed to scolding. He was gone before Meyers could tell him not to let the door hit him in the ass.

"I'll be with you in a moment, Mr. Ross," Meyers said without looking up, waving at the chairs in front of his desk. "Take a seat."

I sat and Meyers returned his focus to the incredibly vital document in front of him, doing his best to send the message the piece of paper contained information that far outdistanced littl' ol' me in importance. I was merely a distraction he would deal with when the more weighty matters that occupied the rest of his precious time were properly handled.

It was all part of the intimidation game, of course—along with the furnishings, the size of the office, and the pictures on the wall. And I guess it worked on some people. As a journalist, you can never let yourself get too awed by someone. You have to remember that anyone, no matter how important they try to make themselves seem, is just as likely to be full of crap as anyone else. That was especially true with someone who went out of their way to impress upon you just how important they are.

So I did what I always do when I'm in a source's office and they're not paying attention to me: I subtly invade their privacy. You can learn all kinds of things from studying someone's desk, especially a large desk like this one, which had so much room for pictures, knickknacks, and top-secret files.

In Meyers's case, I learned he didn't give a crap about his family. Really. There was one picture of him, a mousy woman, and three awkward girls. The rest were pictures of Randy Meyers and his buddies on a variety of exotic vacations: hunting, fishing, scuba diving, skiing, paragliding, skydiving—all macho activities by macho men.

The settings varied from the Caribbean to the Serengeti to the tops of mountains, but there was one constant to all the photos: in each one, Randy Meyers was in the middle. He was clearly the alpha male, bigger and beefier than everyone else, unafraid to throw around his weight.

And sure, I didn't know him. But I knew guys like him and I could see him on those trips. He was the big shot, ordering the

313

most expensive drinks (when someone else was buying), belittling anyone who didn't catch a fish (unless he hadn't), bossing around the strippers and whores (because he was too inept with women for the pickup game).

My decision to dislike the man had been thoroughly cemented.

Once I was done with the vacation pictures, I moved on to the top-secret files, doing my best to read them upside down, hoping to see the name Irving Wallace pop out of one of them. But there didn't appear to be anything of use or importance. Even the supposedly vital document Meyers had in front of him was a letdown. It was a goddamn receipt for an airline flight.

Now I was getting steamed. While I was sitting there waiting, losing precious time against deadline, this jerk was planning another vacation with his idiot buddies. I started clearing my throat, shifting my weight, and making other not-so-subtle signs of impatience. But Randall N. Meyers was paying me no mind whatsoever, to the point it was getting downright bizarre.

How long had I been sitting there? I wanted to look at what time it was on my cell phone. But, of course, I couldn't. The square-jaws downstairs had taken it from me.

Finally, Meyers looked up.

"Sorry about that," he said, with a weighty sigh. "I hope Monty was courteous."

"Yeah, he was a gem," I said. "You must have sent him to all the best obedience schools."

A brief look of amusement passed over Meyers's face, then faded.

"Do your editors know you're here?" he asked.

"I ran out before I had a chance to tell anyone," I said. "But don't worry. If I tell them we've got a good story, they'll back me."

"Very good," he said. "Excellent."

He leaned back in his chair, crossing one thick leg over the other. Even reclined, his stomach spilled out over the top of his belt.

"So, heck of a week, huh?" he said casually.

"Sure was."

"Your articles have been excellent. You're really some writer."

"Thank you."

"You put certain things together faster than my detectives. Maybe I ought to hire you," he said, then added a guffaw.

I smiled but didn't laugh. I usually reserve laughing for things that are, you know, funny. I recognized this as the portion of the conversation where he was trying to establish friendly relations with me. But I wanted to get on to the productive part of the conversation. We each possessed information of indeterminate value to the other. Neither of us would give it up willingly without getting something in return. There would be some bluffing, some casual-sounding questions that weren't actually so casual, some false leads tossed out there just for fun. I was curious who was going to mention the name Irving Wallace first.

"So, I've always wondered this," Meyers continued. "When you work on a story like that, do you work alone or are you part of a team?"

"If it's an important story, we usually have several reporters on it."

"But the person whose name is at the top. They're the one who knows the most? Or no."

"The person with the lead byline is the one who has contributed the most reporting. But that can change from day to day, article to article."

"I see," Meyers said. "But when you have new ideas, you share them with your fellow reporters?"

"It depends whether you need another reporter's help in fleshing it out. Sometimes you share, sometimes you don't."

"Which was it this time?"

"A bit of both," I said.

"I see," he said, again. And I was, quite frankly, a little perplexed by his questions. Had he really brought me here to talk about newspaper politics?

Meyers's hand was resting on his shoulder holster, his fingers absentmindedly tracing the butt of his gun. Really, why was the gun even necessary? This had to be the most secure building in Newark. Was he worried the janitors were plotting against him?

For that matter, when was the last time he'd used the thing? It made me almost sad for him: the paperwork warrior, still hauling around his piece like he was on the front lines.

"So where has your investigation led you with the Ludlow Street murders?" he asked.

I stared at him, unable to hide my incredulity any longer. "I thought that's why I was here."

"Oh?" he said, putting down his legs and sitting up suddenly, like I'd said something to unsettle him.

"Yeah, you called this meeting, right? Or I should say Pete, or Monty, or whatever his name is—he called this meeting. He said you guys had a great story to give me?"

"Oh, yes," he said, nodding unconvincingly, purposely not looking at me.

"So . . ." I began, dragging out the word to indicate it was his turn to talk.

"Well, yes. Your articles have certainly caught our attention," he said. "And I said to Agent Sampson that you seemed like the kind of person we could trust. I mean, a good reporter is someone you can trust, right?"

"Absolutely," I said, then pointed to his gun. "You carry that thing. The only thing I come armed with is my credibility."

"Absolutely, absolutely," Meyers said. "Tell me, and you can trust me, how did you deduce that this brand of heroin—what is it called, 'The Stuff'?—how did you figure out that was the connection between all the dealers? It always fascinates me to understand the thought processes a good investigator goes through."

"Well, Randy, it wasn't really much of a deduction," I said, with what I hoped was a patronizing tone. "I'm not an investigator, of course. I'm a newspaper reporter. Which means I'm always trying to tell a story. And to tell a story, you have to keep asking questions until things make sense to you."

"Of course, of course," he said. "And then today's story, that was quite something, you bumping into this young man just hours before he was killed."

"Yeah, it was something, all right," I said.

"And he told you how he got recruited in prison?"

"He did," I said, feeling my annoyance level rise.

"And he had that packet with those photos?"

I nodded.

"Remarkable," he said.

"Sure was."

"Did he tell you anything else before he died?"

"What do you mean?"

"Oh, I don't know. Any theories about who he was working for? Any ideas about who this 'Director' guy is?"

"He had theories and I had theories, yeah."

"Really? What were they?"

Finally, exasperated, I threw my arms in the air.

"Look, Randy, what game are we playing here? Twenty questions for the *Eagle-Examiner* reporter? Because where I come from, information goes both ways. You show me yours, I show you mine. That kind of thing. If you just hauled me in here to quiz me because your own investigation has stalled, I got better things to do than talk to you."

"Hold on there, soldier," Meyers said, holding his hands out like he was a crossing guard.

"I'm not a soldier, and I'm certainly not *your* soldier," I shot back. "We can play games with the sourcing and that crap later. Right now, I'm leaving if you don't answer a very simple question for me: do you know who the Director is or not?"

I stood up to let him know I was serious, putting my fists on his desk.

And that's when I saw it.

It was just sitting there in plain sight, mixed in with some knickknacks. It was a stamp perched atop an ink pad. You couldn't see the bottom of it, which would have appeared backward anyway. But on the side of the stamp was a sample of its impression.

It was that unmistakable eagle-clutching-syringe design with the scripted lettering underneath.

It was The Stuff's logo.

And there was only one person who could be in possession of that one-of-a-kind stamp—the man who had it imprinted on dime bags by the thousand, the man who stamped it at the top of those memos, the man who killed to protect its reputation for unmatched purity.

The Director.

I looked across the desk with new eyes. It was the man from Red's sketch, all right, with his thick neck, fleshy cheeks, and receding hairline. How had I not seen it when I first entered the room?

Because I had fallen into the mistake of believing Irving Wallace, and only Irving Wallace, was my bad guy. Tina had tried to tell me all the ways Wallace didn't fit, but I wouldn't listen. Hell, Tommy was telling me Wallace was driving a tan-colored vehicle, and I convinced myself it was really white.

Because I *knew* it was a fed.

I just had the wrong fed.

Now that I had the right fed—the one sitting in front of me—I realized I had to keep my face straight and talk my way out of the room as gently as I could. I couldn't let on I knew who he really was.

"Let's slow down a bit here," the Director said. "We can keep things cordial."

"Absolutely," I said, trying to keep my voice from quavering. "And I'm sorry. Like you said, it's been a hectic week. You may have heard I lost my home."

"I did hear that. I'm very sorry about that."

"I lost my cat, too," I said. "I loved that cat. His name was Deadline."

The cat card. I was really playing the cat card again. Anything to cover my retreat.

"Awful, just awful," the Director said. "I'd like to assure you this agency is doing everything it possibly can to bring the person or persons responsible to justice."

"Then let's start at the beginning," I said. "You know where I've been coming from. I've put most of what I know in the newspaper. Why don't you walk me through your investigation a little bit? What led you to the conclusion José de Jesús Encarcerón is behind all this?"

The Director started talking but I was beyond listening. My brain was trained to seek narratives. And now that the Director's once-scattered story was falling into place, it was hard to slow the thoughts streaking through my head. All those questions suddenly had found answers.

Where did 100 percent pure heroin come from? Newark airport. Who was responsible for making seizures at Newark airport? The National Drug Bureau. Who would have unfettered access to the impounded seizures without worrying about chain of custody or being accountable to a higher authority? Field Director Randall N. Meyers.

Who could have more easily skated under, over, and around the detection of all levels of law enforcement? It wouldn't be some lab guy. It would be someone deeply embedded in the agency that was . . . what was the speech Monty/Pete had given me? I couldn't quite summon the language. But it had something to do with being the guys in charge.

Just look at the way the Director had hopped on the Ludlow Street investigations, claiming jurisdiction before the bodies were even stiff. The overburdened Newark cops were all too happy to give it to him, of course. From that point, the Director could spin the investigation any way he wanted, falsifying evidence, pinning it on someone else, or just forgetting to assign any detectives to the case. Talk about guaranteeing the perfect crime: the guy responsible for bringing the perp to justice was the perp himself.

And sure, someone in Washington might notice the Newark office hadn't solved that pesky quadruple homicide. But what would they care? The Director could please his bosses with other successes. He certainly didn't lack for motivation: every time his agents made another successful seizure at Newark airport, it was just more supply for his operation.

The only people who might hold him accountable for the Ludlow Street investigation were the families of the victims— who didn't have much pull or, in some cases, didn't even exist—and the press, i.e., me. And when I came inquiring, all the Director had to do was make up a plausible story. In this case, he had made up some ridiculous, impossible-to-confirm-or-deny fairy tale about José de Jesús Encarcerón—the equivalent of pinning it on the bogeyman. And he had Monty Pete to parrot it for him to the media.

Was L. Pete in on it? Of course he was. He was Wanda's "boss," the little guy with the suit and the badge that Tynesha sucked off. Or at least that was a reasonable guess. After all, he'd offered to take her to a game at Giants Stadium. He had offered to take me to see the Jets—who, of course, play in Giants Stadium. Nice to know L. Pete held me in the same high esteem as his favorite hooker.

Suddenly I became aware the Director was standing, rearing to his full six feet five. He was every ounce of three hundred pounds, but his weight was much more solid than I had first surmised. Lift a Honda? Hell, he could lift a Cadillac.

He was done talking. And he was looking at me like I was supposed to say something.

"That's all very interesting," I said, feeling like the kid in math class who had been caught daydreaming. "What was it that gave it away?"

"That gave what away?"

"You know, what you just said," I said.

"I'm sorry?"

"The thing."

"What thing?"

The Director was staring me down like he was on one of his hunting vacations and I was an antelope at the end of his rifle sight. And—I don't know why this took me so long to figure out—it suddenly dawned on me that's exactly what I was. He hadn't brought me here for a story. And he wasn't tickling that gun on his shoulder because he liked how it felt.

He had lured me into his office to kill me. Right here. Right now.

"Is something the matter?" the Director asked.

My fight-or-flight response was kicking in, and I could feel those ancient juices that had been saving mankind's ass for thousands of years surging through me. I'm not sure what prehistoric generations of the Ross family did a hundred millennia ago when faced with a predator on the plains of Africa. But I knew what I was going to do. There was no fighting this guy, who was big, mean, and, oh yeah, armed.

So I flung myself away from the chair and ran.

In three long strides, I covered that great tract of carpet and made it to his door. I didn't know if he was pulling his weapon, if I was about to feel a bullet in the back of my head, or if my sudden move had caught him by surprise. But I wasn't turning around to check.

I slammed the door behind me, like that would do some good. I knew L. Pete's office was to the left so I cut hard to the right, down the hallway in the opposite direction. I heard the Director's voice from behind the closed door shouting for Monty.

The fifteenth floor of the National Drug Bureau's Newark Field Office was one big rectangle, designed completely without imagination. On the exterior side of the hallway, there were offices. On the interior side, there was a mix of offices and what appeared to be secretaries' stations filled with cubicles.

Maybe there were hiding places, but damn if I could slow down to find a decent one. I raced past the elevators, knowing they weren't going to do me any good: I didn't have time to wait for a car to arrive and, in any event, I didn't have the swipe card to operate one.

The stairs were my only shot. But where were the stairs? I looked around for an exit sign.

"Go that way," I heard the Director shout at Monty. "Guard the stairs."

So much for that.

I disappeared around the next corner just as the Director had rounded the first one. That gave me about a hundred-foot lead on him but I didn't dare round another corner. Eventually, I was going to run into Monty coming from the other direction. No time. I had no time.

I started grabbing at door handles, hoping to find an open office, but none of the doors budged. Goddamn paranoid flatfoot pensioners, locking their offices when they went home at night. Didn't they ever think about the possibility that a desperate newspaper reporter might need to slip under their desks to escape their homicidal boss?

I was on my seventh door when, finally, I found the one that had been left slightly ajar. I slipped in and closed it as softly as I could. I had bought myself time, but how much?

The office was sparse: a desk with a chair, a filing cabinet, a potted plant, and absolutely no place to hide. I reached into my pocket for my cell phone but, of course, it wasn't there. So I tiptoed to the desk phone and picked up. *Hello, 911? I'm trapped in a federal office building where I'm about to be killed by a high-ranking government official. Hello?*

But, no, I couldn't get that far. I couldn't even get a normal dial tone—just this monotone buzz. I looked at the phone in frustration. The screen said: "Enter passkey."

Of course. Uncle Sam wasn't going to stand for anyone making free phone calls. The phone wasn't going to save me.

I looked at the window, but I was fifteen stories up. There was no surviving that kind of fall. So I studied the phone again. Maybe it *might* save me. If I got lucky. I punched in 813. My birthday. What the hell. But the line stayed monotone.

"You have to admit, Carter, my business plan is brilliant, isn't it?" the Director called out. "I mean, have you ever heard of a better brand name for heroin than 'The Stuff.' It's elegant, don't you think? It's going to become the first national heroin brand, you know. It will be like Kleenex, perfectly synonymous with the product it represents."

I kept my ear to the phone and soon the line changed to a fast busy signal, like it had grown tired of waiting for me to push additional buttons. Okay, so maybe it was a four-digit passcode. I tried 8137. Pause. Pause. Fast busy signal.

"You know I'm making more money than I know what to do with?" the Director said, still panting slightly from his sprint. "I'm not sure I could print money as fast as I'm making it. It's all I can do just to get it laundered and shipped offshore."

I keyed in 81378. Pause. Pause. Fast busy signal. Then 081378. This time it went immediately to a fast busy signal. So it was a six-digit code. But even assuming there were a couple hundred employees with passcodes, that made my odds at guessing less than 1 in 1,000.

"You should come join my operation, Carter," the Director went on. "You've been the only one smart enough to catch on to what's happening here. No one else has even come close. Not the FBI. Not those supposed geniuses at the CIA. Not the ATF. The most powerful government in the world and I fooled the whole damn thing. But not you. I could use a man like you. Why don't you come out so we can talk about it? I can make you rich, you know."

I rolled my eyes. If I was smarter than the CIA, what the hell made him think I was dumb enough to step outside the office door and greatly hasten my own demise?

The Director's voice was getting louder—and closer.

"You can't hide forever," he bellowed. "There's not another employee due on this floor until Monday at eight A.M. I've got all the time I need to find you. Come on out and we'll talk this through."

I could hear him opening doors one by one. Obviously, he had some kind of master key and was going office to office looking for me.

"Don't even think of escaping," he called out. "We've got holding cells on every floor. The place is designed so you can't escape. We've hired *experts* to expose flaws in our security system by escaping, and even they couldn't do it."

I was sure I couldn't, either. But I could do a little better job concealing myself. As softly as I could, being mindful that even the slightest squeak could be deadly, I stood up on the desk and slid open one of the ceiling panels. That was always how they did it in the movies, right? Climb up in the ceiling, replace the panel, and you were as good as invisible.

Except, of course, when you were on the top floor and it was just a drop ceiling with nothing above it but a concrete wall. I couldn't even climb around in the space between the real ceiling and the drop ceiling—there was nothing that would come close to supporting my weight.

So, in short, I had no communications, no place to hide, and absolutely no way out.

Sorry, Mrs. Ross. Your boy is flat-out hosed.

There was going to be a showdown, and it was going to come soon. I looked around the room for some kind of weapon, pulling on desk and cabinet drawers to see if there was something sharp inside. A letter opener? A fountain pen? Something?

But even the fed who had been sloppy enough to leave his door slightly ajar had been careful enough to lock everything else tight. So I grabbed the only thing in the room that looked like it could do a little damage: the plant. The pot was made out of terra-cotta, which wasn't exactly known as the world's hardest substance. But maybe if I swung fast enough and connected with something soft and vital, the Director would be the first human being to experience Death by Ficus. Then I could take my chances with Monty.

I hid by the side of the door, hoping the Director might lead with a particularly vulnerable part of his head. I listened as the sound of the Director trying locks inched ever closer. He was perhaps three or four rooms away and closing in fast.

I don't know how long I stood there, ficus in hand, waiting for the end. I was keeping myself so still, so quiet, so alert for any tiny noise that when I finally did hear a sound—a series of loud and thunderous ones—I nearly dropped my plant.

It was a door slamming open and dozens of men rushing onto the floor. There was shouting and struggling and grunting. There were loud orders being barked in rapid succession. Then there was just one voice, and it was asking for me.

"Mr. Ross? This is the Tactical Response Team. Mr. Ross, can you hear me?"

I almost emerged from my hiding spot, but stopped myself. Did I really know who the good guys were? Was this just a ploy by the Director to flush me out? Did he have a Tactical Response Team—or guys who could *pretend* to be a Tactical Response Team—at his disposal?

"Mr. Ross? Mr. Ross? Can you hear me?"

Staying put. I was staying put. And staying quiet.

"I don't know if he's up here. Maybe he's hiding somewhere."

Then I heard a radio squawk and a sweet, squelchy response poured out of it.

"Tell him if he doesn't come out, he's not getting any nooky tonight," Tina Thompson said.

"I surrender," I yelled. "Tell her I surrender."

I walked out of the office to find the hallway filled with men in riot gear. Director Randall Meyers was lying facedown on the floor, his hands and legs bound, his mouth shut. Monty was also bound, but he was whimpering softly.

"Are you okay, Mr. Ross?" one of the riot cops asked me.

"Yeah, yeah," I said. "Sound as a pound."

"Is there any reason you're carrying that tree, sir?" he asked.

I still had a death grip on the ficus.

"This tree and I have been through a lot," I said. "I think I'd like to keep it."

The guy nodded. "Fine by me, sir. You have some friends downstairs who would like to see you."

I rode down the elevator with six heavily armed men, enjoying the knowledge that none of them wanted to shoot me. When I stepped out in the lobby, I was able to put my tree down just in time before Tina and Tommy pounced on me.

"You're an idiot," Tina murmured as she nestled her face in my neck. The three of us stood there for a long minute, clutching each other. I released them when I saw a tall man with a thick head of white hair reaching out to shake my hand.

"Hello, Carter," he said. "Irving Wallace."

I grasped his hand and pumped, still bewildered.

"You? So . . . how . . . what . . . I don't know where to start," I said.

"How about: How did we find you?" Tina suggested.

"Yes. Right. How *did* you find me?"

"I followed you," Tina said, delighted by her own cleverness. "I've been following you all day long. I was sitting five booths behind you at the IHOP and you didn't even notice. You'd make a crummy spy."

"Okay, but how did you know I was in trouble up there?"

"That's where Tommy and I come in," Irving said. "You're lucky that he's a crummy spy, too."

"Aww, come on," Tommy complained. "I wasn't *that* bad."

"I saw him sitting on my street, not looking at anything but my house," Irving said. "I figured he was casing my place to rob it and I wanted to have a little chat with him."

Tommy jumped in.

"I was starting to hightail it out of there, but as Irving got closer he took his hat off," Tommy said. "Suddenly I could tell he wasn't the man from the sketch. Way too much hair. Not nearly enough neck. And he obviously didn't weigh three hundred pounds."

Sure enough, Irving Wallace looked to be two hundred, tops, with a runner's build.

"So I slowed down and talked to him. After I proved to him I wasn't a crook, and he proved to me he wasn't a crook, we started talking like normal law-abiding people," Tommy said. "I told him what I knew. He told me what he knew. And it kind of fell in place."

"I had been suspicious for months," Irving said. "Remember how I told you every sample of heroin comes with its own unique fingerprint? I started noticing that we were getting street samples that looked identical to what the National Drug Bureau had been seizing at the airport."

"And a light went on in your head," I said.

"No, not at first," Wallace said. "I thought it was some strange coincidence or had some kind of benign explanation. But it kept happening. So I started paying careful attention, asking questions, keeping records, that sort of thing. The clincher was actually those samples of 'The Stuff' you gave me. I *knew* I had seen that signature on a shipment that had been seized by the NDB three months ago.

"Anyway," Wallace continued. "I had a guy do some snooping for me and I found out that particular stash was supposed to be in the Newark Field Office's confiscation vault. There's only one person in an NDB field office with free access to the vault: the field director. My snoop called me on Saturday morning to confirm it all. That's when I started calling you."

"And here I thought you were only inviting me to your house for brunch so you could kill me," I said.

The elevator opened and we moved aside to make way for a phalanx of riot police escorting a manacled Randall Meyers, still stoic, out the door. Monty/Pete, still sniveling, was right behind him, also in handcuffs. The lobby filled with the sound of the cops' rubber-soled shoes squeaking on the highly polished marble floor.

"God, I'm glad we nailed him," Irving said. "To think of how that man violated the trust in . . . don't get me started. Anyway, where were we?"

"I was accusing you of wanting to kill me," I said helpfully.

"Oh, right," Irving said. "The real reason we needed to talk in person was so I could show you how exact the match was on those heroin samples. I ended up showing it to Tommy instead."

"I tried to call you and tell you what was going on," Tommy said as they exited. "But your cell phone just kept ringing through to voice mail."

"It had been confiscated," I said.

"Oh. Well, then I called Tina," Tommy said. "I told her 'the Director' from the memo was the field director of the National Drug Bureau's Newark Office and she was like, 'Oh, my God, Carter is there right now.'"

"Actually, I think I said something slightly stronger than that," Tina interjected, snaking her arm around my waist and holding it there.

"That's when Irving called his people and made things happen," Tommy finished.

"Yeah, who *are* those people, anyway?" I asked.

"No comment," Wallace said, smiling. "I just hope the U.S. Attorney is going to be able to put a case together."

"I don't know if it would be considered admissible, but you think a taped confession would help?" I said, drawing the recorder out of my pocket.

Wallace grinned and clapped me on the shoulder. Tina released her grip on me, giving me another kiss on the cheek. "Not to be the bossy editor," she said sweetly, "but you've got a story to write. So stop gabbing with us girls and get your ass in gear."

"There's more of that enlightened management," I said. "Let me collect my things and I'll be out of here."

I grabbed my ficus, aware that I had a houseplant but no house. It was a situation I would have to rectify, if only because I didn't want to go around being so obviously ironic. I had just retrieved my phone from one of the square-jaw boys when it started ringing.

"Carter Ross," I answered.

"Hi, Carter, it's Mrs. Scalabrine from next door," she said.

"Oh, hi."

"I'm sorry to bother you, but you said to call if anyone saw your cat."

"You found Deadline?" I said, feeling my heart lift.

"He's out on the sidewalk right now, pacing back and forth," she said. "I think he's hungry. Want me to feed him?"

"I'm sure he'd like that," I said. "Tell him I'll be home soon."